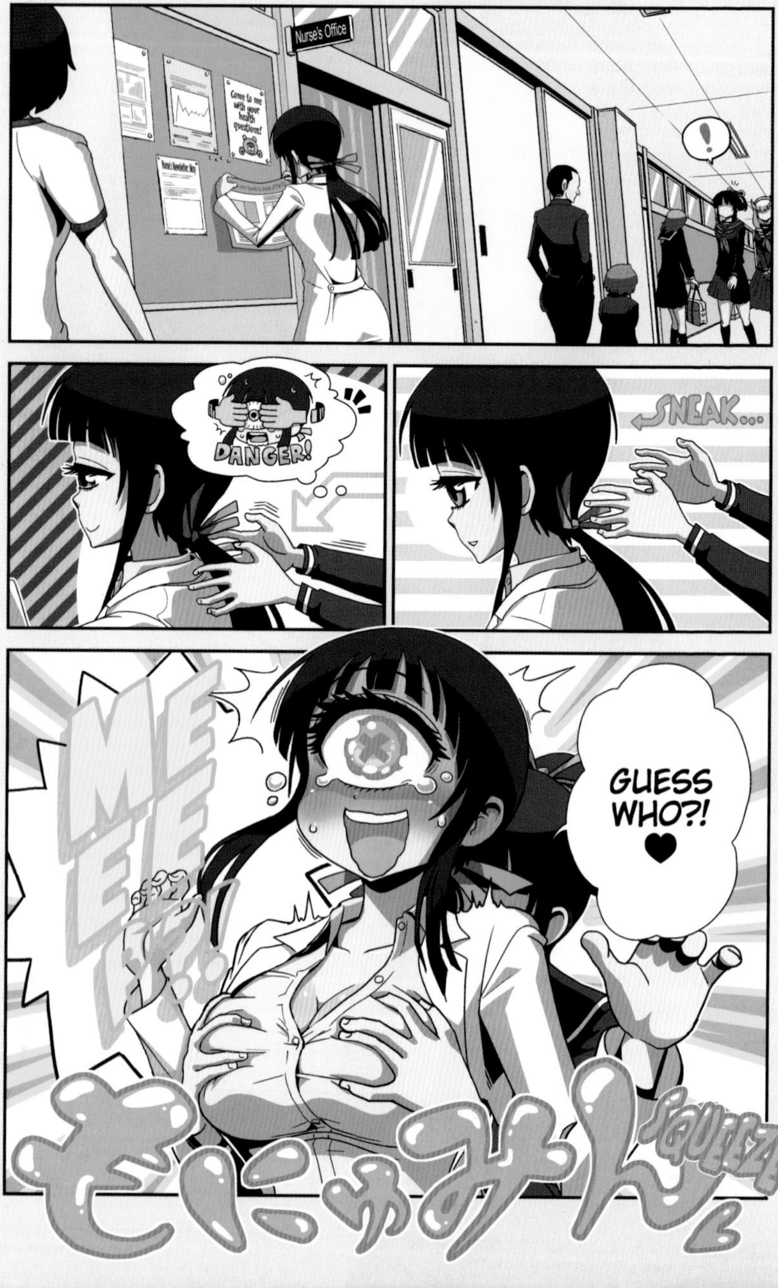
Nurse's Office
Come to me with your health questions!
Nurse's Newsletter: May
!
SNEAK...
DANGER!
GUESS WHO?! ♥
MEEE
SQUEEZE

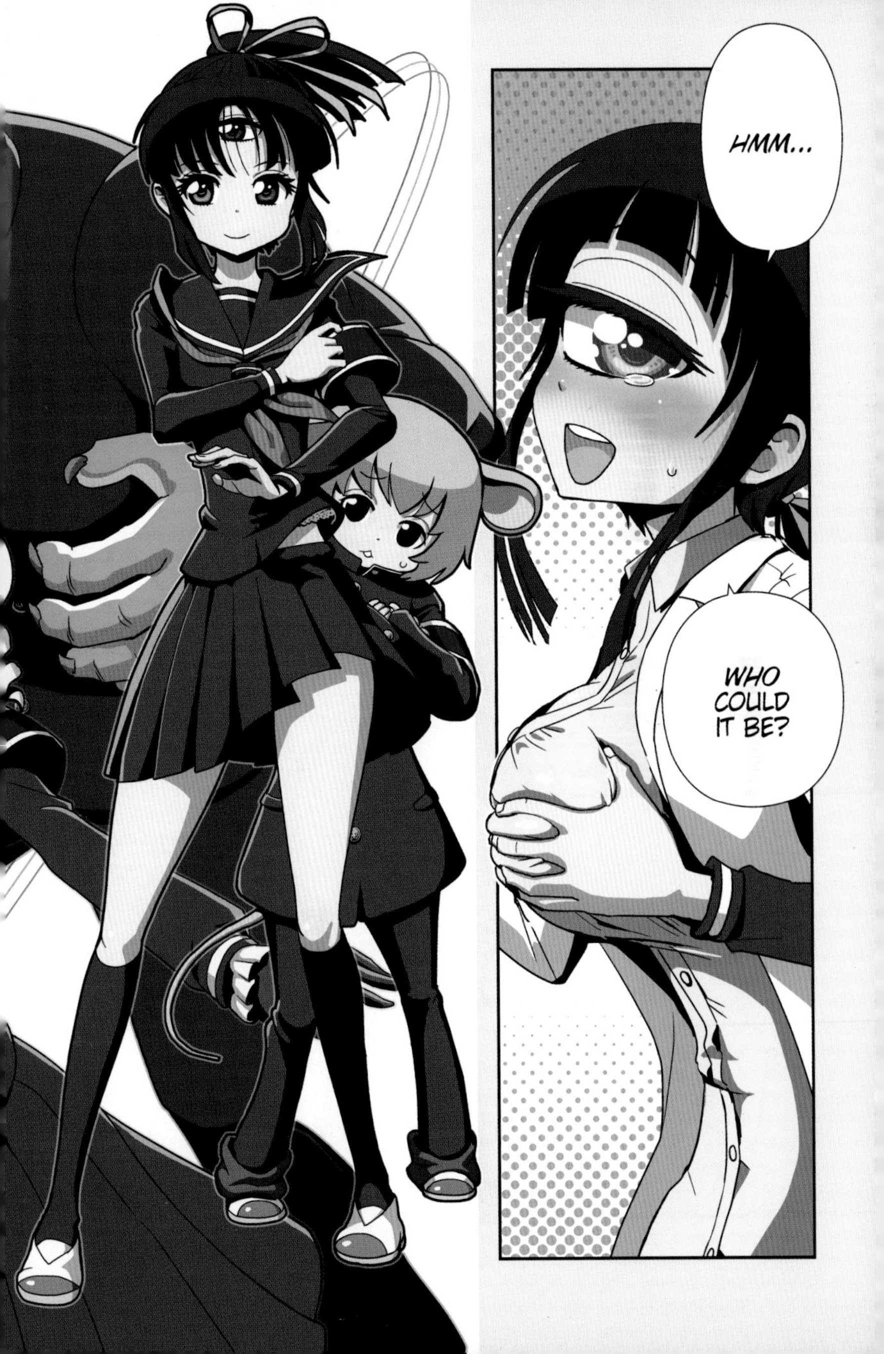
HMM...
WHO COULD IT BE?

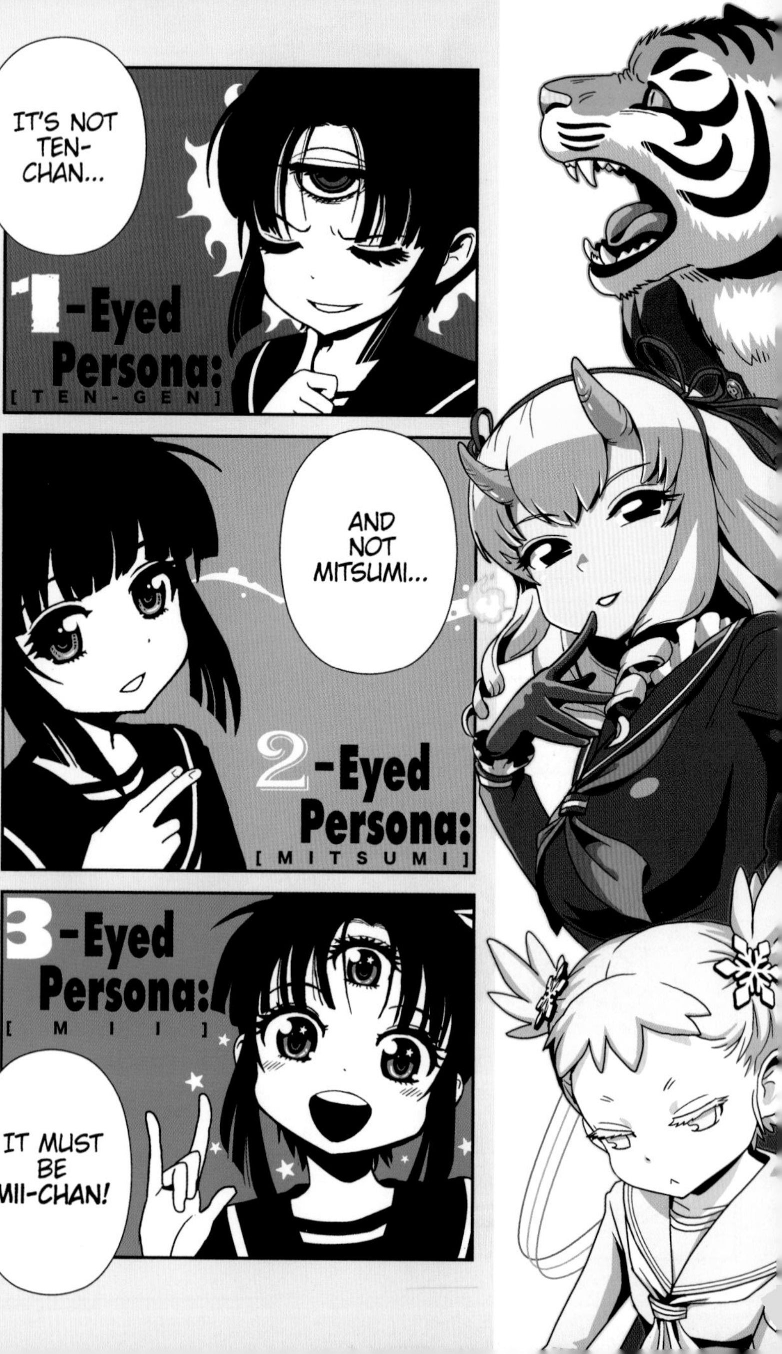
IT'S NOT TEN-CHAN...
1-Eyed Persona:
[TEN-GEN]
AND NOT MITSUMI...
2-Eyed Persona:
[MITSUMI]
3-Eyed Persona:
[MII]
IT MUST BE MII-CHAN!

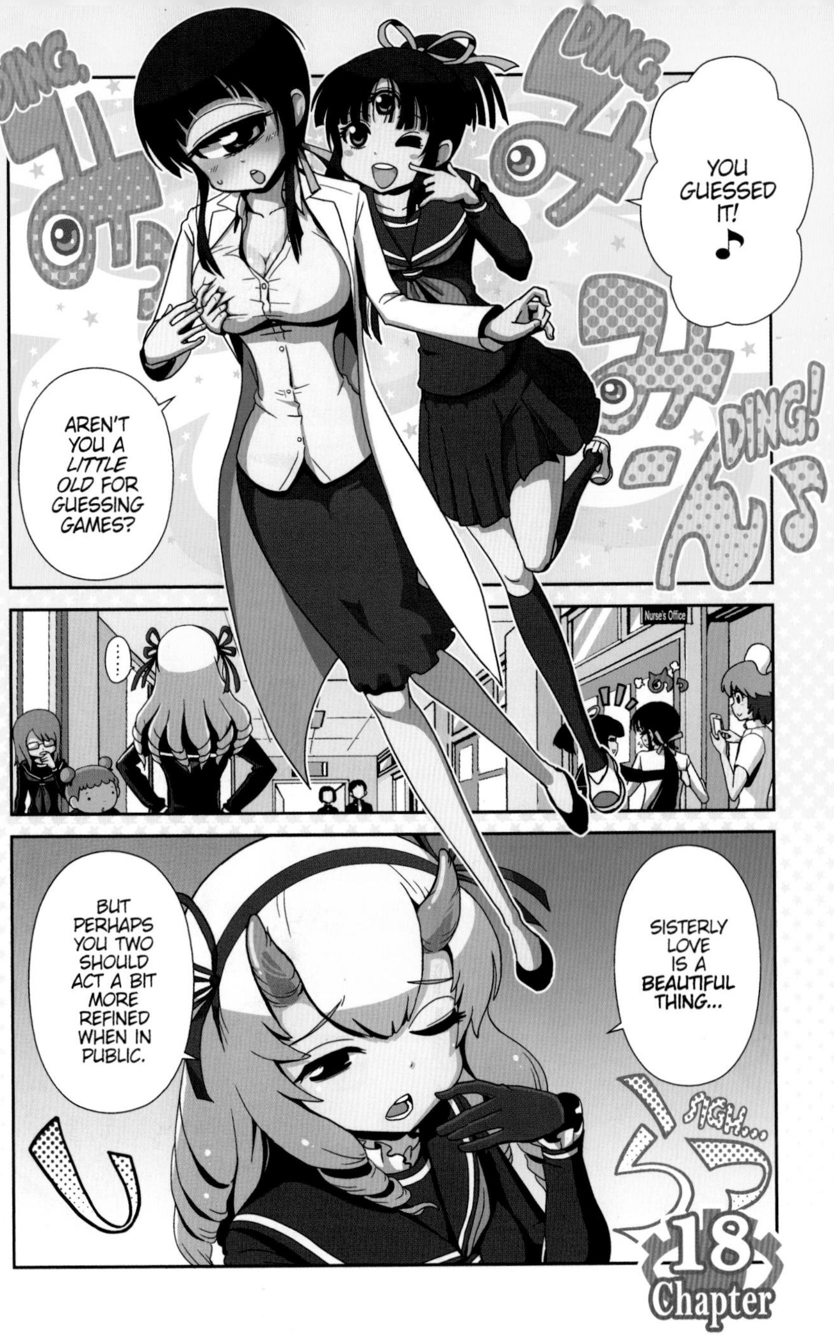
DING.
DING.
YOU GUESSED IT! ♪
DING!
AREN'T YOU A *LITTLE* OLD FOR GUESSING GAMES?
Nurse's Office
......
SISTERLY LOVE IS A BEAUTIFUL THING...
SIGH...
BUT PERHAPS YOU TWO SHOULD ACT A BIT MORE REFINED WHEN IN PUBLIC.
18
Chapter

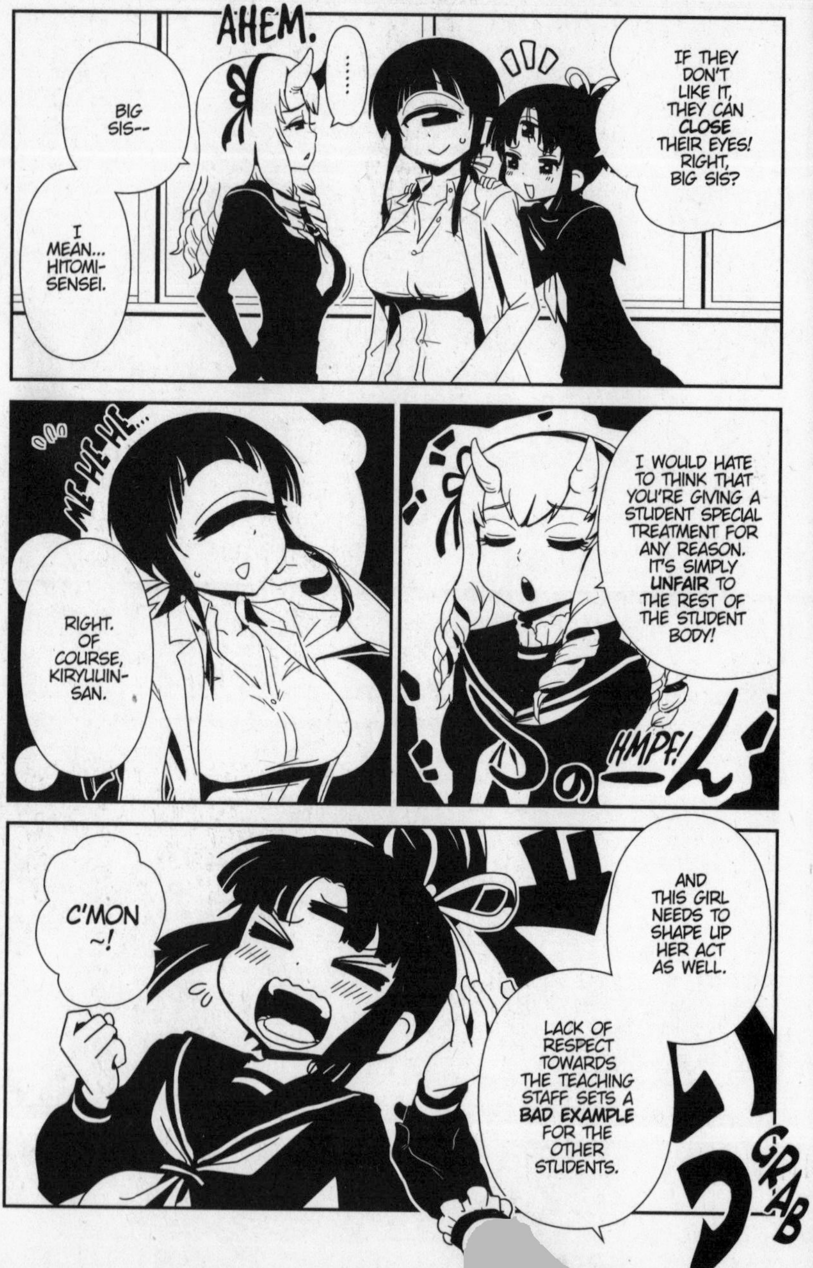
IF THEY DON'T LIKE IT, THEY CAN CLOSE THEIR EYES! RIGHT, BIG SIS?
......
AHEM.
BIG SIS--
I MEAN... HITOMI-SENSEI.
I WOULD HATE TO THINK THAT YOU'RE GIVING A STUDENT SPECIAL TREATMENT FOR ANY REASON. IT'S SIMPLY UNFAIR TO THE REST OF THE STUDENT BODY!
HMPF!
ME HE HE...
RIGHT. OF COURSE, KIRYUUIN-SAN.
AND THIS GIRL NEEDS TO SHAPE UP HER ACT AS WELL.
LACK OF RESPECT TOWARDS THE TEACHING STAFF SETS A BAD EXAMPLE FOR THE OTHER STUDENTS.
GRAB
C'MON ~!

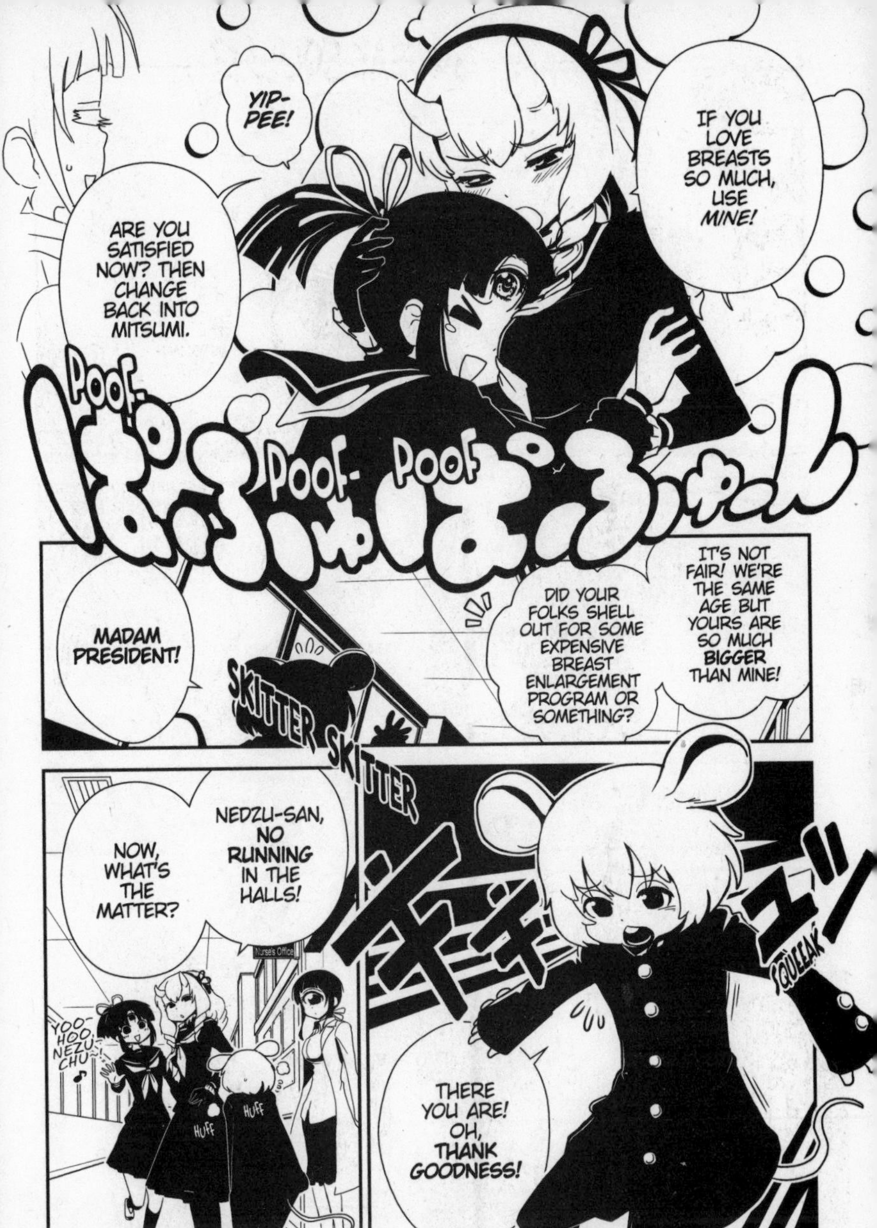
IF YOU LOVE BREASTS SO MUCH, USE MINE!
YIP-PEE!
ARE YOU SATISFIED NOW? THEN CHANGE BACK INTO MITSUMI.
POOF- POOF- POOF
IT'S NOT FAIR! WE'RE THE SAME AGE BUT YOURS ARE SO MUCH BIGGER THAN MINE!
DID YOUR FOLKS SHELL OUT FOR SOME EXPENSIVE BREAST ENLARGEMENT PROGRAM OR SOMETHING?
MADAM PRESIDENT!
SKITTER SKITTER
SQUEAK
THERE YOU ARE! OH, THANK GOODNESS!
NEDZU-SAN, NO RUNNING IN THE HALLS!
NOW, WHAT'S THE MATTER?
Nurse's Office
YOO-HOO, NEZU-CHU~!
HUFF
HUFF

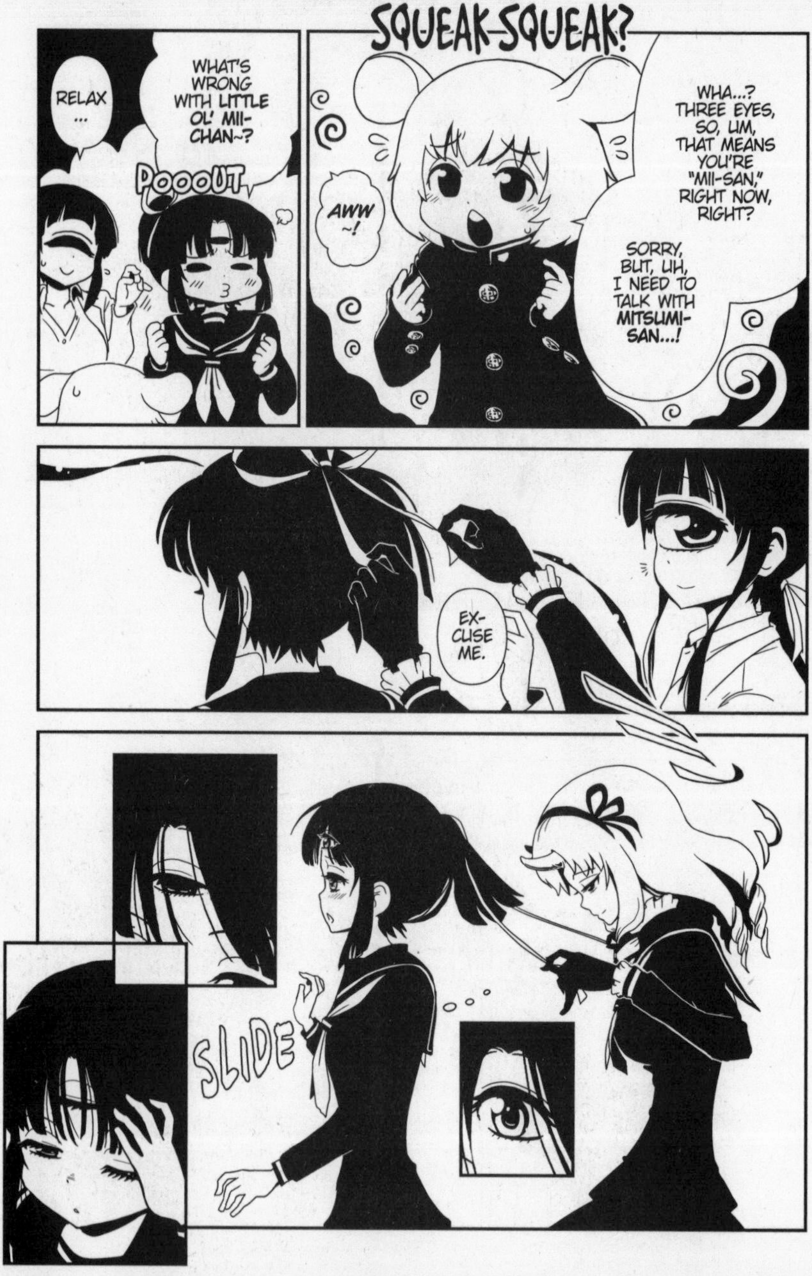
SQUEAK-SQUEAK?
WHA...? THREE EYES, SO, UM, THAT MEANS YOU'RE "MII-SAN," RIGHT NOW, RIGHT?
SORRY, BUT, UH, I NEED TO TALK WITH MITSUMI-SAN...!
AWW~!
WHAT'S WRONG WITH LITTLE OL' MII-CHAN~?
RELAX...
POOOOUT
EX-CUSE ME.
SLIDE

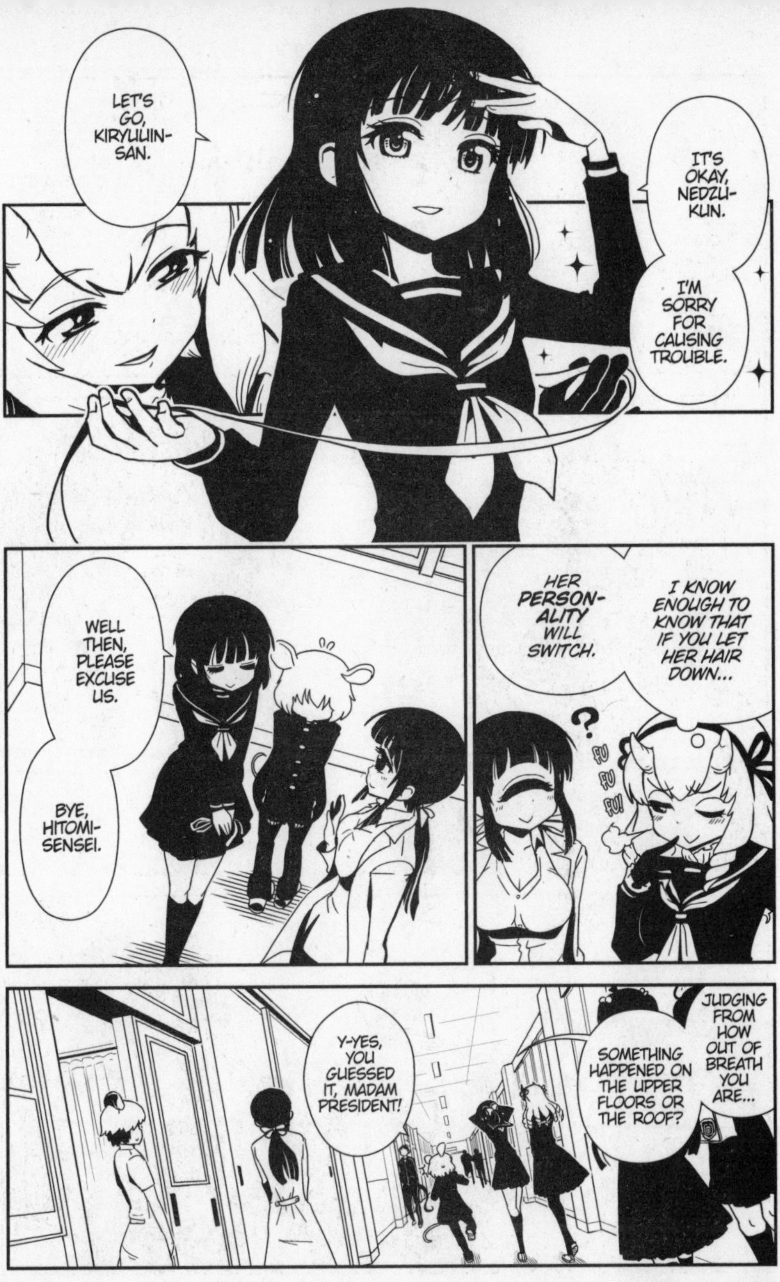
IT'S OKAY, NEDZU-KUN.
I'M SORRY FOR CAUSING TROUBLE.
LET'S GO, KIRYUUIN-SAN.
I KNOW ENOUGH TO KNOW THAT IF YOU LET HER HAIR DOWN...
HER PERSON-ALITY WILL SWITCH.
?
FU FU FU!
WELL THEN, PLEASE EXCUSE US.
BYE, HITOMI-SENSEI.
JUDGING FROM HOW OUT OF BREATH YOU ARE...
SOMETHING HAPPENED ON THE UPPER FLOORS OR THE ROOF?
Y-YES, YOU GUESSED IT, MADAM PRESIDENT!

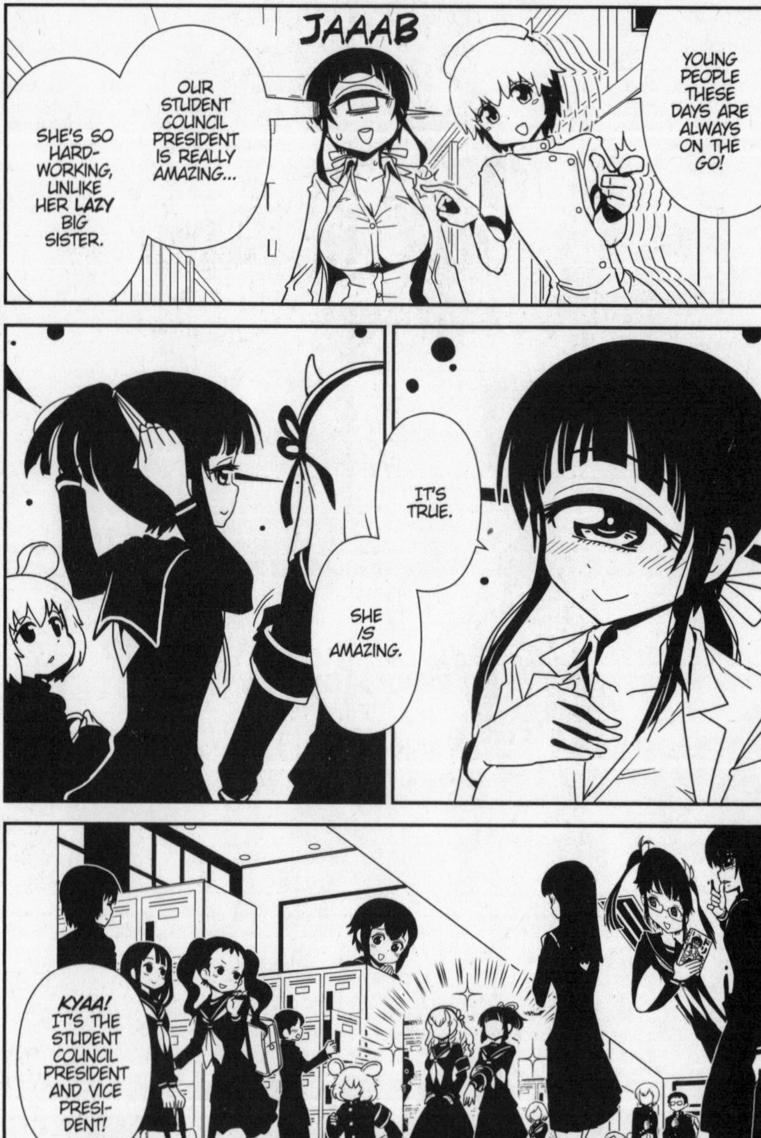
YOUNG PEOPLE THESE DAYS ARE ALWAYS ON THE GO!
JAAAB
OUR STUDENT COUNCIL PRESIDENT IS REALLY AMAZING...
SHE'S SO HARD-WORKING, UNLIKE HER LAZY BIG SISTER.
IT'S TRUE.
SHE IS AMAZING.
KYAA! IT'S THE STUDENT COUNCIL PRESIDENT AND VICE PRESI-DENT!

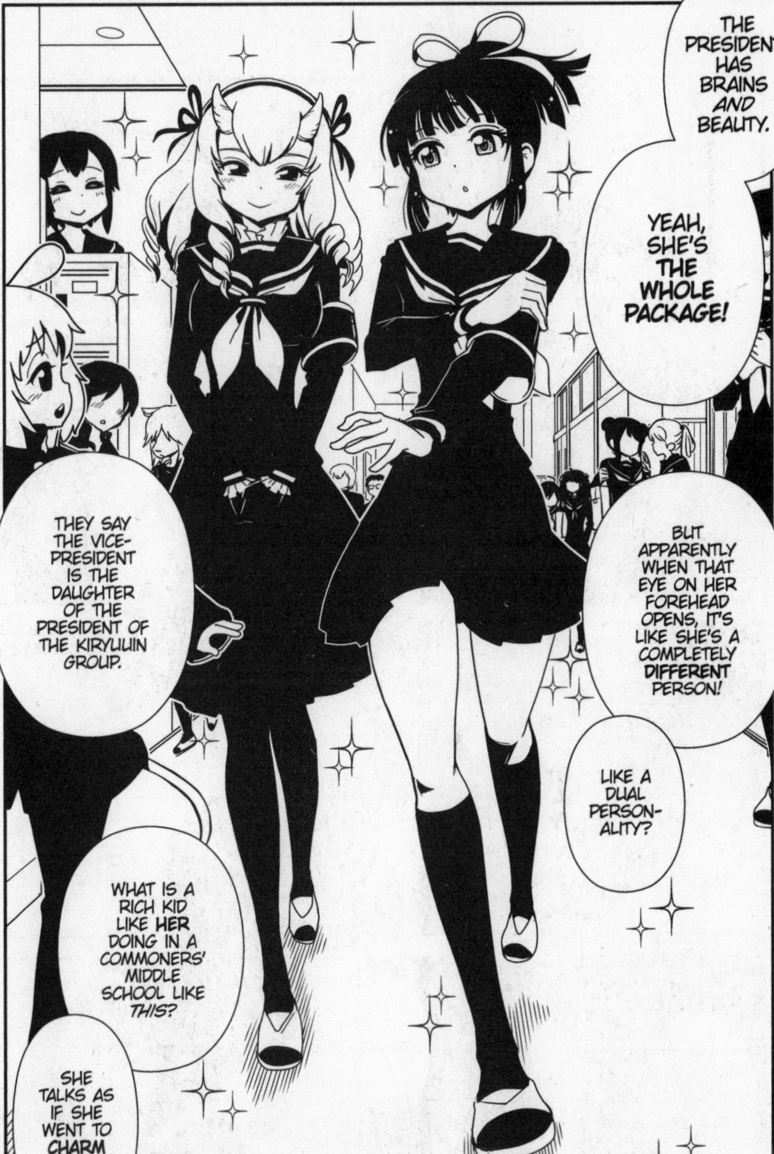
THE PRESIDENT HAS BRAINS *AND* BEAUTY.
YEAH, SHE'S THE WHOLE PACKAGE!
BUT APPARENTLY WHEN THAT EYE ON HER FOREHEAD OPENS, IT'S LIKE SHE'S A COMPLETELY **DIFFERENT** PERSON!
LIKE A DUAL PERSON-ALITY?
THEY SAY THE VICE-PRESIDENT IS THE DAUGHTER OF THE PRESIDENT OF THE KIRYUUIN GROUP.
WHAT IS A RICH KID LIKE **HER** DOING IN A COMMONERS' MIDDLE SCHOOL LIKE *THIS?*
SHE TALKS AS IF SHE WENT TO **CHARM SCHOOL!**

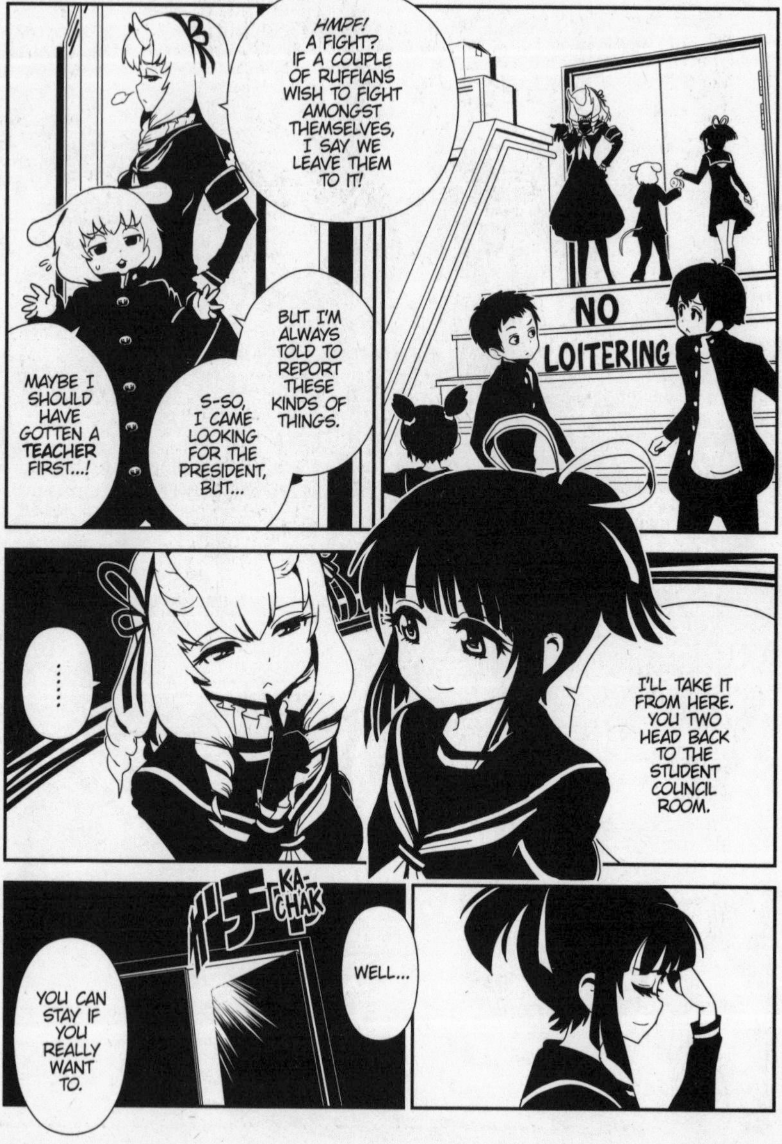
NO LOITERING
HMPF! A FIGHT? IF A COUPLE OF RUFFIANS WISH TO FIGHT AMONGST THEMSELVES, I SAY WE LEAVE THEM TO IT!
BUT I'M ALWAYS TOLD TO REPORT THESE KINDS OF THINGS.
S-SO, I CAME LOOKING FOR THE PRESIDENT, BUT...
MAYBE I SHOULD HAVE GOTTEN A TEACHER FIRST...!
I'LL TAKE IT FROM HERE. YOU TWO HEAD BACK TO THE STUDENT COUNCIL ROOM.
......
WELL...
KA-CHAK
YOU CAN STAY IF YOU REALLY WANT TO.

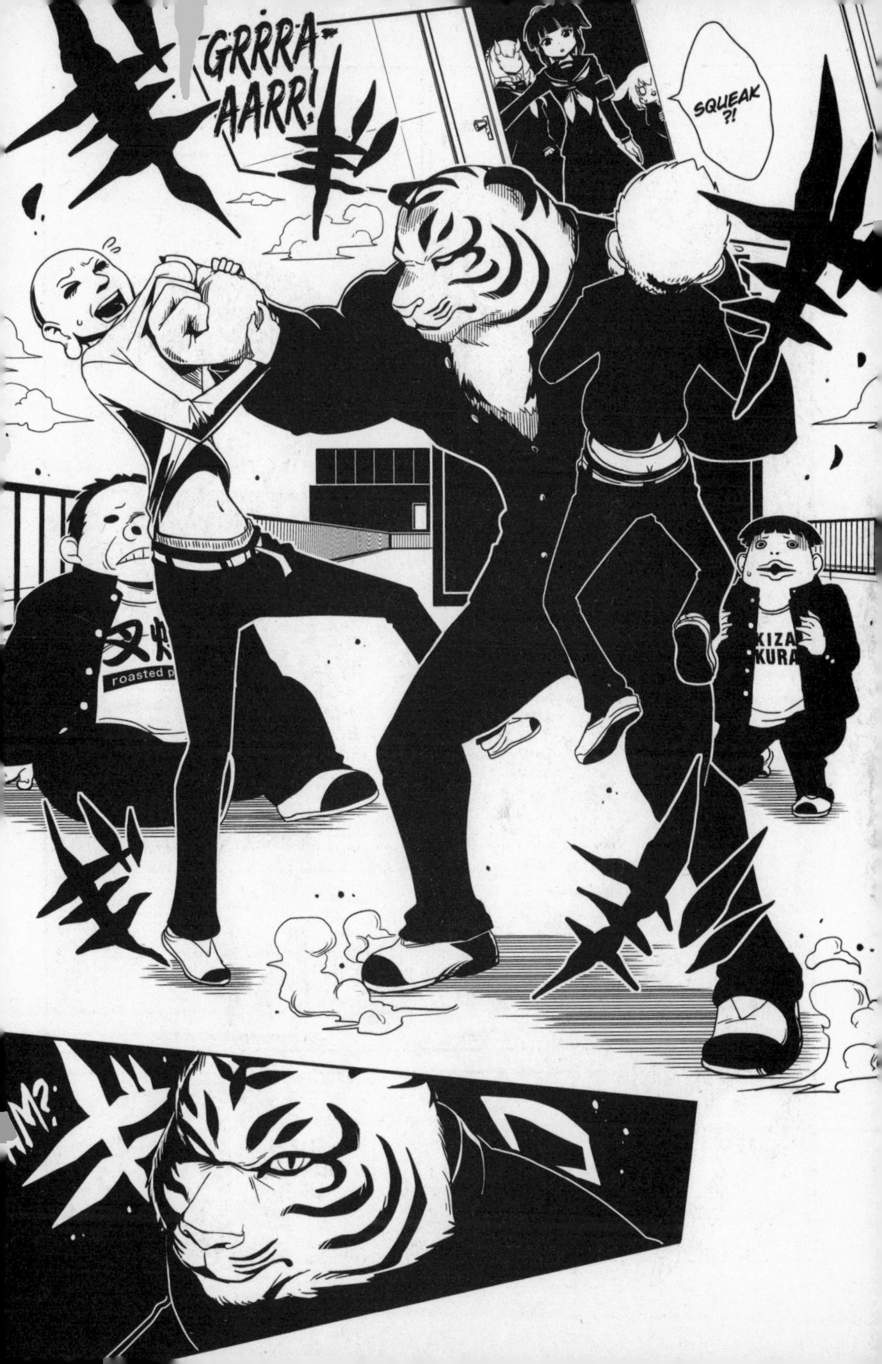
SQUEAK ?!
GRRRA AARR!

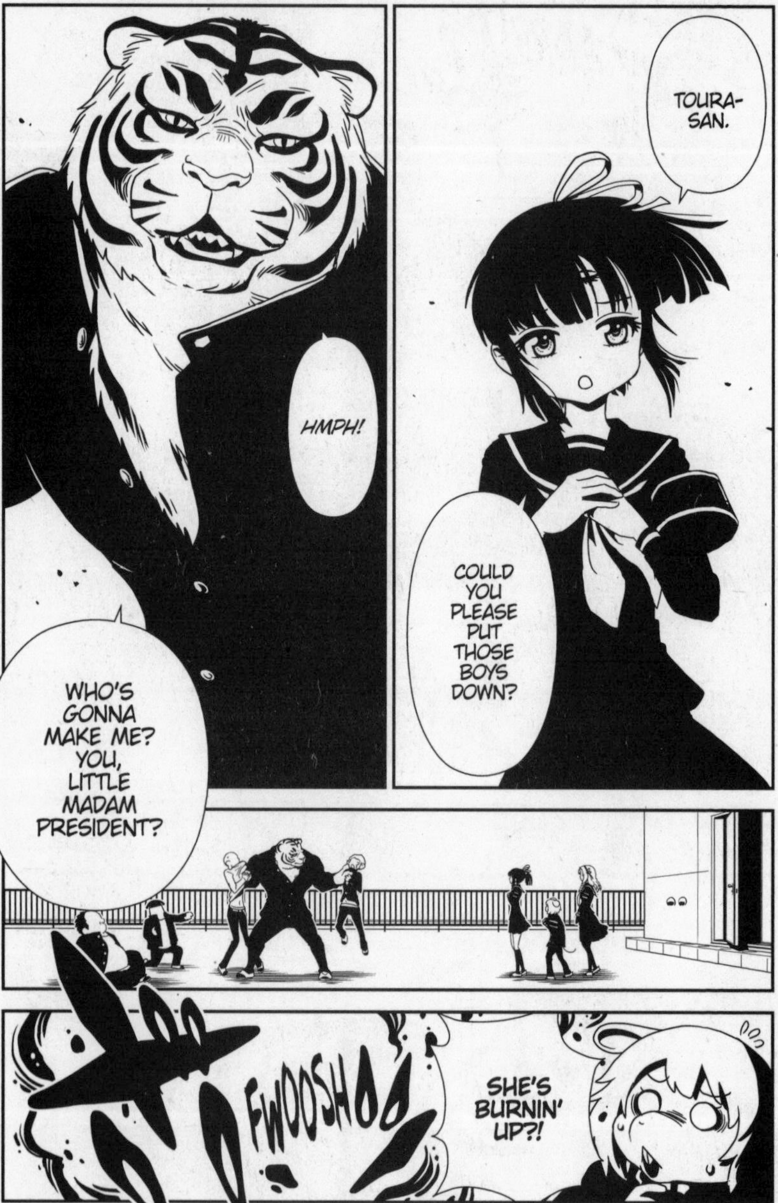
TOURA-SAN.
COULD YOU PLEASE PUT THOSE BOYS DOWN?
HMPH!
WHO'S GONNA MAKE ME? YOU, LITTLE MADAM PRESIDENT?
SHE'S BURNIN' UP?!
FWOOSH

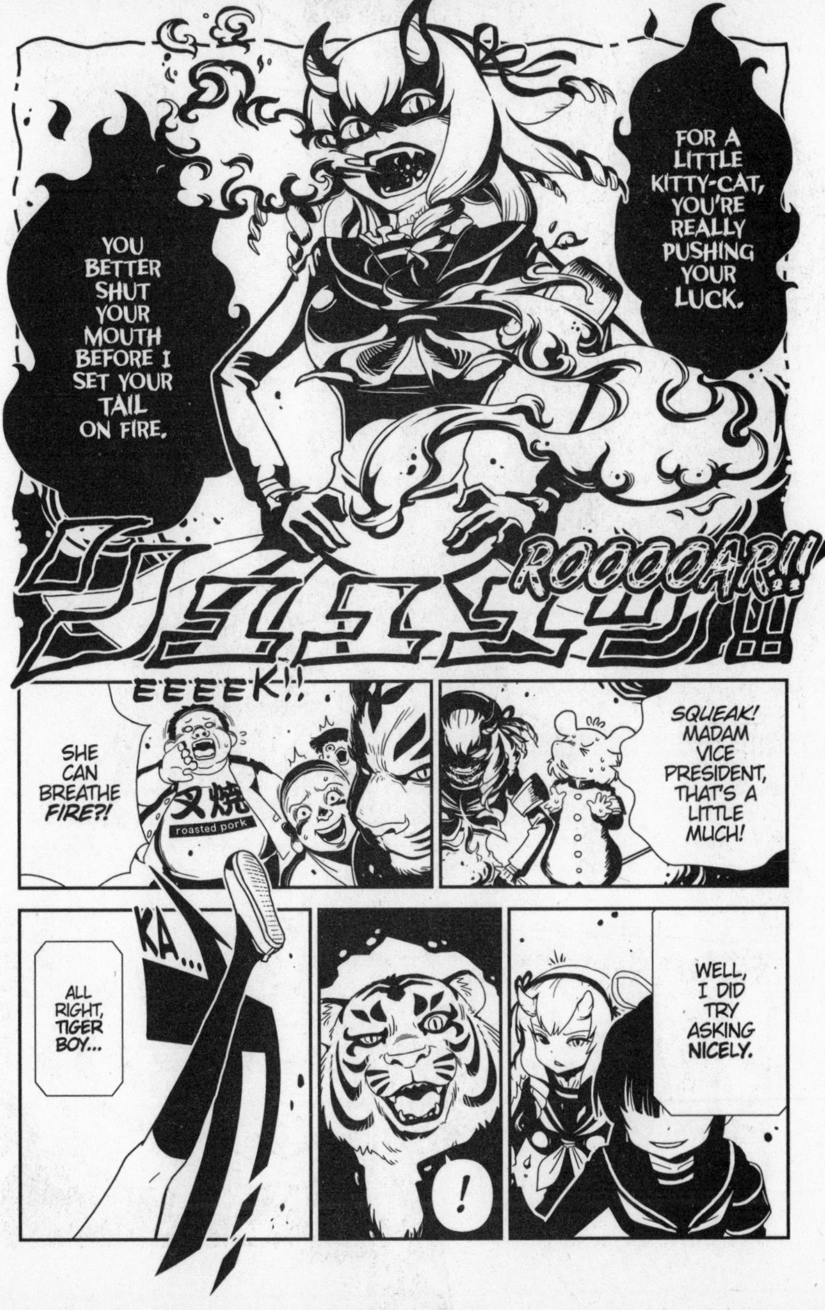

FOR A LITTLE KITTY-CAT, YOU'RE REALLY PUSHING YOUR LUCK.
YOU BETTER SHUT YOUR MOUTH BEFORE I SET YOUR TAIL ON FIRE.
ROOOOAR!!
SQUEAK! MADAM VICE PRESIDENT, THAT'S A LITTLE MUCH!
EEEEK!!
SHE CAN BREATHE FIRE?!
叉焼
roasted pork
WELL, I DID TRY ASKING NICELY.
!
KA...
ALL RIGHT, TIGER BOY...

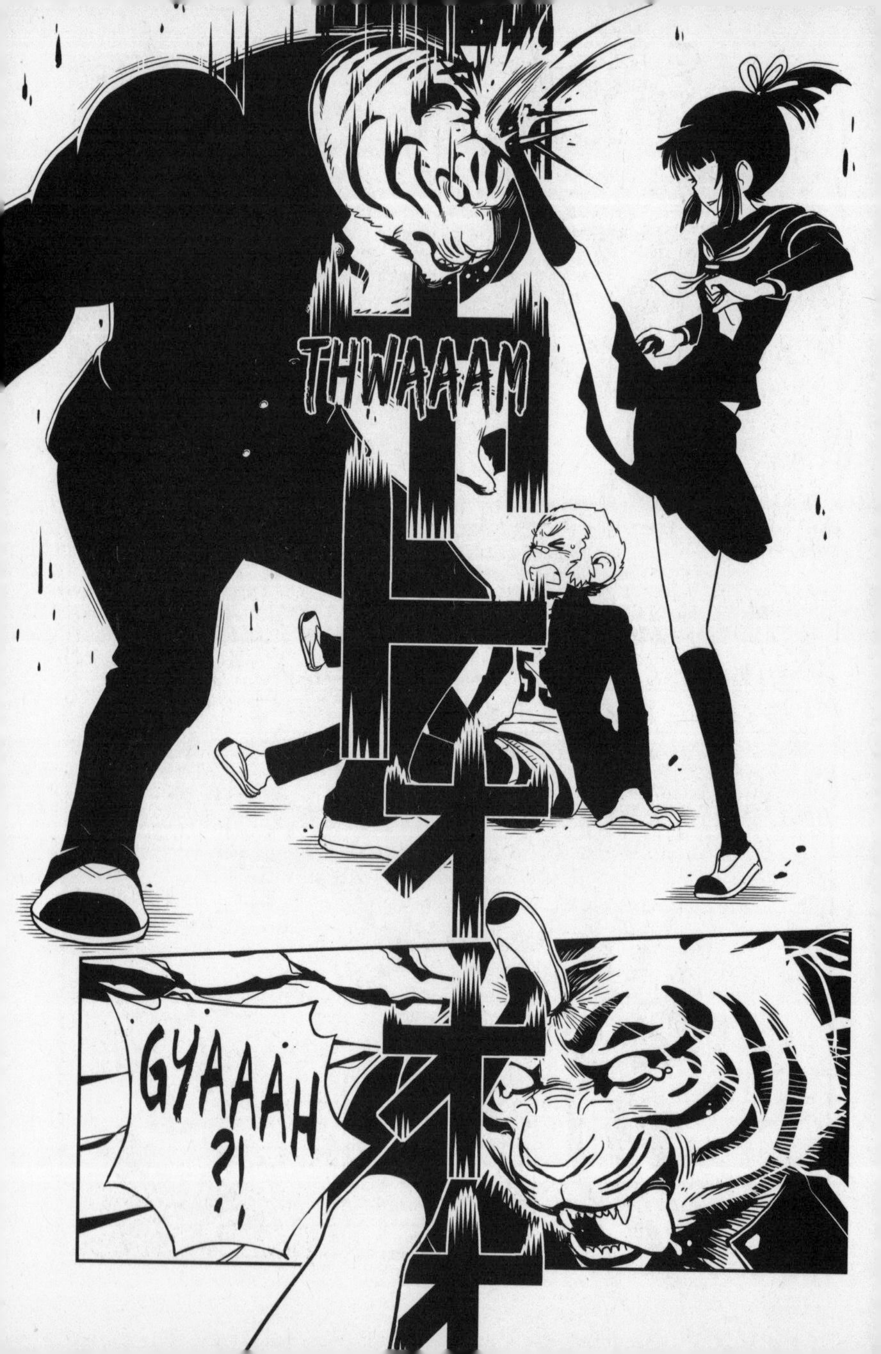
THWAAAM
GYAAAH ?!

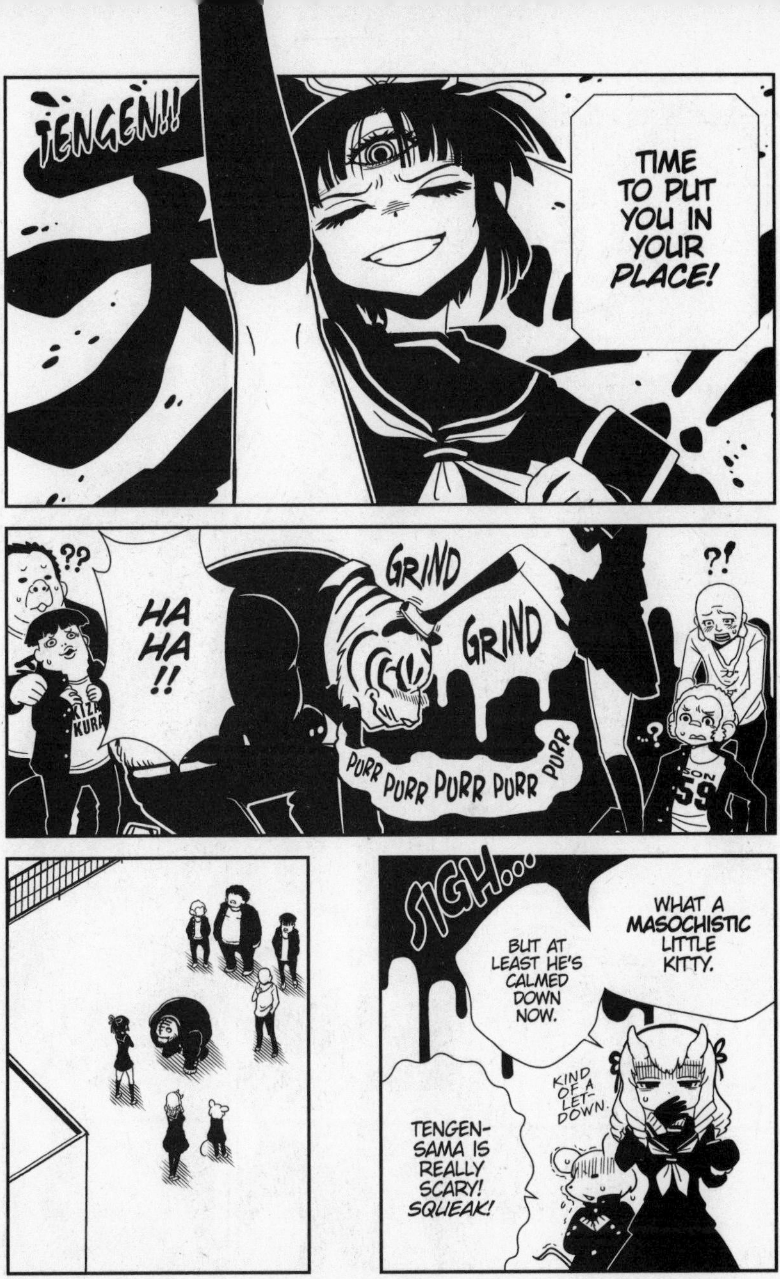
TIME TO PUT YOU IN YOUR PLACE!
TENGEN!!
?!
GRIND
GRIND
HA HA!!
??
PURR PURR PURR PURR PURR
?
SIGH...
WHAT A MASOCHISTIC LITTLE KITTY.
BUT AT LEAST HE'S CALMED DOWN NOW.
KIND OF A LET-DOWN.
TENGEN-SAMA IS REALLY SCARY! SQUEAK!

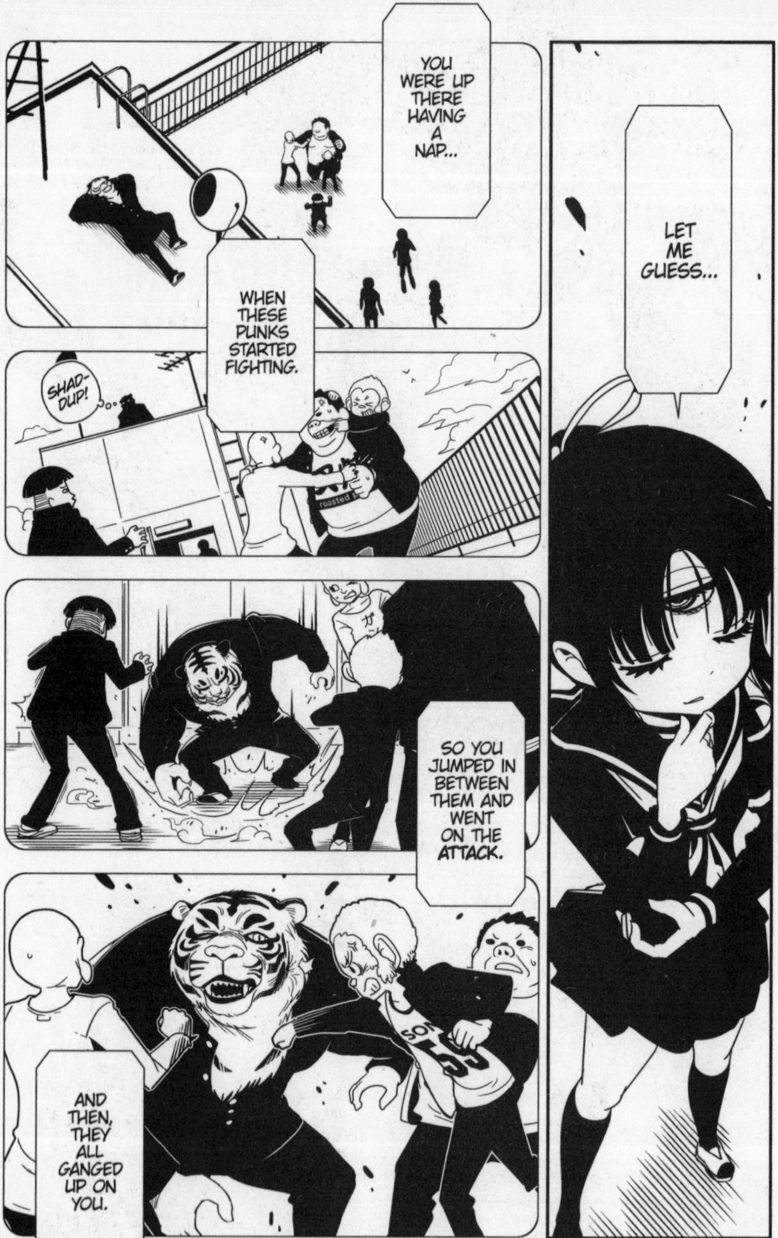
LET ME GUESS...
YOU WERE UP THERE HAVING A NAP...
WHEN THESE PUNKS STARTED FIGHTING.
SHAD-DUP!
SO YOU JUMPED IN BETWEEN THEM AND WENT ON THE ATTACK.
AND THEN, THEY ALL GANGED UP ON YOU.

*The divine ability to see truth.

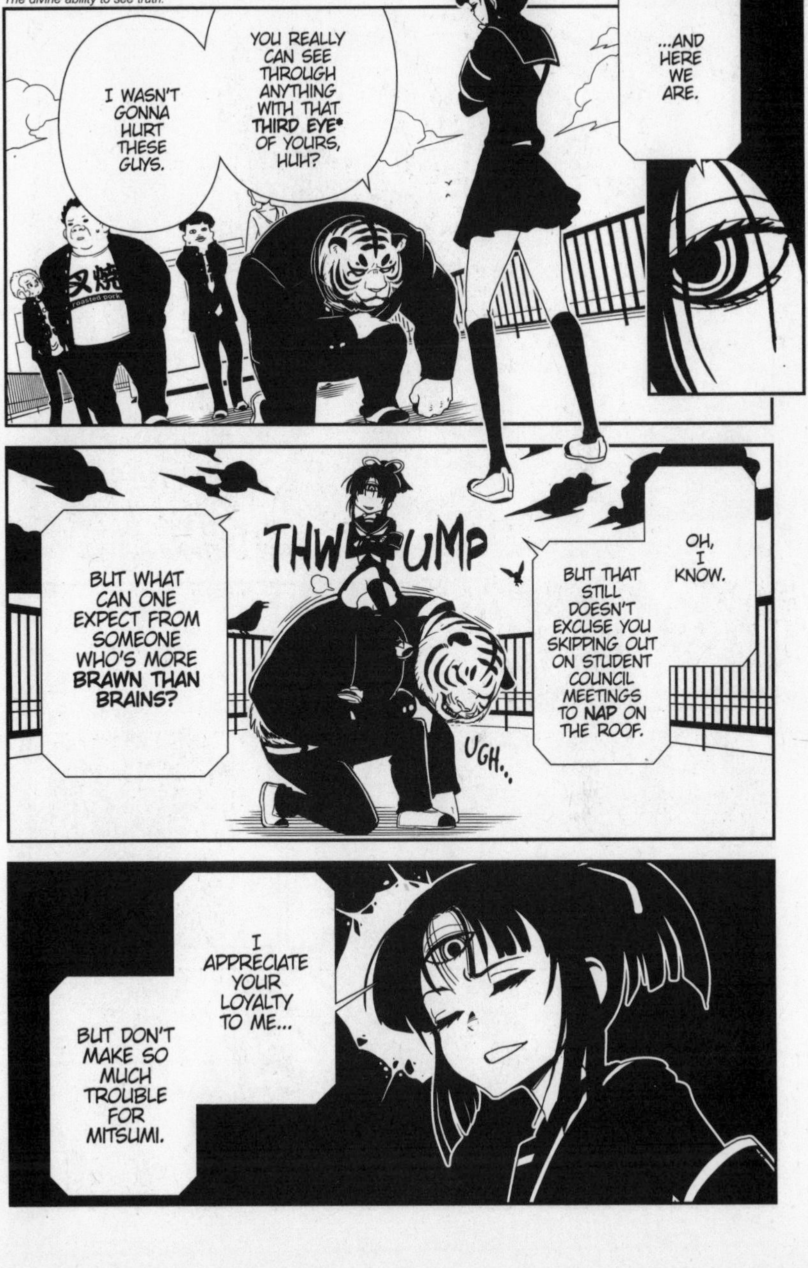
...AND HERE WE ARE.
YOU REALLY CAN SEE THROUGH ANYTHING WITH THAT THIRD EYE* OF YOURS, HUH?
I WASN'T GONNA HURT THESE GUYS.
OH, I KNOW.
BUT THAT STILL DOESN'T EXCUSE YOU SKIPPING OUT ON STUDENT COUNCIL MEETINGS TO NAP ON THE ROOF.
THWUMP
BUT WHAT CAN ONE EXPECT FROM SOMEONE WHO'S MORE BRAWN THAN BRAINS?
UGH...
I APPRECIATE YOUR LOYALTY TO ME...
BUT DON'T MAKE SO MUCH TROUBLE FOR MITSUMI.

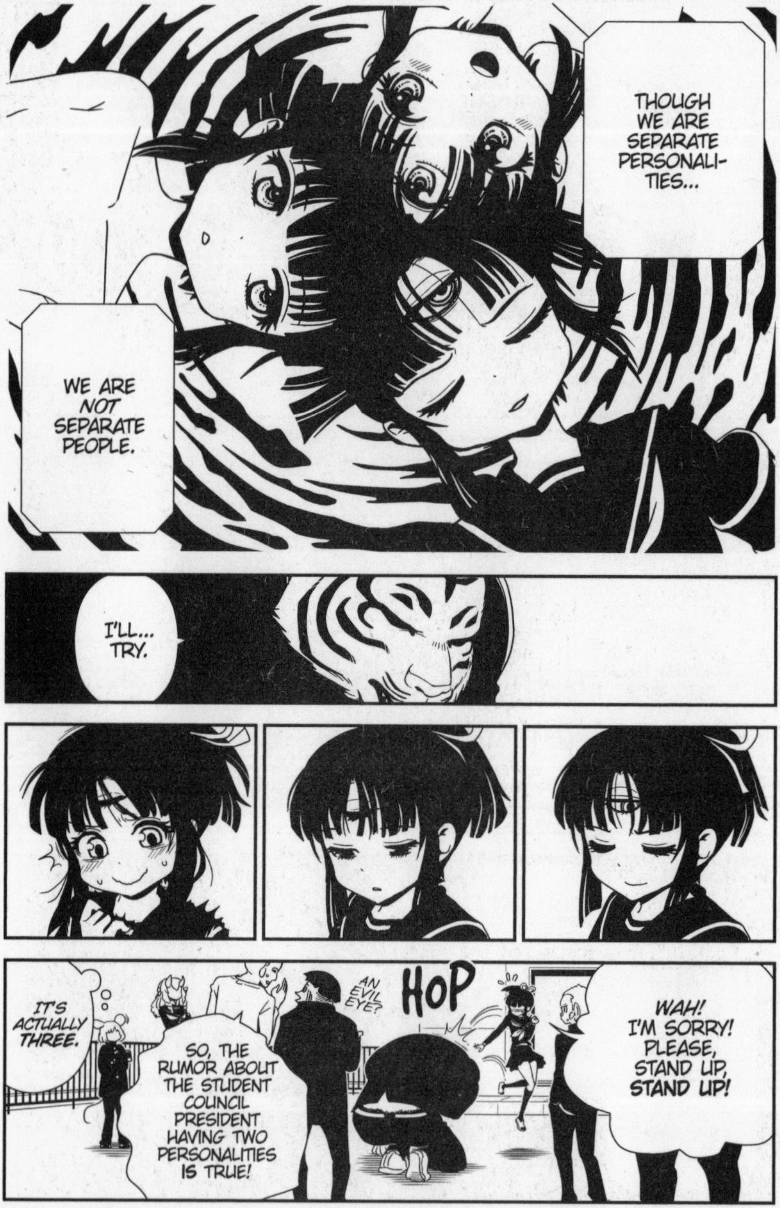
THOUGH WE ARE SEPARATE PERSONALI- TIES...
WE ARE *NOT* SEPARATE PEOPLE.
I'LL... TRY.
WAH! I'M SORRY! PLEASE, STAND UP, STAND UP!
HOP
AN EVIL EYE?
SO, THE RUMOR ABOUT THE STUDENT COUNCIL PRESIDENT HAVING TWO PERSONALITIES IS TRUE!
IT'S ACTUALLY THREE.

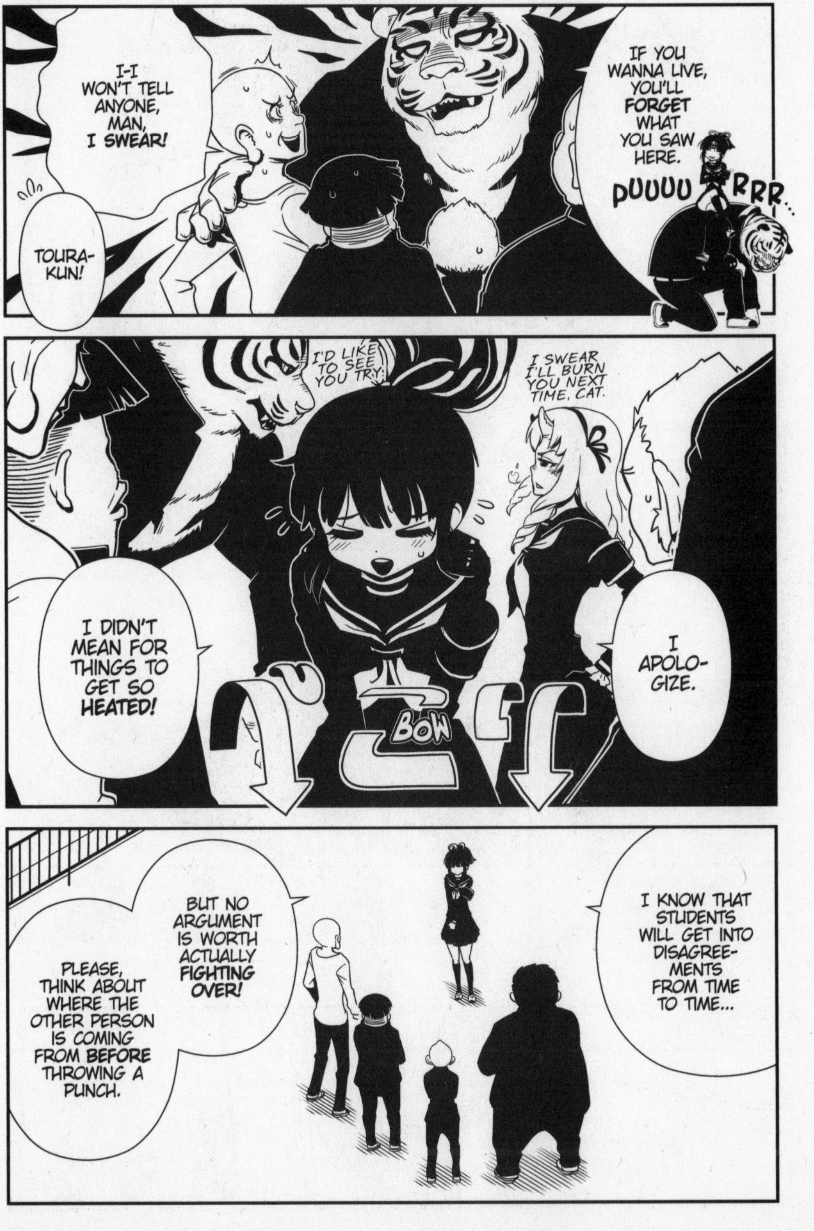
IF YOU WANNA LIVE, YOU'LL FORGET WHAT YOU SAW HERE.
PUUUURRR...
I-I WON'T TELL ANYONE, MAN, I SWEAR!
TOURA-KUN!
I SWEAR I'LL BURN YOU NEXT TIME, CAT.
I'D LIKE TO SEE YOU TRY.
I APOLO-GIZE.
BOW
I DIDN'T MEAN FOR THINGS TO GET SO HEATED!
I KNOW THAT STUDENTS WILL GET INTO DISAGREE-MENTS FROM TIME TO TIME...
BUT NO ARGUMENT IS WORTH ACTUALLY FIGHTING OVER!
PLEASE, THINK ABOUT WHERE THE OTHER PERSON IS COMING FROM BEFORE THROWING A PUNCH.

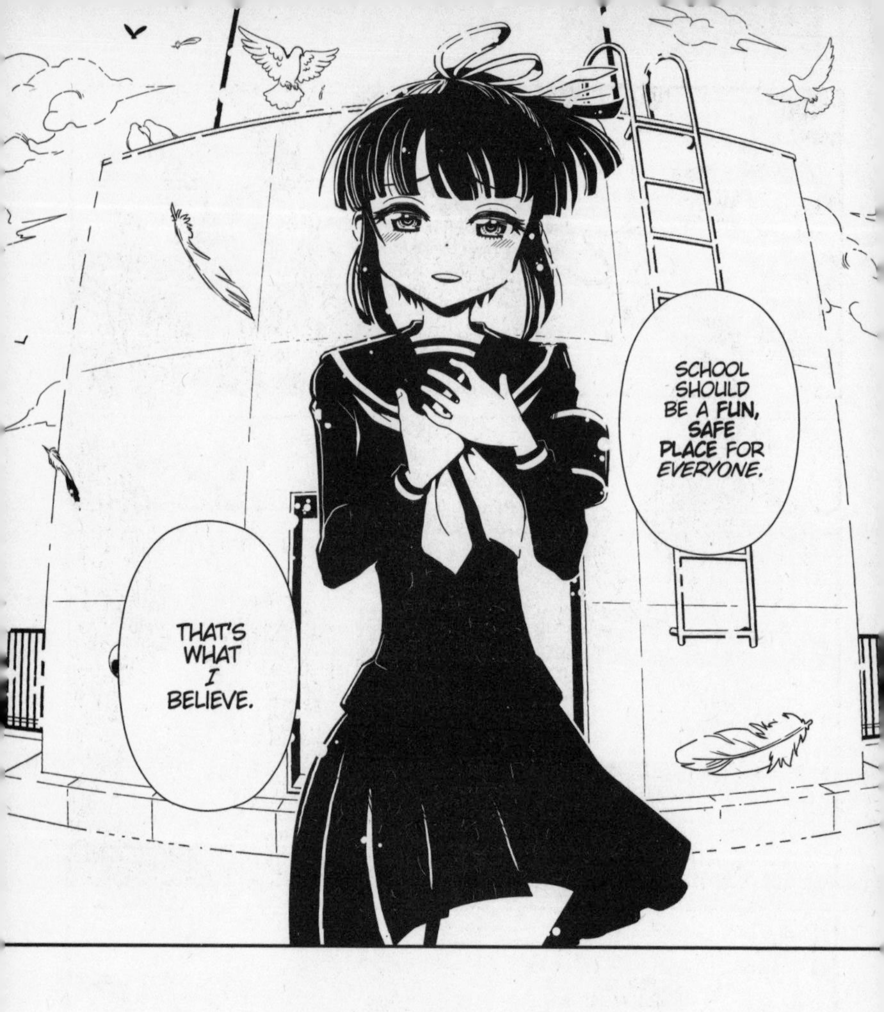
SCHOOL SHOULD BE A FUN, SAFE PLACE FOR EVERYONE.
THAT'S WHAT I BELIEVE.

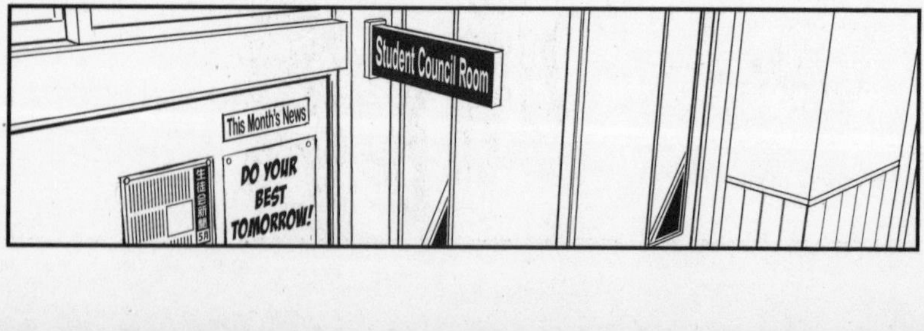
Student Council Room
This Month's News
DO YOUR BEST TOMORROW!

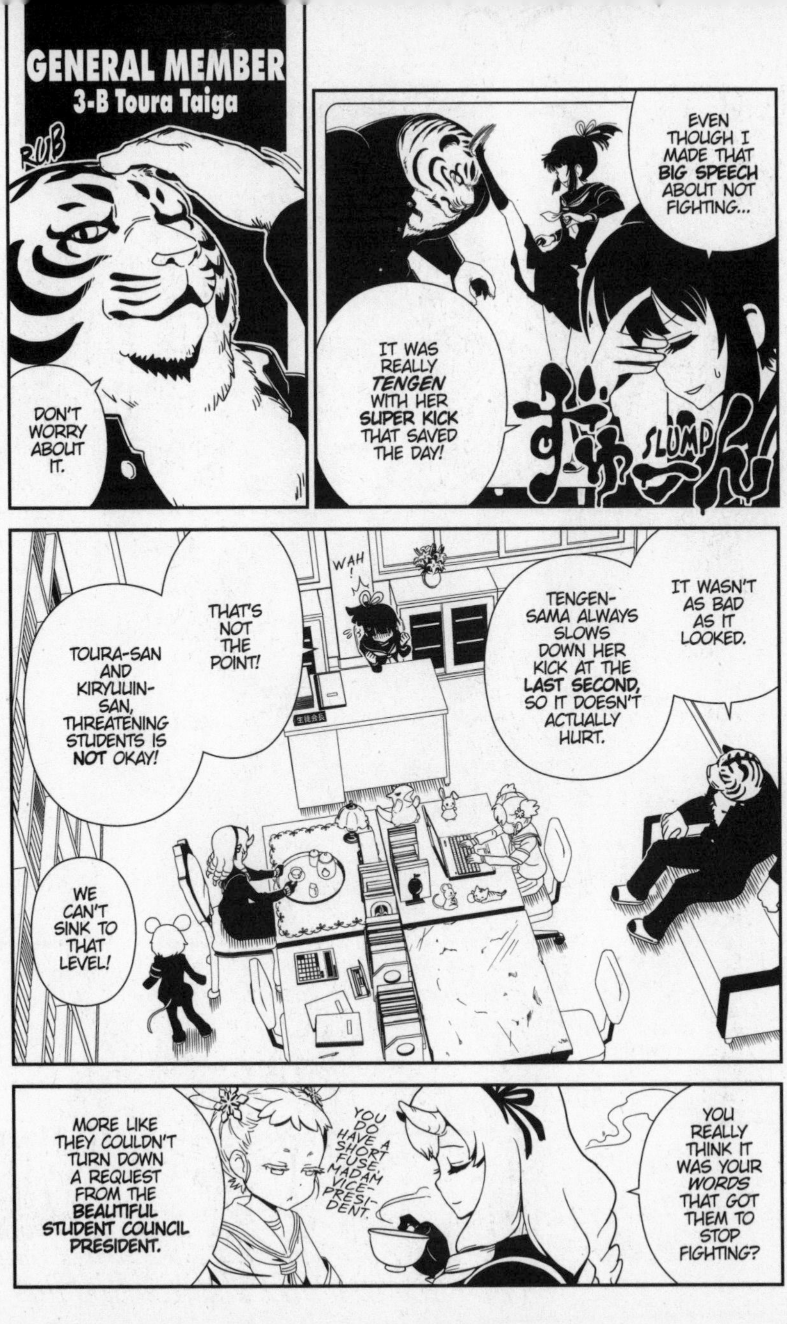
EVEN THOUGH I MADE THAT BIG SPEECH ABOUT NOT FIGHTING...
IT WAS REALLY TENGEN WITH HER SUPER KICK THAT SAVED THE DAY!
SLUMP
GENERAL MEMBER
3-B Toura Taiga
RUB
DON'T WORRY ABOUT IT.
IT WASN'T AS BAD AS IT LOOKED.
TENGEN-SAMA ALWAYS SLOWS DOWN HER KICK AT THE LAST SECOND, SO IT DOESN'T ACTUALLY HURT.
WAH!
生徒会長
THAT'S NOT THE POINT!
TOURA-SAN AND KIRYUUIN-SAN, THREATENING STUDENTS IS NOT OKAY!
WE CAN'T SINK TO THAT LEVEL!
YOU REALLY THINK IT WAS YOUR WORDS THAT GOT THEM TO STOP FIGHTING?
YOU DO HAVE A SHORT FUSE MADAM VICE-PRESIDENT.
MORE LIKE THEY COULDN'T TURN DOWN A REQUEST FROM THE BEAUTIFUL STUDENT COUNCIL PRESIDENT.

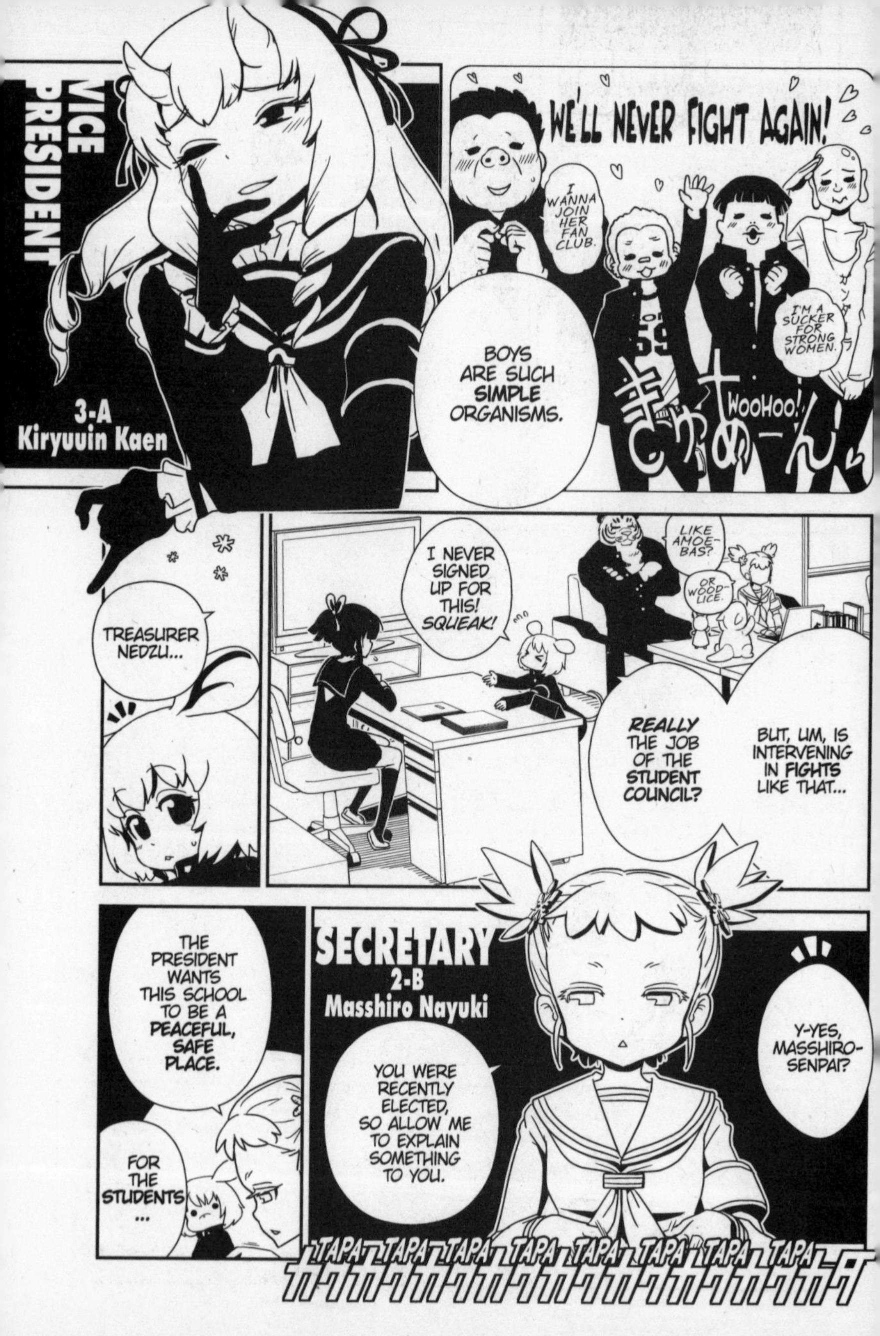
WE'LL NEVER FIGHT AGAIN!
I'M A SUCKER FOR STRONG WOMEN.
I WANNA JOIN HER FAN CLUB.
WOOHOO!
BOYS ARE SUCH SIMPLE ORGANISMS.
VICE PRESIDENT
3-A
Kiryuuin Kaen
LIKE AMOEBAS?
OR WOODLICE.
I NEVER SIGNED UP FOR THIS! SQUEAK!
BUT, UM, IS INTERVENING IN FIGHTS LIKE THAT...
REALLY THE JOB OF THE STUDENT COUNCIL?
TREASURER NEDZU...
Y-YES, MASSHIRO-SENPAI?
SECRETARY
2-B
Masshiro Nayuki
YOU WERE RECENTLY ELECTED, SO ALLOW ME TO EXPLAIN SOMETHING TO YOU.
TAPA TAPA TAPA TAPA TAPA TAPA TAPA TAPA
THE PRESIDENT WANTS THIS SCHOOL TO BE A PEACEFUL, SAFE PLACE.
FOR THE STUDENTS...

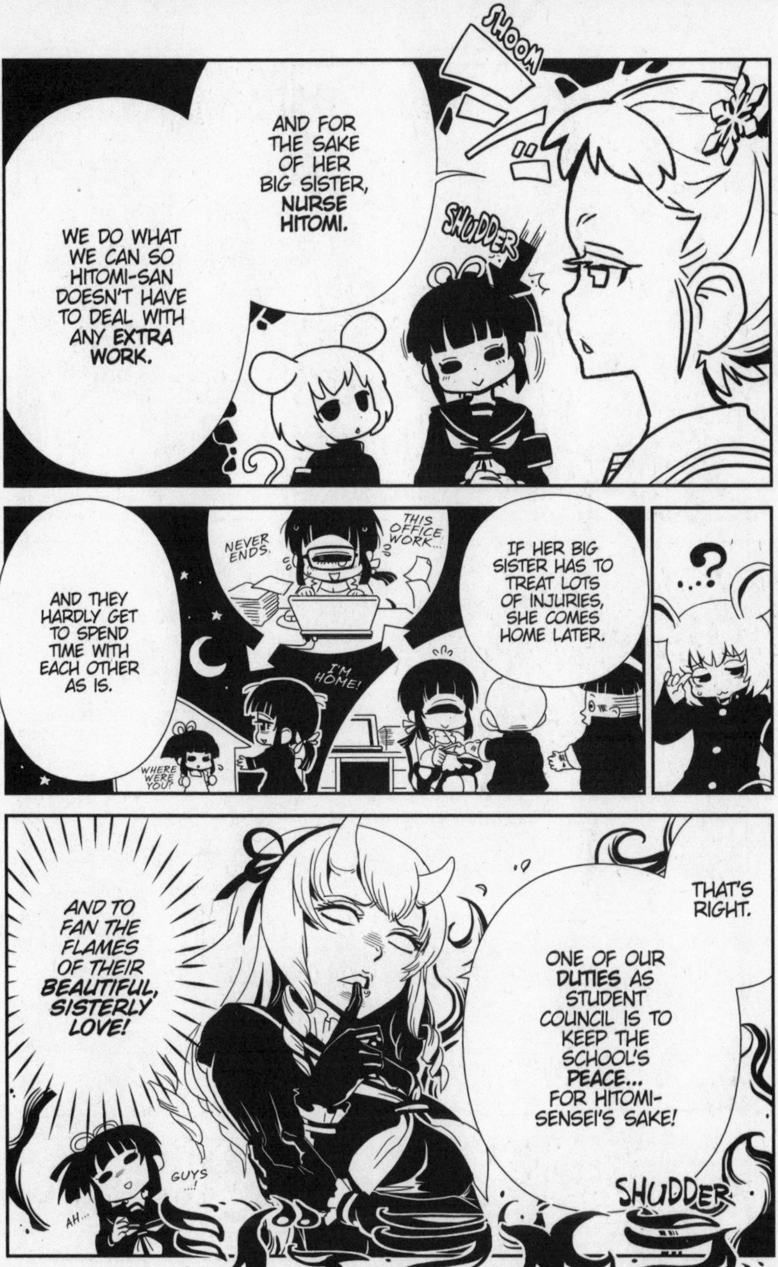
SHOOM
AND FOR THE SAKE OF HER BIG SISTER, NURSE HITOMI.
SHUDDER
WE DO WHAT WE CAN SO HITOMI-SAN DOESN'T HAVE TO DEAL WITH ANY EXTRA WORK.
?
...
IF HER BIG SISTER HAS TO TREAT LOTS OF INJURIES, SHE COMES HOME LATER.
THIS OFFICE WORK...
NEVER ENDS.
AND THEY HARDLY GET TO SPEND TIME WITH EACH OTHER AS IS.
I'M HOME!
WHERE WERE YOU?
THAT'S RIGHT.
ONE OF OUR DUTIES AS STUDENT COUNCIL IS TO KEEP THE SCHOOL'S PEACE... FOR HITOMI-SENSEI'S SAKE!
SHUDDER
AND TO FAN THE FLAMES OF THEIR BEAUTIFUL, SISTERLY LOVE!
GUYS ...!
AH...

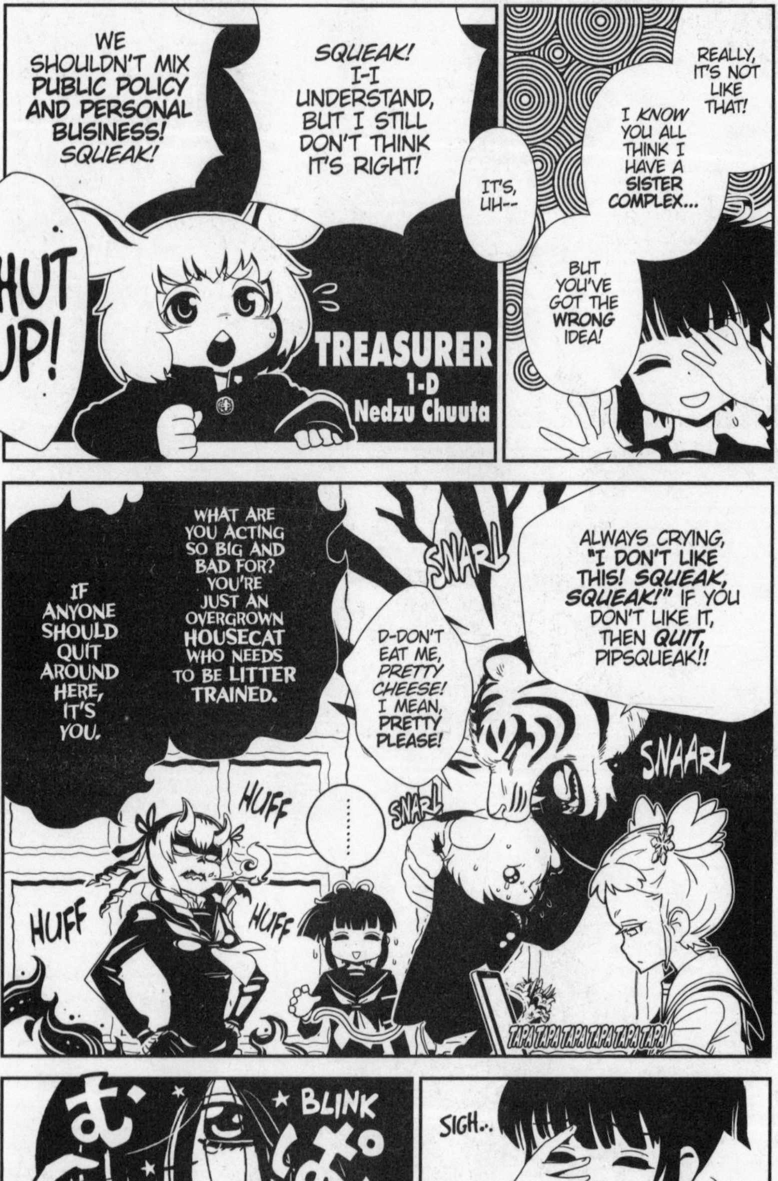
REALLY, IT'S NOT LIKE THAT!
I *KNOW* YOU ALL THINK I HAVE A **SISTER COMPLEX...**
IT'S, UH--
BUT YOU'VE GOT THE **WRONG** IDEA!
SQUEAK! I-I UNDERSTAND, BUT I STILL DON'T THINK IT'S RIGHT!
WE SHOULDN'T MIX **PUBLIC POLICY AND PERSONAL BUSINESS!** *SQUEAK!*
SHUT UP!
TREASURER
1-D
Nedzu Chuuta
ALWAYS CRYING, **"I DON'T LIKE THIS! *SQUEAK, SQUEAK!*"** IF YOU DON'T LIKE IT, THEN ***QUIT,*** PIPSQUEAK!!
SNARL
D-DON'T EAT ME, *PRETTY* CHEESE! I MEAN, *PRETTY* PLEASE!
WHAT ARE YOU ACTING SO BIG AND BAD FOR? YOU'RE JUST AN OVERGROWN **HOUSECAT** WHO NEEDS TO BE **LITTER TRAINED.**
IF ANYONE SHOULD QUIT AROUND HERE, IT'S YOU.
SNAARL
SNARL
HUFF
......
HUFF
HUFF
TAPA TAPA TAPA TAPA TAPA TAPA
SIGH..
★ BLINK
むぱ

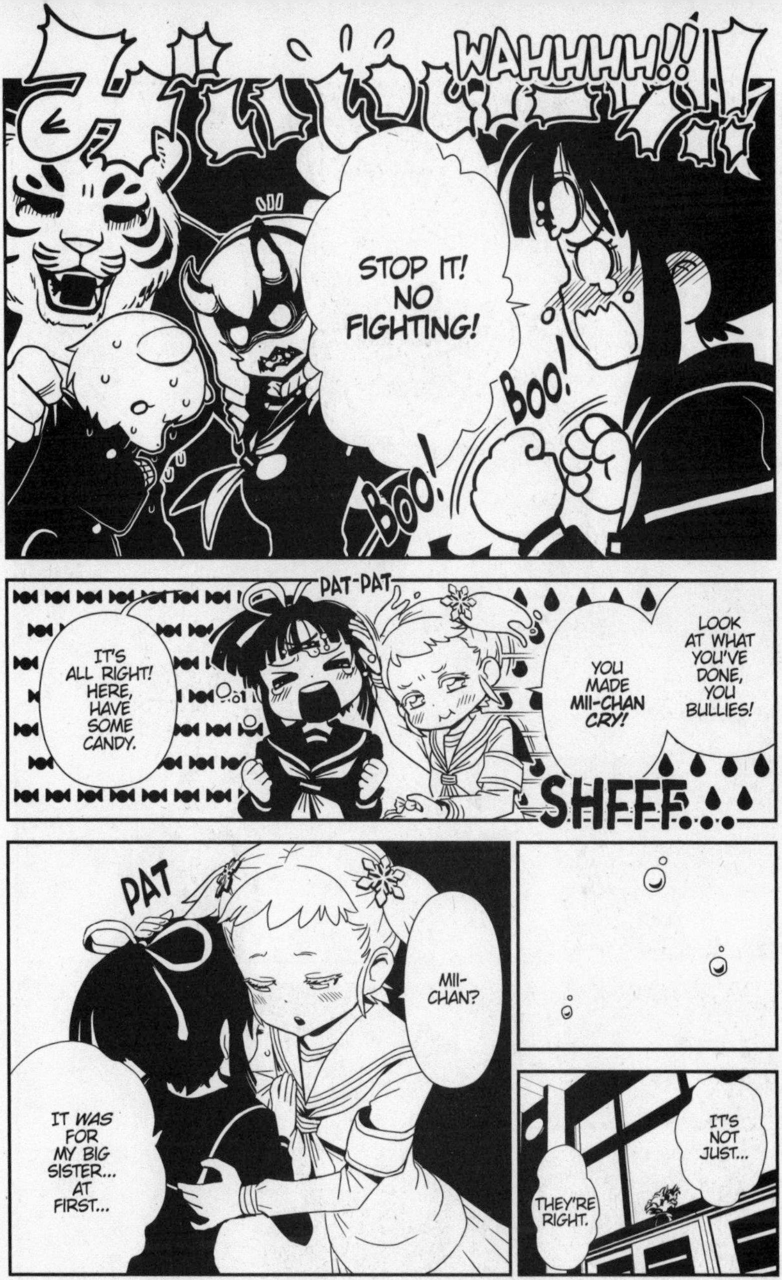
WAHHHH!!!
STOP IT! NO FIGHTING!
BOO!
BOO!
PAT-PAT
LOOK AT WHAT YOU'VE DONE, YOU BULLIES!
YOU MADE MII-CHAN CRY!
SHFFF...
IT'S ALL RIGHT! HERE, HAVE SOME CANDY.
IT'S NOT JUST...
THEY'RE RIGHT.
PAT
MII-CHAN?
IT WAS FOR MY BIG SISTER... AT FIRST...

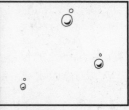

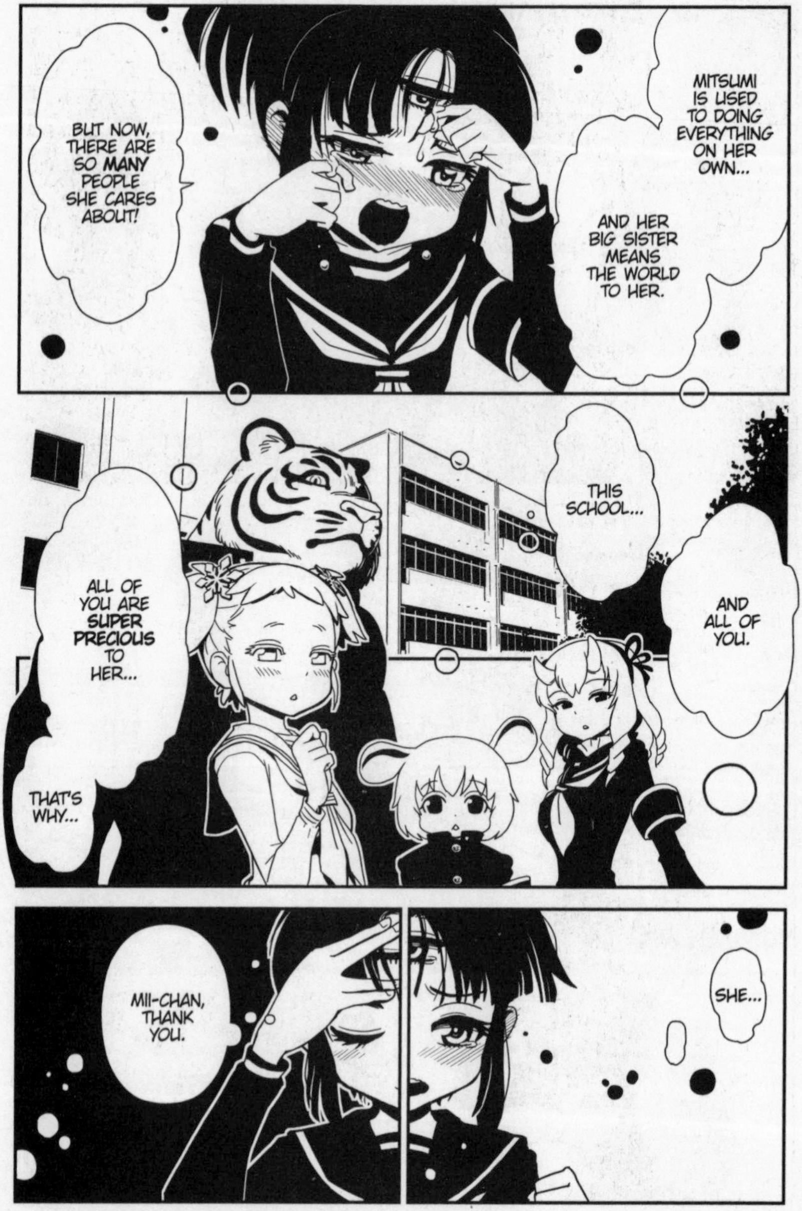
MITSUMI IS USED TO DOING EVERYTHING ON HER OWN...
AND HER BIG SISTER MEANS THE WORLD TO HER.
BUT NOW, THERE ARE SO MANY PEOPLE SHE CARES ABOUT!
THIS SCHOOL...
AND ALL OF YOU.
ALL OF YOU ARE SUPER PRECIOUS TO HER...
THAT'S WHY...
SHE...
MII-CHAN, THANK YOU.

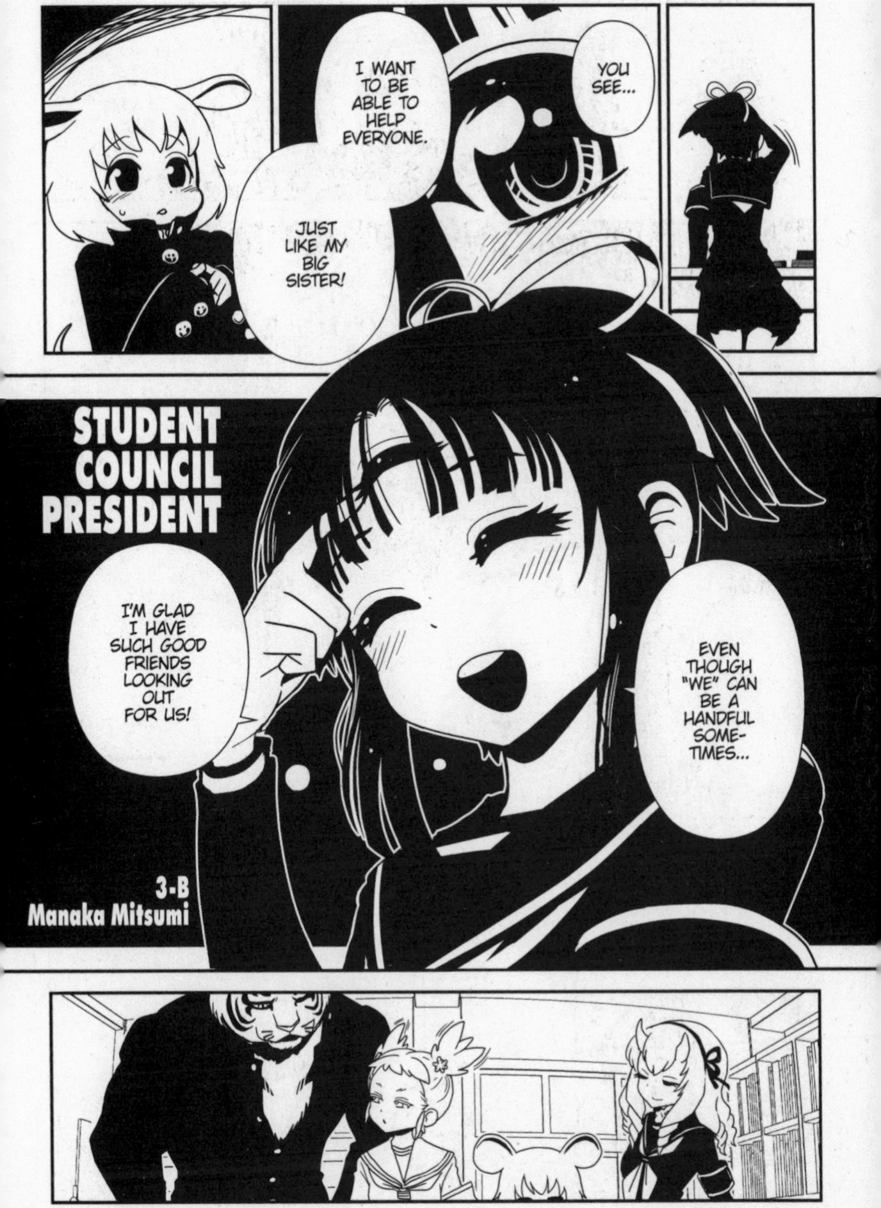
YOU SEE...
I WANT TO BE ABLE TO HELP EVERYONE.
JUST LIKE MY BIG SISTER!
STUDENT COUNCIL PRESIDENT
EVEN THOUGH "WE" CAN BE A HANDFUL SOMETIMES...
I'M GLAD I HAVE SUCH GOOD FRIENDS LOOKING OUT FOR US!
3-B
Manaka Mitsumi

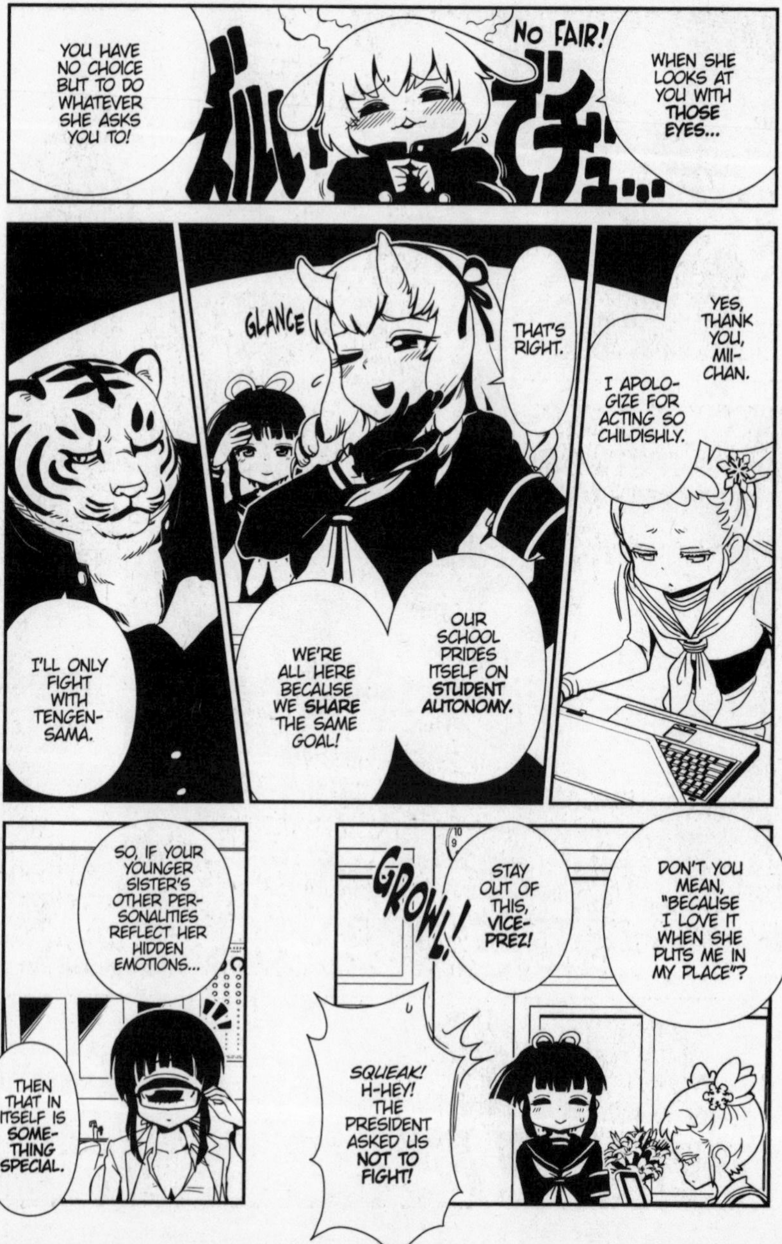
WHEN SHE LOOKS AT YOU WITH THOSE EYES...
NO FAIR!
YOU HAVE NO CHOICE BUT TO DO WHATEVER SHE ASKS YOU TO!
YES, THANK YOU, MII-CHAN.
I APOLO-GIZE FOR ACTING SO CHILDISHLY.
THAT'S RIGHT.
GLANCE
OUR SCHOOL PRIDES ITSELF ON STUDENT AUTONOMY.
WE'RE ALL HERE BECAUSE WE SHARE THE SAME GOAL!
I'LL ONLY FIGHT WITH TENGEN-SAMA.
DON'T YOU MEAN, "BECAUSE I LOVE IT WHEN SHE PUTS ME IN MY PLACE"?
STAY OUT OF THIS, VICE-PREZ!
GROWL!
SQUEAK! H-HEY! THE PRESIDENT ASKED US NOT TO FIGHT!
SO, IF YOUR YOUNGER SISTER'S OTHER PER-SONALITIES REFLECT HER HIDDEN EMOTIONS...
THEN THAT IN ITSELF IS SOME-THING SPECIAL.

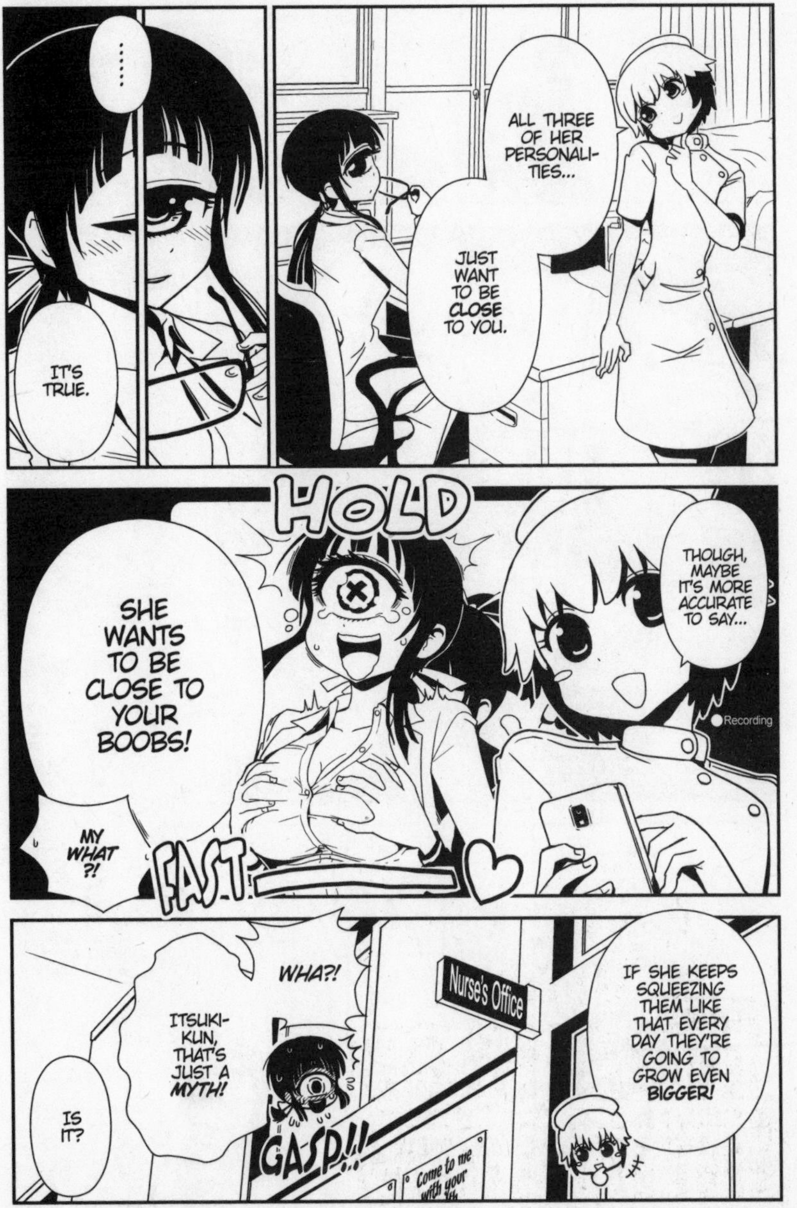
ALL THREE OF HER PERSONALITIES...
JUST WANT TO BE CLOSE TO YOU.
......
IT'S TRUE.
HOLD
THOUGH, MAYBE IT'S MORE ACCURATE TO SAY...
SHE WANTS TO BE CLOSE TO YOUR BOOBS!
Recording
MY WHAT?!
FAST
IF SHE KEEPS SQUEEZING THEM LIKE THAT EVERY DAY THEY'RE GOING TO GROW EVEN BIGGER!
Nurse's Office
WHA?!
ITSUKI-KUN, THAT'S JUST A MYTH!
GASP!!
Come to me with your
IS IT?

NURSE HITOMI'S Monster Infirmary

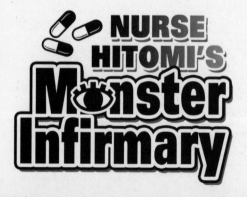

Student Council Executive Officers

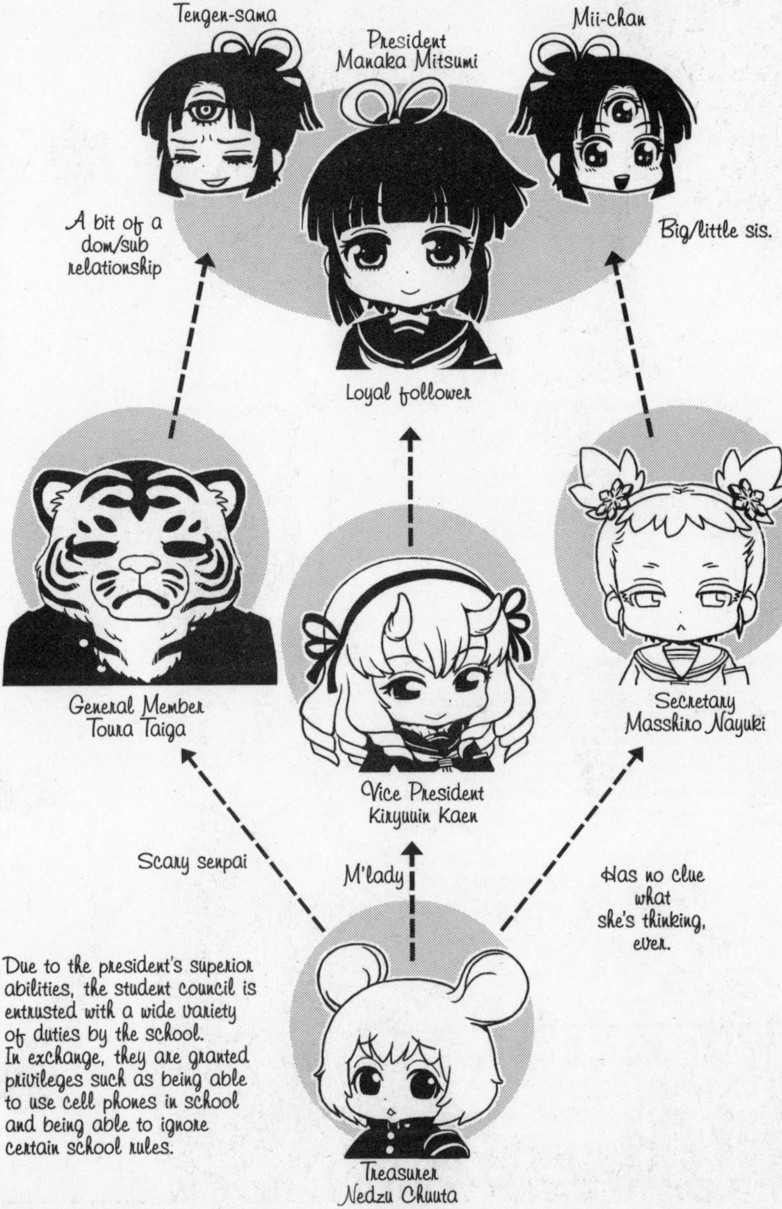
Tengen-sama
President
Manaka Mitsumi
Mii-chan
A bit of a dom/sub relationship
Big/little sis.
Loyal follower
General Member
Toura Taiga
Secretary
Masshiro Nayuki
Vice President
Kiryuuin Kaen
Scary senpai
M'lady
Has no clue what she's thinking, ever.
Treasurer
Nedzu Chuuta

Due to the president's superior abilities, the student council is entrusted with a wide variety of duties by the school.
In exchange, they are granted privileges such as being able to use cell phones in school and being able to ignore certain school rules.

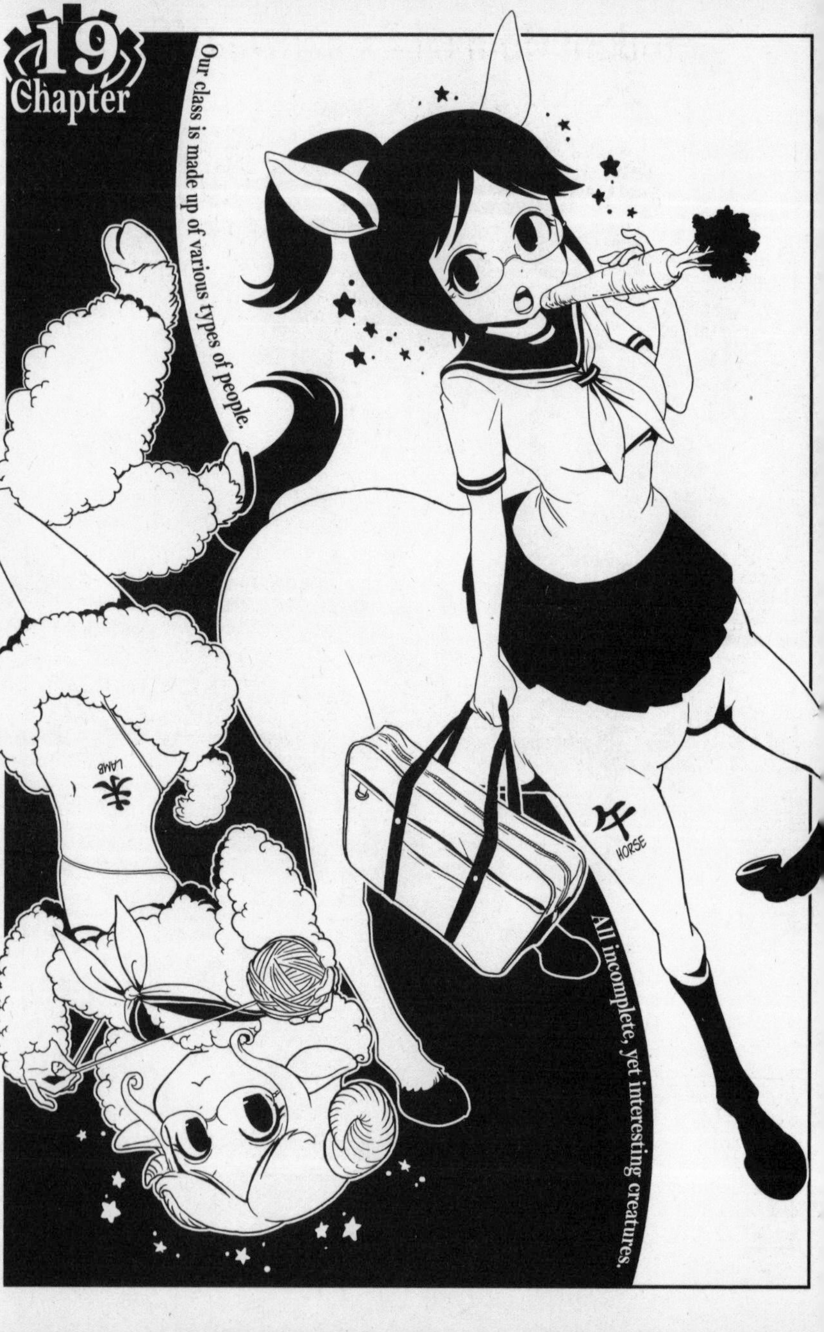
19
Chapter
Our class is made up of various types of people.
All incomplete, yet interesting creatures.
羊
LAMB
午
HORSE

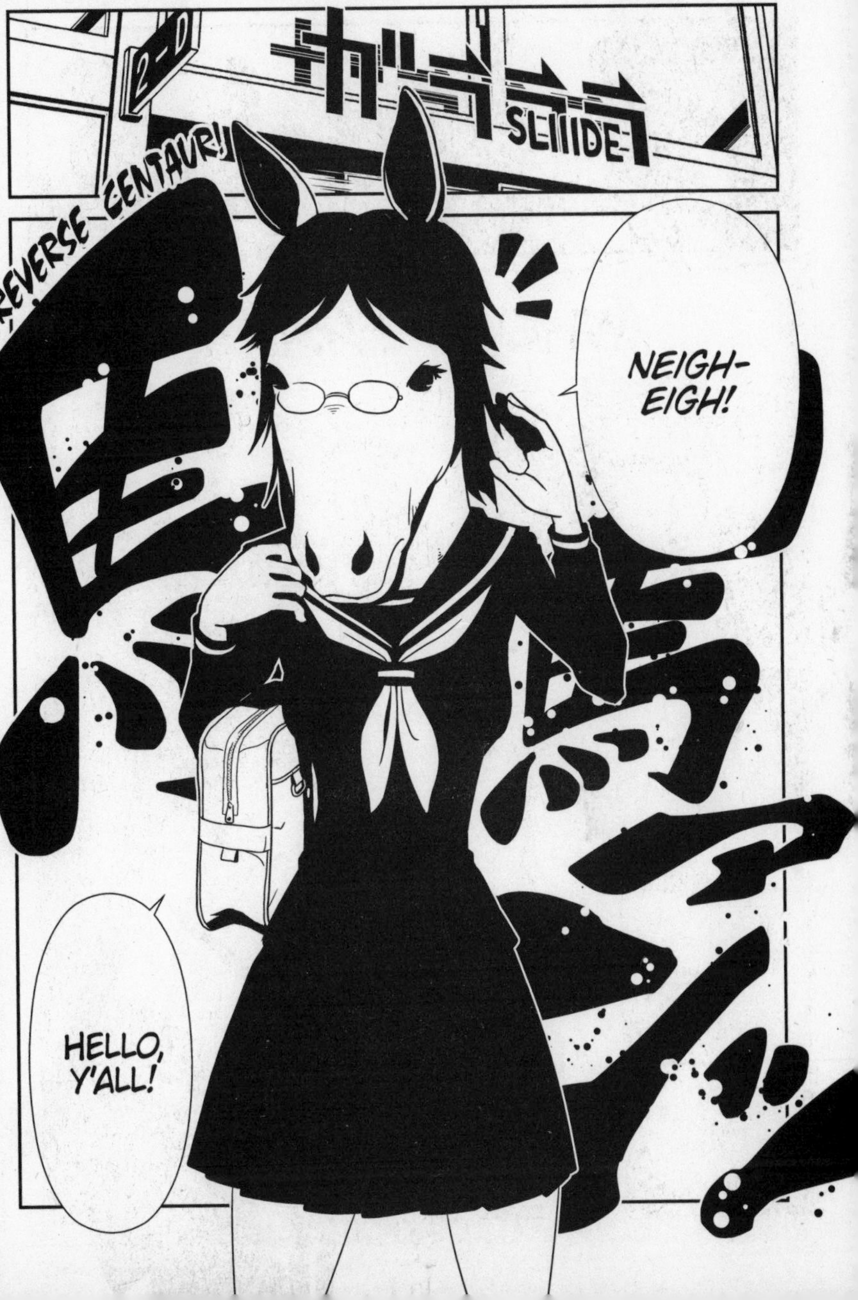
2-D
SLIIIDE
NEIGH-EIGH!
REVERSE CENTAUR!
HELLO, Y'ALL!

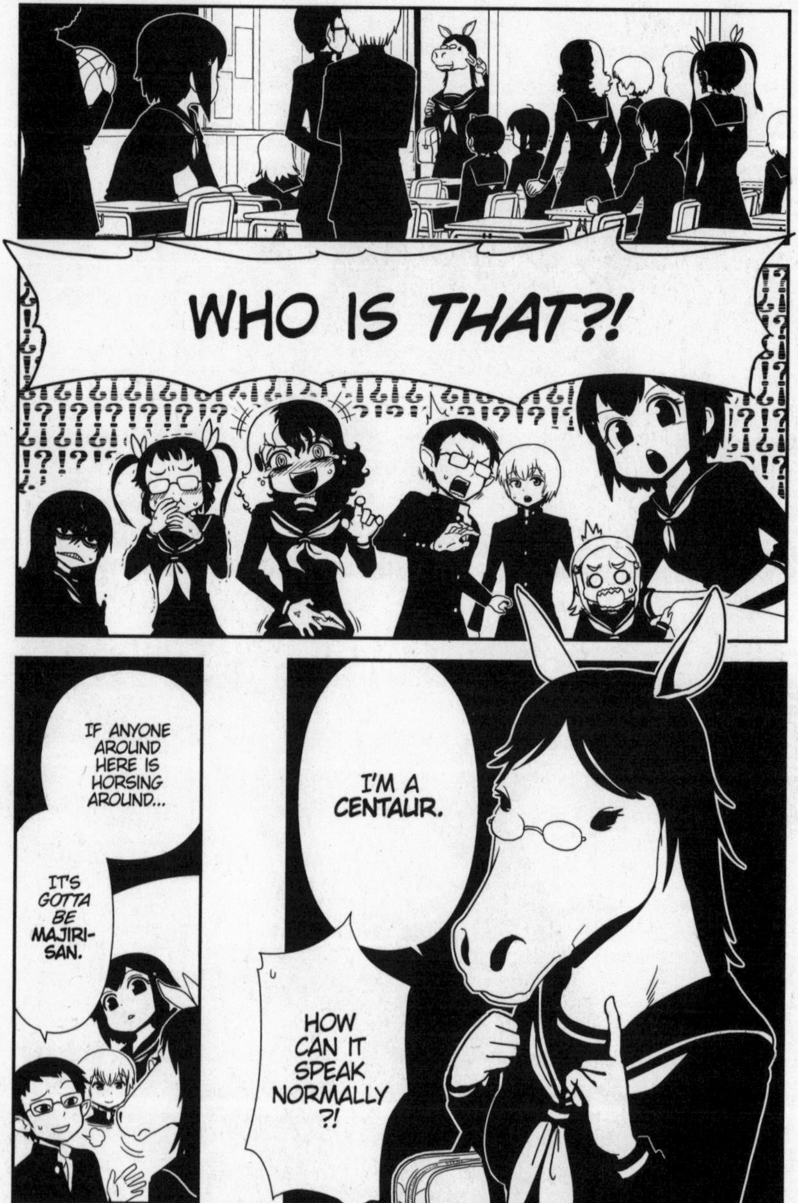
WHO IS THAT?!
I'M A CENTAUR.
HOW CAN IT SPEAK NORMALLY?!
IF ANYONE AROUND HERE IS HORSING AROUND...
IT'S GOTTA BE MAJIRI-SAN.

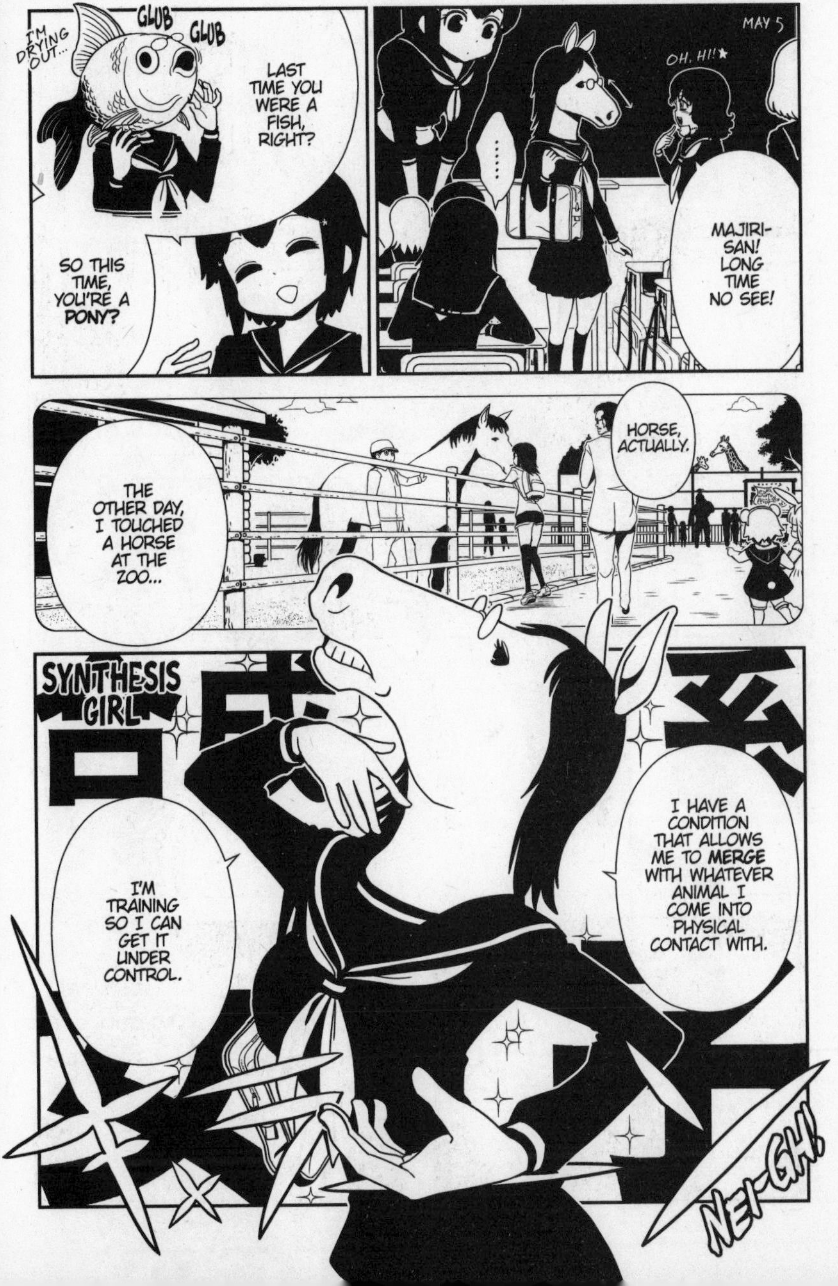
MAY 5
OH, HI!★
MAJIRI-SAN! LONG TIME NO SEE!
......
LAST TIME YOU WERE A FISH, RIGHT?
GLUB GLUB
I'M DRYING OUT...
SO THIS TIME, YOU'RE A PONY?
HORSE, ACTUALLY.
THE OTHER DAY, I TOUCHED A HORSE AT THE ZOO...
SYNTHESIS GIRL
I HAVE A CONDITION THAT ALLOWS ME TO MERGE WITH WHATEVER ANIMAL I COME INTO PHYSICAL CONTACT WITH.
I'M TRAINING SO I CAN GET IT UNDER CONTROL.
NEI-GH!

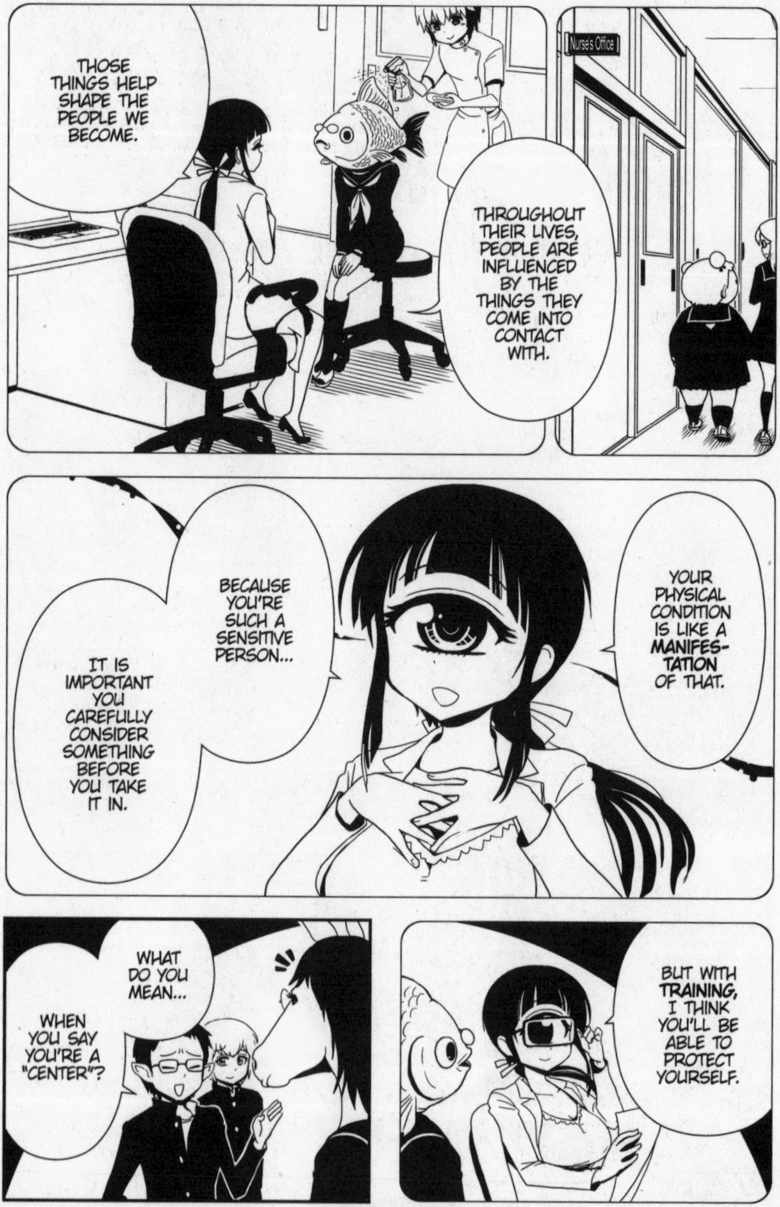
Nurse's Office
THROUGHOUT THEIR LIVES, PEOPLE ARE INFLUENCED BY THE THINGS THEY COME INTO CONTACT WITH.
THOSE THINGS HELP SHAPE THE PEOPLE WE BECOME.
YOUR PHYSICAL CONDITION IS LIKE A **MANIFESTATION** OF THAT.
BECAUSE YOU'RE SUCH A SENSITIVE PERSON...
IT IS IMPORTANT YOU CAREFULLY CONSIDER SOMETHING BEFORE YOU TAKE IT IN.
BUT WITH **TRAINING**, I THINK YOU'LL BE ABLE TO PROTECT YOURSELF.
WHAT DO YOU MEAN...
WHEN YOU SAY YOU'RE A "CENTER"?

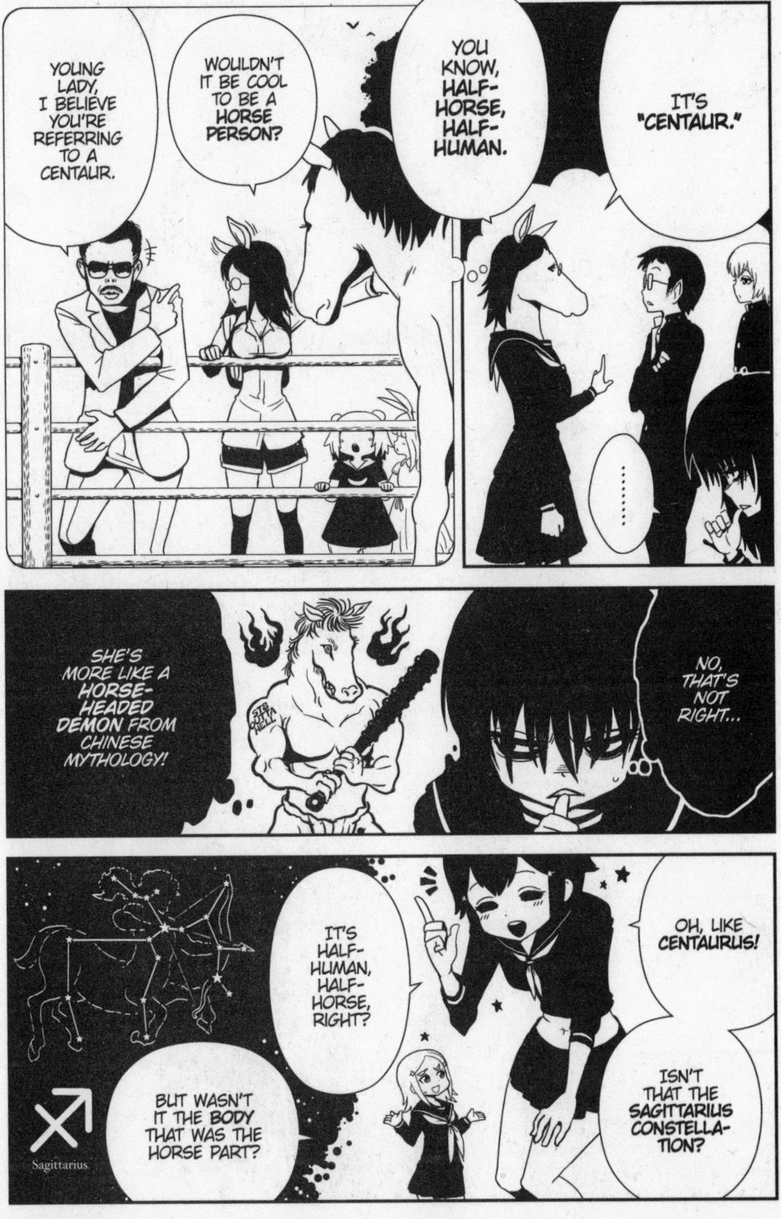
IT'S "CENTAUR."
YOU KNOW, HALF-HORSE, HALF-HUMAN.
......
WOULDN'T IT BE COOL TO BE A HORSE PERSON?
YOUNG LADY, I BELIEVE YOU'RE REFERRING TO A CENTAUR.
NO, THAT'S NOT RIGHT...
STB OUTTA HELL
SHE'S MORE LIKE A HORSE-HEADED DEMON FROM CHINESE MYTHOLOGY!
OH, LIKE CENTAURUS!
IT'S HALF-HUMAN, HALF-HORSE, RIGHT?
ISN'T THAT THE SAGITTARIUS CONSTELLATION?
BUT WASN'T IT THE BODY THAT WAS THE HORSE PART?
Sagittarius

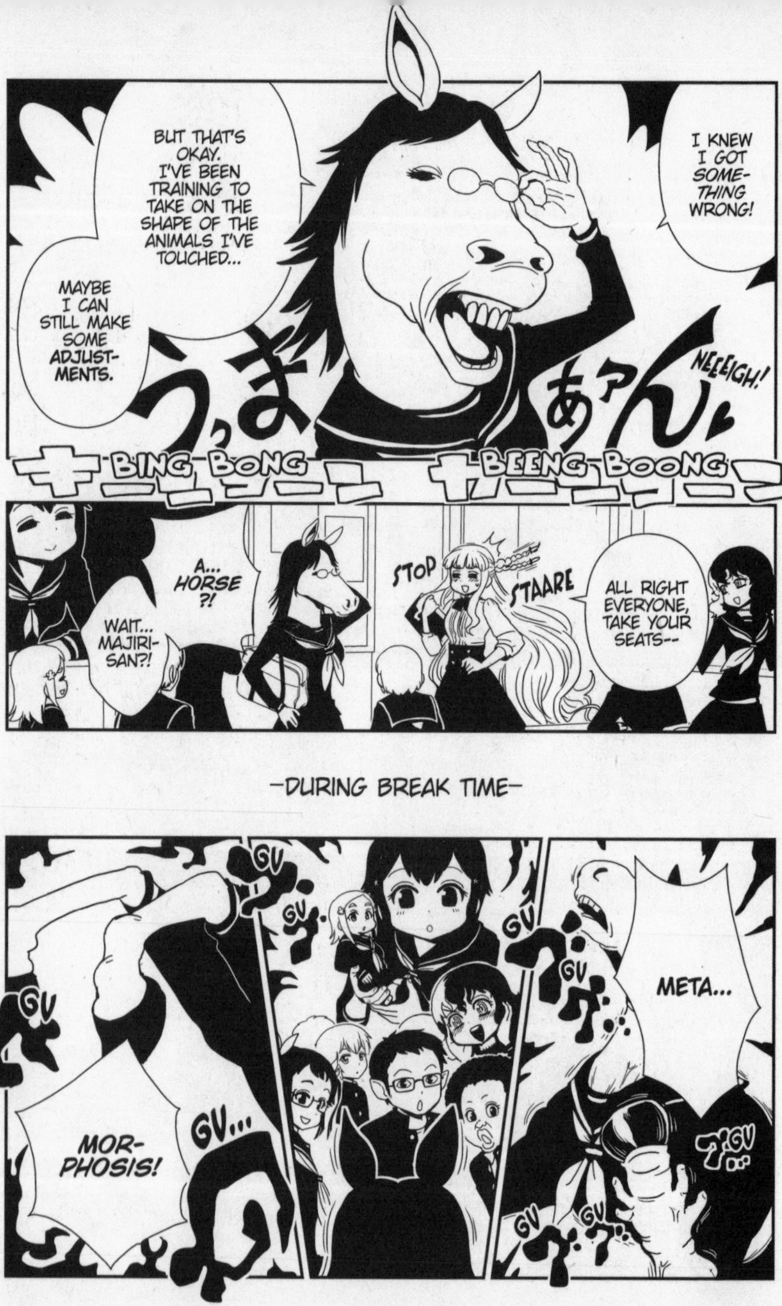
I KNEW I GOT SOME-THING WRONG!
BUT THAT'S OKAY. I'VE BEEN TRAINING TO TAKE ON THE SHAPE OF THE ANIMALS I'VE TOUCHED...
MAYBE I CAN STILL MAKE SOME ADJUST-MENTS.
NEEEIGH!
うまぁん
BEENG BOONG
BING BONG
ALL RIGHT EVERYONE, TAKE YOUR SEATS--
STOP
STAARE
A... HORSE?!
WAIT... MAJIRI-SAN?!
-DURING BREAK TIME-
META...
GV
GV...
MOR-PHOSIS!

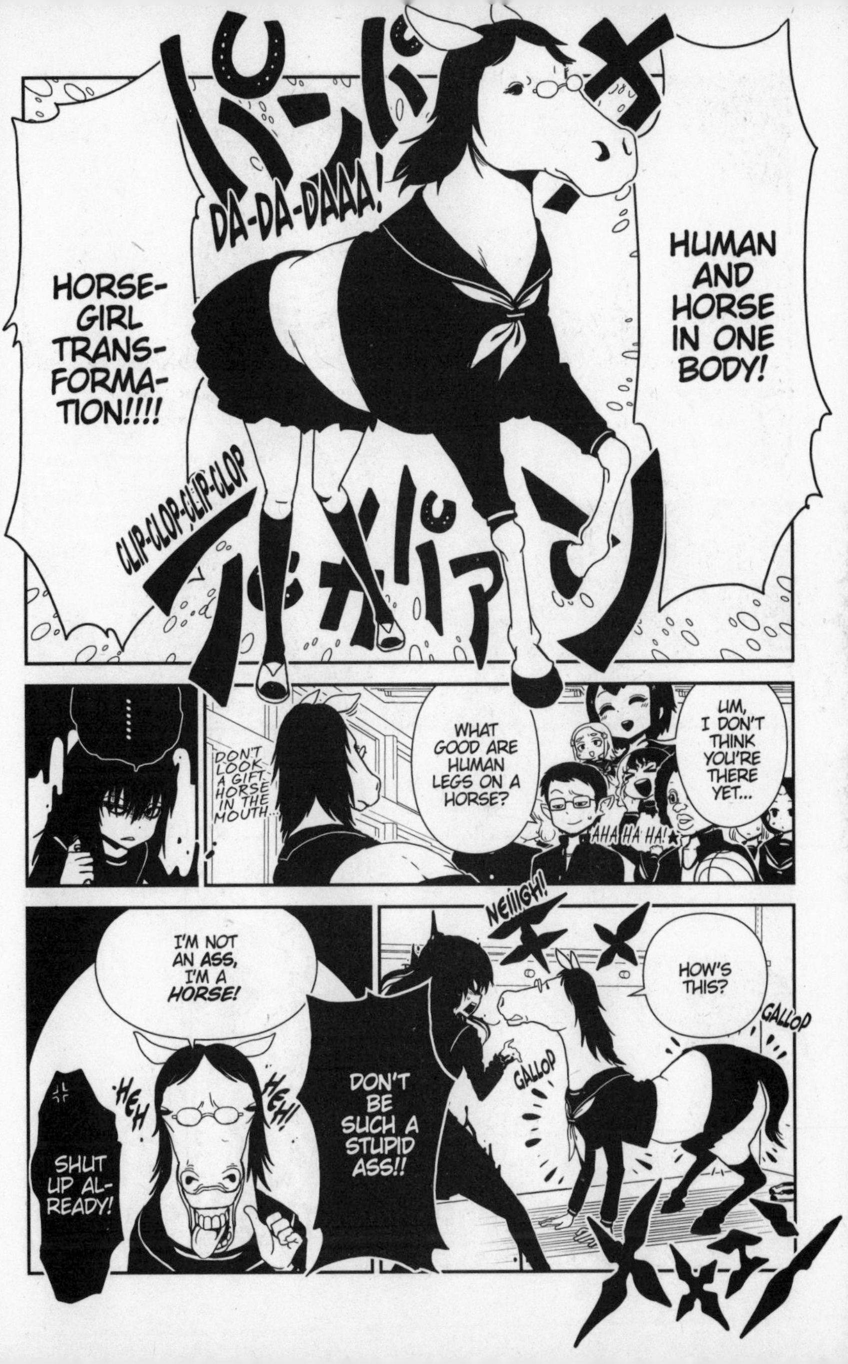
HUMAN AND HORSE IN ONE BODY!
DA-DA-DAAA!
HORSE-GIRL TRANS-FORMA-TION!!!!!
CLIP-CLOP-CLIP-CLOP
UM, I DON'T THINK YOU'RE THERE YET...
WHAT GOOD ARE HUMAN LEGS ON A HORSE?
AHA HA HA!
DON'T LOOK A GIFT HORSE IN THE MOUTH...
......
NEIIIGH!
HOW'S THIS?
GALLOP
GALLOP
DON'T BE SUCH A STUPID ASS!!
I'M NOT AN ASS, I'M A HORSE!
HEH HEH!
SHUT UP AL-READY!

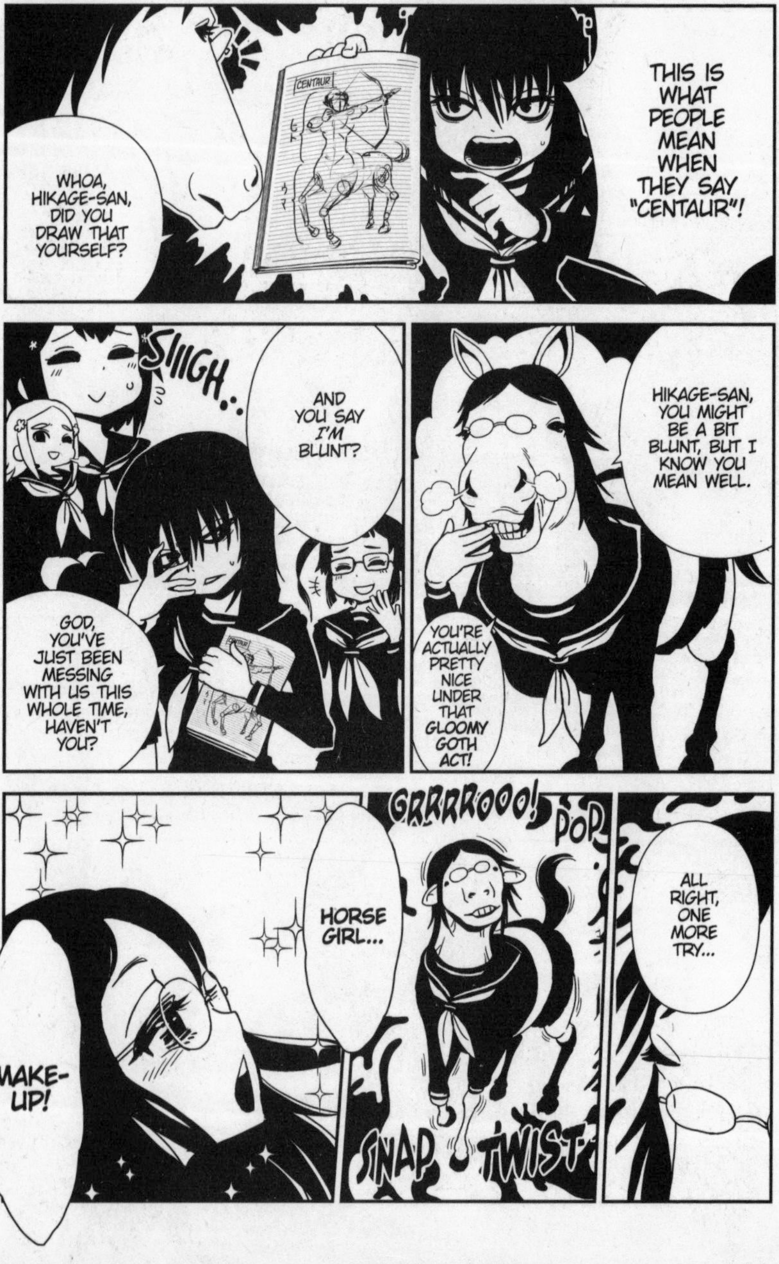
THIS IS WHAT PEOPLE MEAN WHEN THEY SAY "CENTAUR"!
CENTAUR
WHOA, HIKAGE-SAN, DID YOU DRAW THAT YOURSELF?
HIKAGE-SAN, YOU MIGHT BE A BIT BLUNT, BUT I KNOW YOU MEAN WELL.
YOU'RE ACTUALLY PRETTY NICE UNDER THAT GLOOMY GOTH ACT!
AND YOU SAY *I'M* BLUNT?
SIIIGH...
GOD, YOU'VE JUST BEEN MESSING WITH US THIS WHOLE TIME, HAVEN'T YOU?
ALL RIGHT, ONE MORE TRY...
POP
GRRRROOO!
HORSE GIRL...
SNAP
TWIST
MAKE-UP!

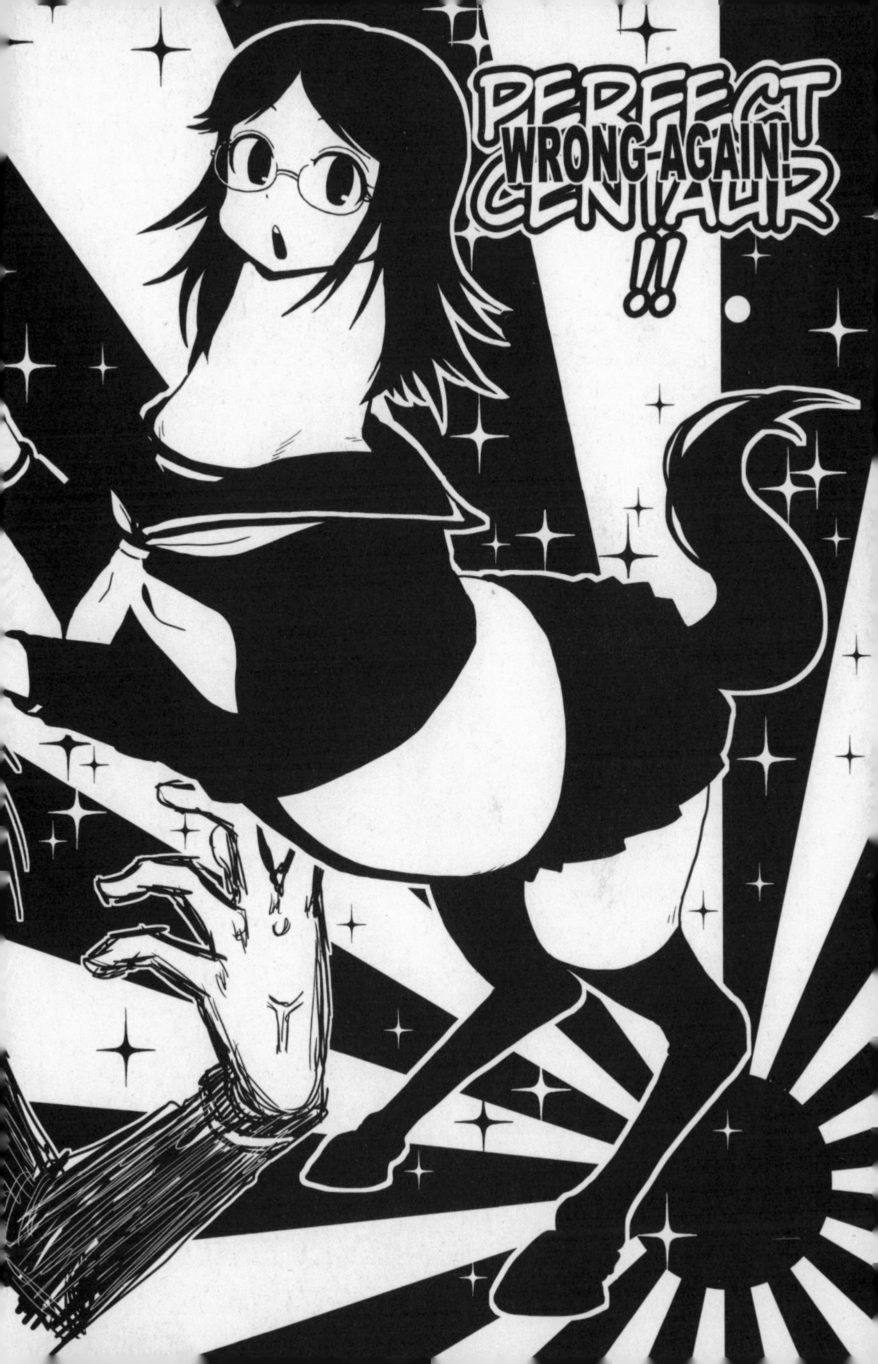
PERFECT
WRONG-AGAIN!
CENTAUR
!!

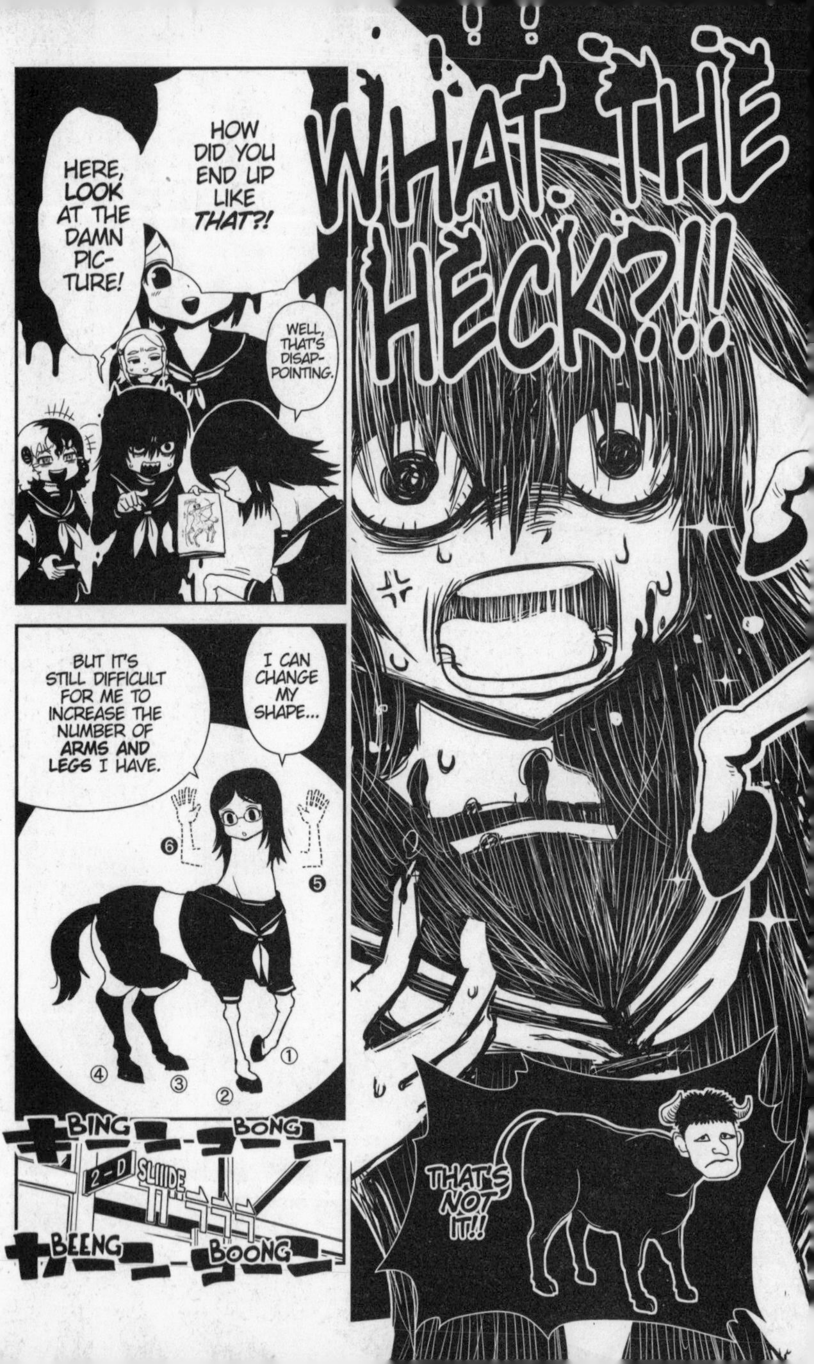

!!
WHAT THE HECK?!!
THAT'S NOT IT!!
HOW DID YOU END UP LIKE *THAT?!*
HERE, LOOK AT THE DAMN PIC-TURE!
WELL, THAT'S DISAP-POINTING.
I CAN CHANGE MY SHAPE...
BUT IT'S STILL DIFFICULT FOR ME TO INCREASE THE NUMBER OF **ARMS AND LEGS** I HAVE.
6
5
1
2
3
4
BING
BONG
2-D
SLIIDE
BEENG
BOONG

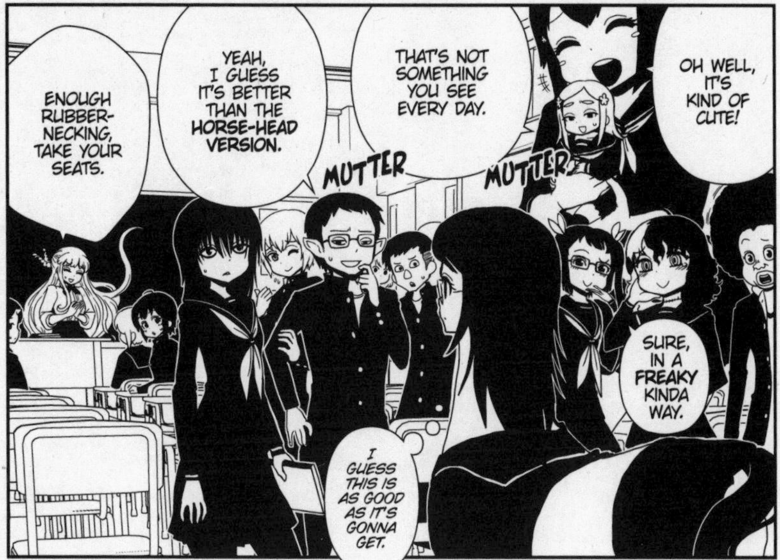
OH WELL, IT'S KIND OF CUTE!
THAT'S NOT SOMETHING YOU SEE EVERY DAY.
MUTTER
YEAH, I GUESS IT'S BETTER THAN THE HORSE-HEAD VERSION.
MUTTER
ENOUGH RUBBER-NECKING, TAKE YOUR SEATS.
SURE, IN A FREAKY KINDA WAY.
I GUESS THIS IS AS GOOD AS IT'S GONNA GET.

-THE NEXT DAY-

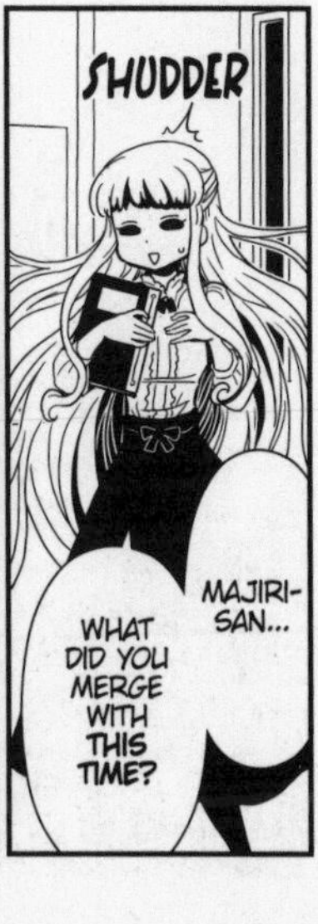
SHUDDER
MAJIRI-SAN...
WHAT DID YOU MERGE WITH THIS TIME?

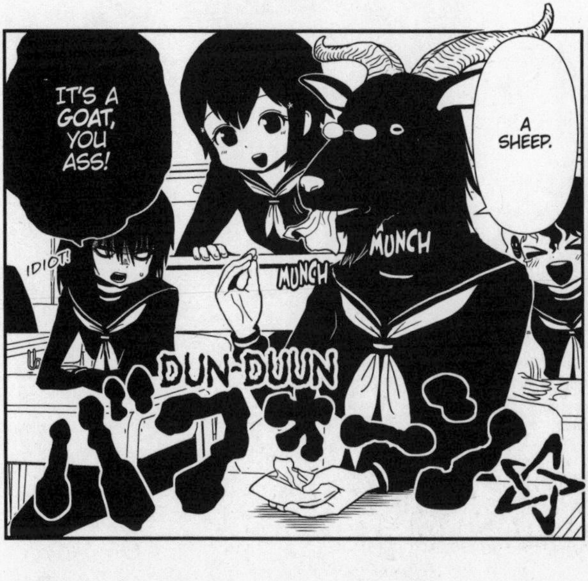
A SHEEP.
MUNCH
MUNCH
IT'S A GOAT, YOU ASS!
IDIOT!
DUN-DUUN

NURSE HITOMI'S

Monster Infirmary

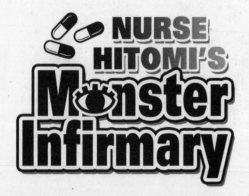

Student Health Record

May 201X

Class 2-D

Majiri Kirameki

Synthesis Girl

- She has a condition where she takes on the traits of animals she's come in contact with.

- While she can make some adjustments as to how the new form will blend with her existing body, the transformation has limits based on her total mass and her skeletal structure.

- Since anything she's wearing at the time will affect the transformation, her glasses become one with her face.

- Touching another human returns her to normal.

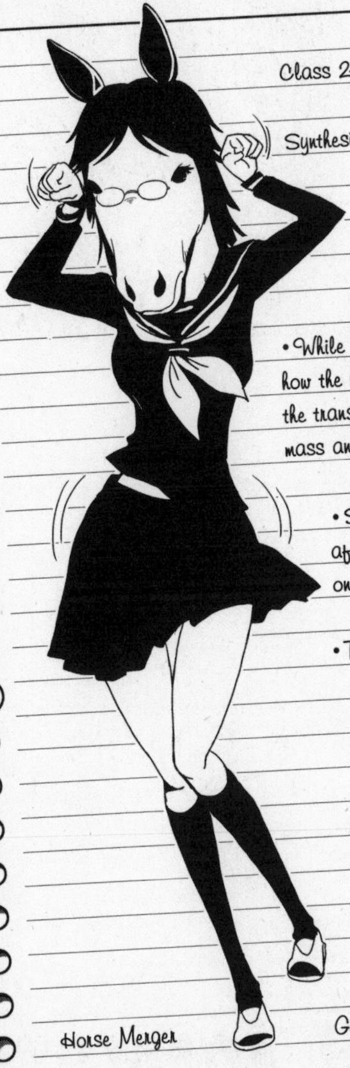

Horse Merger

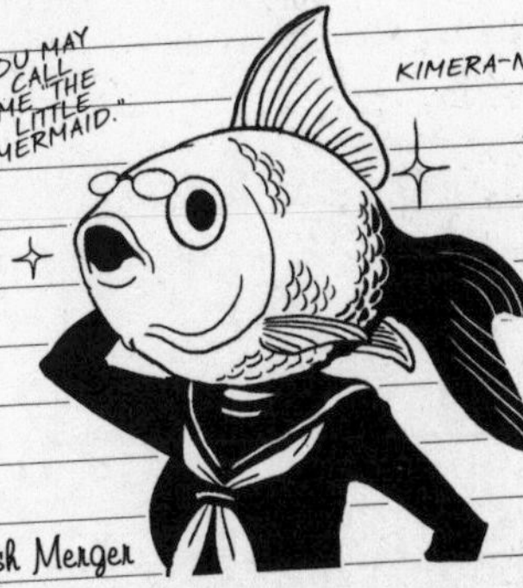
YOU MAY CALL ME "THE LITTLE MERMAID."
KIMERA-N

Goldfish Merger

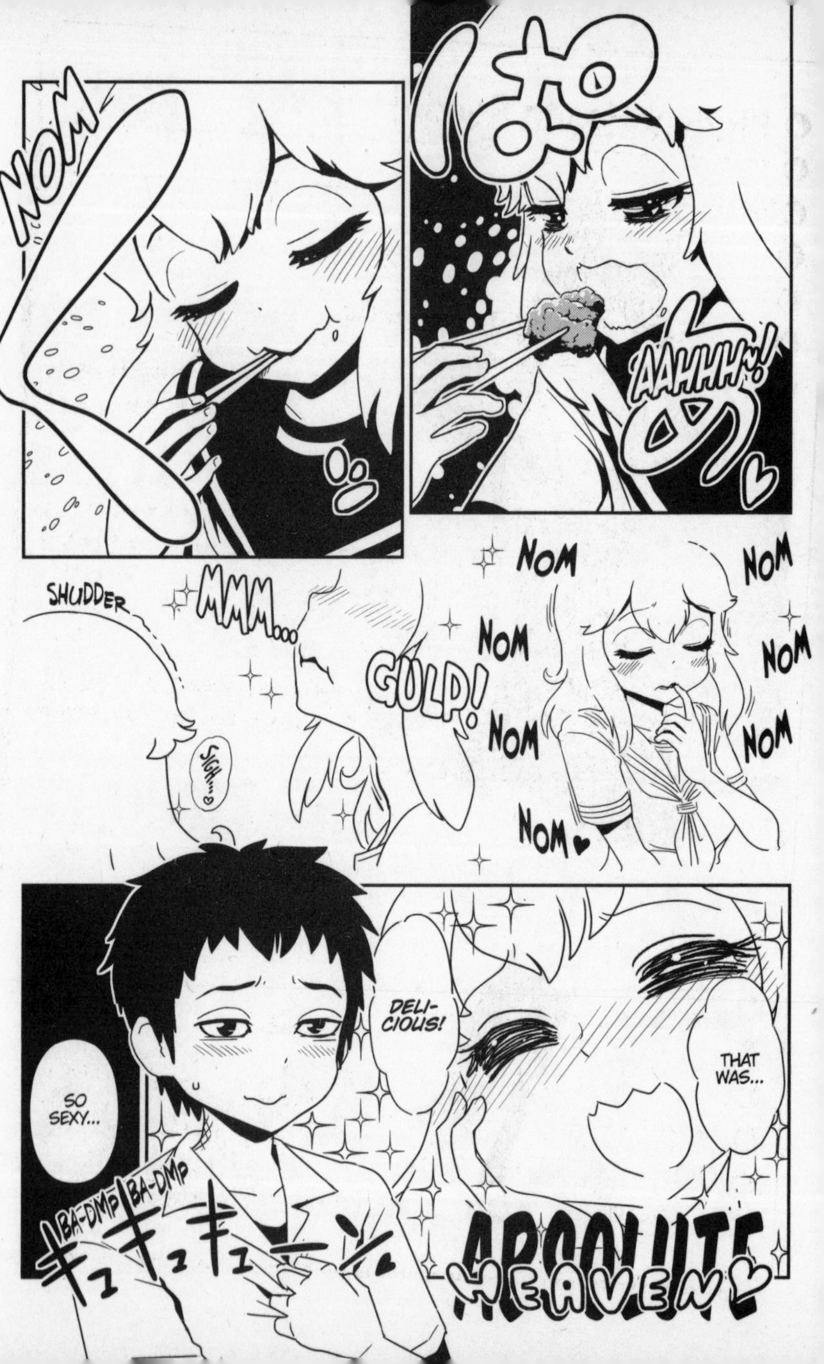
AAHHH~!
NOM
MMM...
GULP!
NOM
NOM
NOM
NOM
NOM
NOM
NOM♥
SHUDDER
SIGH...♥
THAT WAS...
DELICIOUS!
ABSOLUTE HEAVEN♥
SO SEXY...
BA-DMP BA-DMP
キュキュキュー

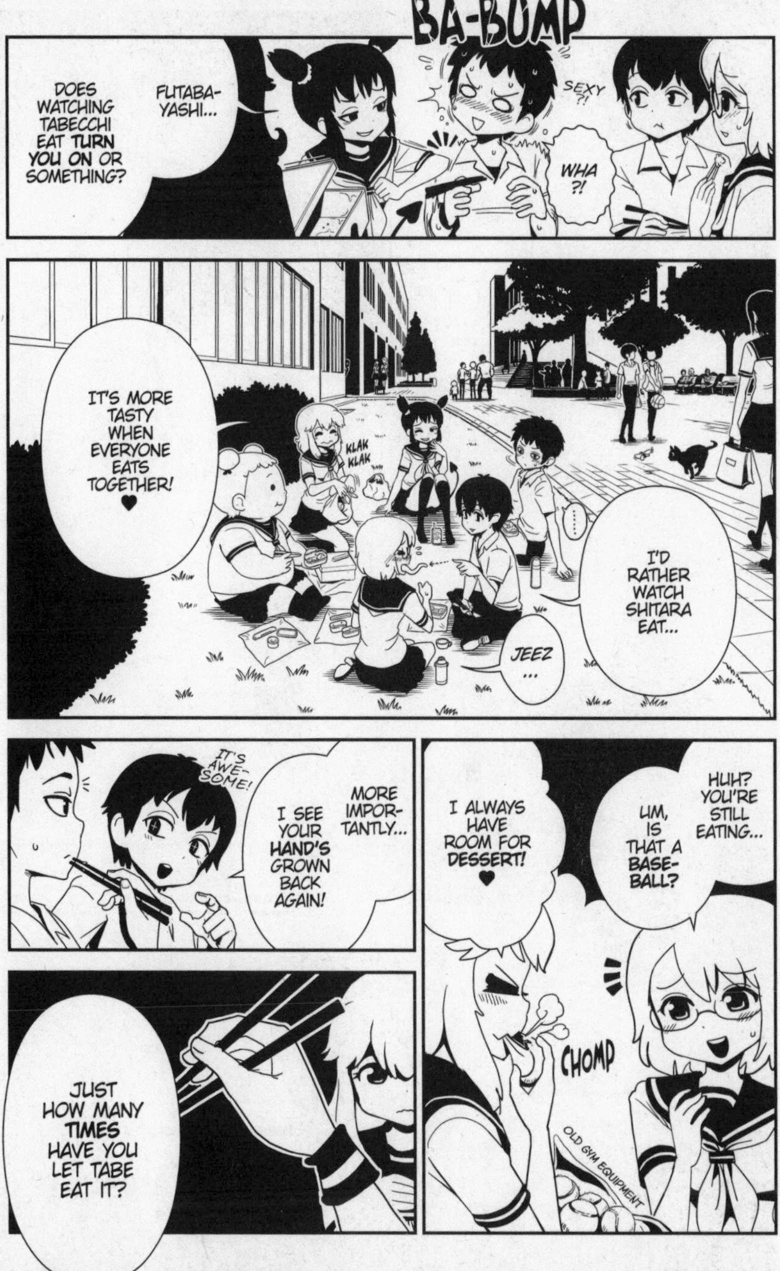
BA-BUMP
SEXY ?!
WHA ?!
FUTABA-YASHI...
DOES WATCHING TABECCHI EAT TURN YOU ON OR SOMETHING?
I'D RATHER WATCH SHITARA EAT...
...
JEEZ ...
KLAK KLAK
IT'S MORE TASTY WHEN EVERYONE EATS TOGETHER! ♥
HUH? YOU'RE STILL EATING...
UM, IS THAT A BASE-BALL?
I ALWAYS HAVE ROOM FOR DESSERT! ♥
CHOMP
OLD GYM EQUIPMENT
MORE IMPOR-TANTLY...
I SEE YOUR HAND'S GROWN BACK AGAIN!
IT'S AWE-SOME!
JUST HOW MANY TIMES HAVE YOU LET TABE EAT IT?

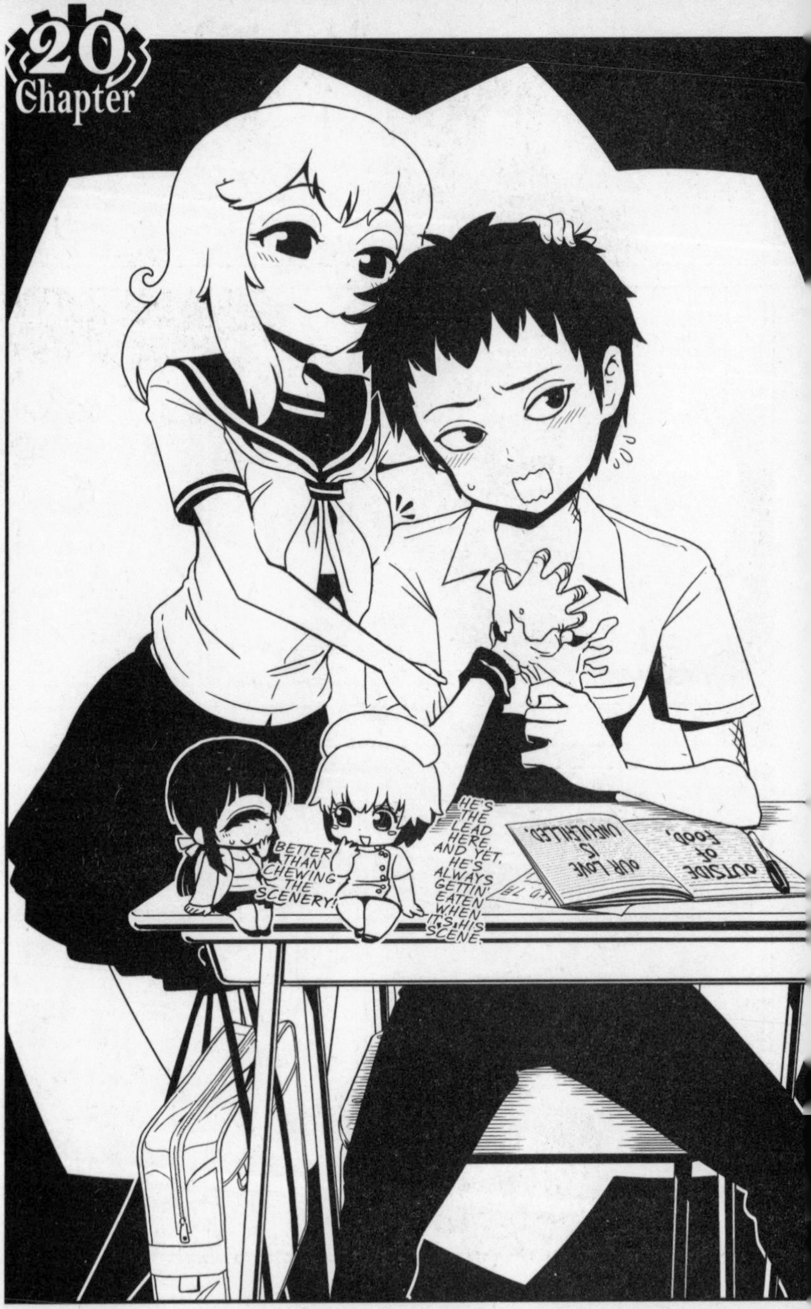
20
Chapter
OUTSIDE OF FOOD, OUR LOVE IS UNFULFILLED.
HE'S THE LEAD HERE, AND YET, HE'S ALWAYS GETTIN' EATEN WHEN IT'S HIS SCENE.
BETTER THAN CHEWING THE SCENERY!

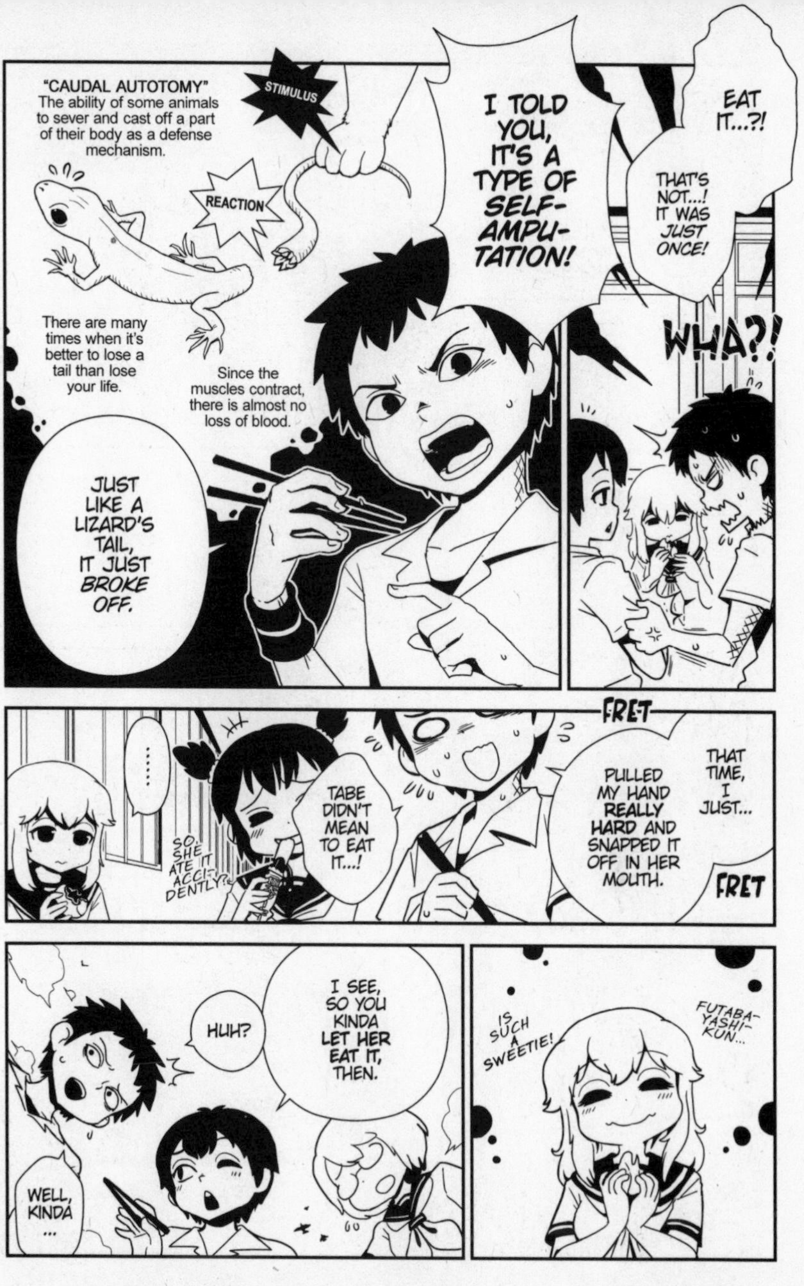

EAT IT...?!
THAT'S NOT...! IT WAS JUST ONCE!
WHA?!
I TOLD YOU, IT'S A TYPE OF SELF-AMPUTATION!
STIMULUS
REACTION
"CAUDAL AUTOTOMY" The ability of some animals to sever and cast off a part of their body as a defense mechanism.
There are many times when it's better to lose a tail than lose your life.
Since the muscles contract, there is almost no loss of blood.
JUST LIKE A LIZARD'S TAIL, IT JUST BROKE OFF.
THAT TIME, I JUST...
FRET
PULLED MY HAND REALLY HARD AND SNAPPED IT OFF IN HER MOUTH.
FRET
TABE DIDN'T MEAN TO EAT IT...!
SO, SHE ATE IT ACCIDENTLY?!
......
FUTABAYASHI-KUN...
IS SUCH A SWEETIE!
I SEE, SO YOU KINDA LET HER EAT IT, THEN.
HUH?
WELL, KINDA ...

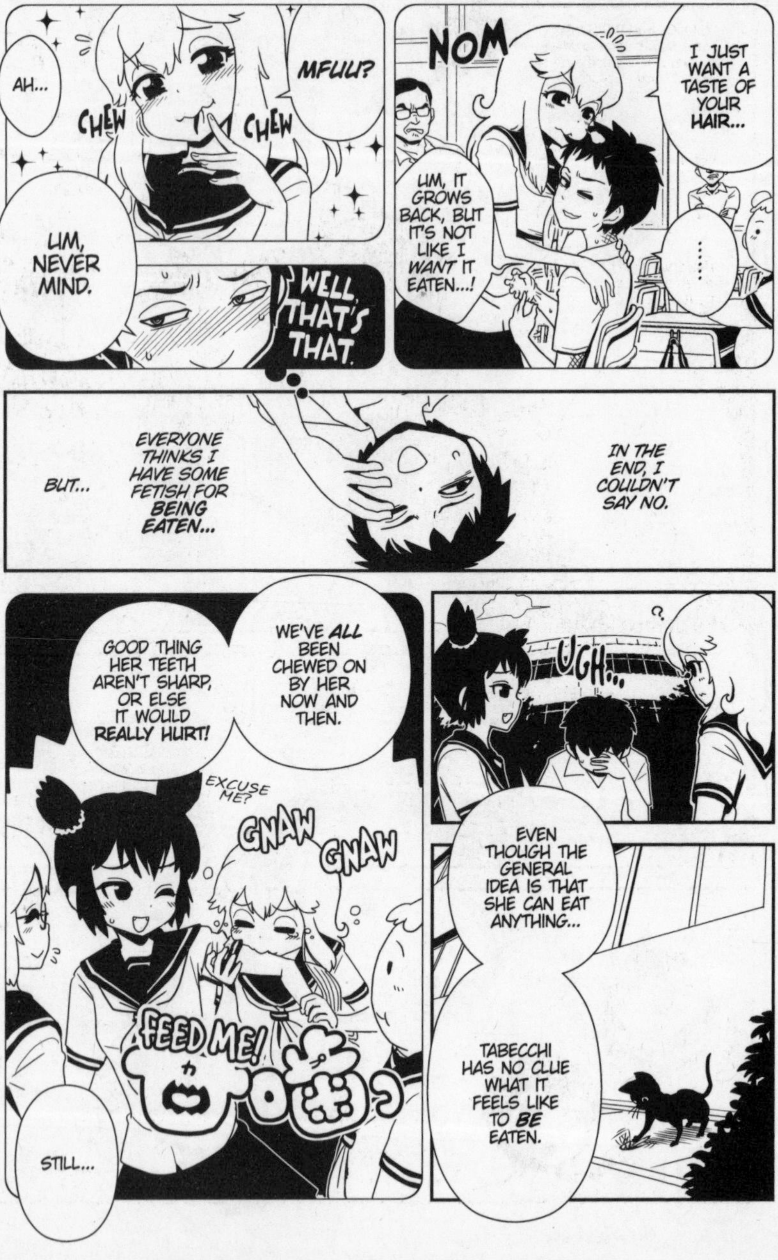
NOM
I JUST WANT A TASTE OF YOUR HAIR...
UM, IT GROWS BACK, BUT IT'S NOT LIKE I *WANT* IT EATEN...!
......
MFUU?
AH...
CHEW CHEW
WELL, THAT'S THAT.
UM, NEVER MIND.
IN THE END, I COULDN'T SAY NO.
EVERYONE THINKS I HAVE SOME FETISH FOR **BEING EATEN...**
BUT...
?
UGH...
EVEN THOUGH THE GENERAL IDEA IS THAT SHE CAN EAT ANYTHING...
TABECCHI HAS NO CLUE WHAT IT FEELS LIKE TO *BE* EATEN.
WE'VE *ALL* BEEN CHEWED ON BY HER NOW AND THEN.
GOOD THING HER TEETH AREN'T SHARP, OR ELSE IT WOULD **REALLY HURT!**
EXCUSE ME?
GNAW GNAW
FEED ME!
STILL...

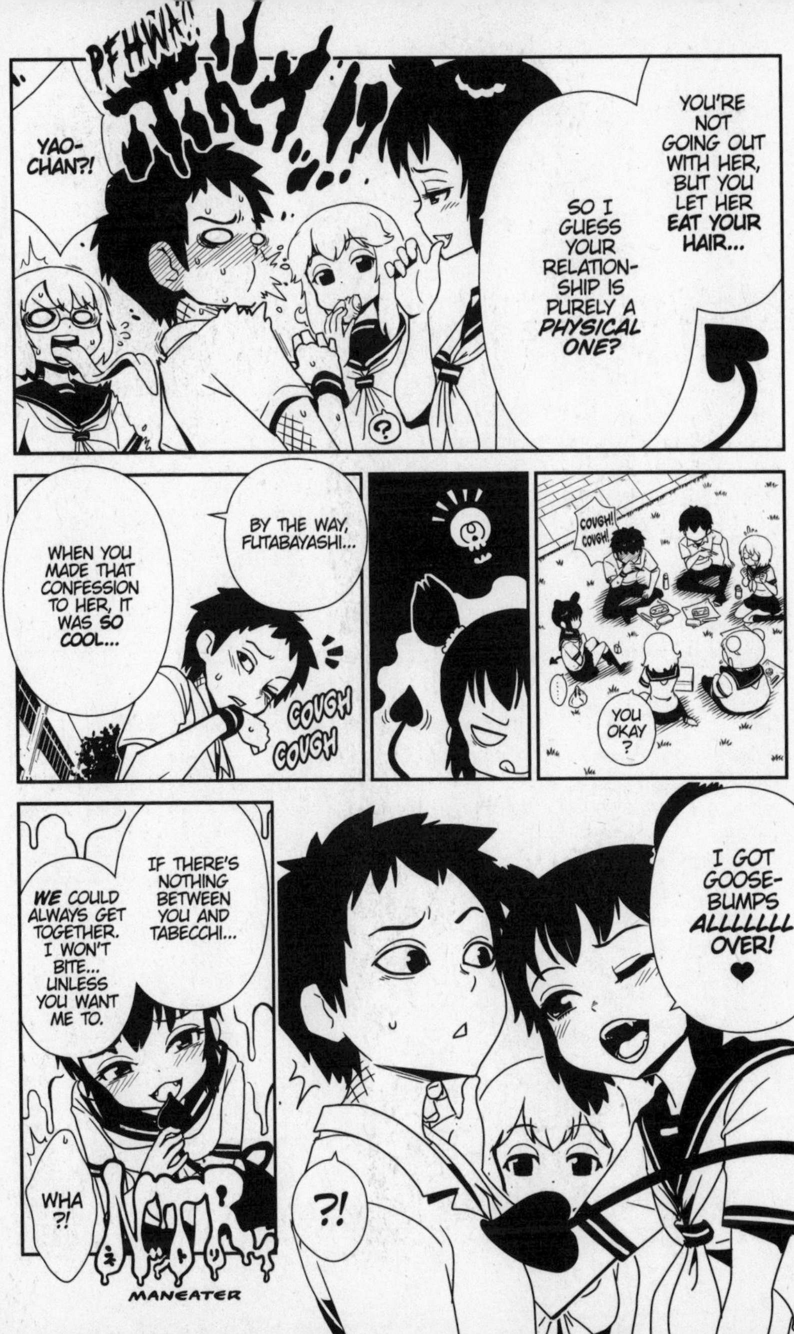
YOU'RE NOT GOING OUT WITH HER, BUT YOU LET HER EAT YOUR HAIR...
SO I GUESS YOUR RELATIONSHIP IS PURELY A PHYSICAL ONE?
PFHWA!!
YAO-CHAN?!
?
COUGH! COUGH!
YOU OKAY?
......
BY THE WAY, FUTABAYASHI...
WHEN YOU MADE THAT CONFESSION TO HER, IT WAS SO COOL...
COUGH COUGH
I GOT GOOSE-BUMPS ALLLLLLL OVER! ♥
?!
IF THERE'S NOTHING BETWEEN YOU AND TABECCHI...
WE COULD ALWAYS GET TOGETHER. I WON'T BITE... UNLESS YOU WANT ME TO.
WHA?!
MANEATER

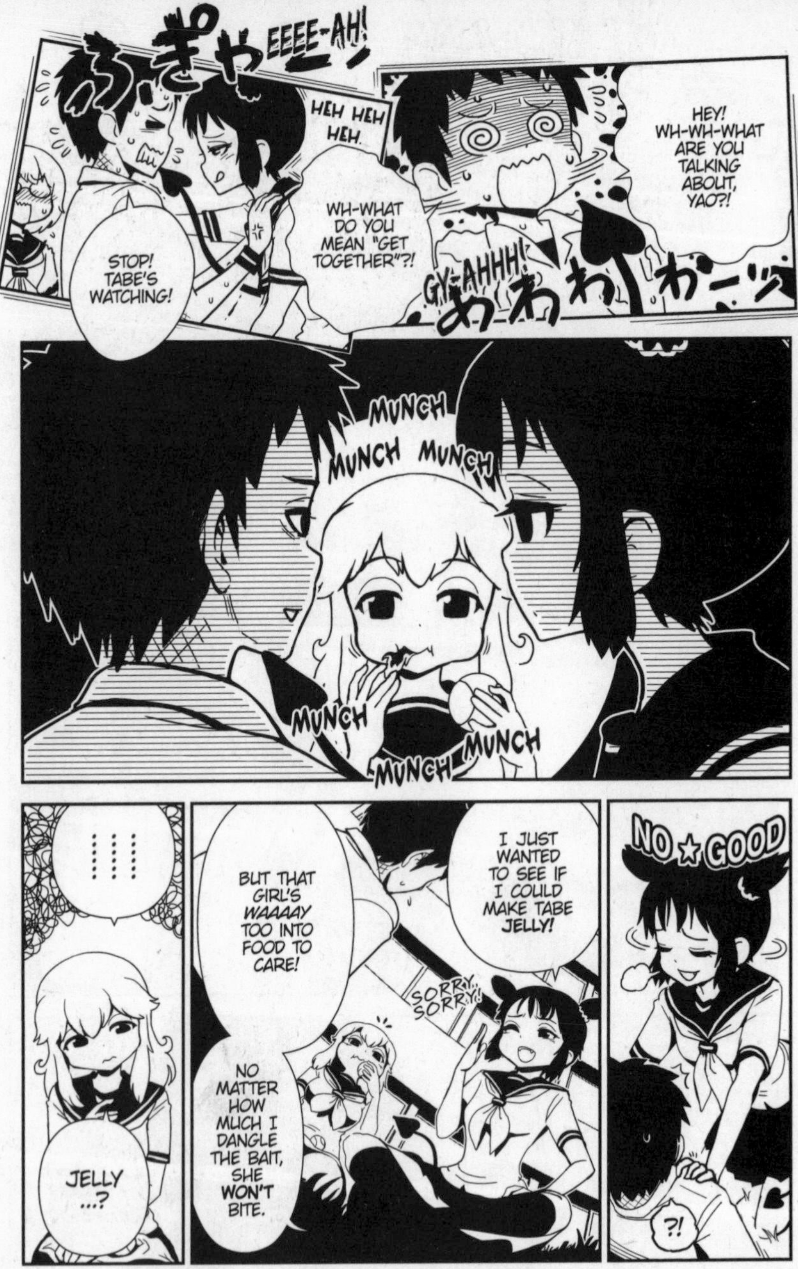
HEY! WH-WH-WHAT ARE YOU TALKING ABOUT, YAO?!
GY-AHHH!
わわわ わーッ
HEH HEH HEH.
WH-WHAT DO YOU MEAN "GET TOGETHER"?!
ふぎゃ EEEE-AH!
STOP! TABE'S WATCHING!
MUNCH
MUNCH MUNCH
MUNCH
MUNCH MUNCH
NO ☆ GOOD
?!
I JUST WANTED TO SEE IF I COULD MAKE TABE JELLY!
SORRY, SORRY!
BUT THAT GIRL'S *WAAAAY* TOO INTO FOOD TO CARE!
NO MATTER HOW MUCH I DANGLE THE BAIT, SHE **WON'T** BITE.
......
JELLY ...?

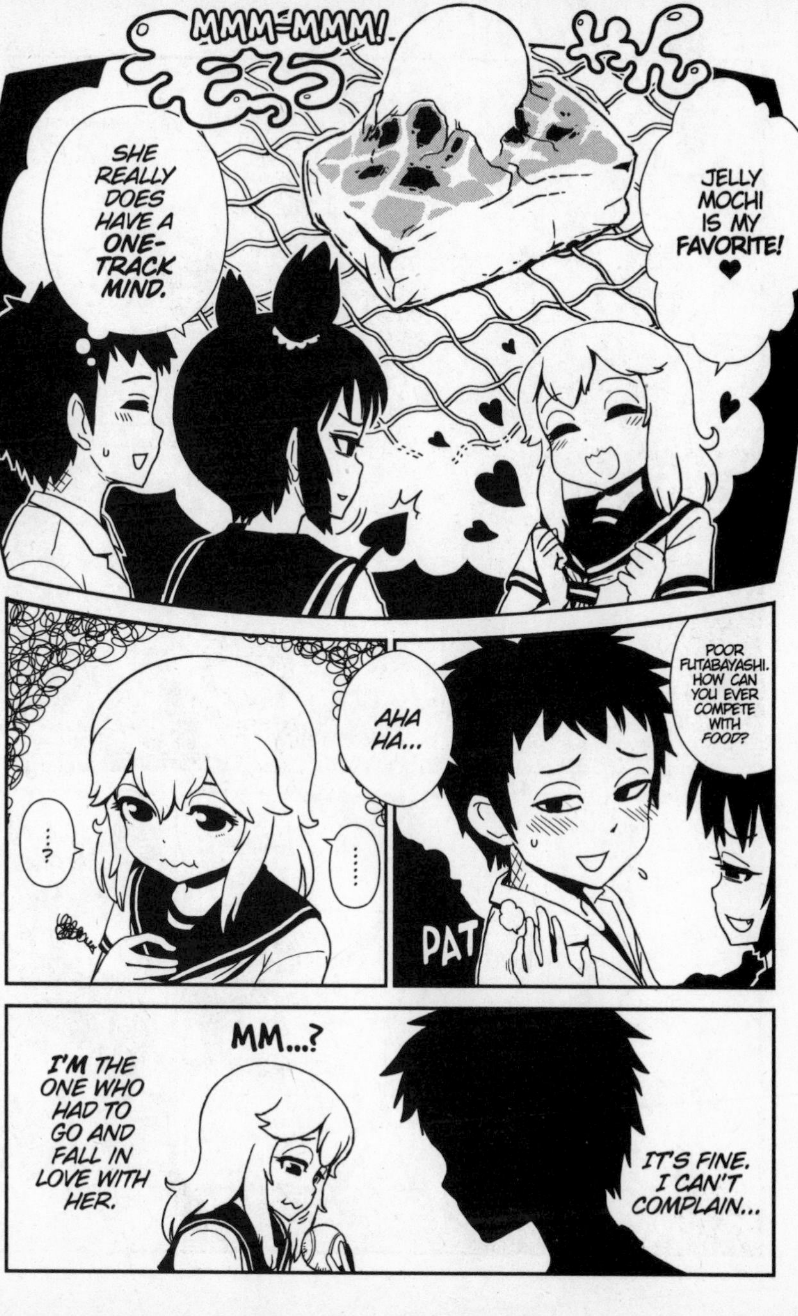
MMM-MMM!
JELLY MOCHI IS MY FAVORITE! ♥
SHE REALLY DOES HAVE A ONE-TRACK MIND.
POOR FUTABAYASHI. HOW CAN YOU EVER COMPETE WITH FOOD?
AHA HA...
PAT
......
...?
MM...?
IT'S FINE. I CAN'T COMPLAIN...
I'M THE ONE WHO HAD TO GO AND FALL IN LOVE WITH HER.

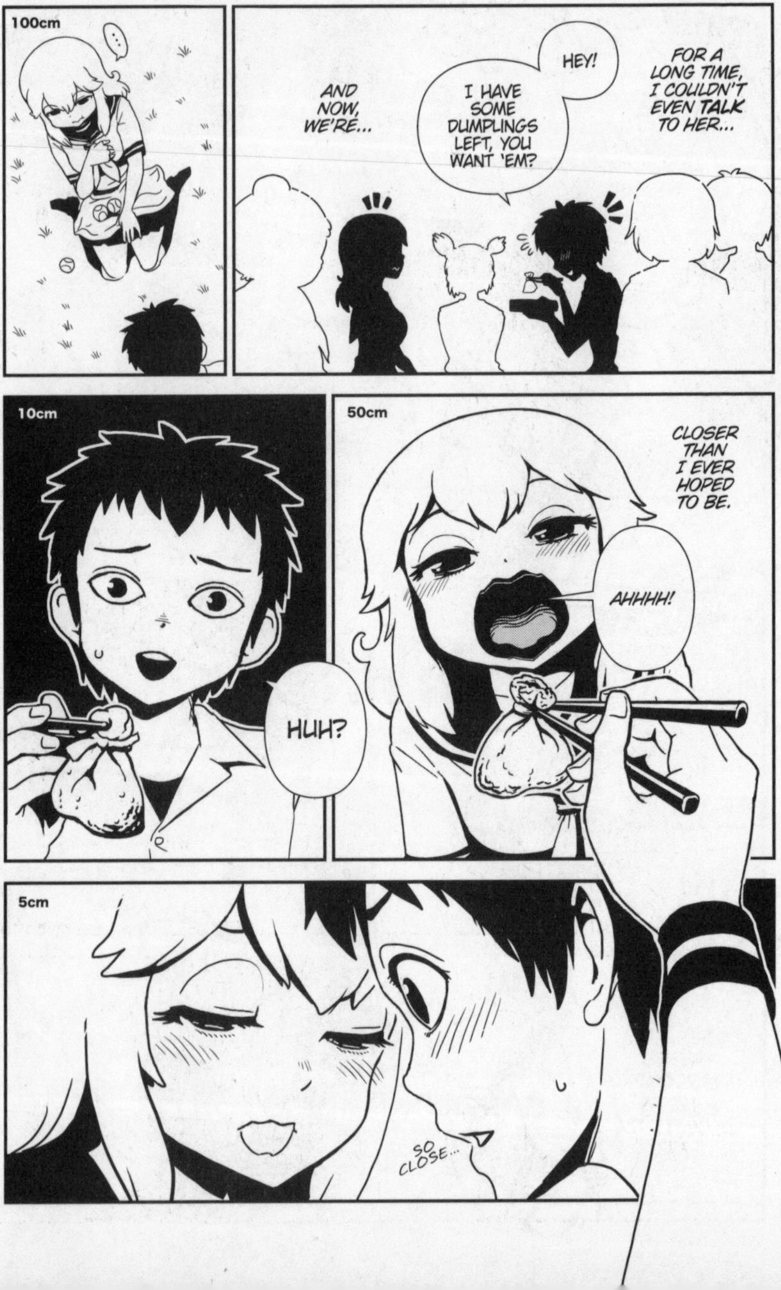
FOR A LONG TIME, I COULDN'T EVEN TALK TO HER...
HEY!
I HAVE SOME DUMPLINGS LEFT, YOU WANT 'EM?
AND NOW, WE'RE...
100cm
...
50cm
CLOSER THAN I EVER HOPED TO BE.
AHHHH!
10cm
HUH?
5cm
SO CLOSE...

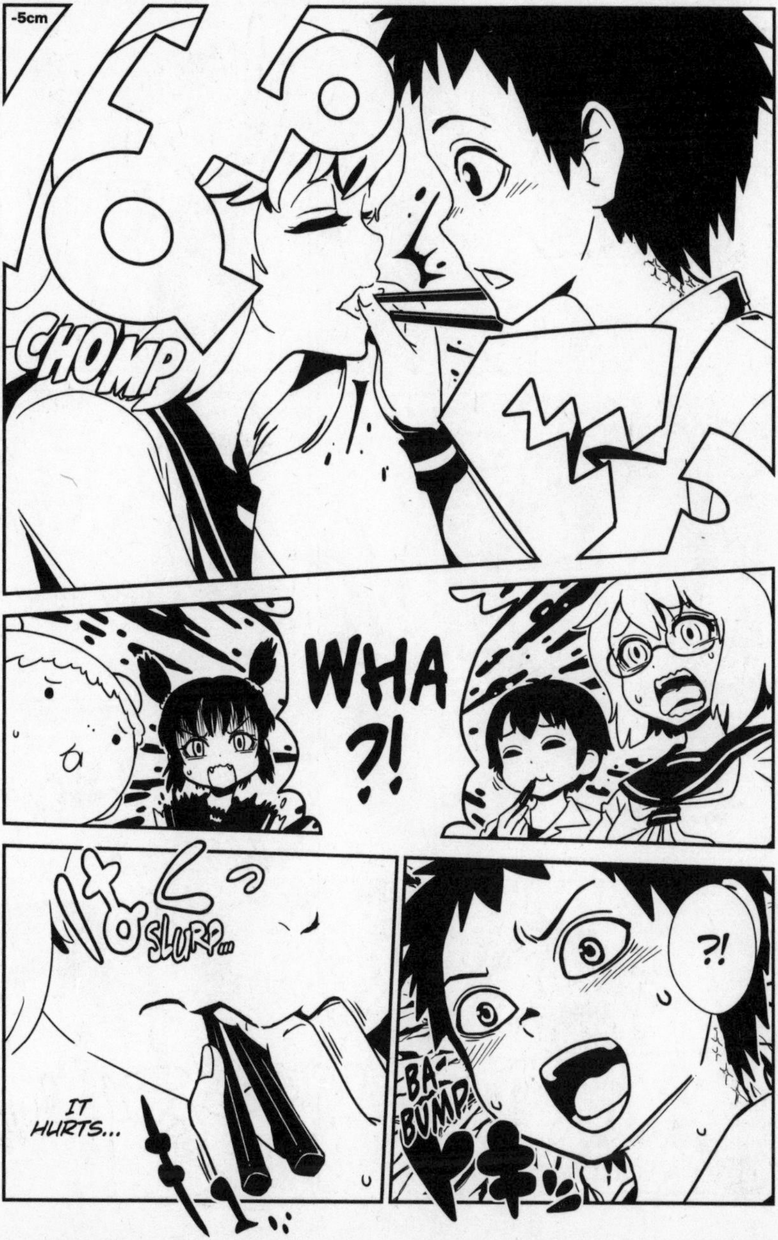
-5cm
CHOMP
WHA ?!
SLURP...
IT HURTS...
?!
BA-BUMP

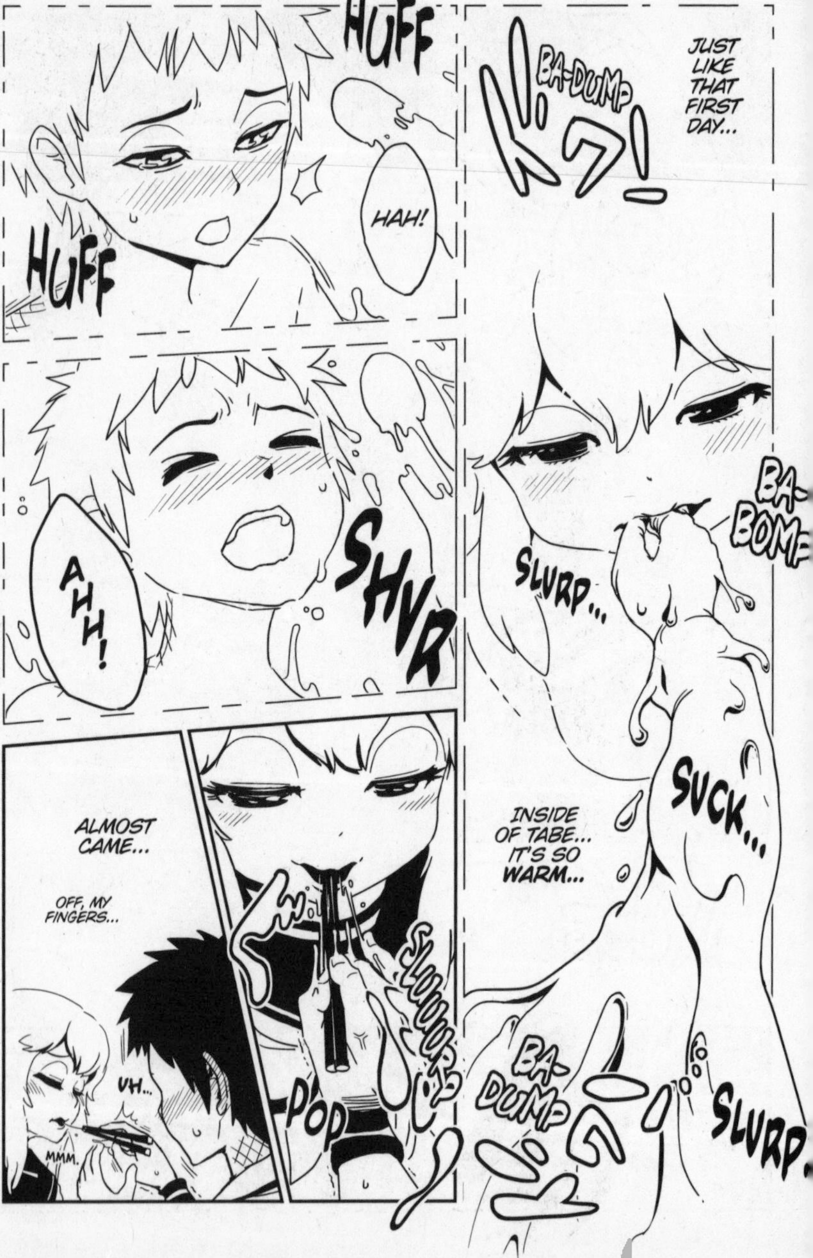
BA-DUMP
JUST LIKE THAT FIRST DAY...
BA-BOMP
SLURP...
SUCK...
INSIDE OF TABE... IT'S SO WARM...
BA-DUMP
SLURP.
HUFF
HAH!
HUFF
SHVR
AHH!
SLUUURP
POP
ALMOST CAME...
OFF, MY FINGERS...
UH...
MMM.

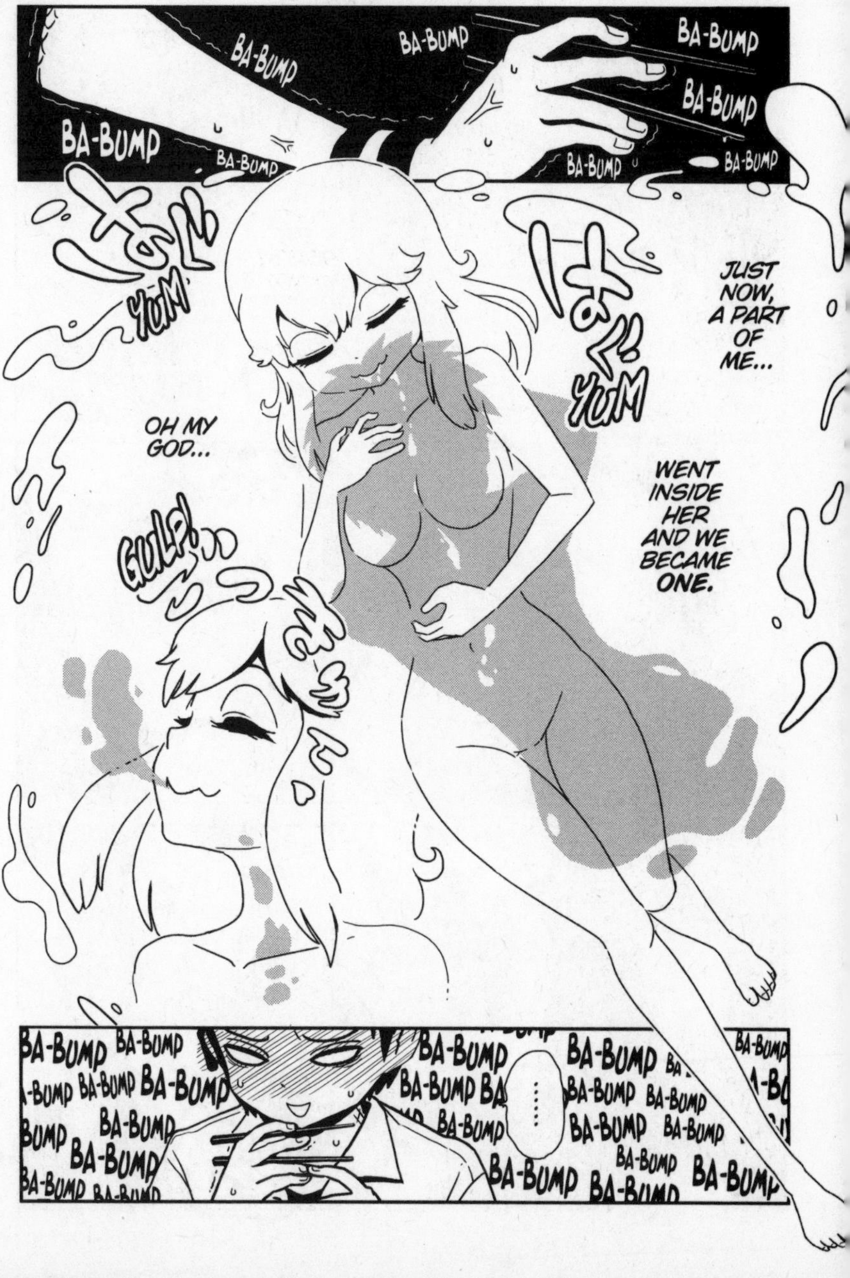
BA-BUMP
BA-BUMP
BA-BUMP
BA-BUMP
BA-BUMP
BA-BUMP
BA-BUMP
BA-BUMP
JUST NOW, A PART OF ME...
YUM
WENT INSIDE HER AND WE BECAME ONE.
YUM
OH MY GOD...
GULP!
BA-BUMP
......

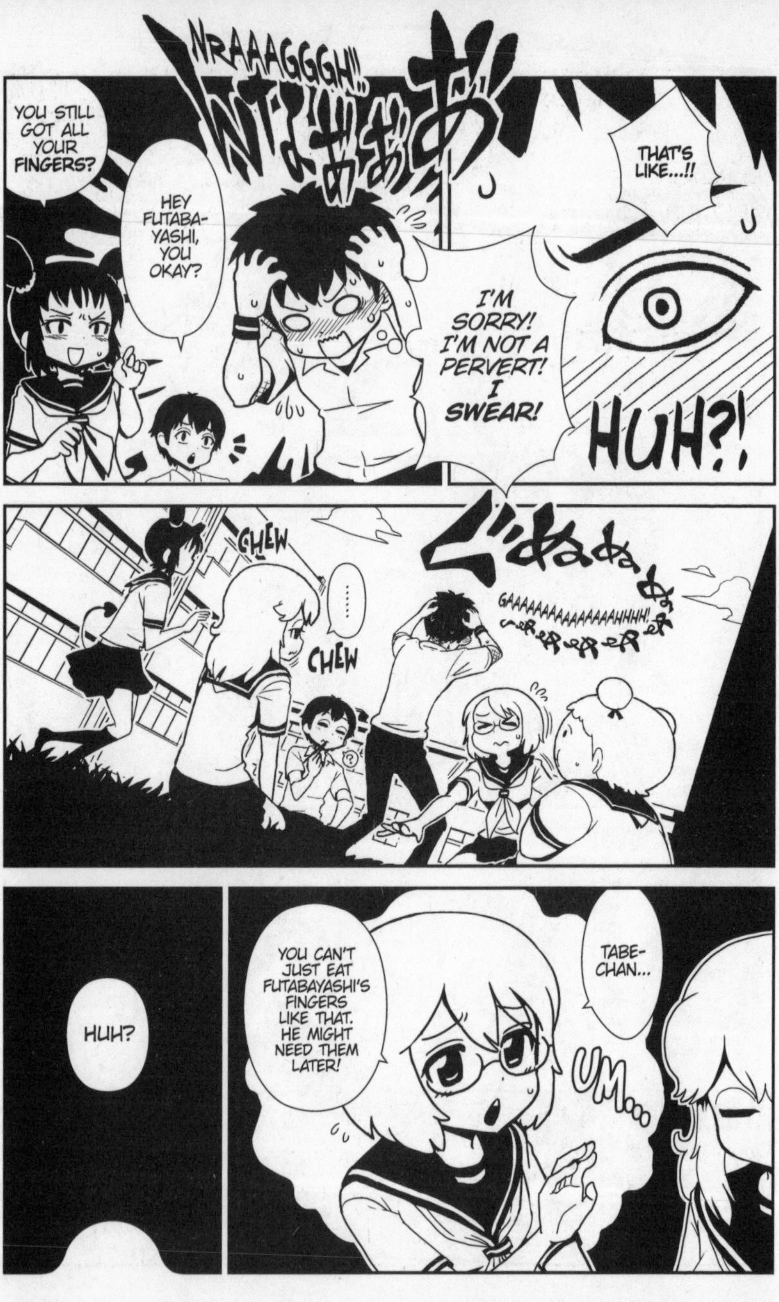
THAT'S LIKE...!!
HUH?!
NRAAAGGGH!!
I'M SORRY! I'M NOT A PERVERT! I SWEAR!
HEY FUTABAYASHI, YOU OKAY?
YOU STILL GOT ALL YOUR FINGERS?
GAAAAAAAAAAAAAAAAHHHH!
CHEW
......
CHEW
TABE-CHAN...
UM...
YOU CAN'T JUST EAT FUTABAYASHI'S FINGERS LIKE THAT. HE MIGHT NEED THEM LATER!
HUH?

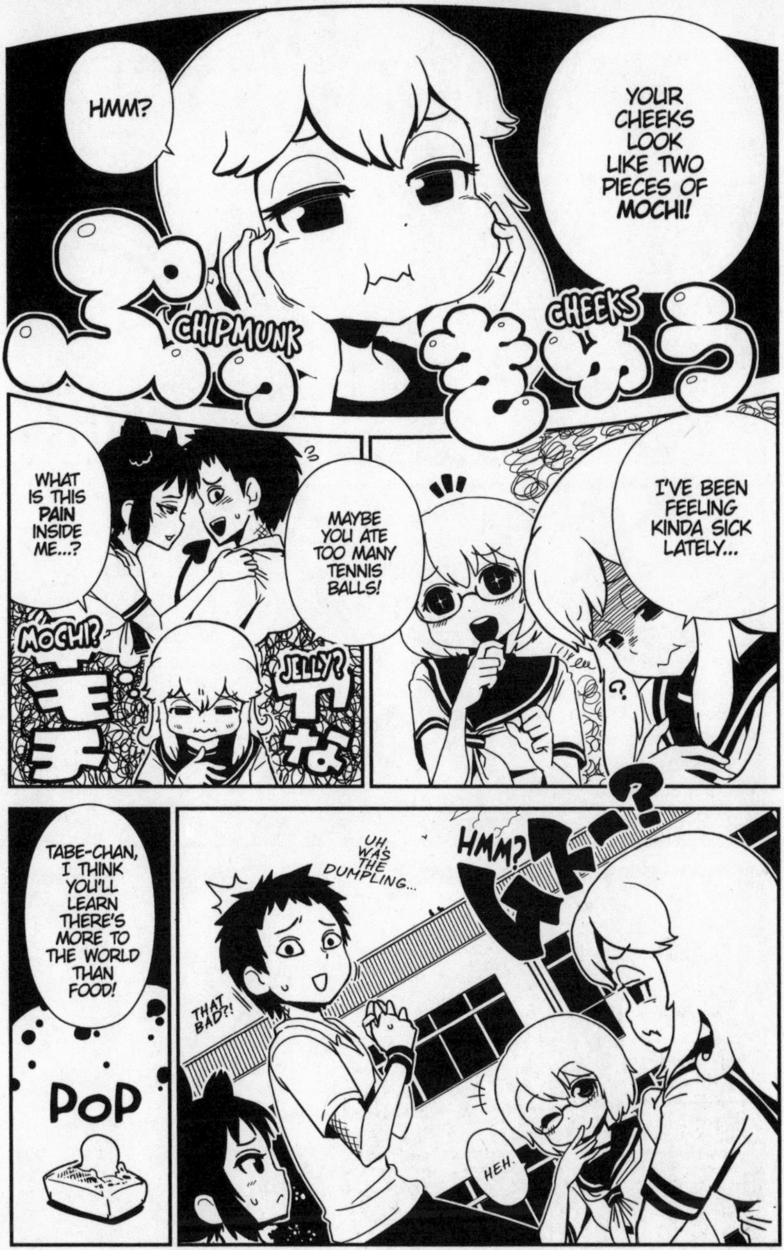
YOUR CHEEKS LOOK LIKE TWO PIECES OF MOCHI!
HMM?
CHIPMUNK CHEEKS
I'VE BEEN FEELING KINDA SICK LATELY...
MAYBE YOU ATE TOO MANY TENNIS BALLS!
WHAT IS THIS PAIN INSIDE ME...?
JELLY?
MOCHI?
HMM?
UH, WAS THE DUMPLING...
THAT BAD?!
HEH.
TABE-CHAN, I THINK YOU'LL LEARN THERE'S MORE TO THE WORLD THAN FOOD!
POP

NURSE HITOMI'S Monster Infirmary

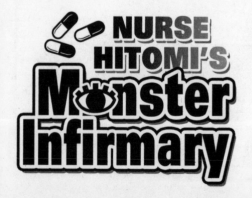

Student Health Record

Jul 201X

Class 2-A Futabayashi Kageto

Regeneration Boy

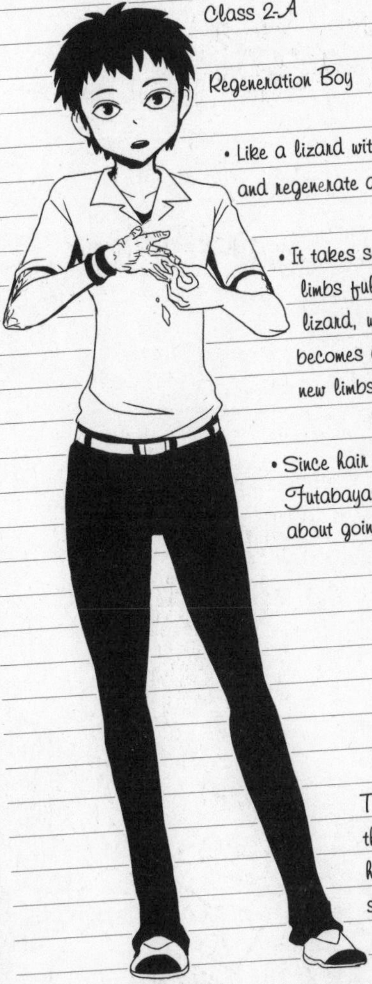

- Like a lizard with its detachable tail, he can sever and regenerate a part of his body at will.

- It takes several days of shedding before his limbs fully regenerate. As opposed to a lizard, where the bone in the regenerated tail becomes cartilage, his bones grow back. His new limbs are just as good as the old ones.

- Since hair has high regenerative abilities, Futabayashi-san will never have to worry about going bald.

The skin on the back of his neck is scaly.

"IT'S NOT LIKE I WANT TO GET EATEN OR ANYTHING... ...REALLY."

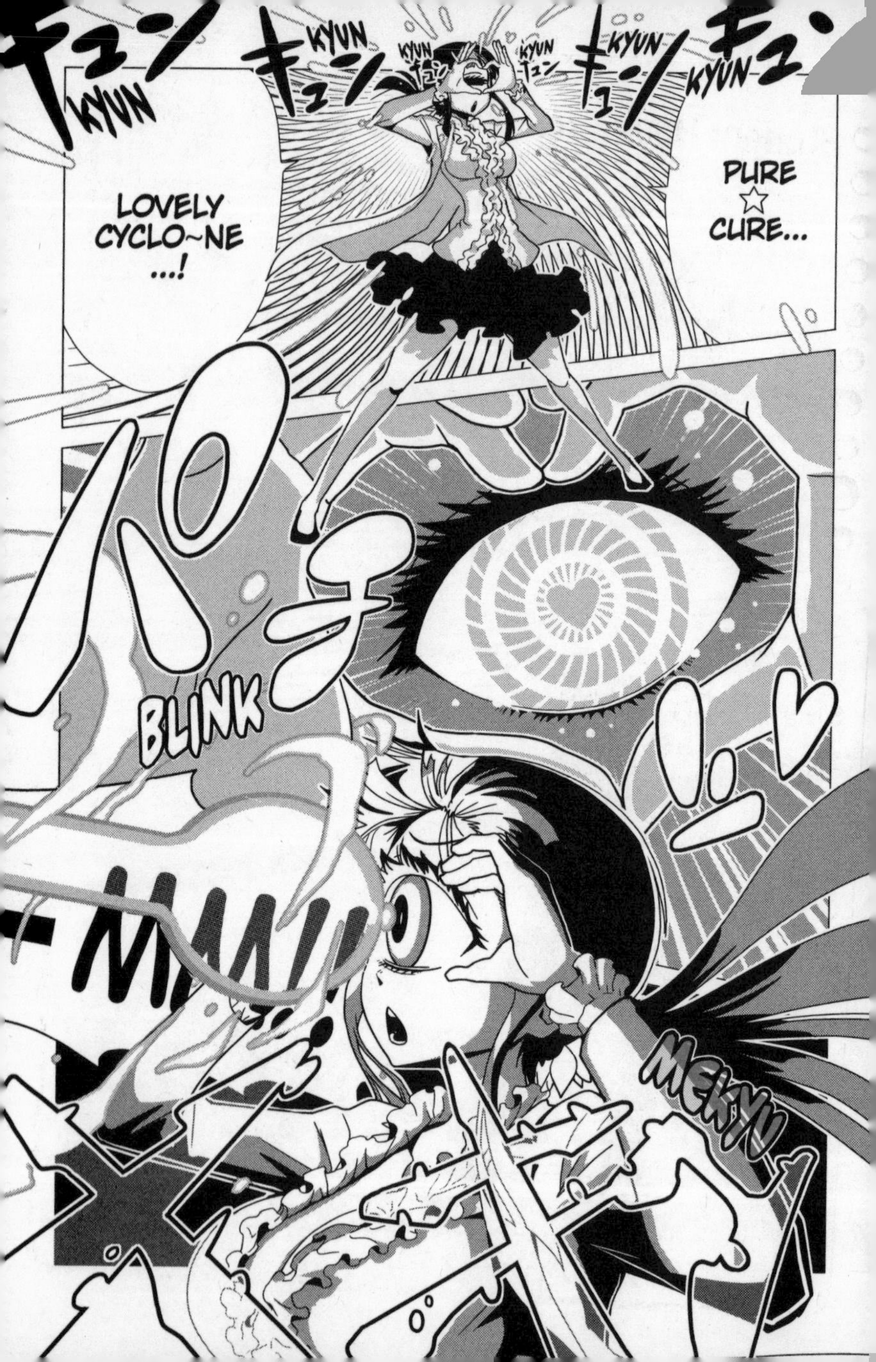
KYUN
KYUN
KYUN
KYUN
KYUN
KYUN
KYUN
PURE ☆ CURE...
LOVELY CYCLO~NE ...!
MEKYU
BLINK

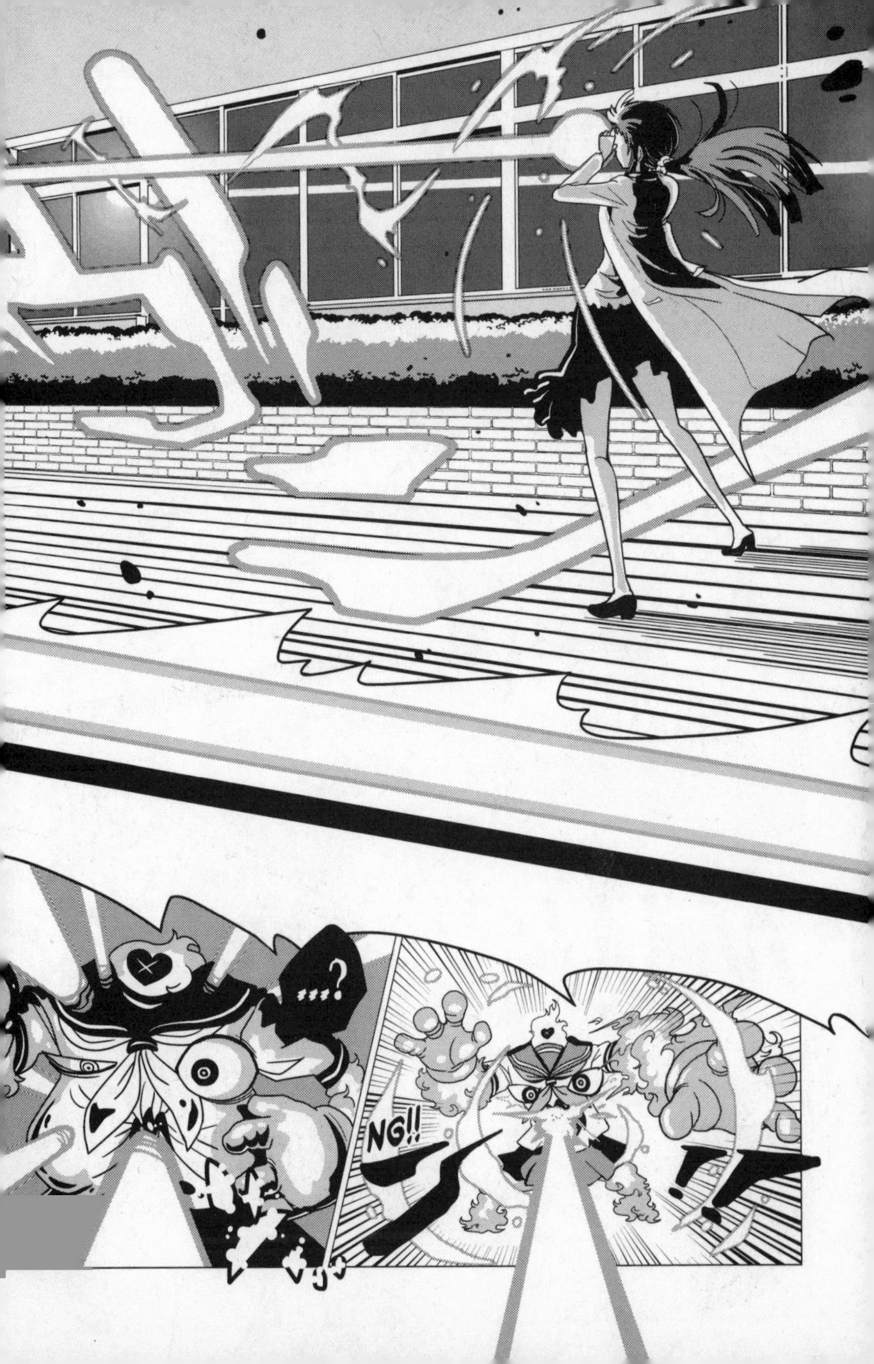
NG!!
?

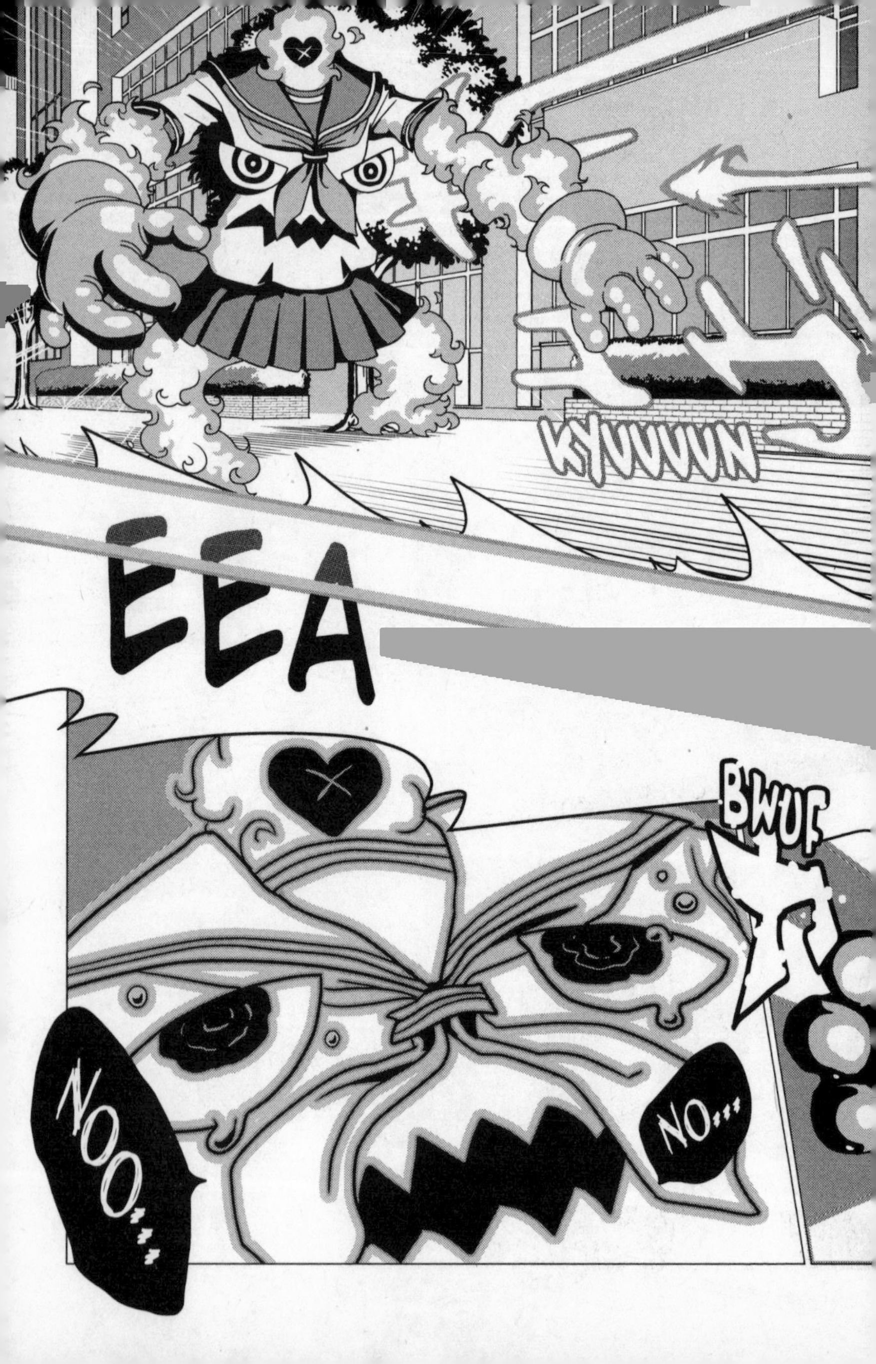
KYUUUUN
EEA
BWUF
NO...
NOO...

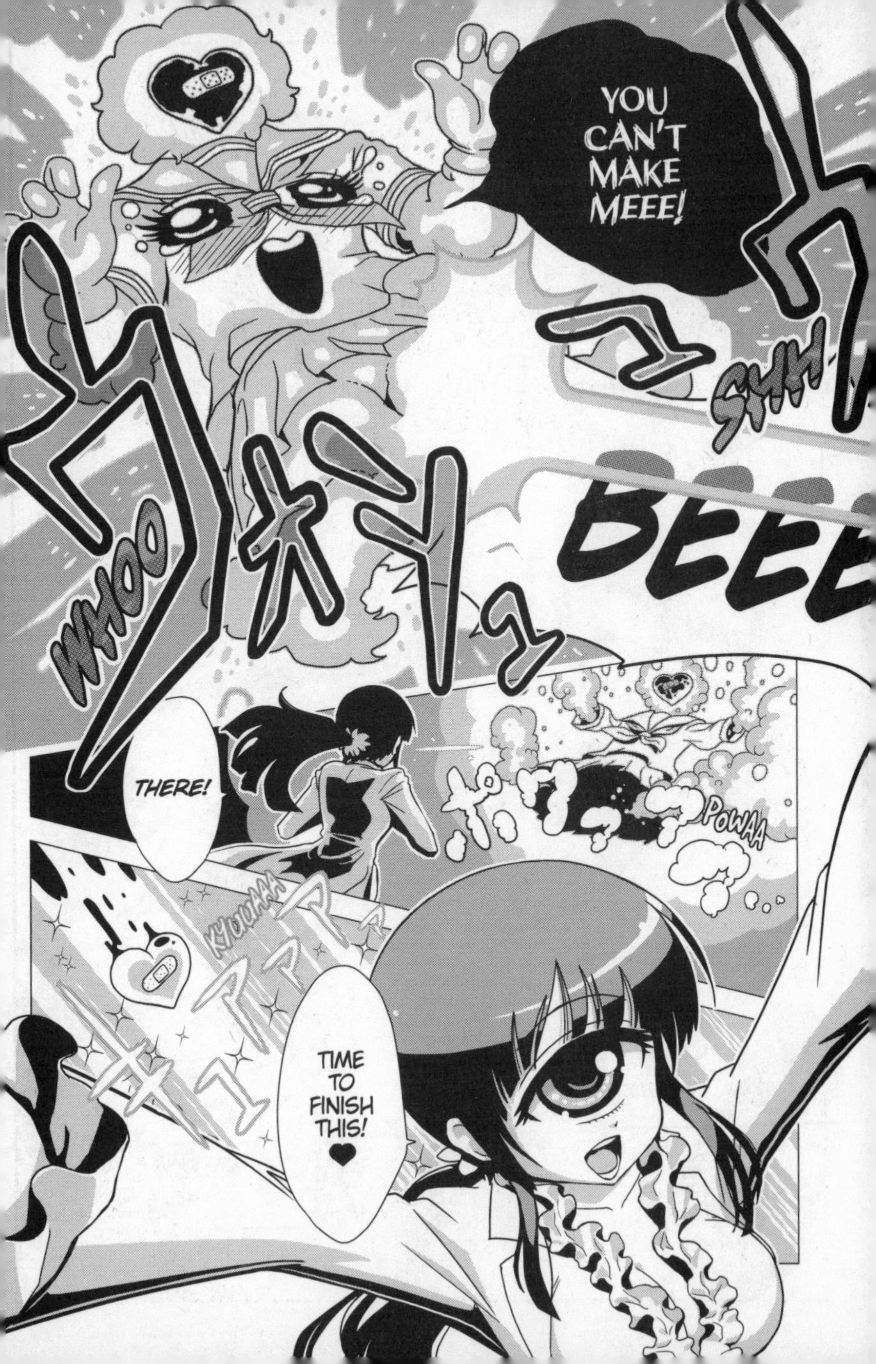
YOU CAN'T MAKE MEEE!
SYUN
BEEE
WHOO
POWAA
THERE!
KYUUAAA
TIME TO FINISH THIS! ♥

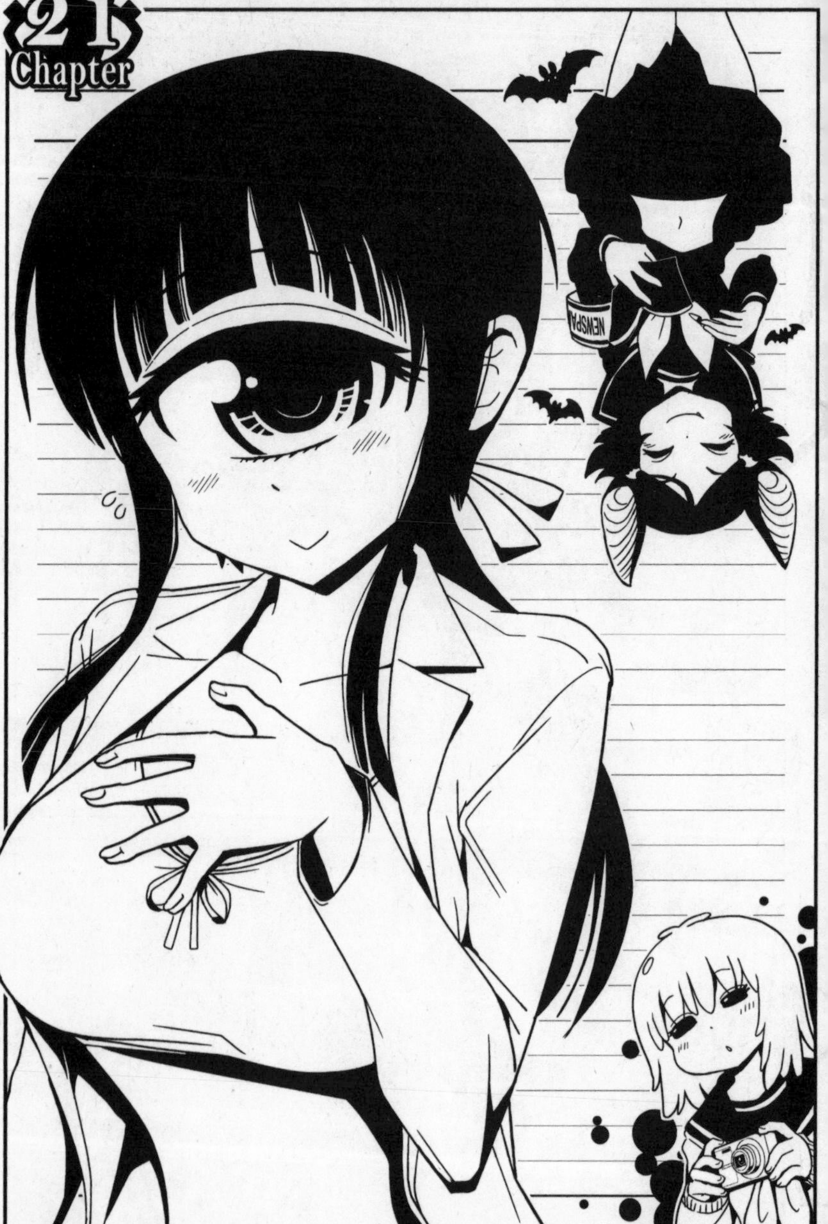
21
Chapter
NEWSPA

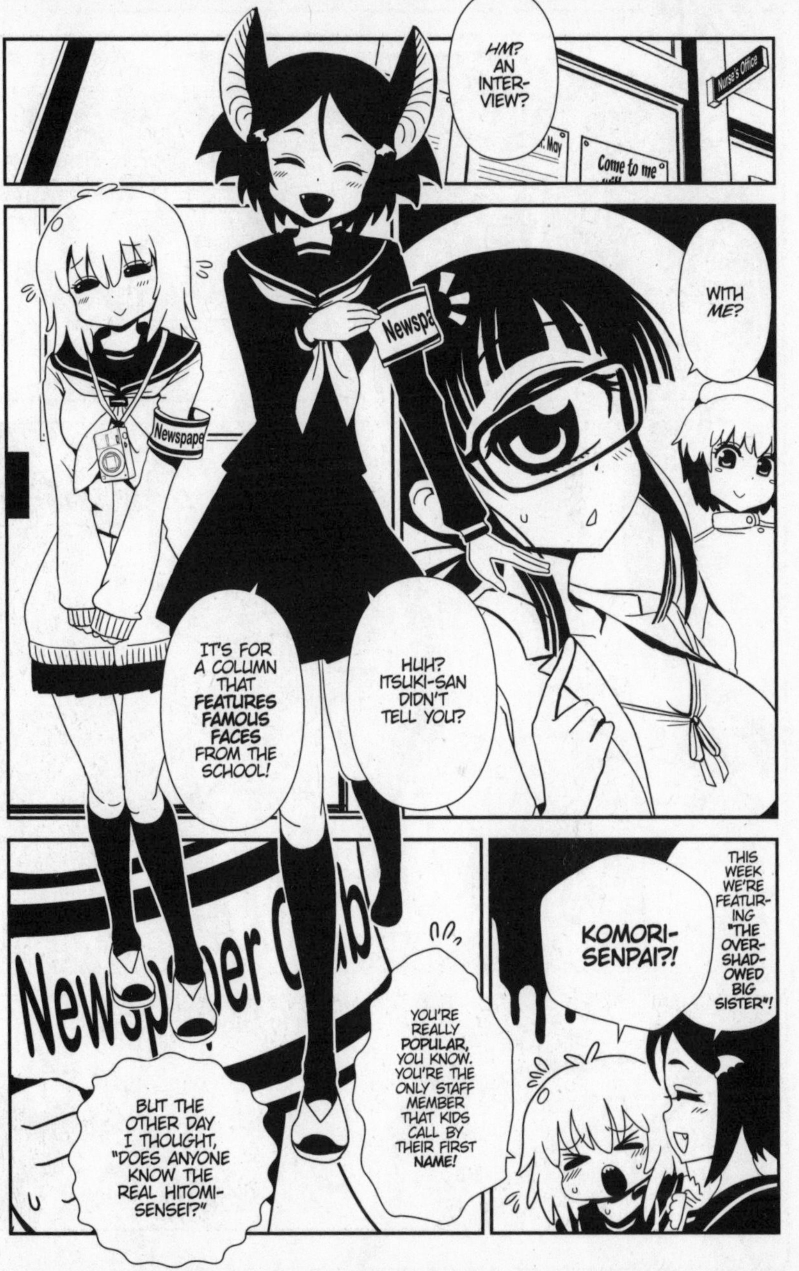
Nurse's Office
Come to me
HM? AN INTER-VIEW?
WITH ME?
HUH? ITSUKI-SAN DIDN'T TELL YOU?
IT'S FOR A COLUMN THAT FEATURES FAMOUS FACES FROM THE SCHOOL!
THIS WEEK WE'RE FEATURING "THE OVER-SHADOWED BIG SISTER"!
KOMORI-SENPAI?!
YOU'RE REALLY POPULAR, YOU KNOW. YOU'RE THE ONLY STAFF MEMBER THAT KIDS CALL BY THEIR FIRST NAME!
BUT THE OTHER DAY I THOUGHT, "DOES ANYONE KNOW THE REAL HITOMI-SENSEI?"

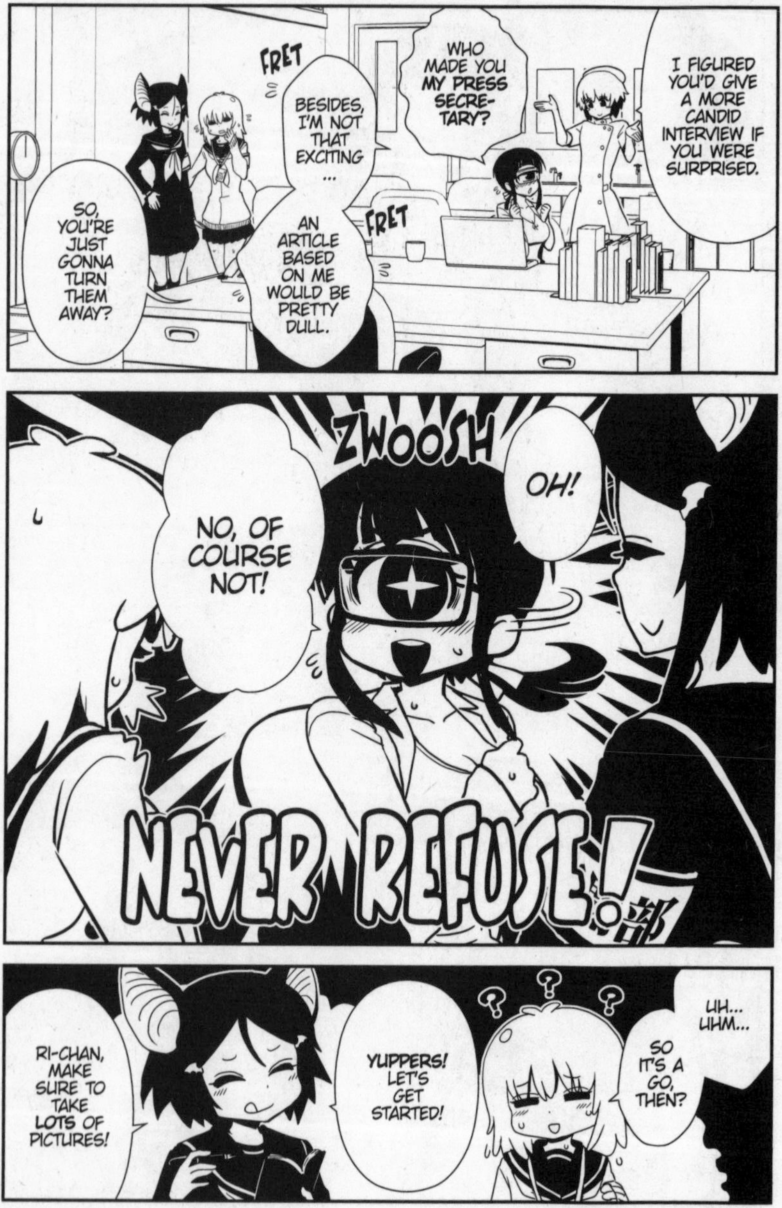
I FIGURED YOU'D GIVE A MORE CANDID INTERVIEW IF YOU WERE SURPRISED.
WHO MADE YOU MY PRESS SECRETARY?
FRET
BESIDES, I'M NOT THAT EXCITING ...
AN ARTICLE BASED ON ME WOULD BE PRETTY DULL.
FRET
SO, YOU'RE JUST GONNA TURN THEM AWAY?
OH!
ZWOOSH
NO, OF COURSE NOT!
NEVER REFUSE!
UH... UHM...
SO IT'S A GO, THEN?
YUPPERS! LET'S GET STARTED!
RI-CHAN, MAKE SURE TO TAKE LOTS OF PICTURES!

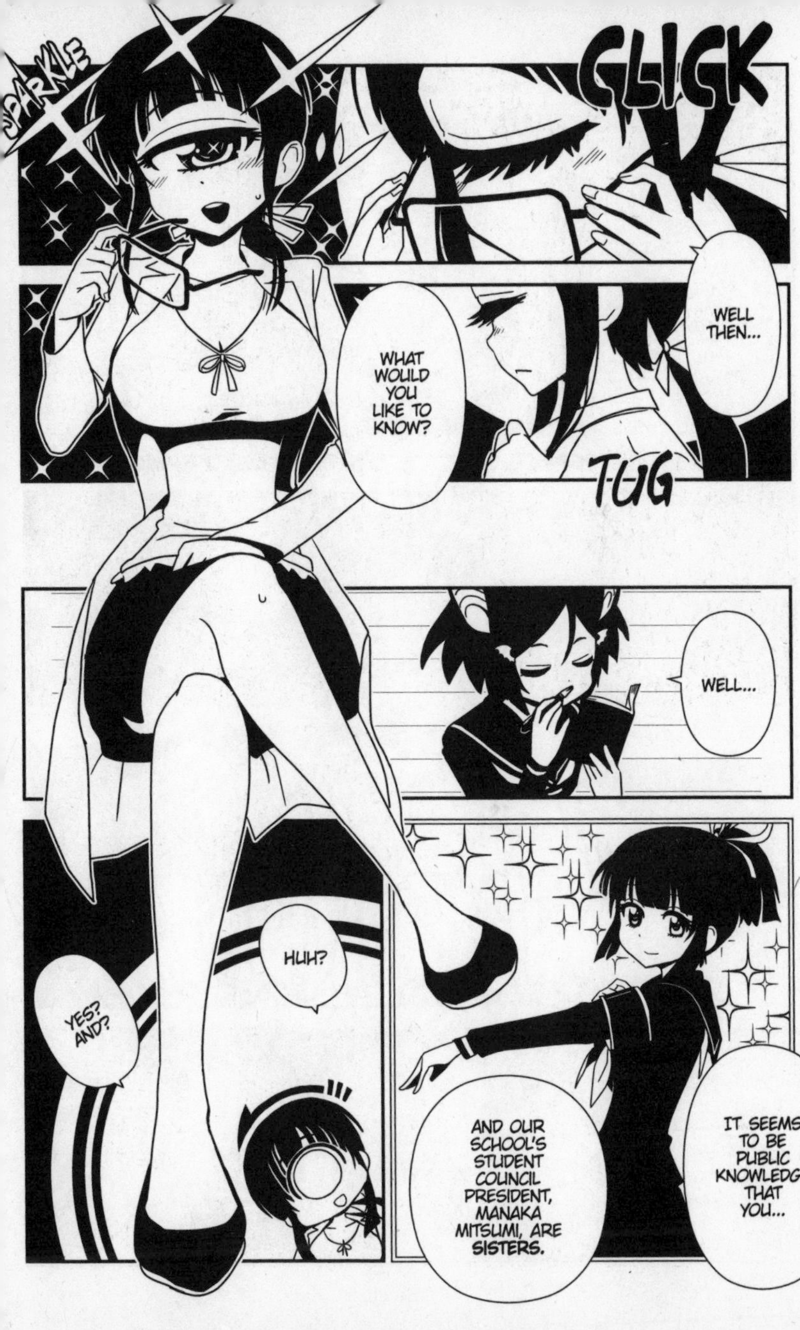
CLICK
WELL THEN...
TUG
WELL...
IT SEEMS TO BE PUBLIC KNOWLEDGE THAT YOU...
AND OUR SCHOOL'S STUDENT COUNCIL PRESIDENT, MANAKA MITSUMI, ARE SISTERS.
HUH?
YES? AND?
SPARKLE
WHAT WOULD YOU LIKE TO KNOW?

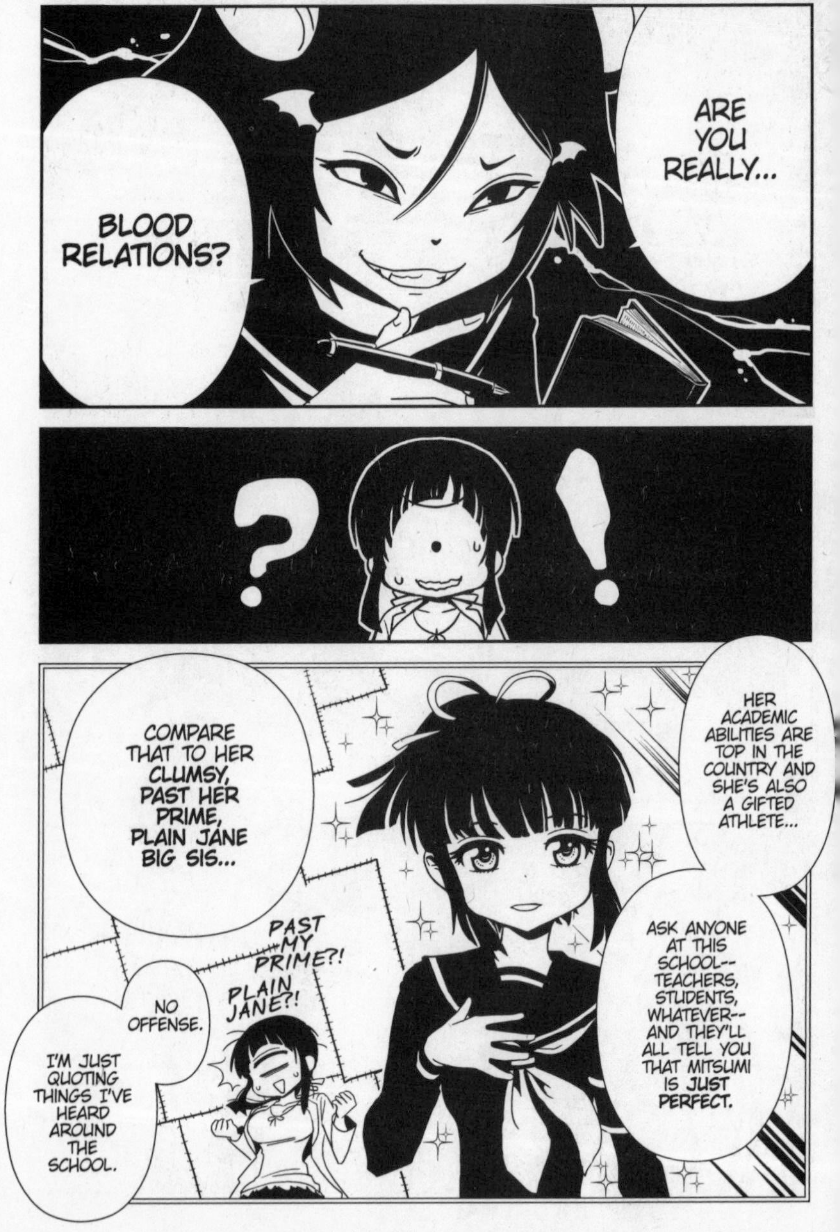
ARE YOU REALLY...
BLOOD RELATIONS?
HER ACADEMIC ABILITIES ARE TOP IN THE COUNTRY AND SHE'S ALSO A GIFTED ATHLETE...
ASK ANYONE AT THIS SCHOOL-- TEACHERS, STUDENTS, WHATEVER-- AND THEY'LL ALL TELL YOU THAT MITSUMI IS JUST PERFECT.
COMPARE THAT TO HER CLUMSY, PAST HER PRIME, PLAIN JANE BIG SIS...
PAST MY PRIME?!
PLAIN JANE?!
NO OFFENSE.
I'M JUST QUOTING THINGS I'VE HEARD AROUND THE SCHOOL.

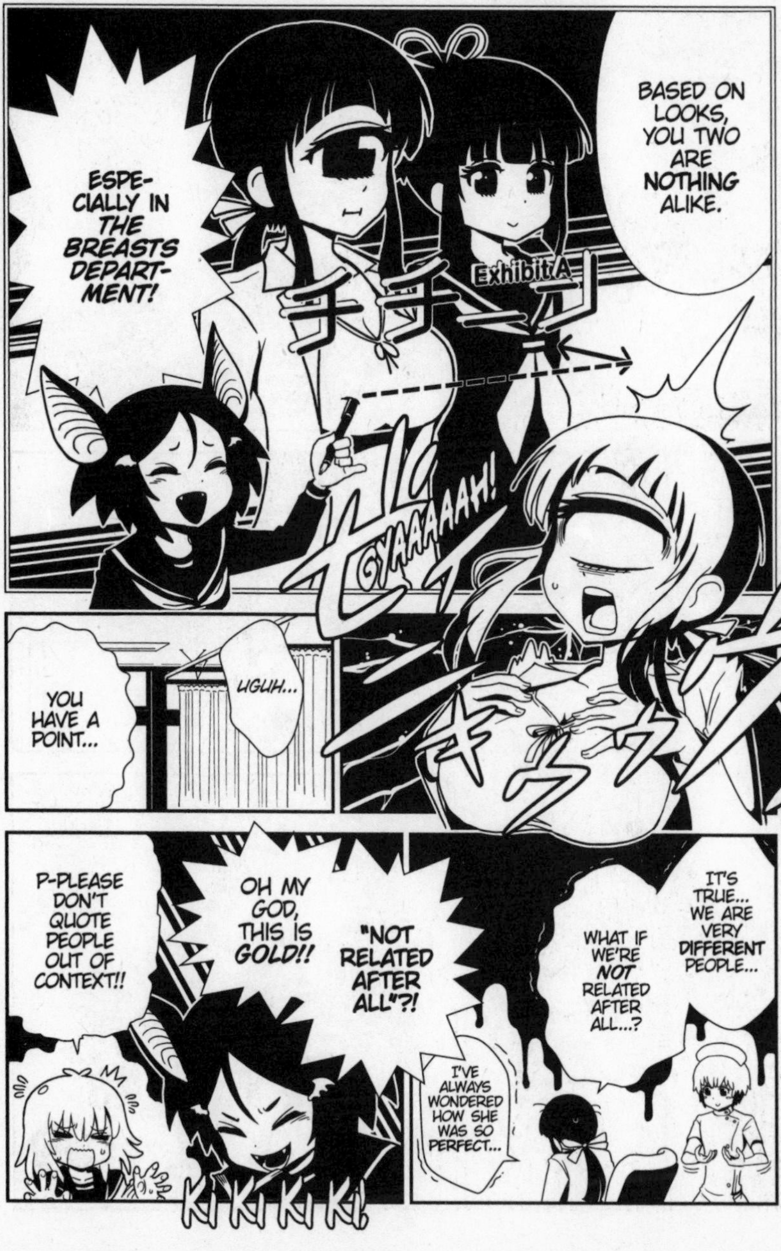
BASED ON LOOKS, YOU TWO ARE NOTHING ALIKE.
ESPE-CIALLY IN THE BREASTS DEPART-MENT!
Exhibit A
GYAAAAAH!
UGUH...
YOU HAVE A POINT...
IT'S TRUE... WE ARE VERY DIFFERENT PEOPLE...
WHAT IF WE'RE NOT RELATED AFTER ALL...?
I'VE ALWAYS WONDERED HOW SHE WAS SO PERFECT...
OH MY GOD, THIS IS GOLD!!
"NOT RELATED AFTER ALL"?!
P-PLEASE DON'T QUOTE PEOPLE OUT OF CONTEXT!!
KI KI KI KI!

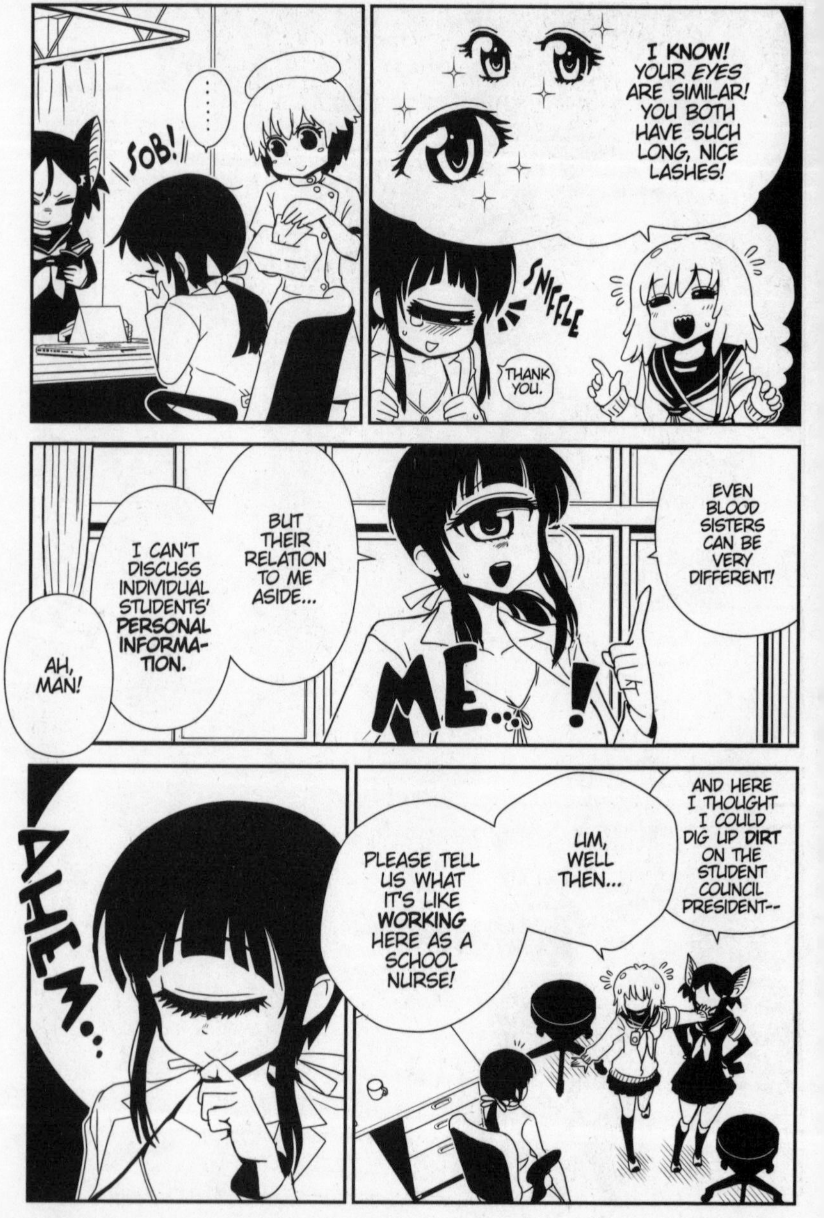
I KNOW! YOUR EYES ARE SIMILAR! YOU BOTH HAVE SUCH LONG, NICE LASHES!
SNIFFLE
THANK YOU.
SOB!
......
EVEN BLOOD SISTERS CAN BE VERY DIFFERENT!
ME...!
BUT THEIR RELATION TO ME ASIDE...
I CAN'T DISCUSS INDIVIDUAL STUDENTS' PERSONAL INFORMATION.
AH, MAN!
AND HERE I THOUGHT I COULD DIG UP DIRT ON THE STUDENT COUNCIL PRESIDENT--
UM, WELL THEN...
PLEASE TELL US WHAT IT'S LIKE WORKING HERE AS A SCHOOL NURSE!
AHEM...

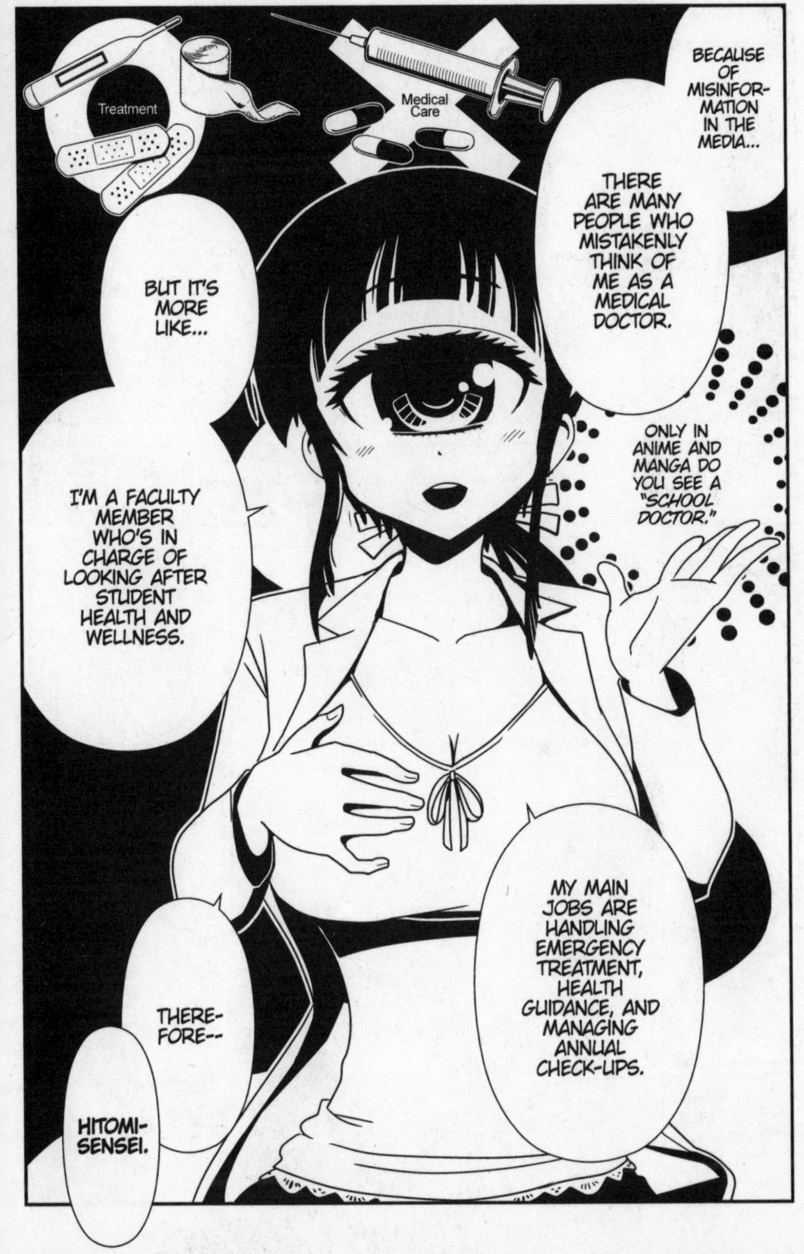
BECAUSE OF MISINFORMATION IN THE MEDIA...
Medical Care
Treatment
THERE ARE MANY PEOPLE WHO MISTAKENLY THINK OF ME AS A MEDICAL DOCTOR.
ONLY IN ANIME AND MANGA DO YOU SEE A "SCHOOL DOCTOR."
BUT IT'S MORE LIKE...
I'M A FACULTY MEMBER WHO'S IN CHARGE OF LOOKING AFTER STUDENT HEALTH AND WELLNESS.
MY MAIN JOBS ARE HANDLING EMERGENCY TREATMENT, HEALTH GUIDANCE, AND MANAGING ANNUAL CHECK-UPS.
THERE-FORE--
HITOMI-SENSEI.

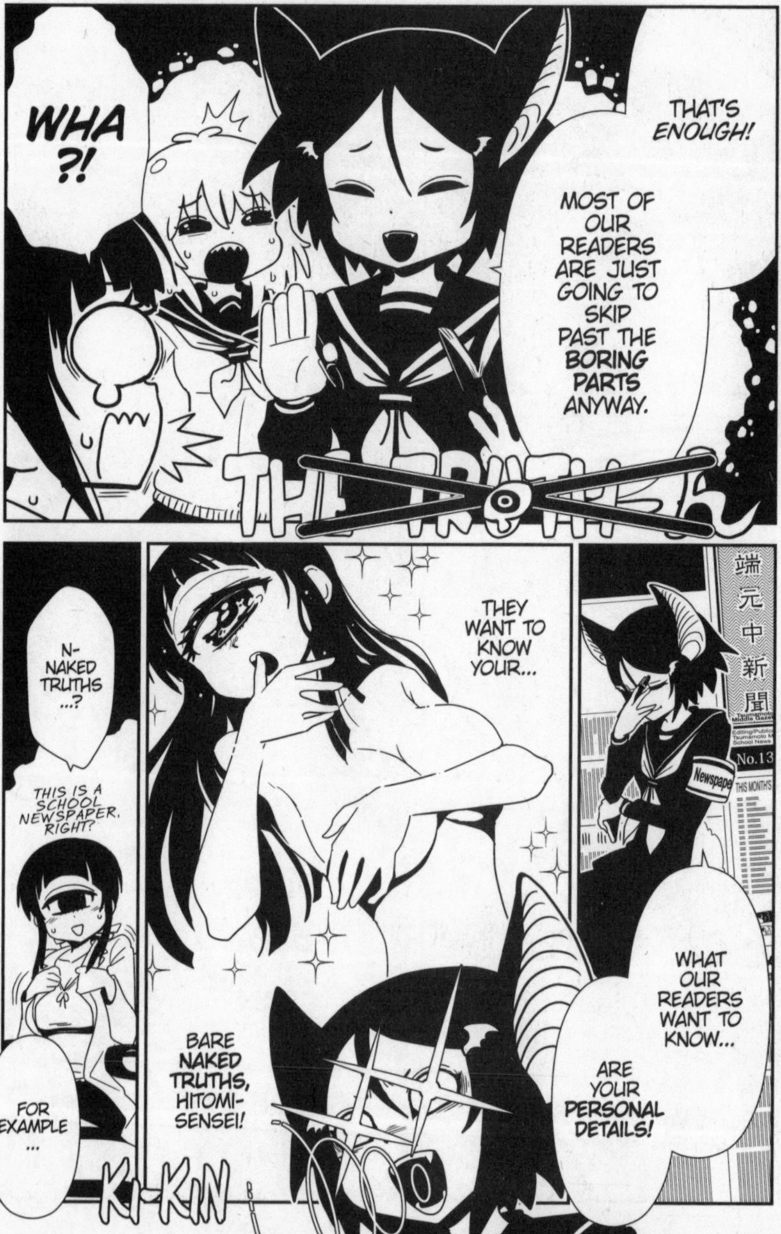
THAT'S ENOUGH!
MOST OF OUR READERS ARE JUST GOING TO SKIP PAST THE BORING PARTS ANYWAY.
WHA ?!
端元中新聞
No.13
Newspaper
THEY WANT TO KNOW YOUR...
BARE NAKED TRUTHS, HITOMI-SENSEI!
N-NAKED TRUTHS ...?
THIS IS A SCHOOL NEWSPAPER, RIGHT?
WHAT OUR READERS WANT TO KNOW...
ARE YOUR PERSONAL DETAILS!
KI-KIN
FOR EXAMPLE ...

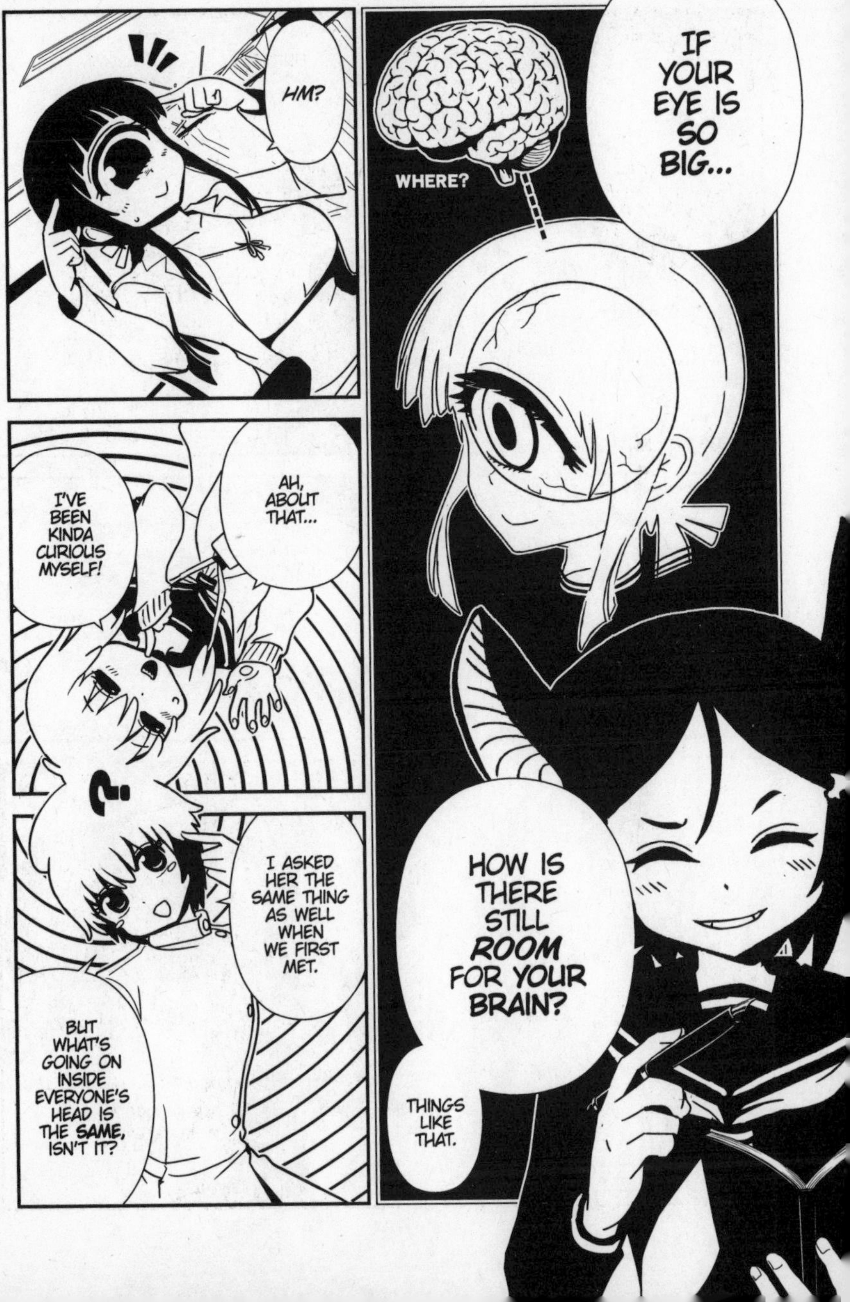
IF YOUR EYE IS SO BIG...
WHERE?
HOW IS THERE STILL *ROOM* FOR YOUR BRAIN?
THINGS LIKE THAT.
HM?
AH, ABOUT THAT...
I'VE BEEN KINDA CURIOUS MYSELF!
I ASKED HER THE SAME THING AS WELL WHEN WE FIRST MET.
BUT WHAT'S GOING ON INSIDE EVERYONE'S HEAD IS THE SAME, ISN'T IT?

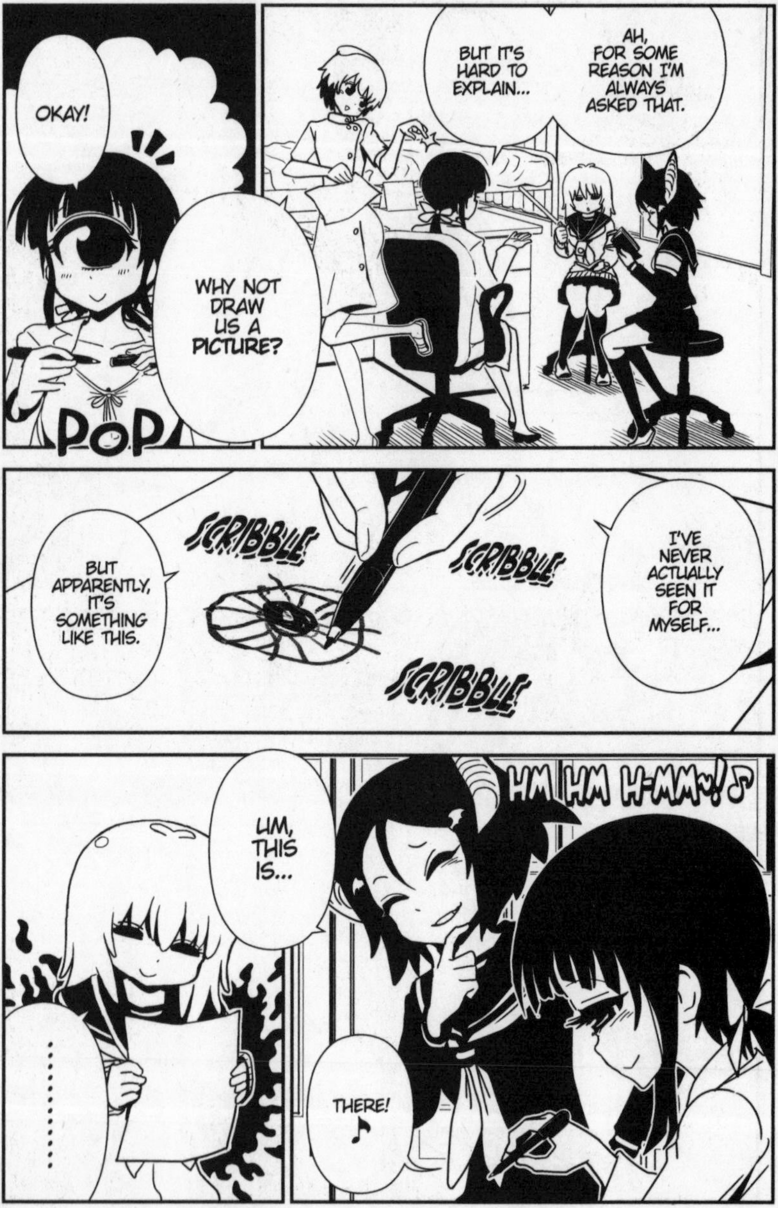
AH, FOR SOME REASON I'M ALWAYS ASKED THAT.
BUT IT'S HARD TO EXPLAIN...
WHY NOT DRAW US A PICTURE?
OKAY!
POP
I'VE NEVER ACTUALLY SEEN IT FOR MYSELF...
SCRIBBLE
SCRIBBLE
SCRIBBLE
BUT APPARENTLY, IT'S SOMETHING LIKE THIS.
HM HM H-MM~!♪
THERE! ♪
UM, THIS IS...
....

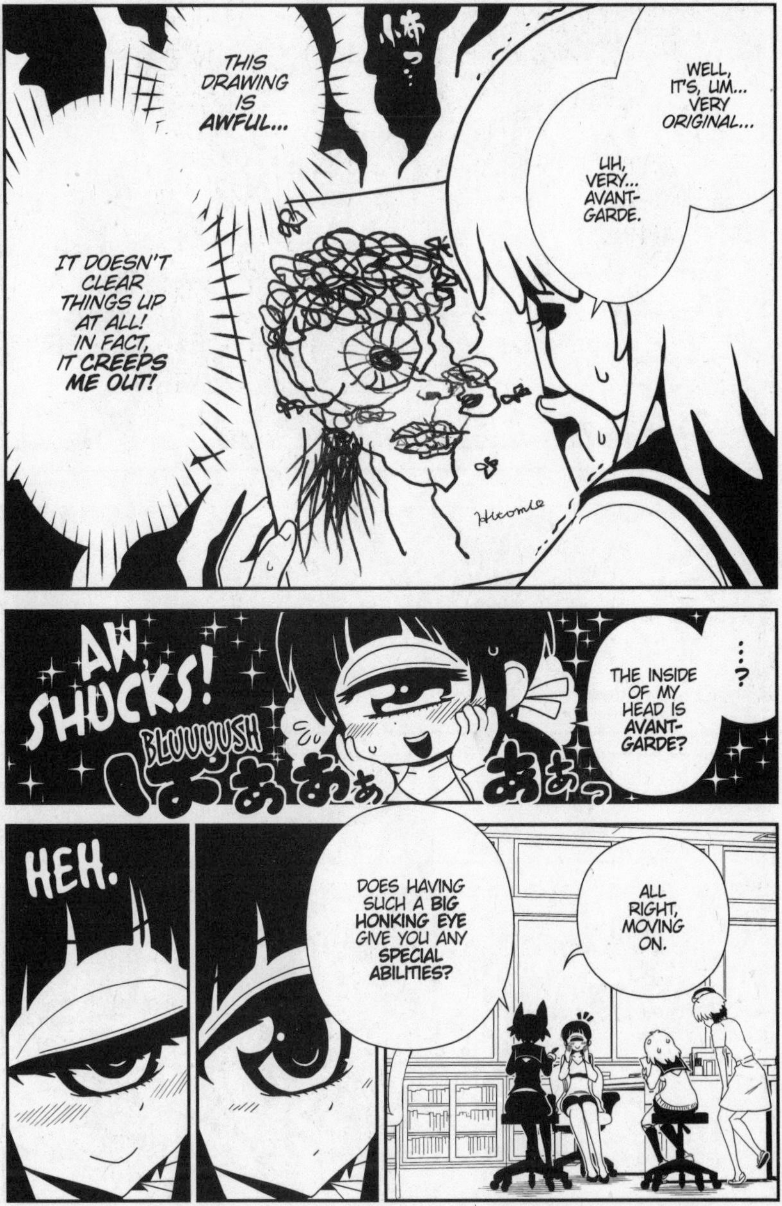
WELL, IT'S, UM... VERY ORIGINAL...
UH, VERY... AVANT-GARDE.
THIS DRAWING IS AWFUL...
IT DOESN'T CLEAR THINGS UP AT ALL! IN FACT, IT CREEPS ME OUT!
...?
THE INSIDE OF MY HEAD IS AVANT-GARDE?
AW SHUCKS!
BLUUUUSH
ALL RIGHT, MOVING ON.
DOES HAVING SUCH A BIG HONKING EYE GIVE YOU ANY SPECIAL ABILITIES?
HEH.

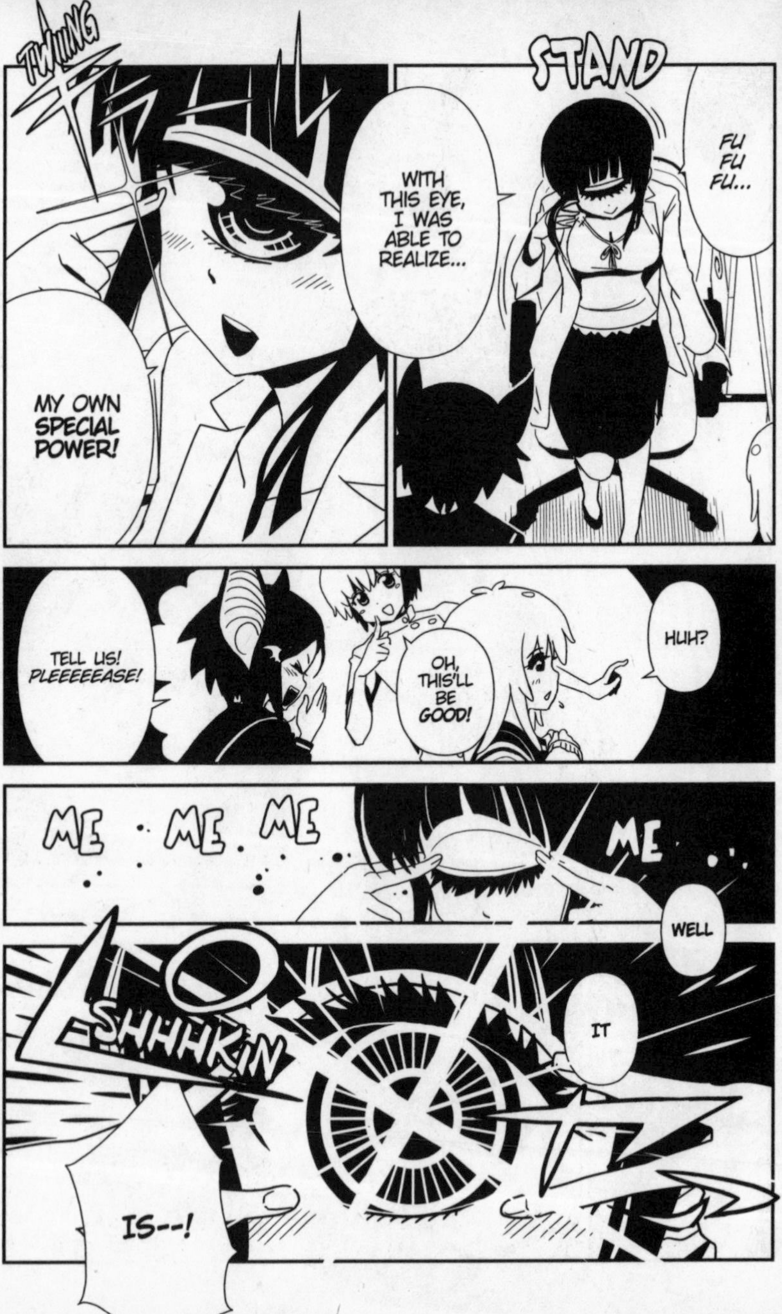
STAND
FU FU FU...
WITH THIS EYE, I WAS ABLE TO REALIZE...
TWIIING
MY OWN SPECIAL POWER!
HUH?
OH, THIS'LL BE GOOD!
TELL US! PLEEEEEASE!
ME ME ME
ME
WELL
IT
SHHHKIN
IS--!

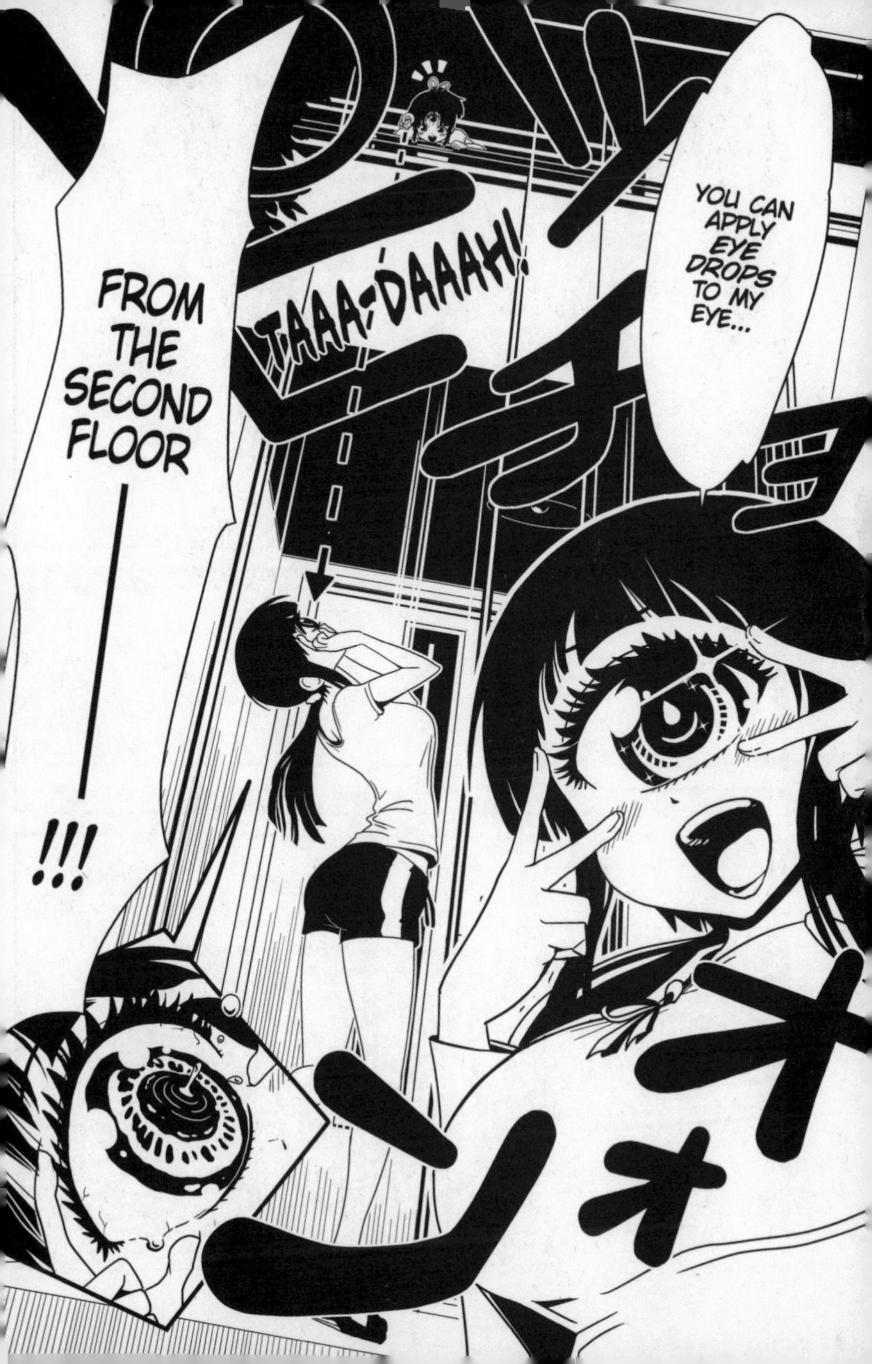
YOU CAN APPLY EYE DROPS TO MY EYE...
TAAA-DAAAH!
FROM THE SECOND FLOOR———!!!

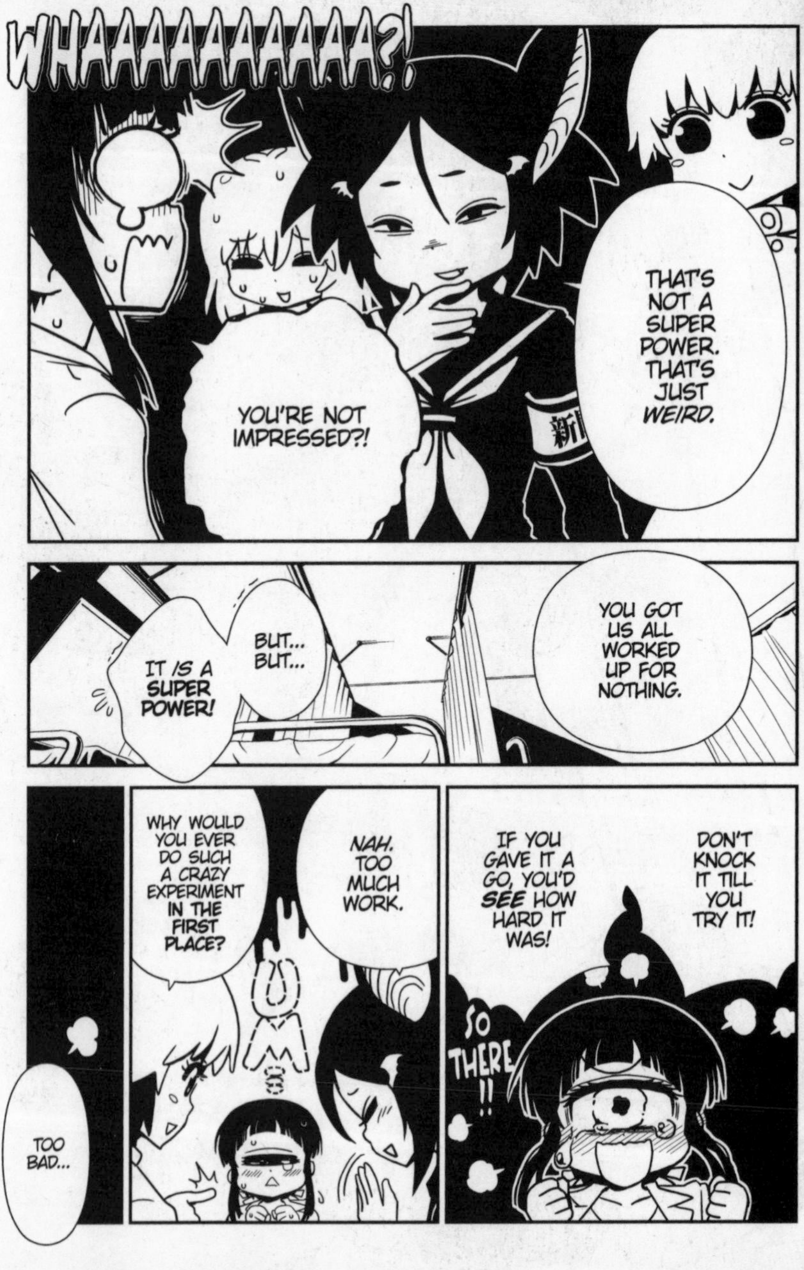
WHAAAAAAAAAA?!
THAT'S NOT A SUPER POWER. THAT'S JUST *WEIRD.*
YOU'RE NOT IMPRESSED?!
YOU GOT US ALL WORKED UP FOR NOTHING.
BUT... BUT...
IT *IS* A SUPER POWER!
DON'T KNOCK IT TILL YOU TRY IT!
IF YOU GAVE IT A GO, YOU'D *SEE* HOW HARD IT WAS!
SO THERE!!
NAH. TOO MUCH WORK.
WHY WOULD YOU EVER DO SUCH A CRAZY EXPERIMENT IN THE FIRST PLACE?
TOO BAD...

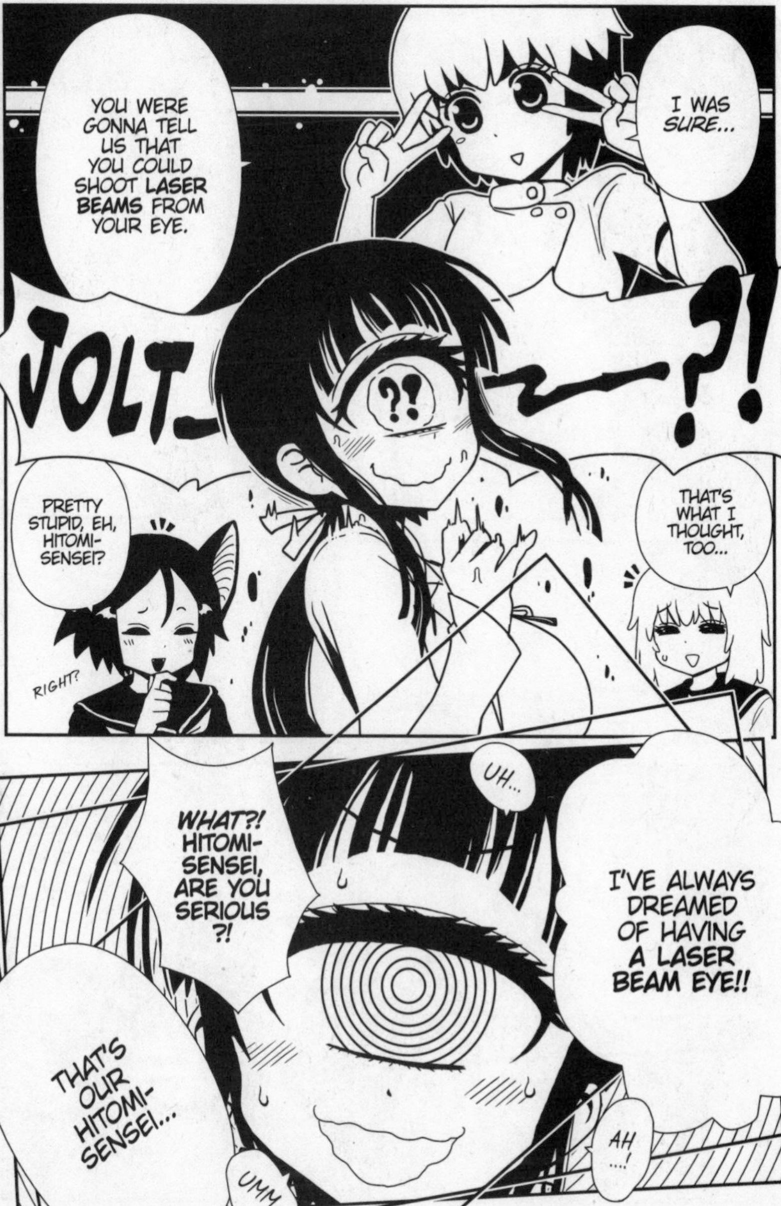
I WAS SURE...
YOU WERE GONNA TELL US THAT YOU COULD SHOOT LASER BEAMS FROM YOUR EYE.
JOLT—?!
THAT'S WHAT I THOUGHT, TOO...
PRETTY STUPID, EH, HITOMI-SENSEI?
RIGHT?
UH...
I'VE ALWAYS DREAMED OF HAVING A LASER BEAM EYE!!
WHAT?! HITOMI-SENSEI, ARE YOU SERIOUS?!
AH...!
THAT'S OUR HITOMI-SENSEI...
UMM...

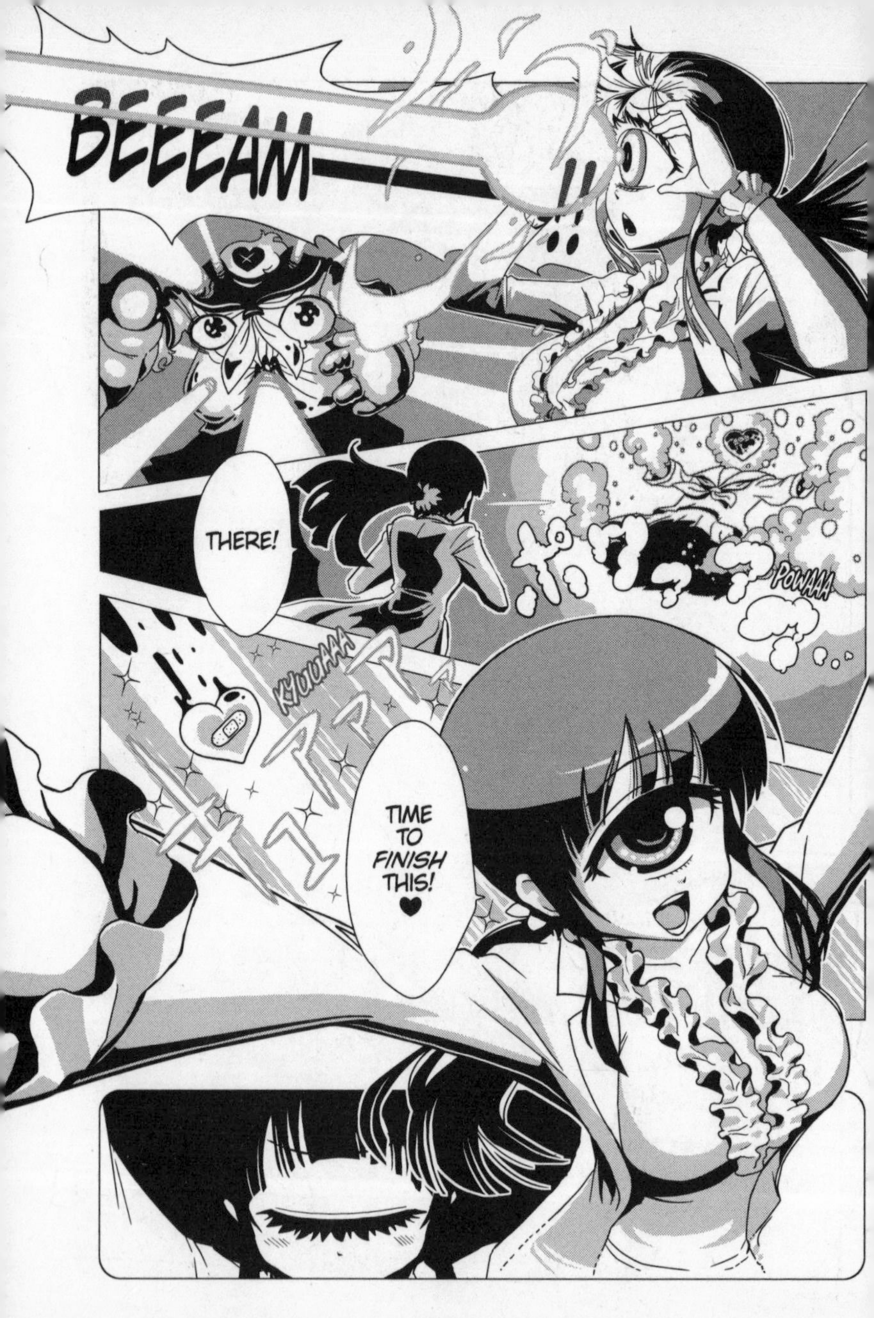
BEEEAM
POWAAA
THERE!
TIME TO FINISH THIS! ♥
KYOUAAA

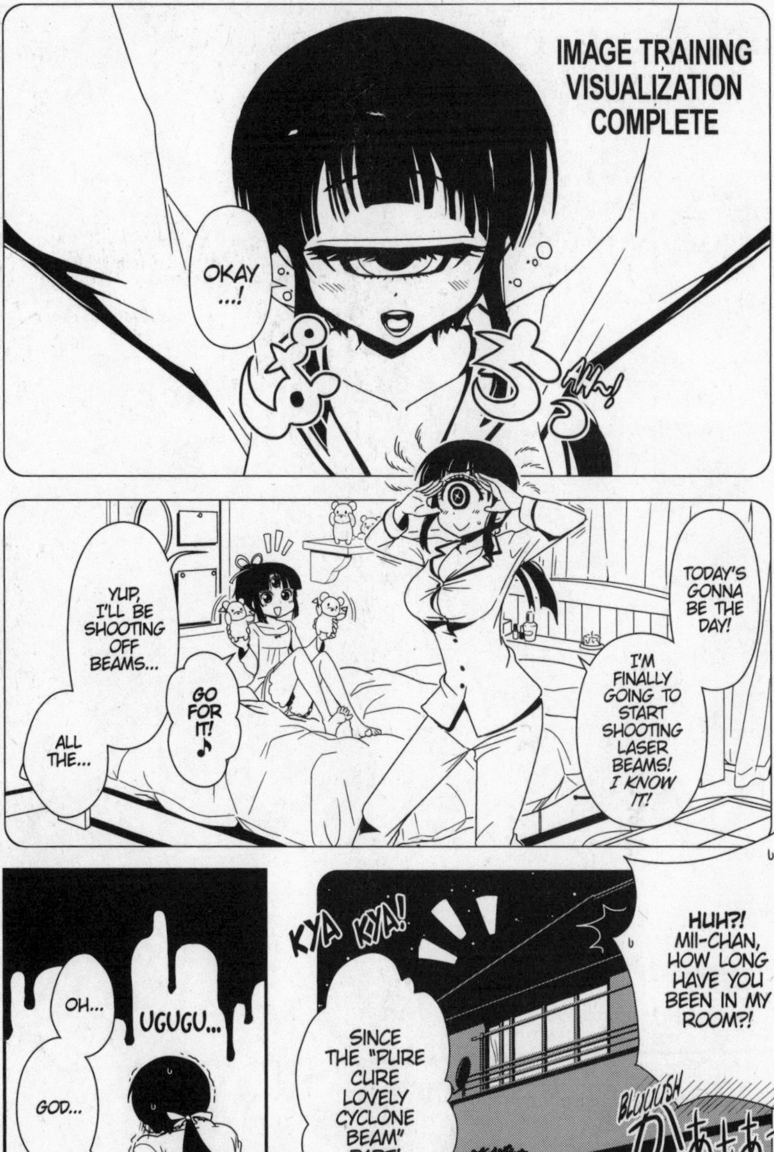
IMAGE TRAINING VISUALIZATION COMPLETE
OKAY ...!
AH~!
TODAY'S GONNA BE THE DAY!
I'M FINALLY GOING TO START SHOOTING LASER BEAMS! I KNOW IT!
GO FOR IT! ♪
YUP, I'LL BE SHOOTING OFF BEAMS...
ALL THE...
HUH?! MII-CHAN, HOW LONG HAVE YOU BEEN IN MY ROOM?!
KYA KYA!
SINCE THE "PURE CURE LOVELY CYCLONE BEAM" PART! ♪
BLUUUSH
かあああっ
UGUGU...
OH...
GOD...

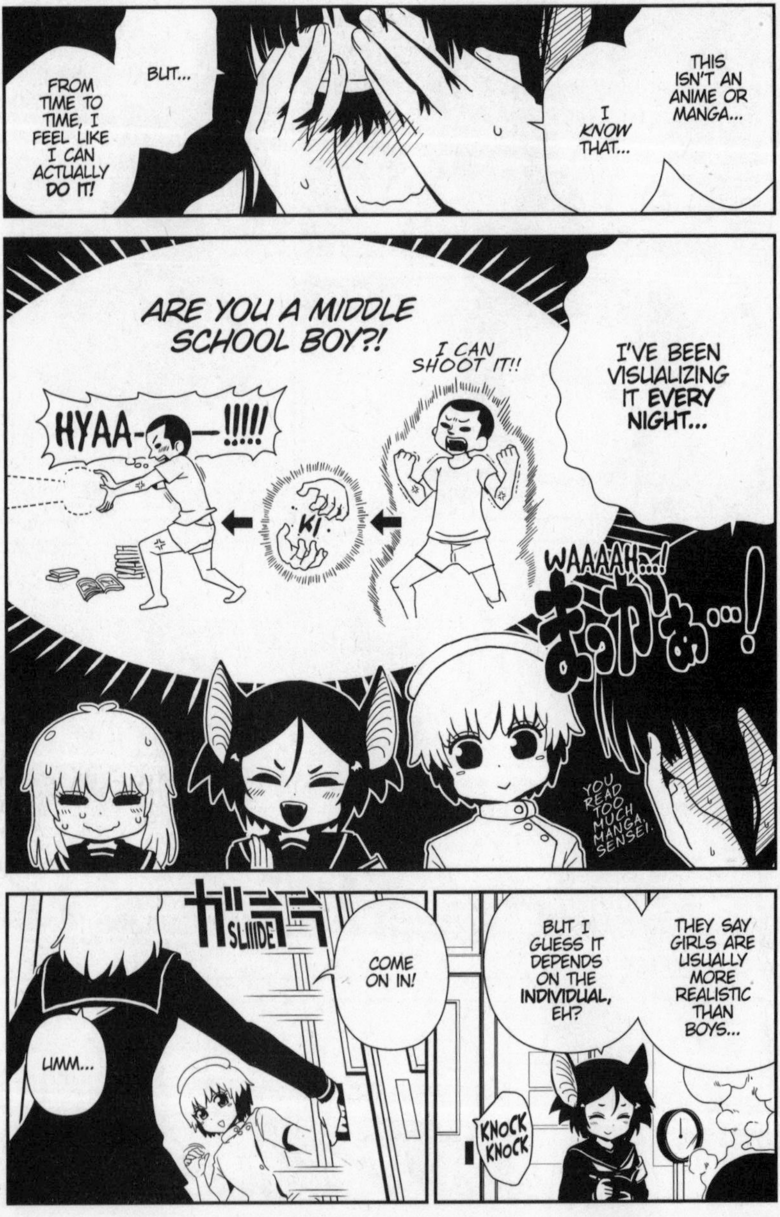
THIS ISN'T AN ANIME OR MANGA...
I KNOW THAT...
BUT...
FROM TIME TO TIME, I FEEL LIKE I CAN ACTUALLY DO IT!
I'VE BEEN VISUALIZING IT EVERY NIGHT...
I CAN SHOOT IT!!
KI
HYAA-——!!!!!
ARE YOU A MIDDLE SCHOOL BOY?!
WAAAAH...!
まっかぁ…!
YOU READ TOO MUCH MANGA, SENSEI.
THEY SAY GIRLS ARE USUALLY MORE REALISTIC THAN BOYS...
BUT I GUESS IT DEPENDS ON THE INDIVIDUAL, EH?
KNOCK KNOCK
SLIIIDE
COME ON IN!
UMM...

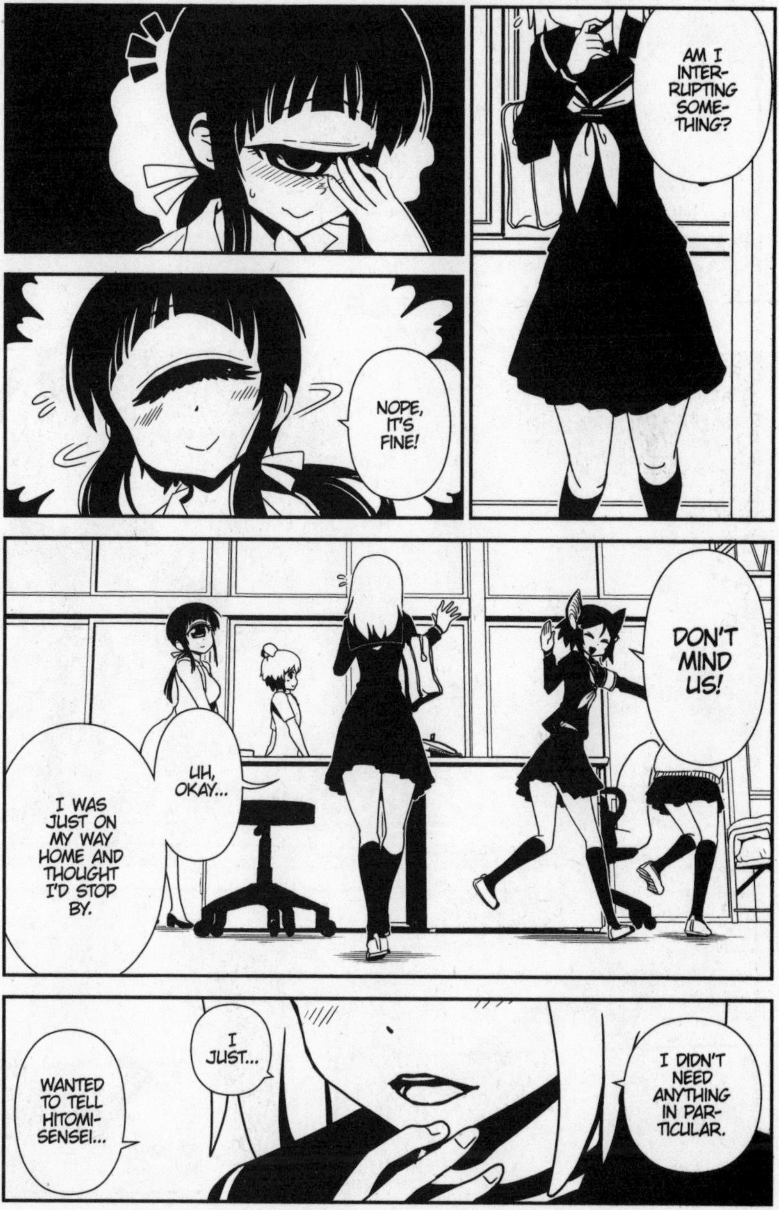
AM I INTERRUPTING SOMETHING?
NOPE, IT'S FINE!
DON'T MIND US!
UH, OKAY...
I WAS JUST ON MY WAY HOME AND THOUGHT I'D STOP BY.
I DIDN'T NEED ANYTHING IN PARTICULAR.
I JUST...
WANTED TO TELL HITOMI-SENSEI...

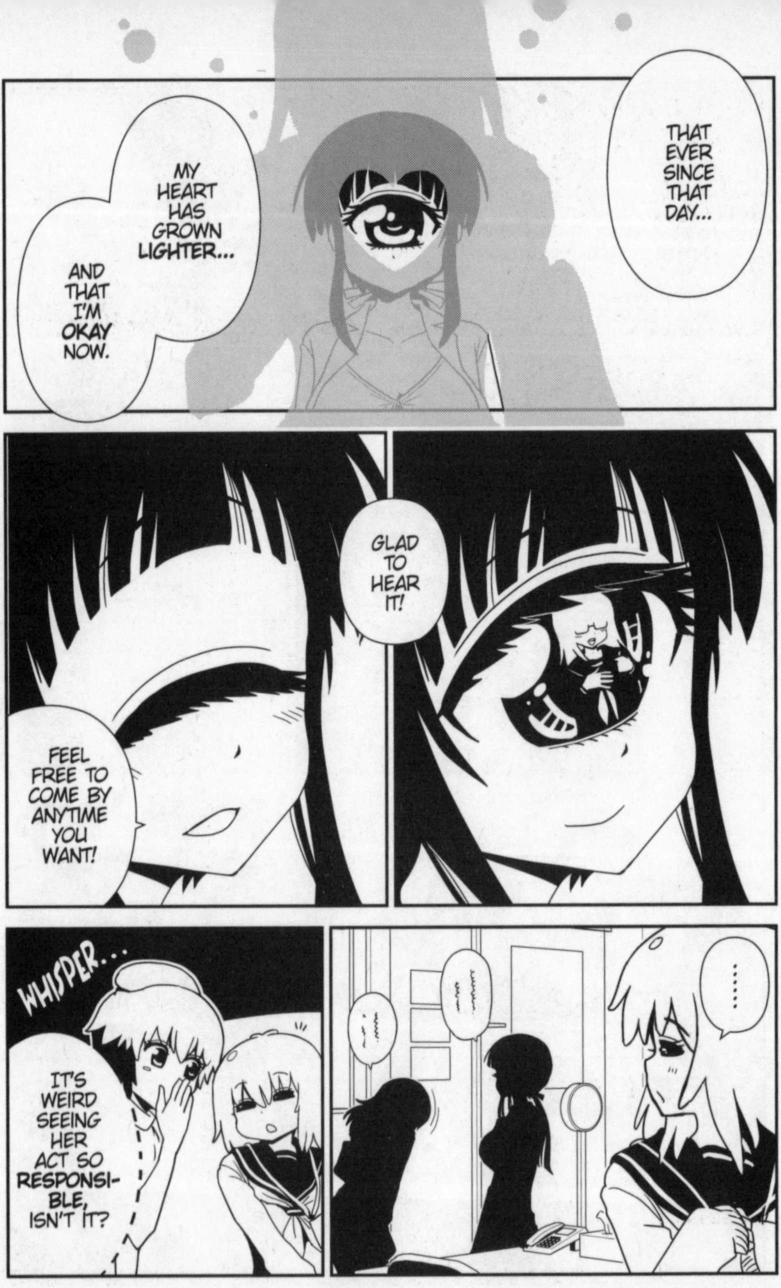
THAT EVER SINCE THAT DAY...
MY HEART HAS GROWN LIGHTER...
AND THAT I'M OKAY NOW.
GLAD TO HEAR IT!
FEEL FREE TO COME BY ANYTIME YOU WANT!
......
WHISPER...
IT'S WEIRD SEEING HER ACT SO RESPONSIBLE, ISN'T IT?

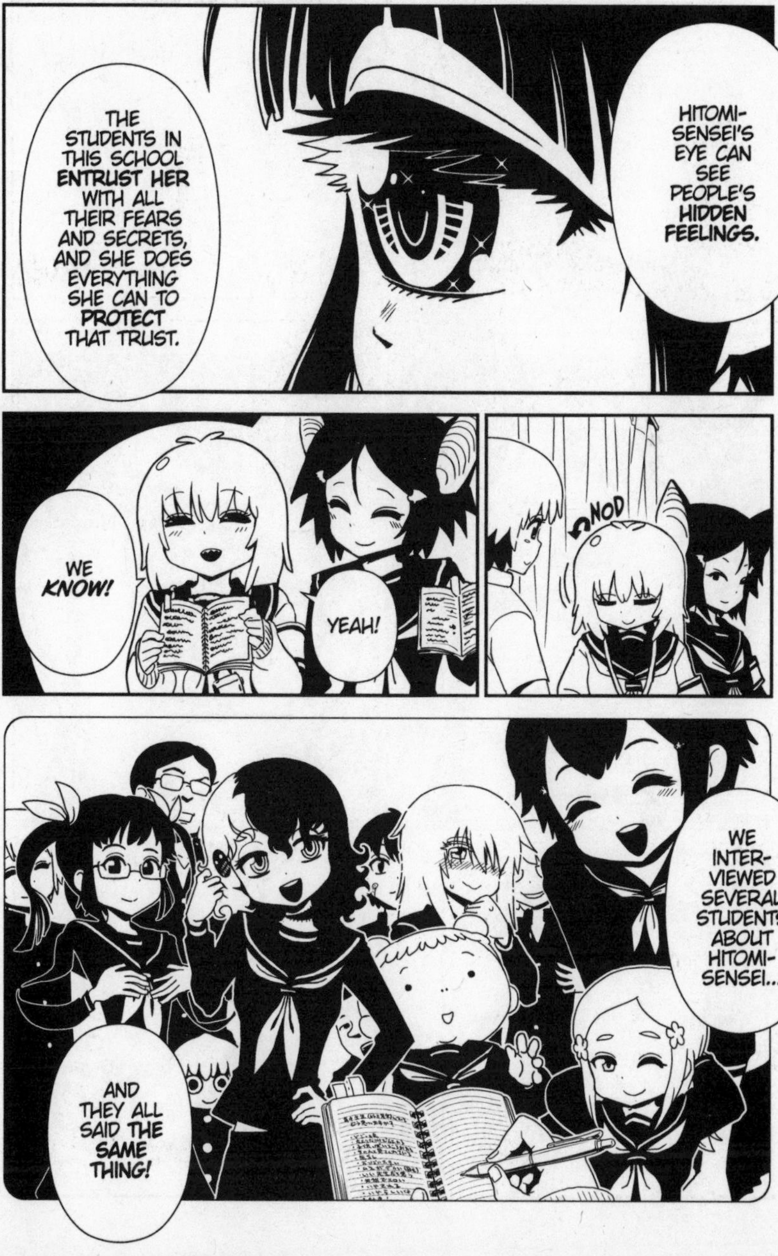
HITOMI-SENSEI'S EYE CAN SEE PEOPLE'S HIDDEN FEELINGS.
THE STUDENTS IN THIS SCHOOL ENTRUST HER WITH ALL THEIR FEARS AND SECRETS, AND SHE DOES EVERYTHING SHE CAN TO PROTECT THAT TRUST.
NOD
WE KNOW!
YEAH!
WE INTERVIEWED SEVERAL STUDENTS ABOUT HITOMI-SENSEI...
AND THEY ALL SAID THE SAME THING!

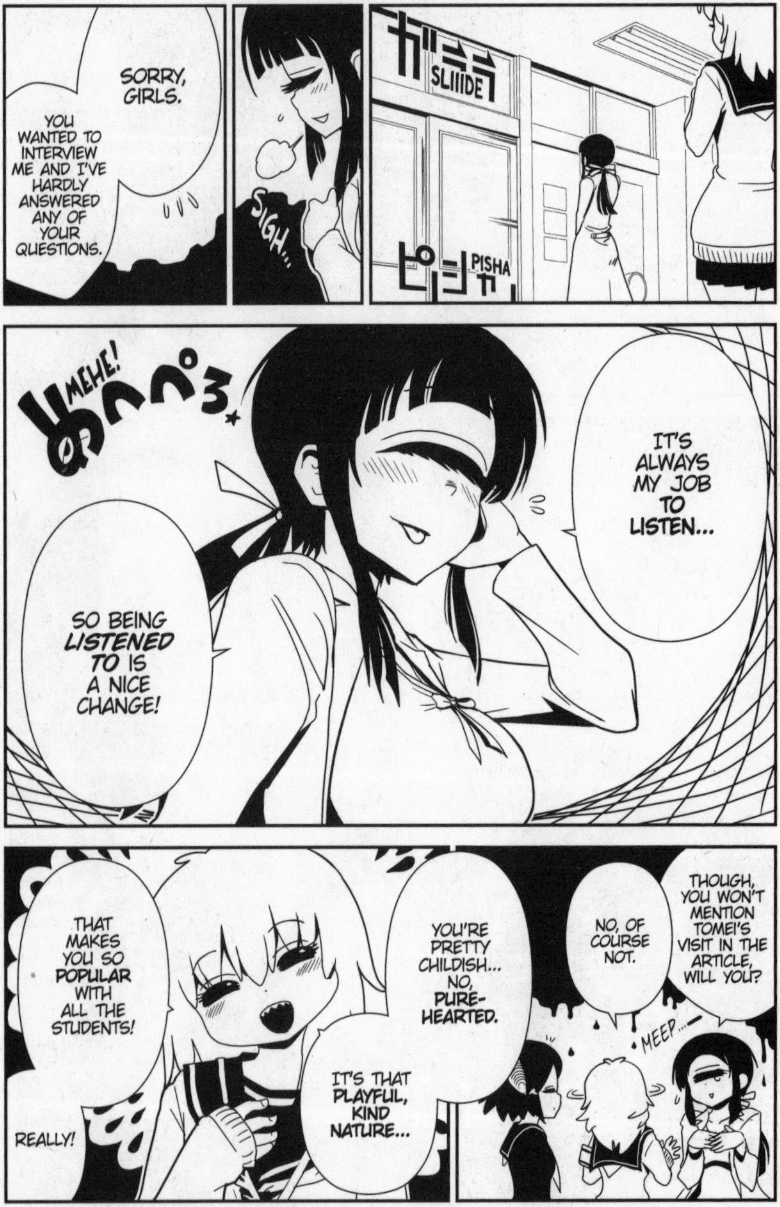
SLIIIDE
PISHA
SIGH...
SORRY, GIRLS.
YOU WANTED TO INTERVIEW ME AND I'VE HARDLY ANSWERED ANY OF YOUR QUESTIONS.
IT'S ALWAYS MY JOB TO LISTEN...
SO BEING LISTENED TO IS A NICE CHANGE!
MEHE!
THOUGH, YOU WON'T MENTION TOMEI'S VISIT IN THE ARTICLE, WILL YOU?
NO, OF COURSE NOT.
MEEP...
YOU'RE PRETTY CHILDISH... NO, PURE-HEARTED.
IT'S THAT PLAYFUL, KIND NATURE...
THAT MAKES YOU SO POPULAR WITH ALL THE STUDENTS!
REALLY!

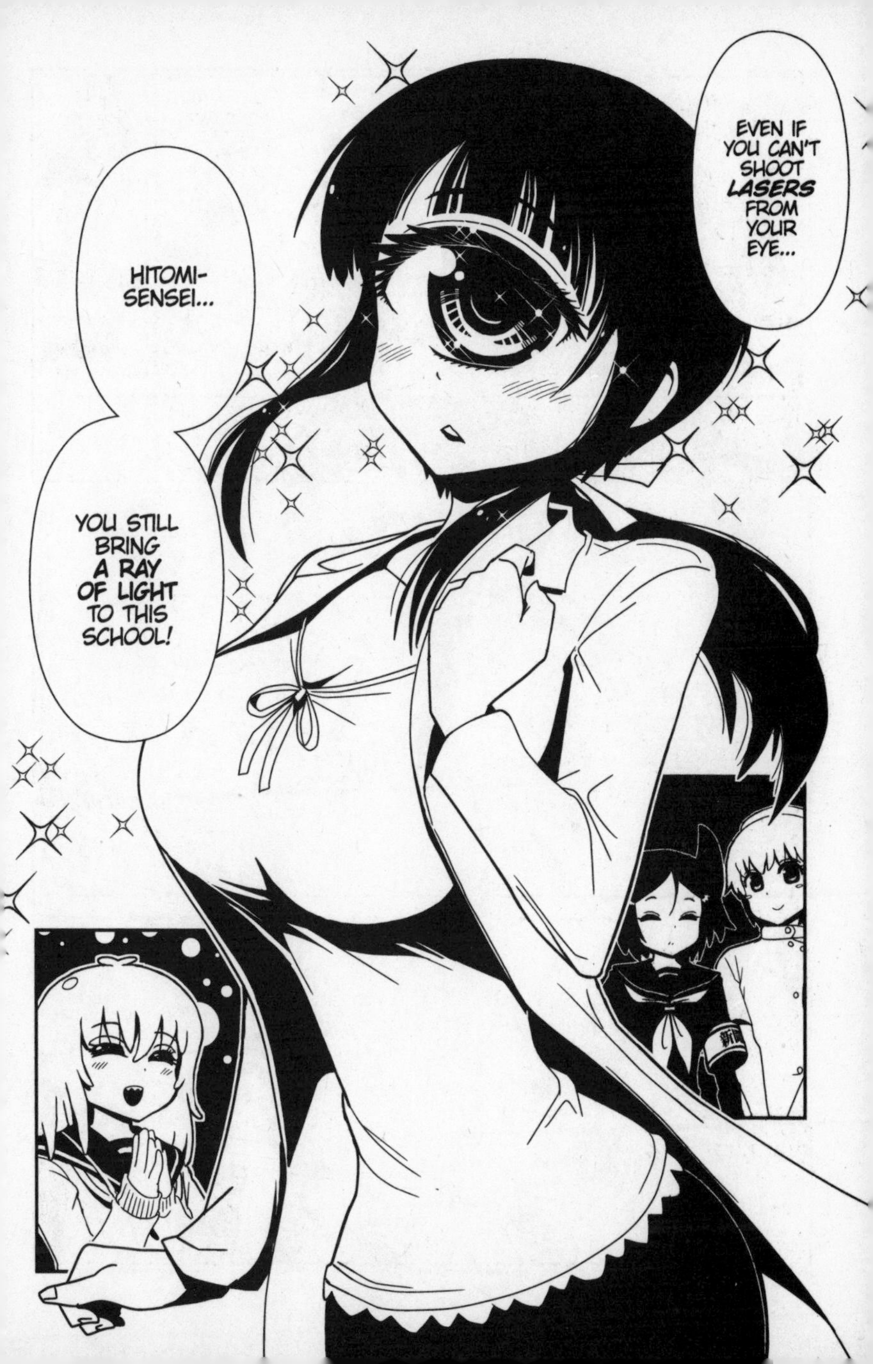
EVEN IF YOU CAN'T SHOOT **LASERS** FROM YOUR EYE...
HITOMI-SENSEI...
YOU STILL BRING **A RAY OF LIGHT** TO THIS SCHOOL!

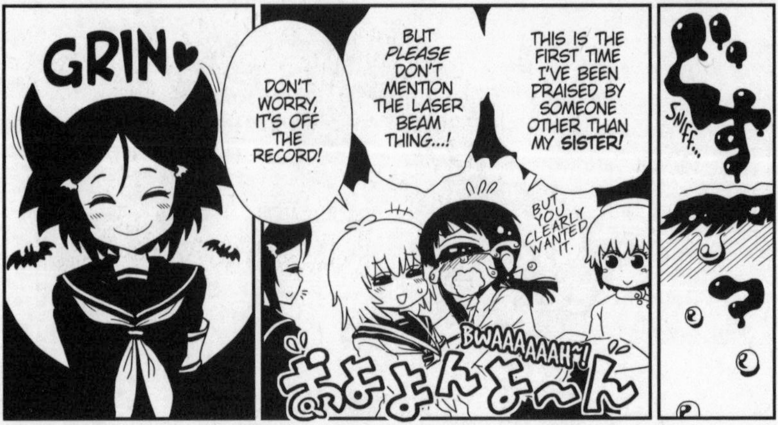
ぐす
SNIFF...
?
THIS IS THE FIRST TIME I'VE BEEN PRAISED BY SOMEONE OTHER THAN MY SISTER!
BUT *PLEASE* DON'T MENTION THE LASER BEAM THING...!
DON'T WORRY, IT'S OFF THE RECORD!
BUT YOU CLEARLY WANTED IT.
BWAAAAAAAH~!
およよんよ〜ん
GRIN

-THE NEXT DAY-

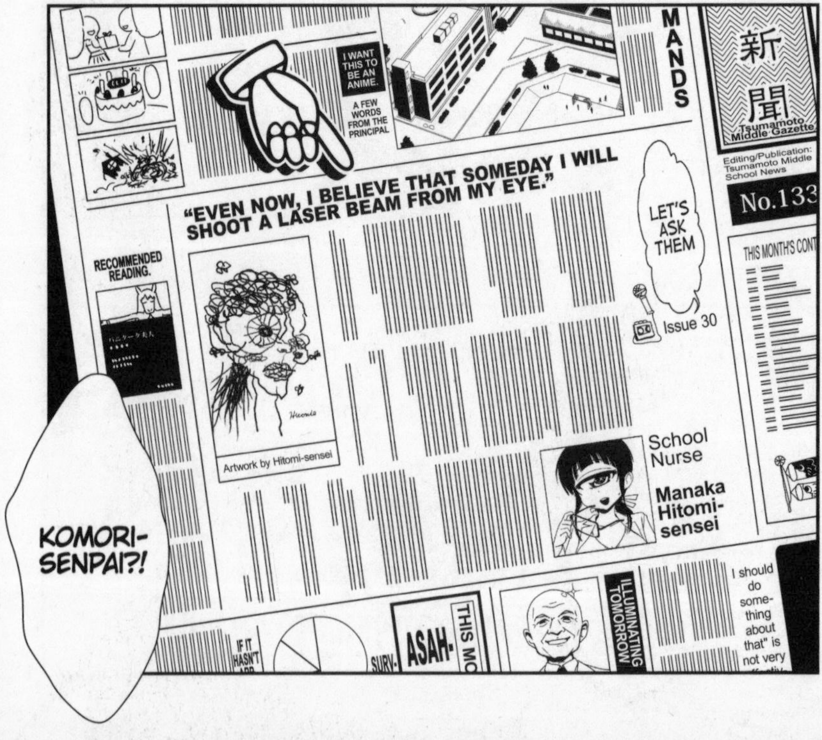
新聞
Tsumamoto Middle Gazette
Editing/Publication: Tsumamoto Middle School News
No.133
MANDS
I WANT THIS TO BE AN ANIME.
A FEW WORDS FROM THE PRINCIPAL
"EVEN NOW, I BELIEVE THAT SOMEDAY I WILL SHOOT A LASER BEAM FROM MY EYE."
LET'S ASK THEM
Issue 30
THIS MONTH'S CONT
RECOMMENDED READING.
Artwork by Hitomi-sensei
School Nurse
Manaka Hitomi-sensei
I should do something about that" is not very
ILLUMINATING TOMORROW
THIS MO
ASAH-
SURV-
IF IT HASN'T
KOMORI-SENPAI?!

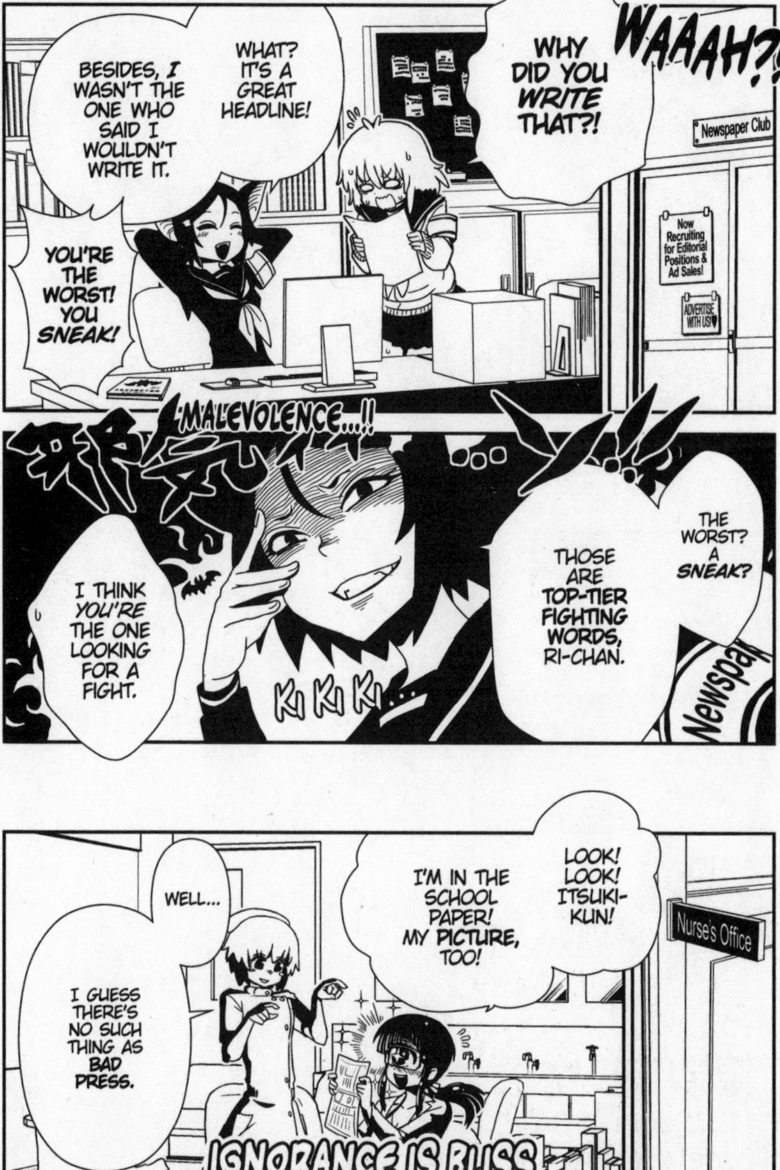
WAAAH?!
WHY DID YOU WRITE THAT?!
Newspaper Club
Now Recruiting for Editorial Positions & Ad Sales!
ADVERTISE WITH US!♥
WHAT? IT'S A GREAT HEADLINE!
BESIDES, I WASN'T THE ONE WHO SAID I WOULDN'T WRITE IT.
YOU'RE THE WORST! YOU SNEAK!
THE WORST? A SNEAK?
THOSE ARE TOP-TIER FIGHTING WORDS, RI-CHAN.
MALEVOLENCE...!!
KI KI KI
I THINK YOU'RE THE ONE LOOKING FOR A FIGHT.
Nurse's Office
LOOK! LOOK! ITSUKI-KUN!
I'M IN THE SCHOOL PAPER! MY PICTURE, TOO!
WELL...
I GUESS THERE'S NO SUCH THING AS BAD PRESS.
IGNORANCE IS BLISS

NURSE HITOMI'S Monster Infirmary

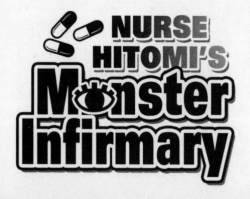

“EVEN NOW, I BELIEVE THAT SOMEDAY I WILL SHOOT A LASER BEAM FROM MY EYE.”

LET'S ASK THEM

Issue 30

Artwork by Hitomi-sensei

“There are many people who mistakenly think of me as a medical doctor. But it's more like I'm a faculty member who's in charge of looking after student health and wellness.”

Sharing her vast knowledge without me even asking for it, Hitomi-sensei covers her one large eye, then crosses her legs with the poise of an actress. Manaka-sensei, the school nurse known to students as “Hitomi-sensei,” is supposedly the older sister of our school's student council president, Manaka Mitsumi. While the little sister is skilled in both academics and sports and is a perfect superhuman loved by both teachers and students, the older sister is just a basic klutz.

Could these two women, one flat-chested, the other stacked, truly be related by blood? Hitomi-sensei seemed perplexed by this question at first, but finally confessed that she too often wondered if “we aren't related at all.” In a way, that in itself answers the question.

Another question one might have is in regards to the inside of Hitomi-sensei's head. With an eye that large, where on earth does her brain fit? Sensei drew a picture, though it raises more questions than it answers. This unique art piece depicts the inside of her head (image at left). Who knew that our school nurse was also an artist?

“I have my own special power.”

After creating that hair-raising artwork, the master painter boasts of a special ability that would make use of her large eyeball. This technique turns out to be the ability “to have eye drops administered from the second floor.” Hitomi-sensei insisted that this is quite a difficult feat to pull off. We humble reporters shall bow to her wisdom in this case.

However, Hitomi-sensei's quest for special abilities would not end there. Influenced by manga or sci-fi films, she believes “a beam will come out of her eye” if she just tries hard enough.

Every day without fail, Hitomi-sensei trains so that she can shoot a beam from her eye.

“Even now, I believe that someday I WILL shoot a laser beam from my eye,” Hitomi-sensei said confidently, her eye shining brightly. (By Komori Kiki)

School Nurse

Manaka Hitomi-sensei

IT'S NOT THE MOST FLATTERING ARTICLE...
......
BUT SHE SEEMS HAPPY WITH IT, SO IT'S FINE.
SO DON'T ATTACK THE NEWSPAPER CLUB, OKAY, TENGEN?
SCRAP BOOK

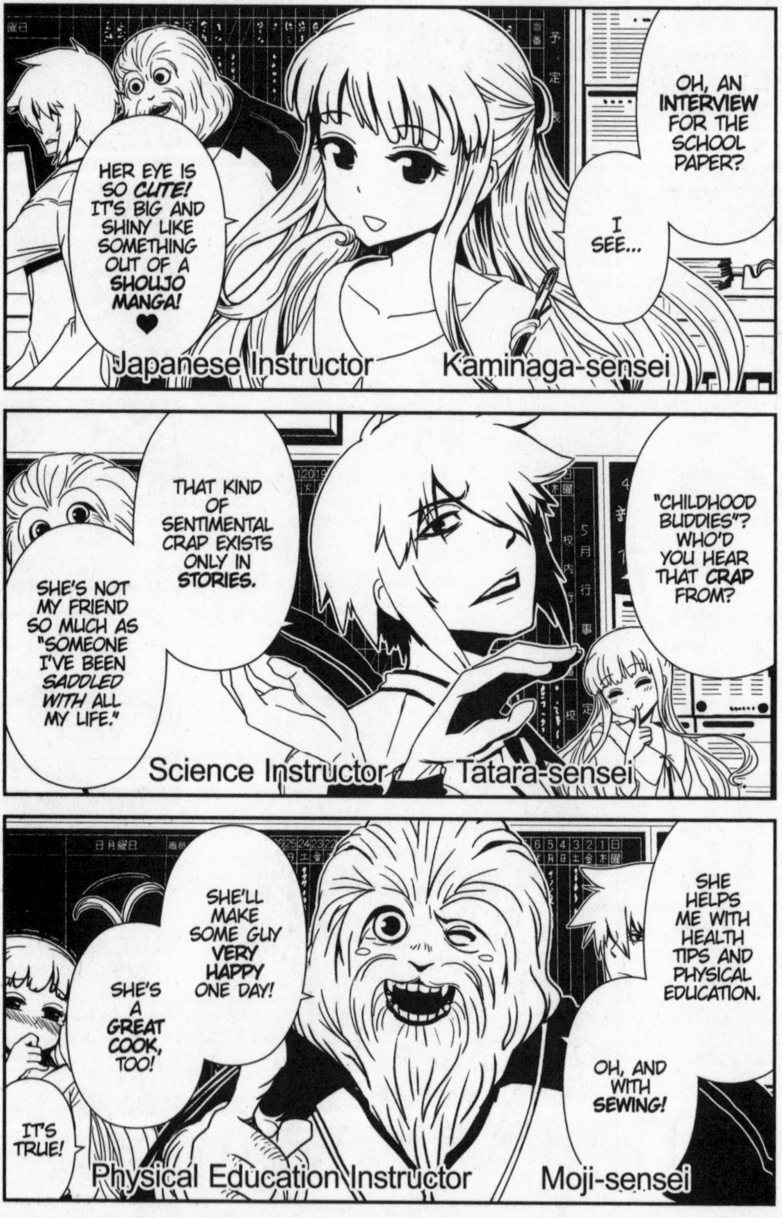
OH, AN INTERVIEW FOR THE SCHOOL PAPER?
I SEE...
HER EYE IS SO CUTE! IT'S BIG AND SHINY LIKE SOMETHING OUT OF A SHOUJO MANGA! ♥
Japanese Instructor Kaminaga-sensei
"CHILDHOOD BUDDIES"? WHO'D YOU HEAR THAT CRAP FROM?
THAT KIND OF SENTIMENTAL CRAP EXISTS ONLY IN STORIES.
SHE'S NOT MY FRIEND SO MUCH AS "SOMEONE I'VE BEEN SADDLED WITH ALL MY LIFE."
Science Instructor Tatara-sensei
SHE HELPS ME WITH HEALTH TIPS AND PHYSICAL EDUCATION.
OH, AND WITH SEWING!
SHE'LL MAKE SOME GUY VERY HAPPY ONE DAY!
SHE'S A GREAT COOK, TOO!
IT'S TRUE!
Physical Education Instructor Moji-sensei

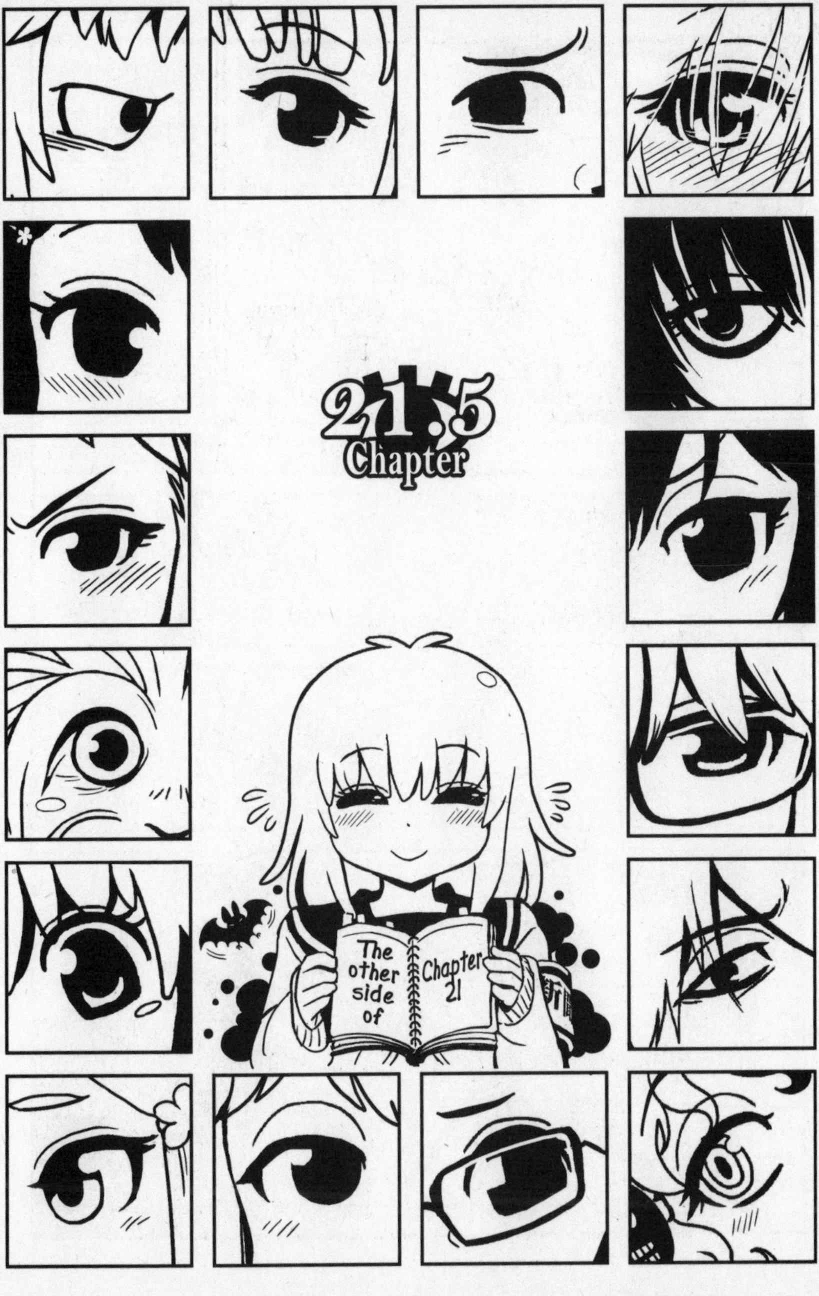
21.5
Chapter
The other side of
Chapter 21

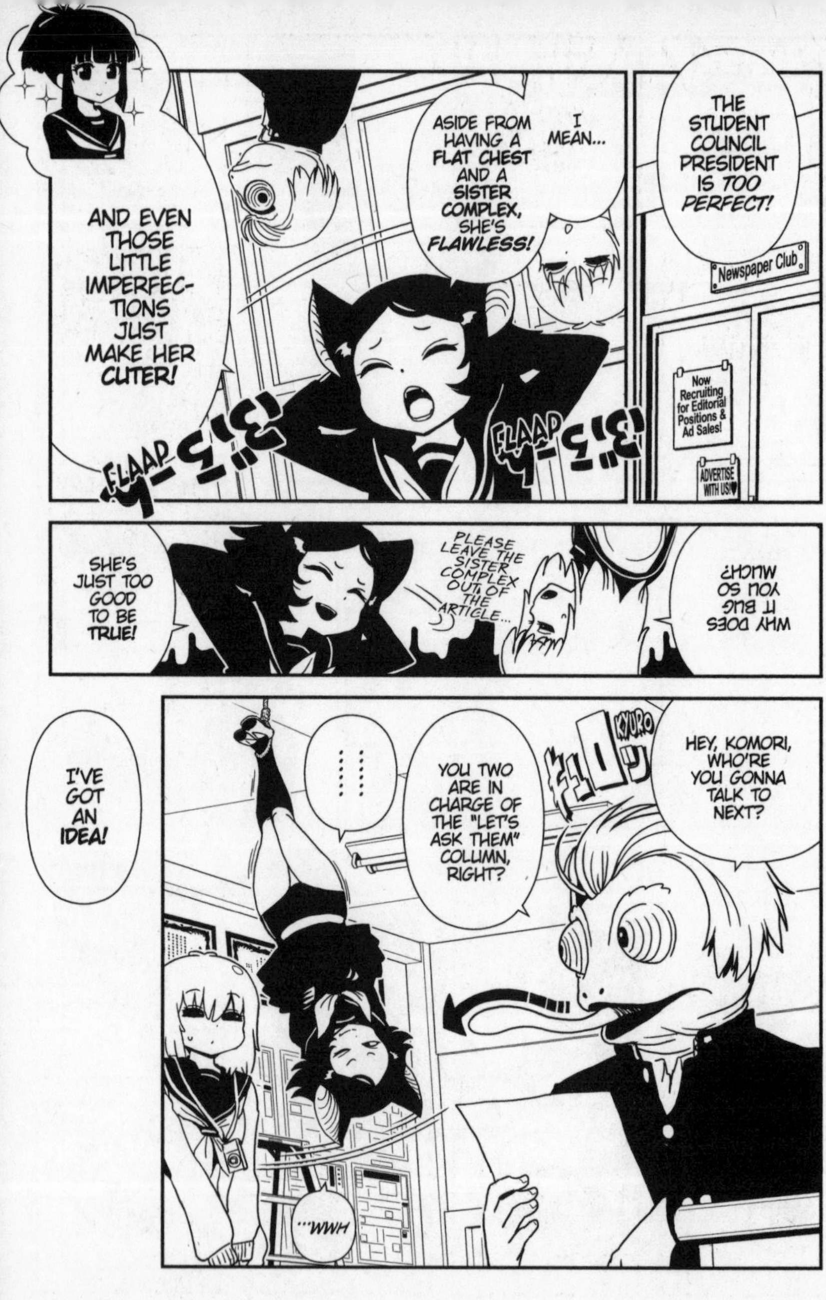
THE STUDENT COUNCIL PRESIDENT IS TOO PERFECT!
Newspaper Club
Now Recruiting for Editorial Positions & Ad Sales!
ADVERTISE WITH US!♥
I MEAN...
ASIDE FROM HAVING A FLAT CHEST AND A SISTER COMPLEX, SHE'S FLAWLESS!
FLAAP
FLAAP
AND EVEN THOSE LITTLE IMPERFECTIONS JUST MAKE HER CUTER!
WHY DOES IT BUG YOU SO MUCH?
PLEASE LEAVE THE SISTER COMPLEX OUT OF THE ARTICLE...
SHE'S JUST TOO GOOD TO BE TRUE!
HEY, KOMORI, WHO'RE YOU GONNA TALK TO NEXT?
KYURO
YOU TWO ARE IN CHARGE OF THE "LET'S ASK THEM" COLUMN, RIGHT?
......
HMM...
I'VE GOT AN IDEA!

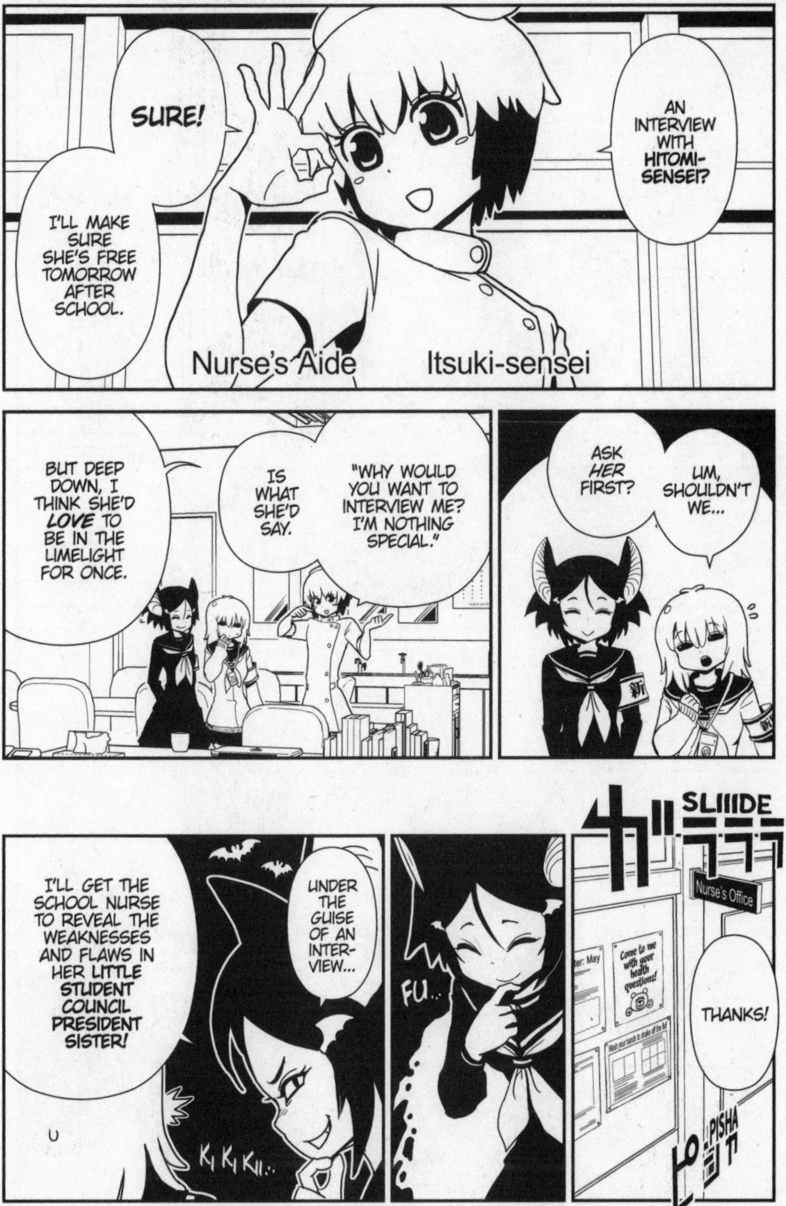
AN INTERVIEW WITH HITOMI-SENSEI?
SURE!
I'LL MAKE SURE SHE'S FREE TOMORROW AFTER SCHOOL.
Nurse's Aide Itsuki-sensei
UM, SHOULDN'T WE...
ASK HER FIRST?
"WHY WOULD YOU WANT TO INTERVIEW ME? I'M NOTHING SPECIAL."
IS WHAT SHE'D SAY.
BUT DEEP DOWN, I THINK SHE'D LOVE TO BE IN THE LIMELIGHT FOR ONCE.
SLIIIDE
Nurse's Office
Come to me with your health questions!
THANKS!
PISHA
FU...
UNDER THE GUISE OF AN INTER-VIEW...
I'LL GET THE SCHOOL NURSE TO REVEAL THE WEAKNESSES AND FLAWS IN HER LITTLE STUDENT COUNCIL PRESIDENT SISTER!
KI KI KII...

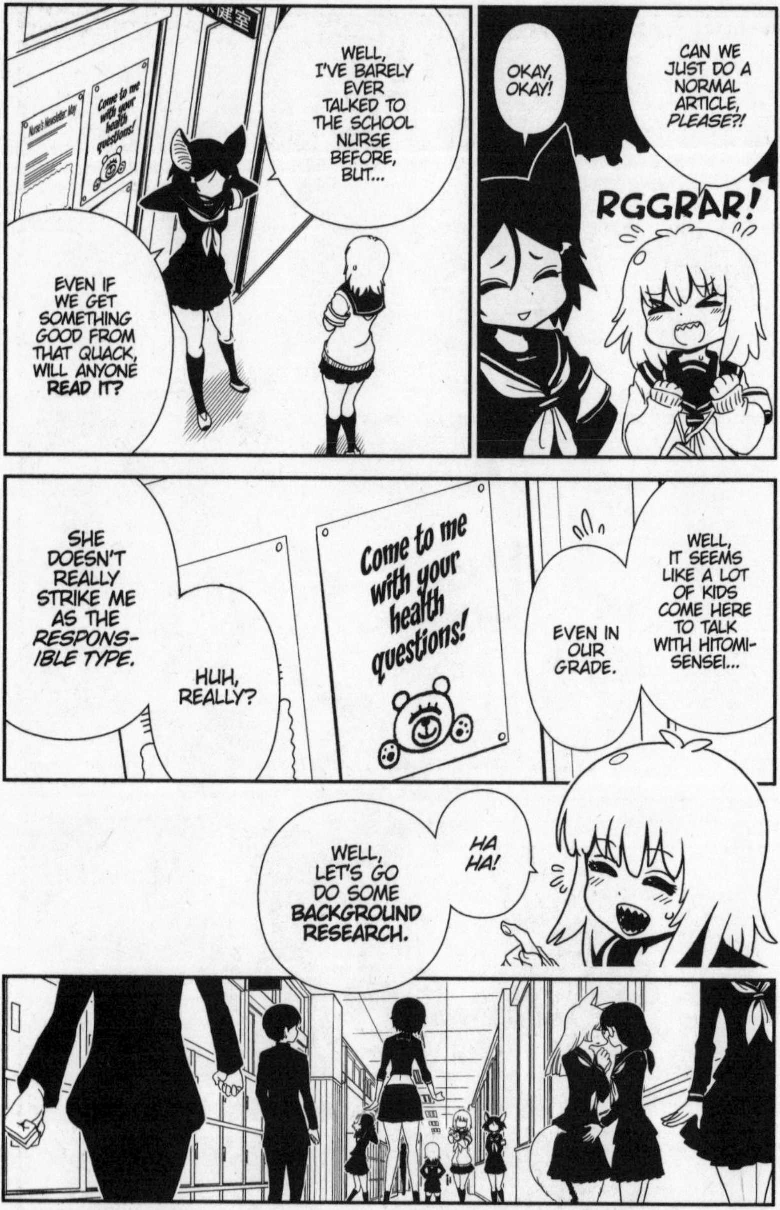
CAN WE JUST DO A NORMAL ARTICLE, PLEASE?!
OKAY, OKAY!
RGGRAR!
保健室
WELL, I'VE BARELY EVER TALKED TO THE SCHOOL NURSE BEFORE, BUT...
Come to me with your health questions!
Nurse's Newsletter: May
EVEN IF WE GET SOMETHING GOOD FROM THAT QUACK, WILL ANYONE READ IT?
WELL, IT SEEMS LIKE A LOT OF KIDS COME HERE TO TALK WITH HITOMI-SENSEI...
EVEN IN OUR GRADE.
Come to me with your health questions!
HUH, REALLY?
SHE DOESN'T REALLY STRIKE ME AS THE *RESPONSIBLE TYPE.*
HA HA!
WELL, LET'S GO DO SOME BACKGROUND RESEARCH.

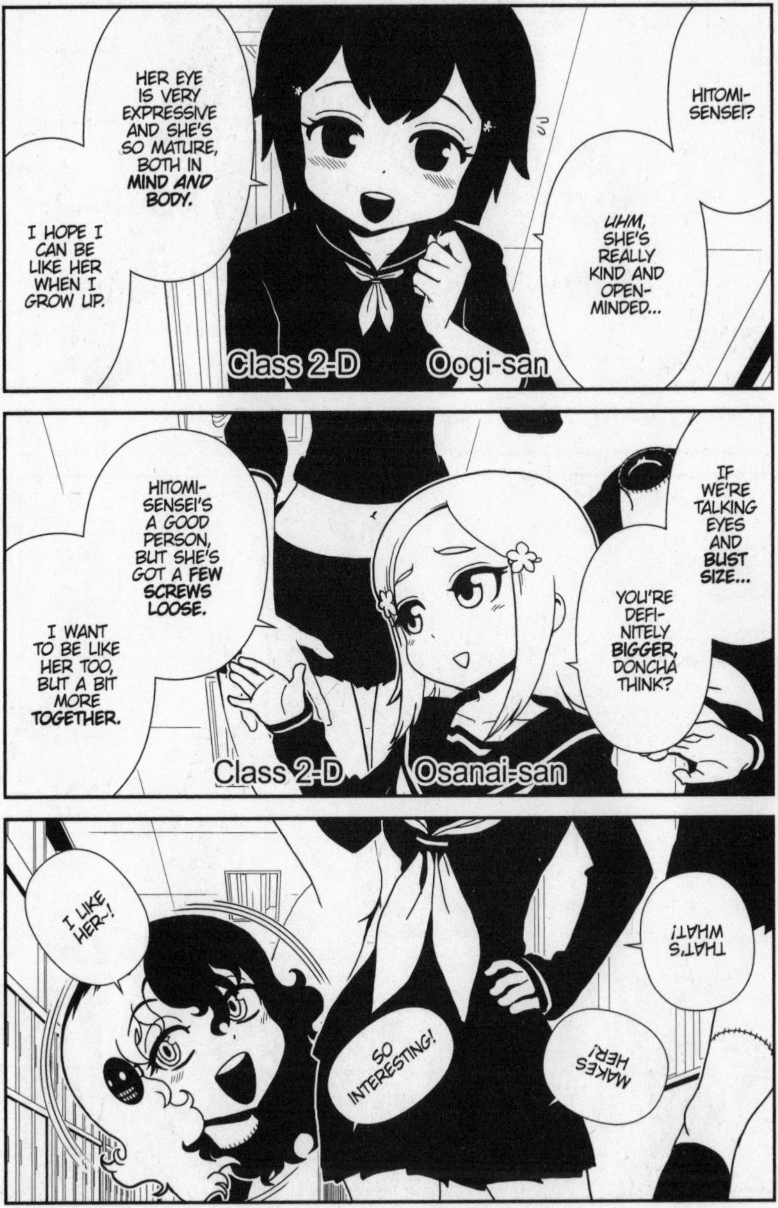
HITOMI-SENSEI?
UHM, SHE'S REALLY KIND AND OPEN-MINDED...
HER EYE IS VERY EXPRESSIVE AND SHE'S SO MATURE, BOTH IN **MIND *AND* BODY.**
I HOPE I CAN BE LIKE HER WHEN I GROW UP.
Class 2-D Oogi-san
IF WE'RE TALKING EYES AND **BUST SIZE...**
YOU'RE DEFINITELY **BIGGER,** DONCHA THINK?
HITOMI-SENSEI'S A GOOD PERSON, BUT SHE'S GOT A FEW **SCREWS LOOSE.**
I WANT TO BE LIKE HER TOO, BUT A BIT MORE **TOGETHER.**
Class 2-D Osanai-san
THAT'S WHAT!
MAKES HER!
SO INTERESTING!
I LIKE HER~!

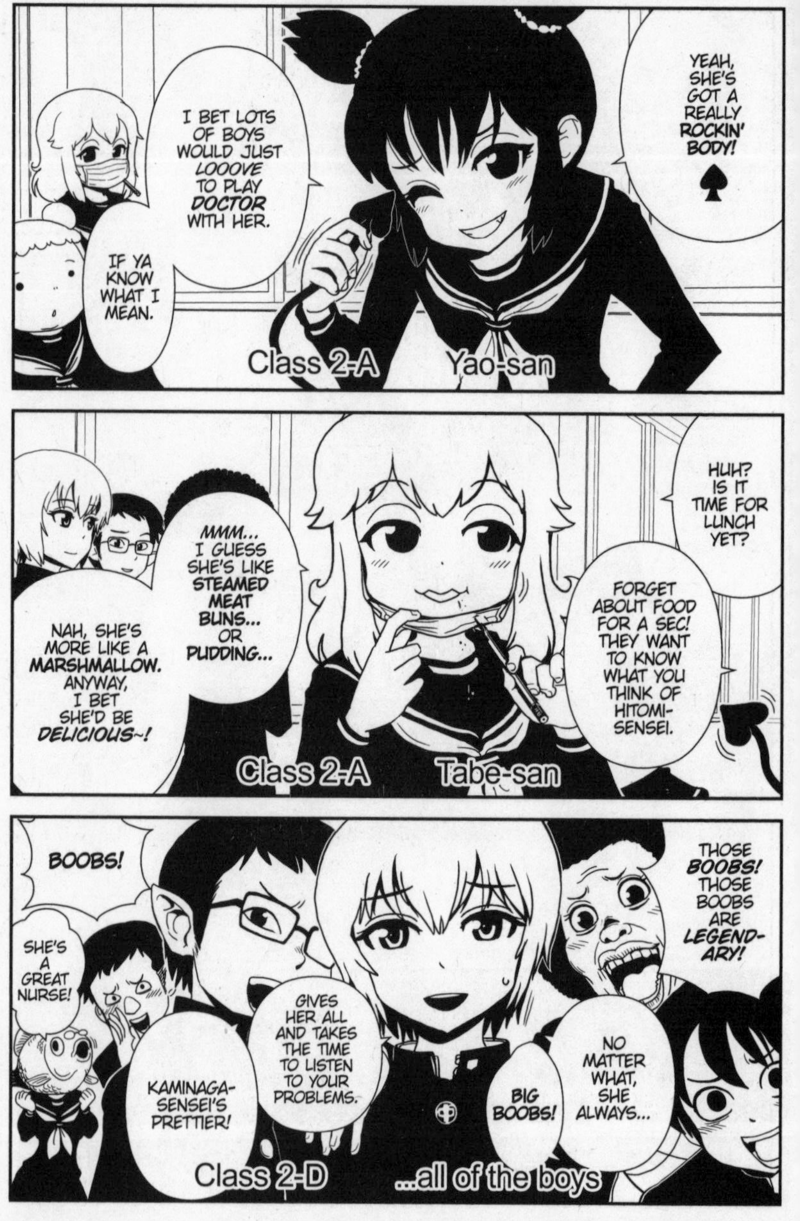
YEAH, SHE'S GOT A REALLY ROCKIN' BODY! ♠
I BET LOTS OF BOYS WOULD JUST LOOOVE TO PLAY DOCTOR WITH HER.
IF YA KNOW WHAT I MEAN.
Class 2-A Yao-san
HUH? IS IT TIME FOR LUNCH YET?
FORGET ABOUT FOOD FOR A SEC! THEY WANT TO KNOW WHAT YOU THINK OF HITOMI-SENSEI.
MMM... I GUESS SHE'S LIKE STEAMED MEAT BUNS... OR PUDDING...
NAH, SHE'S MORE LIKE A MARSHMALLOW. ANYWAY, I BET SHE'D BE DELICIOUS~!
Class 2-A Tabe-san
THOSE BOOBS! THOSE BOOBS ARE LEGENDARY!
BOOBS!
SHE'S A GREAT NURSE!
NO MATTER WHAT, SHE ALWAYS...
BIG BOOBS!
GIVES HER ALL AND TAKES THE TIME TO LISTEN TO YOUR PROBLEMS.
KAMINAGA-SENSEI'S PRETTIER!
Class 2-D ...all of the boys

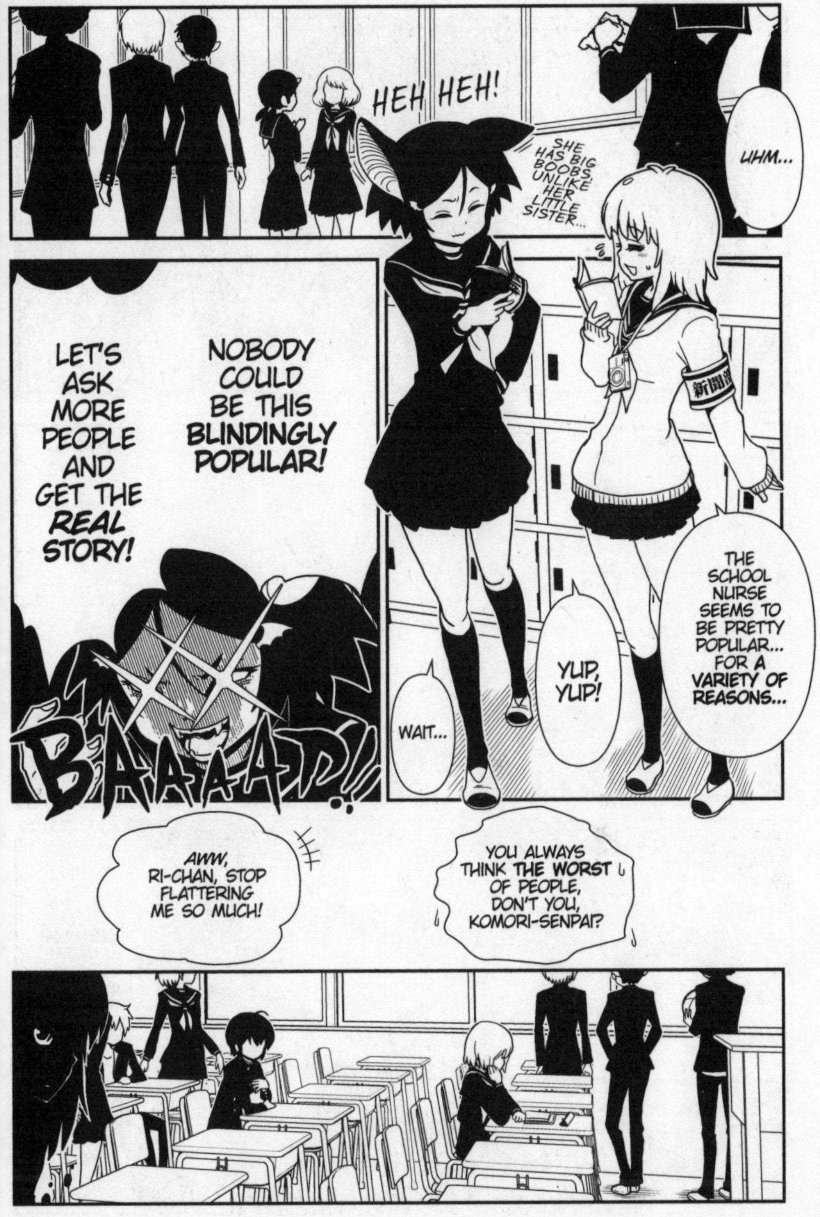
UHM...
SHE HAS BIG BOOBS, UNLIKE HER LITTLE SISTER...
HEH HEH!
THE SCHOOL NURSE SEEMS TO BE PRETTY POPULAR... FOR A VARIETY OF REASONS...
YUP, YUP!
WAIT...
NOBODY COULD BE THIS BLINDINGLY POPULAR!
LET'S ASK MORE PEOPLE AND GET THE REAL STORY!
BAAAD!!
YOU ALWAYS THINK THE WORST OF PEOPLE, DON'T YOU, KOMORI-SENPAI?
AWW, RI-CHAN, STOP FLATTERING ME SO MUCH!

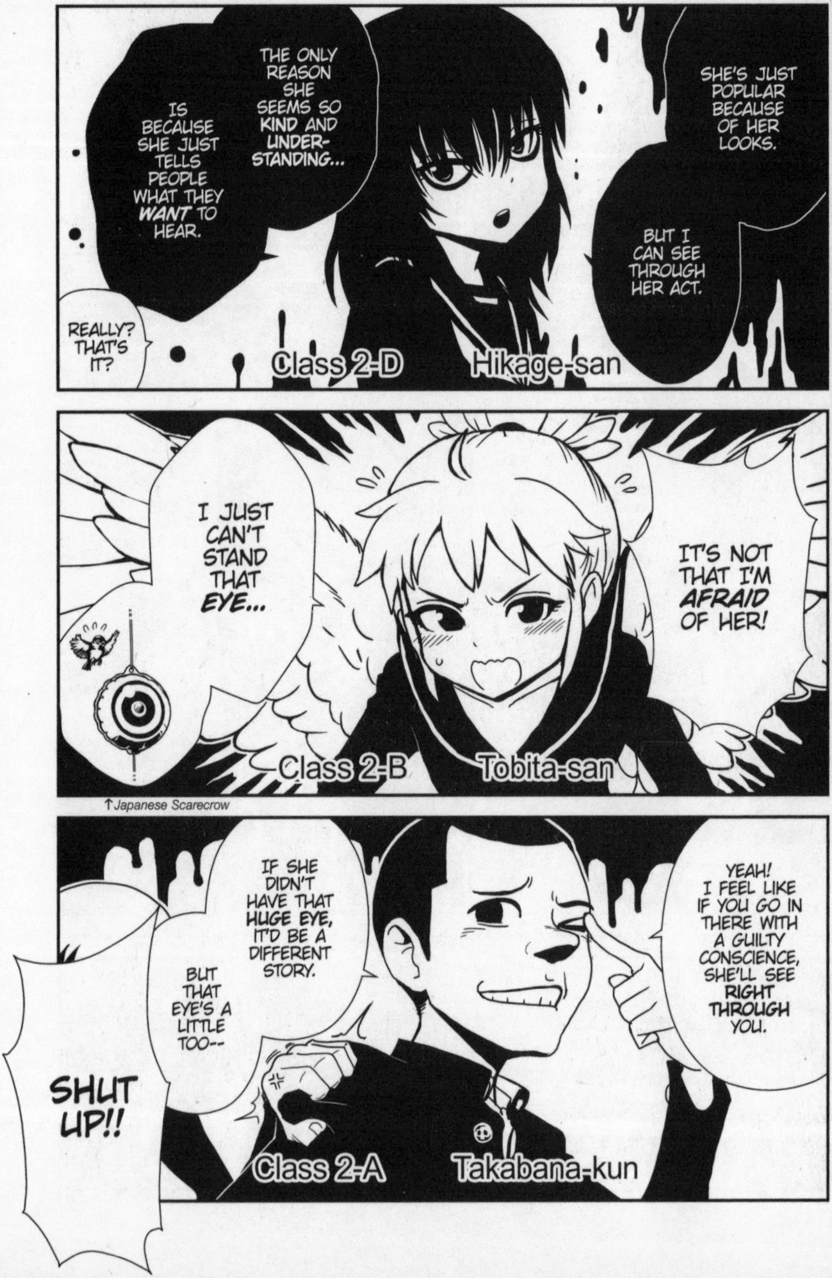
SHE'S JUST POPULAR BECAUSE OF HER LOOKS.
BUT I CAN SEE THROUGH HER ACT.
THE ONLY REASON SHE SEEMS SO KIND AND UNDER-STANDING...
IS BECAUSE SHE JUST TELLS PEOPLE WHAT THEY WANT TO HEAR.
REALLY? THAT'S IT?
Class 2-D Hikage-san
IT'S NOT THAT I'M AFRAID OF HER!
I JUST CAN'T STAND THAT EYE...
Class 2-B Tobita-san
↑Japanese Scarecrow
YEAH! I FEEL LIKE IF YOU GO IN THERE WITH A GUILTY CONSCIENCE, SHE'LL SEE RIGHT THROUGH YOU.
IF SHE DIDN'T HAVE THAT HUGE EYE, IT'D BE A DIFFERENT STORY.
BUT THAT EYE'S A LITTLE TOO--
SHUT UP!!
Class 2-A Takabana-kun

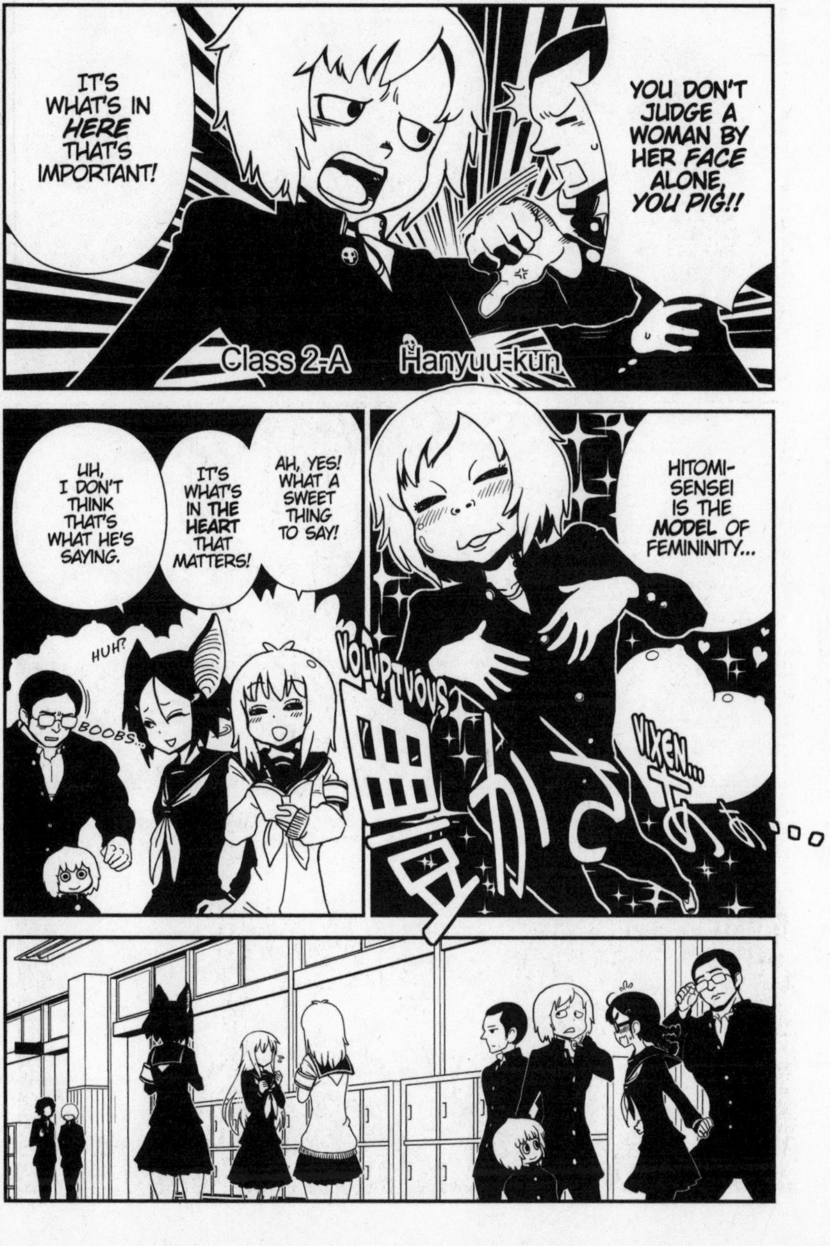
YOU DON'T JUDGE A WOMAN BY HER *FACE* ALONE, *YOU PIG!!*
IT'S WHAT'S IN *HERE* THAT'S IMPORTANT!
Class 2-A Hanyuu-kun
HITOMI-SENSEI IS THE MODEL OF FEMININITY...
VIXEN...
VOLUPTUOUS
AH, YES! WHAT A SWEET THING TO SAY!
IT'S WHAT'S IN THE HEART THAT MATTERS!
UH, I DON'T THINK THAT'S WHAT HE'S SAYING.
HUH?
BOOBS...

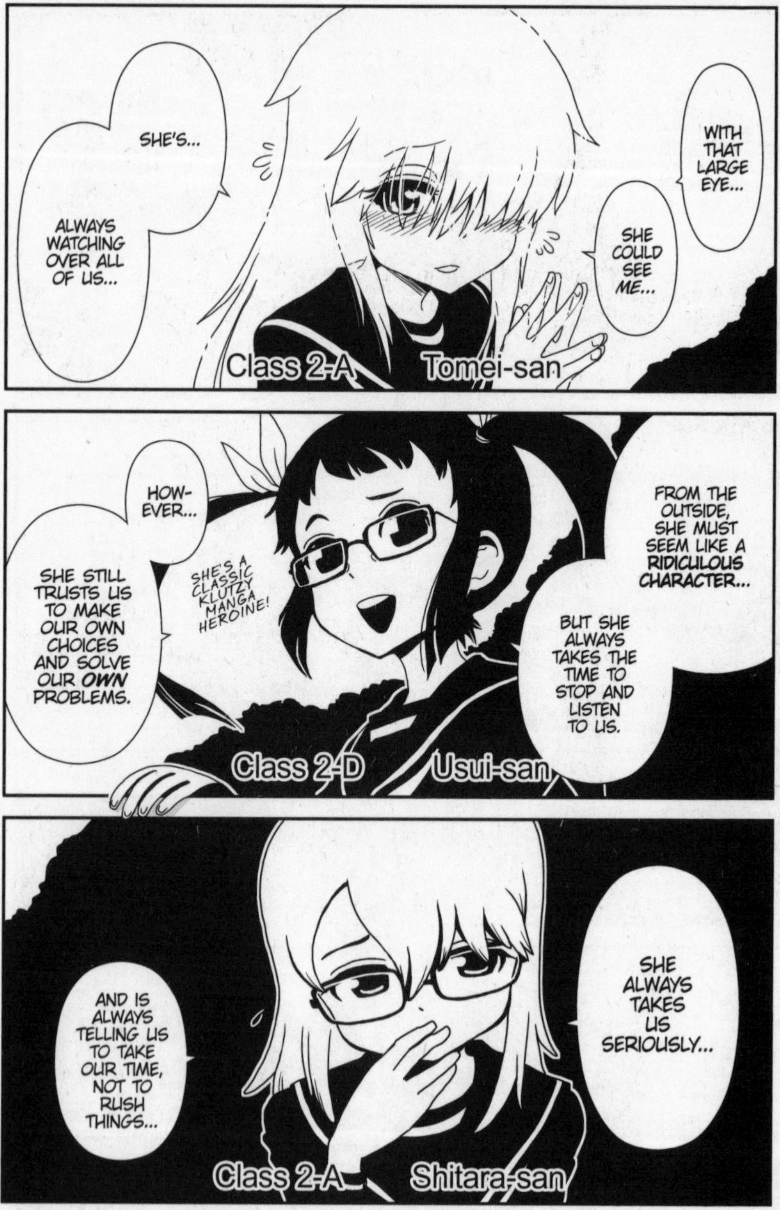
WITH THAT LARGE EYE...
SHE COULD SEE ME...
SHE'S...
ALWAYS WATCHING OVER ALL OF US...
Class 2-A Tomei-san
FROM THE OUTSIDE, SHE MUST SEEM LIKE A RIDICULOUS CHARACTER...
BUT SHE ALWAYS TAKES THE TIME TO STOP AND LISTEN TO US.
SHE'S A CLASSIC KLUTZY MANGA HEROINE!
HOW-EVER...
SHE STILL TRUSTS US TO MAKE OUR OWN CHOICES AND SOLVE OUR *OWN* PROBLEMS.
Class 2-D Usui-san
SHE ALWAYS TAKES US SERIOUSLY...
AND IS ALWAYS TELLING US TO TAKE OUR TIME, NOT TO RUSH THINGS...
Class 2-A Shitara-san

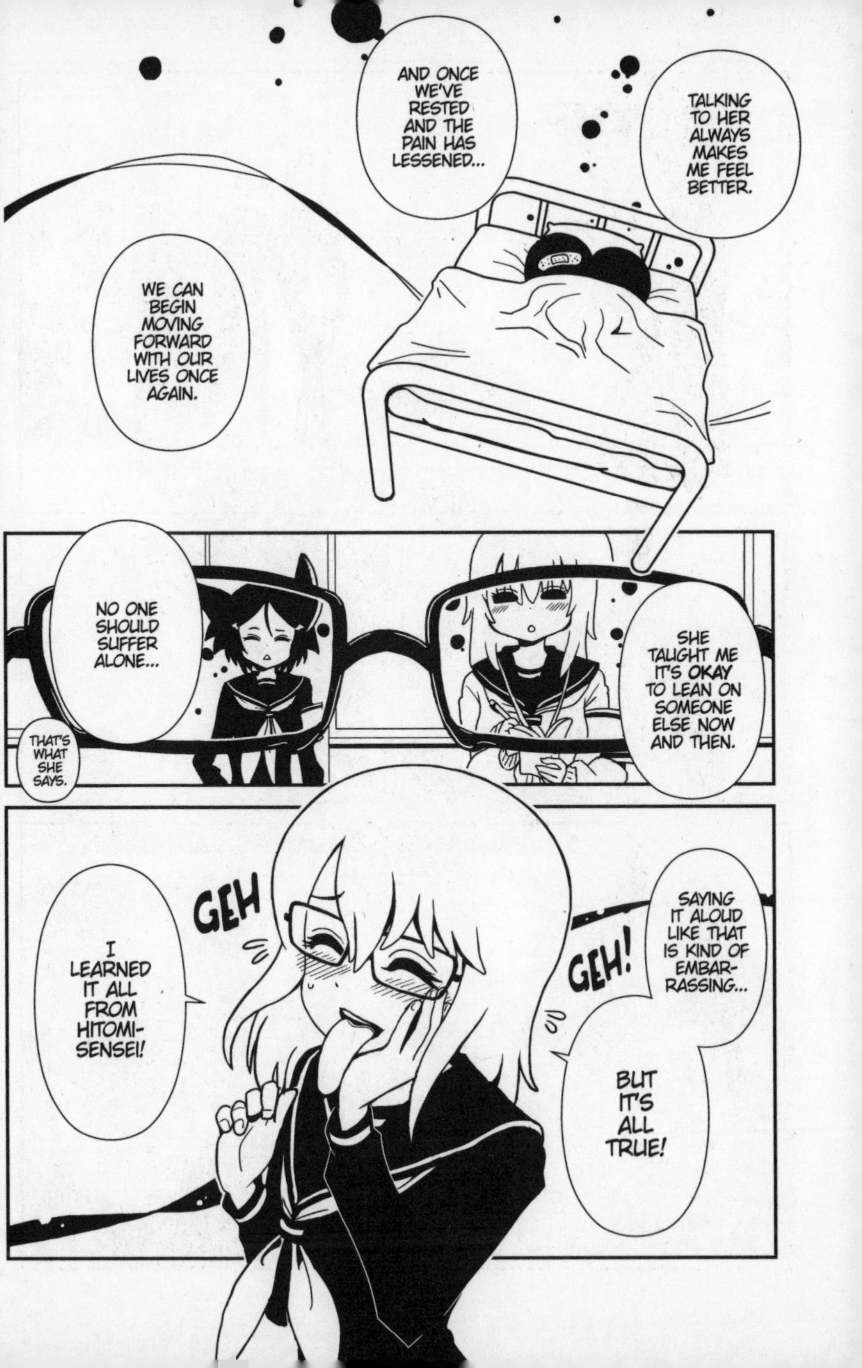
TALKING TO HER ALWAYS MAKES ME FEEL BETTER.
AND ONCE WE'VE RESTED AND THE PAIN HAS LESSENED...
WE CAN BEGIN MOVING FORWARD WITH OUR LIVES ONCE AGAIN.
SHE TAUGHT ME IT'S OKAY TO LEAN ON SOMEONE ELSE NOW AND THEN.
NO ONE SHOULD SUFFER ALONE...
THAT'S WHAT SHE SAYS.
SAYING IT ALOUD LIKE THAT IS KIND OF EMBARRASSING...
GEH!
GEH
BUT IT'S ALL TRUE!
I LEARNED IT ALL FROM HITOMI-SENSEI!

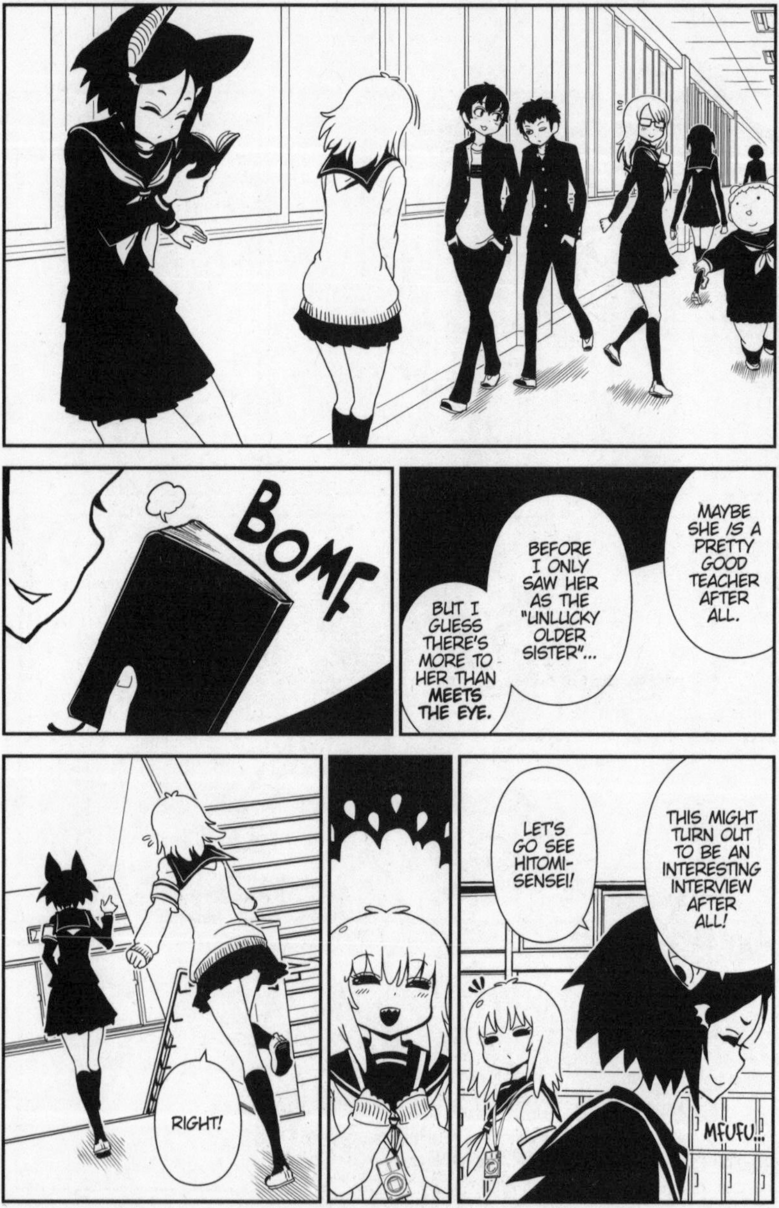
MAYBE SHE IS A PRETTY GOOD TEACHER AFTER ALL.
BEFORE I ONLY SAW HER AS THE "UNLUCKY OLDER SISTER"...
BUT I GUESS THERE'S MORE TO HER THAN MEETS THE EYE.
BOMF
THIS MIGHT TURN OUT TO BE AN INTERESTING INTERVIEW AFTER ALL!
LET'S GO SEE HITOMI-SENSEI!
MFUFU...
RIGHT!

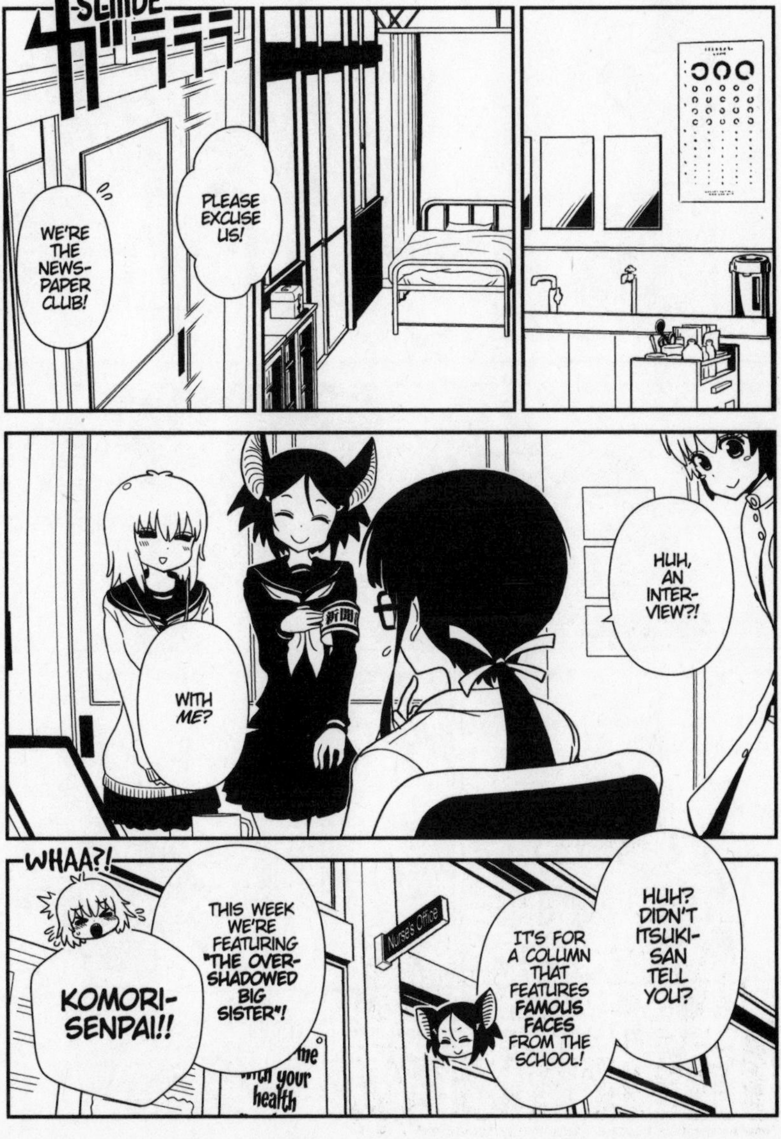
SLIIIDE ガラララ
PLEASE EXCUSE US!
WE'RE THE NEWSPAPER CLUB!
HUH, AN INTERVIEW?!
WITH ME?
HUH? DIDN'T ITSUKI-SAN TELL YOU?
IT'S FOR A COLUMN THAT FEATURES FAMOUS FACES FROM THE SCHOOL!
Nurse's Office
THIS WEEK WE'RE FEATURING "THE OVER-SHADOWED BIG SISTER"!
KOMORI-SENPAI!!
WHAA?!
with your health

NURSE HITOMI'S Monster Infirmary

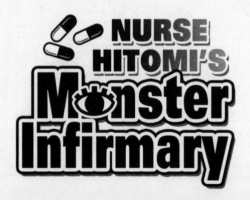

Student Health Record

May 201X

Class 2-D

Komori Kiki

Bat-Eared Girl

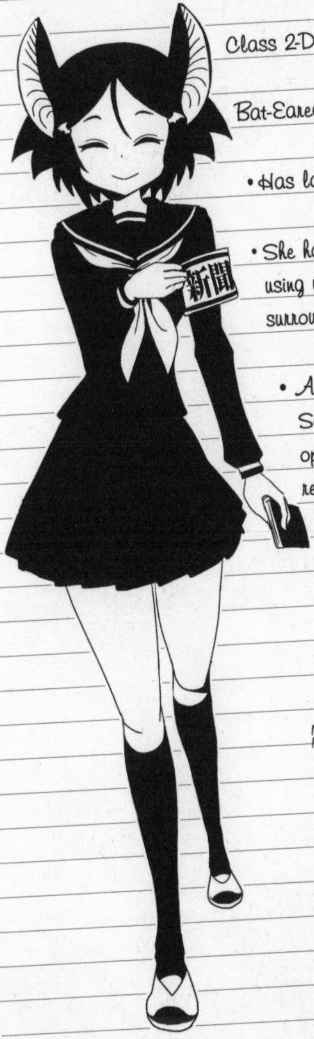

新聞

- Has large ears like a bat.
- She has the ability of echolocation: using ultrasonic waves she can assess her surroundings, even in pitch darkness.
- A member of the Newspaper Club. School paper aside, her ears are always open for gossip and she enjoys seeing the reaction to her articles.

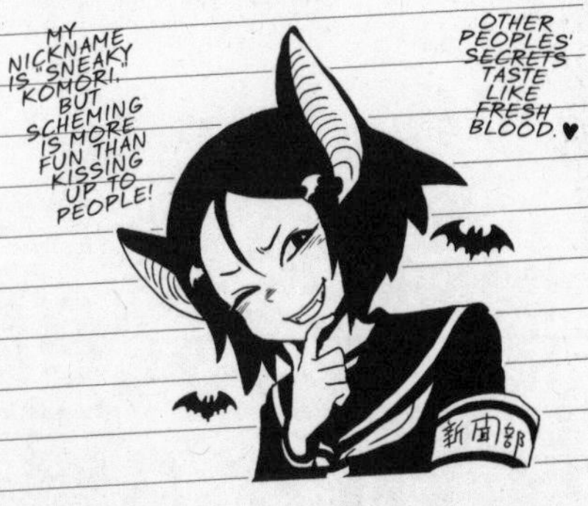

OTHER PEOPLES' SECRETS TASTE LIKE FRESH BLOOD.♥
MY NICKNAME IS "SNEAKY KOMORI." BUT SCHEMING IS MORE FUN THAN KISSING UP TO PEOPLE!
新聞部

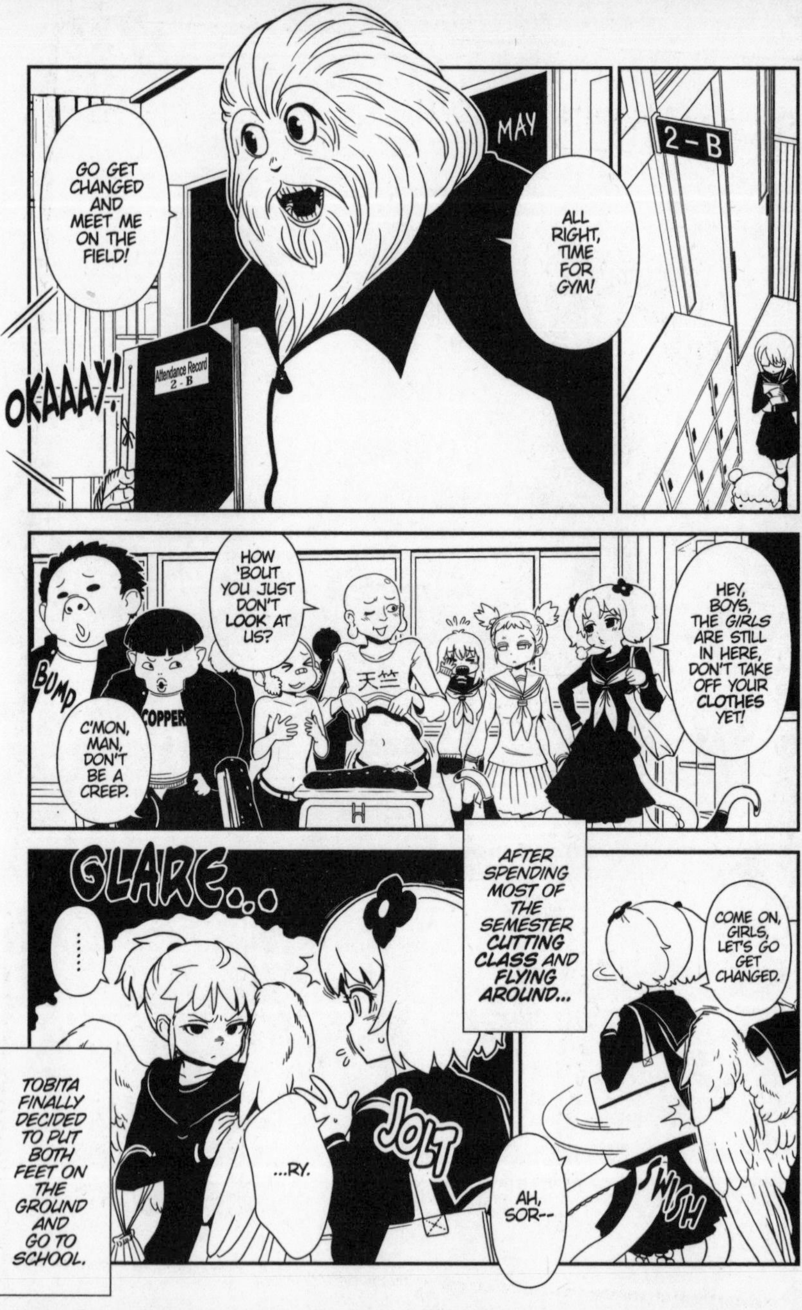
2 - B
MAY
ALL RIGHT, TIME FOR GYM!
GO GET CHANGED AND MEET ME ON THE FIELD!
OKAAAY!
Attendance Record 2 - B
HEY, BOYS, THE GIRLS ARE STILL IN HERE, DON'T TAKE OFF YOUR CLOTHES YET!
HOW 'BOUT YOU JUST DON'T LOOK AT US?
天竺
BUMP
COPPERS
C'MON, MAN, DON'T BE A CREEP.
COME ON, GIRLS, LET'S GO GET CHANGED.
SWISH
AH, SOR--
AFTER SPENDING MOST OF THE SEMESTER CUTTING CLASS AND FLYING AROUND...
GLARE...
......
JOLT
...RY.
TOBITA FINALLY DECIDED TO PUT BOTH FEET ON THE GROUND AND GO TO SCHOOL.

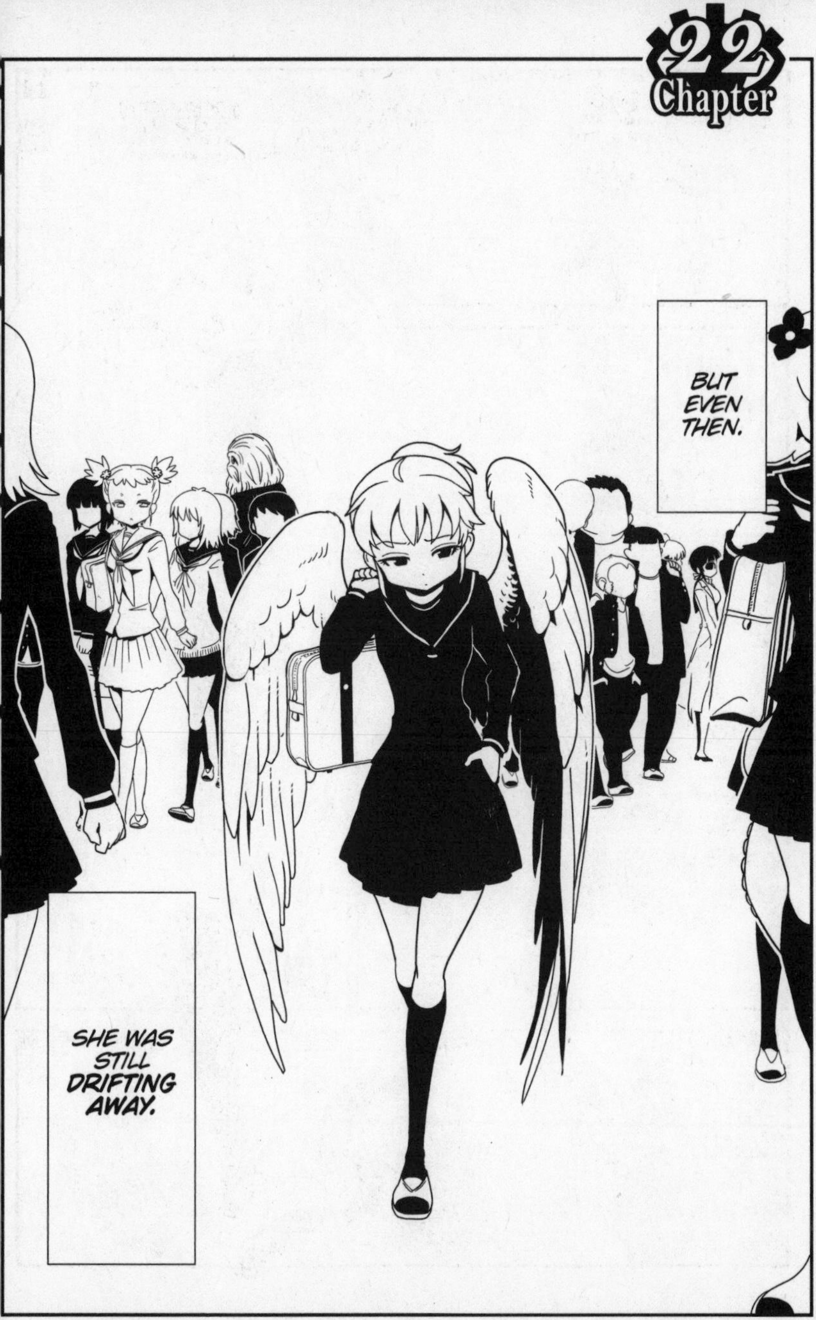
22
Chapter
BUT EVEN THEN.
SHE WAS STILL DRIFTING AWAY.

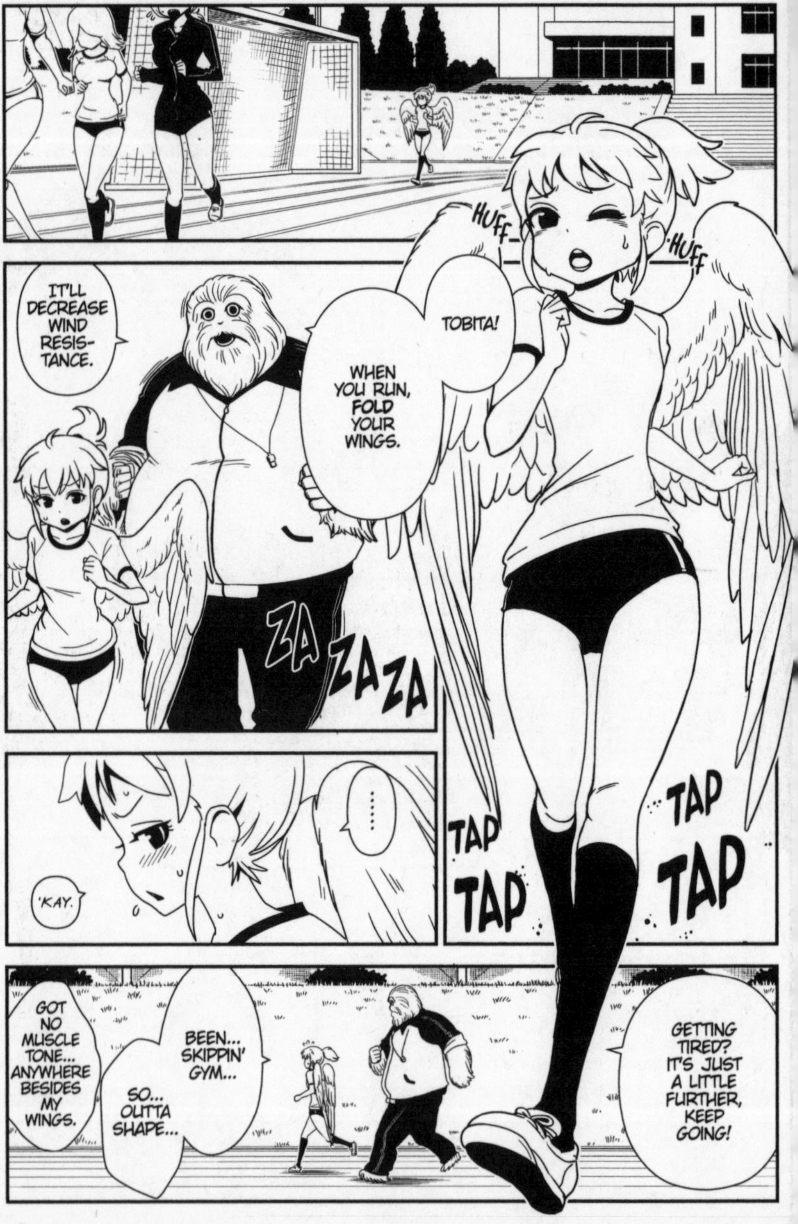
HUFF HUFF
TAP TAP TAP TAP
TOBITA!
WHEN YOU RUN, FOLD YOUR WINGS.
IT'LL DECREASE WIND RESIS-TANCE.
ZA ZA ZA
......
'KAY.
GETTING TIRED? IT'S JUST A LITTLE FURTHER, KEEP GOING!
BEEN... SKIPPIN' GYM...
SO... OUTTA SHAPE...
GOT NO MUSCLE TONE... ANYWHERE BESIDES MY WINGS.

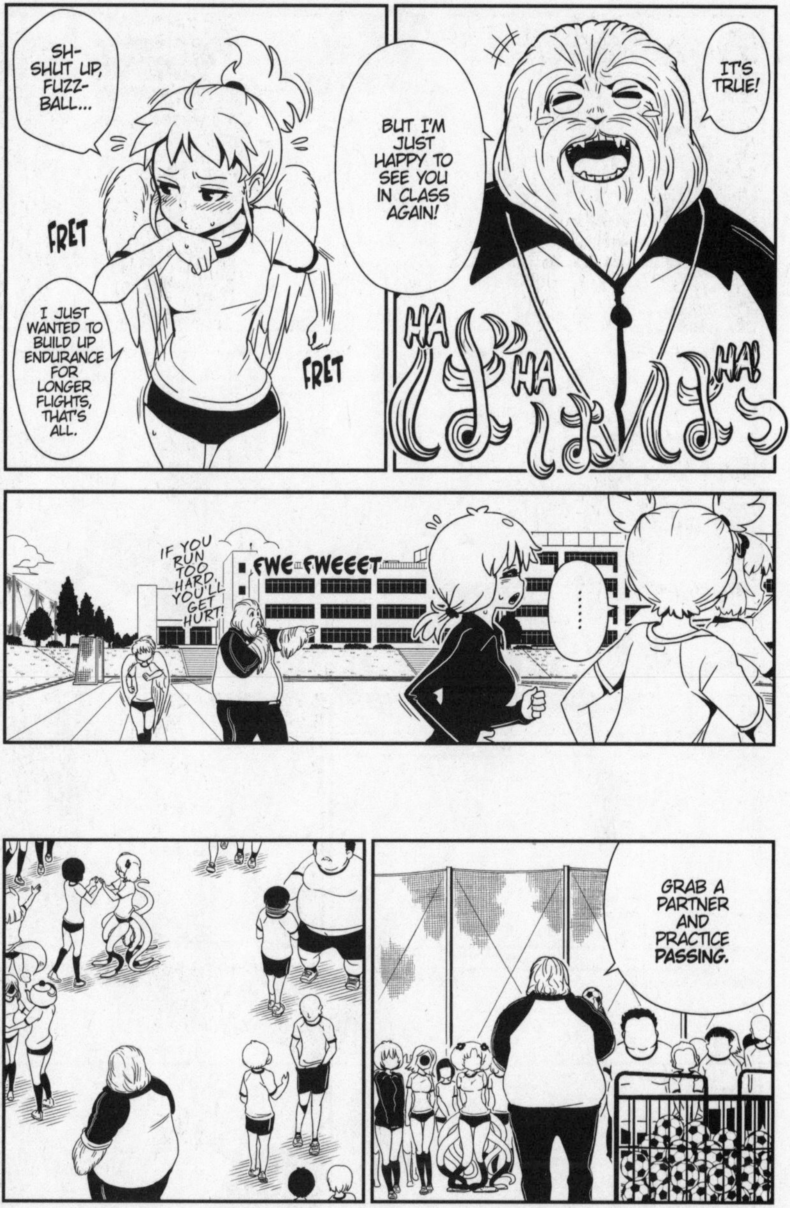
IT'S TRUE!
BUT I'M JUST HAPPY TO SEE YOU IN CLASS AGAIN!
HA HA HA HA!
SH- SHUT UP, FUZZ-BALL...
FRET
I JUST WANTED TO BUILD UP ENDURANCE FOR LONGER FLIGHTS, THAT'S ALL.
FRET
......
FWE FWEEET
IF YOU RUN TOO HARD, YOU'LL GET HURT!
GRAB A PARTNER AND PRACTICE PASSING.

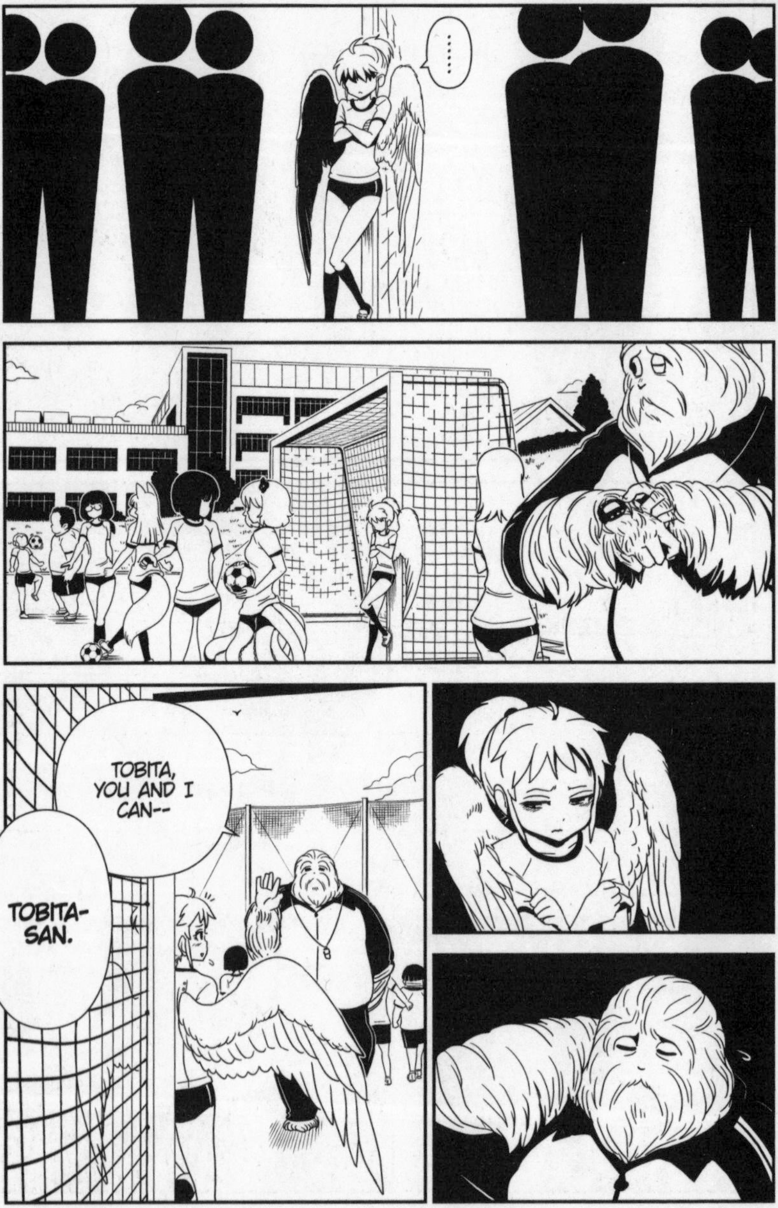
……
TOBITA, YOU AND I CAN--
TOBITA-SAN.

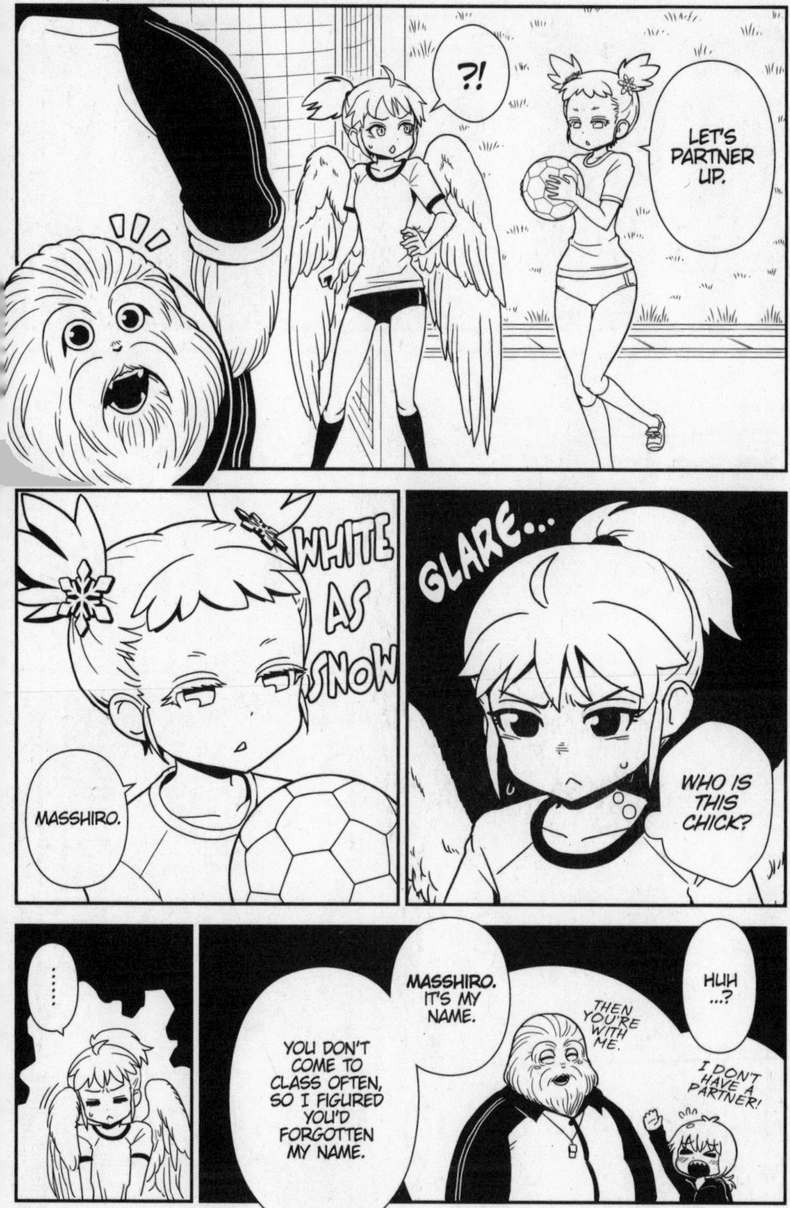
LET'S PARTNER UP.
?!
GLARE...
WHO IS THIS CHICK?
WHITE AS SNOW
MASSHIRO.
HUH ...?
I DON'T HAVE A PARTNER!
THEN YOU'RE WITH ME.
MASSHIRO. IT'S MY NAME.
YOU DON'T COME TO CLASS OFTEN, SO I FIGURED YOU'D FORGOTTEN MY NAME.
......

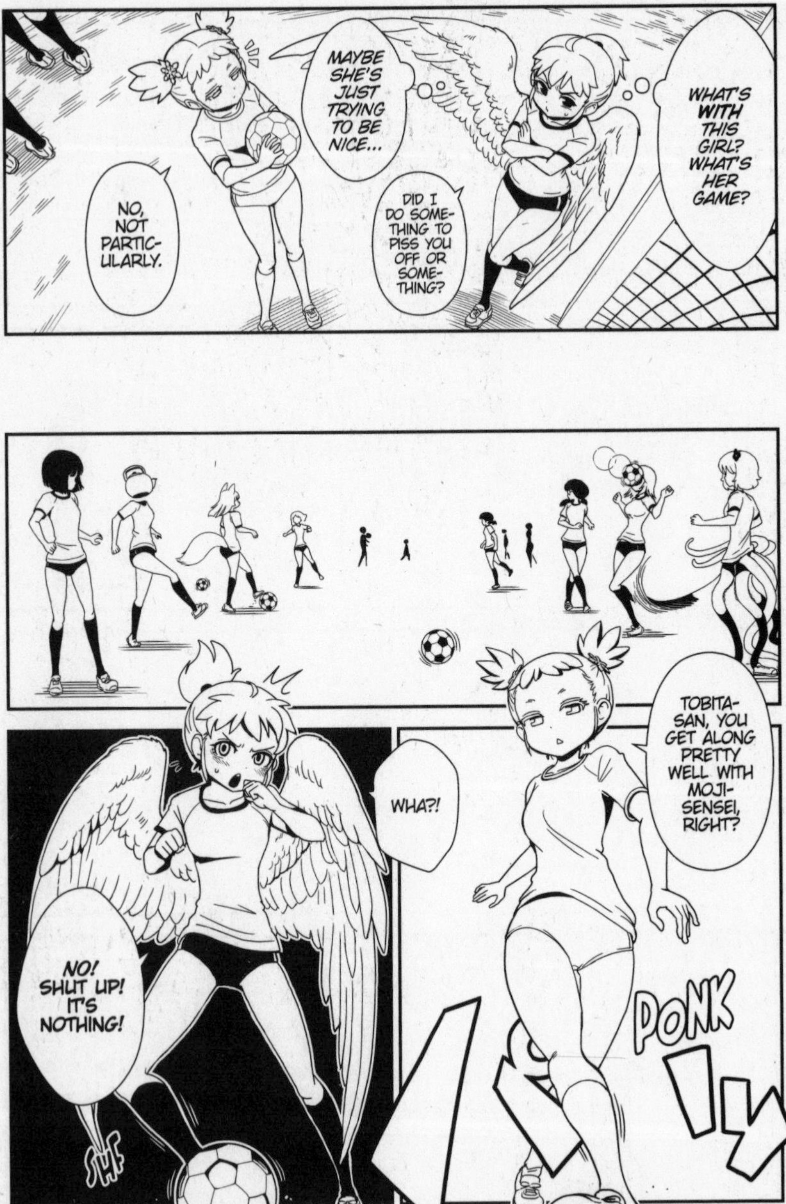
WHAT'S WITH THIS GIRL? WHAT'S HER GAME?
MAYBE SHE'S JUST TRYING TO BE NICE...
DID I DO SOME-THING TO PISS YOU OFF OR SOME-THING?
NO, NOT PARTIC-ULARLY.
TOBITA-SAN, YOU GET ALONG PRETTY WELL WITH MOJI-SENSEI, RIGHT?
WHA?!
PONK
NO! SHUT UP! IT'S NOTHING!
SHF

MOJI-SENSEI'S PRETTY COOL, ISN'T HE?
HUH?
WHAT DID YOU...?
SERIOUSLY, WHAT'S UP WITH HER?
NARL NARL
I LIKE MOJI-SENSEI.

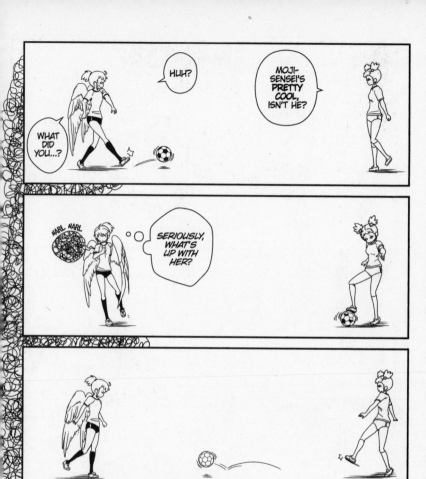

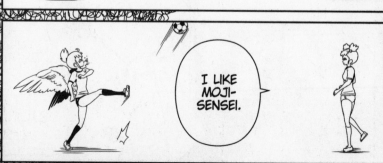

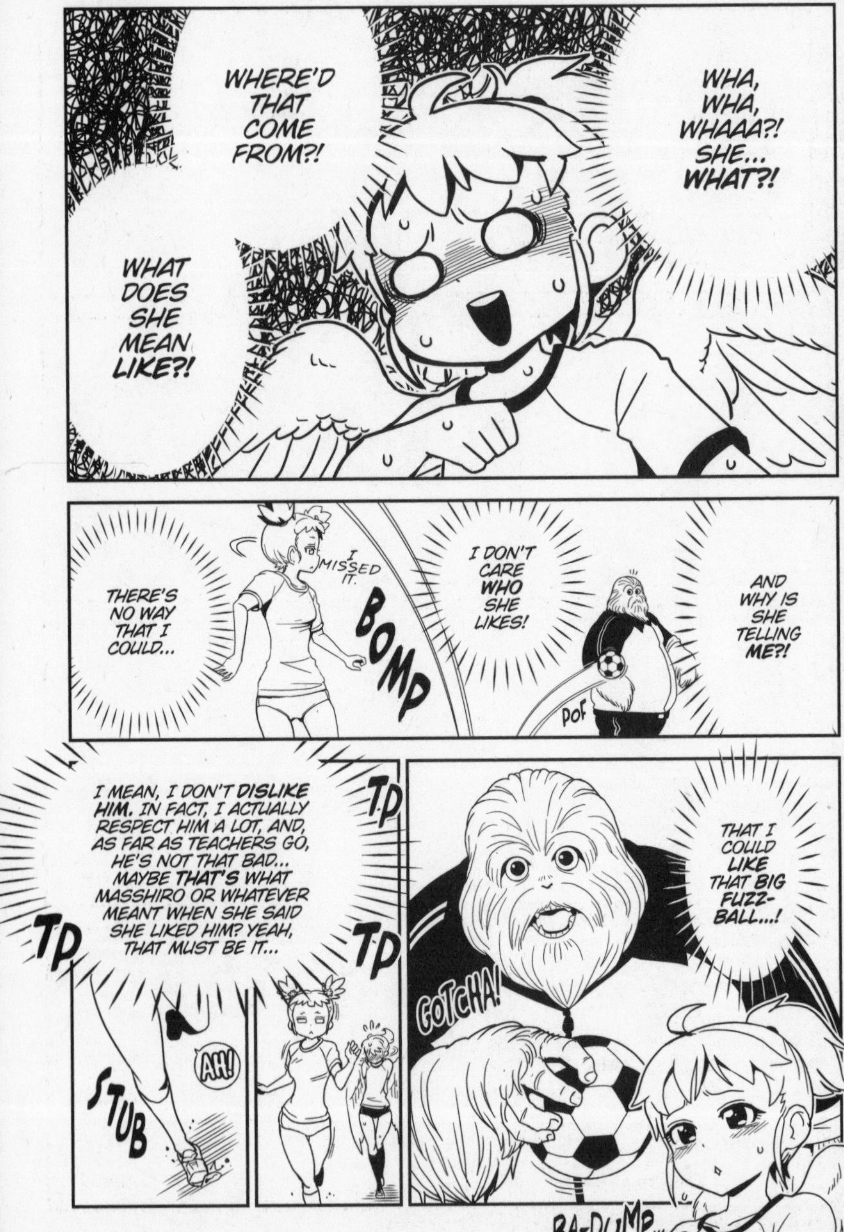
WHA, WHA, WHAAA?! SHE... WHAT?!
WHERE'D THAT COME FROM?!
WHAT DOES SHE MEAN LIKE?!
AND WHY IS SHE TELLING ME?!
I DON'T CARE WHO SHE LIKES!
I MISSED IT.
BOMP
POF
THERE'S NO WAY THAT I COULD...
THAT I COULD LIKE THAT BIG FUZZ-BALL...!
GOTCHA!
BA-DUMP...
I MEAN, I DON'T DISLIKE HIM. IN FACT, I ACTUALLY RESPECT HIM A LOT, AND, AS FAR AS TEACHERS GO, HE'S NOT THAT BAD... MAYBE THAT'S WHAT MASSHIRO OR WHATEVER MEANT WHEN SHE SAID SHE LIKED HIM? YEAH, THAT MUST BE IT...
TP
TP
TP
AH!
STUB

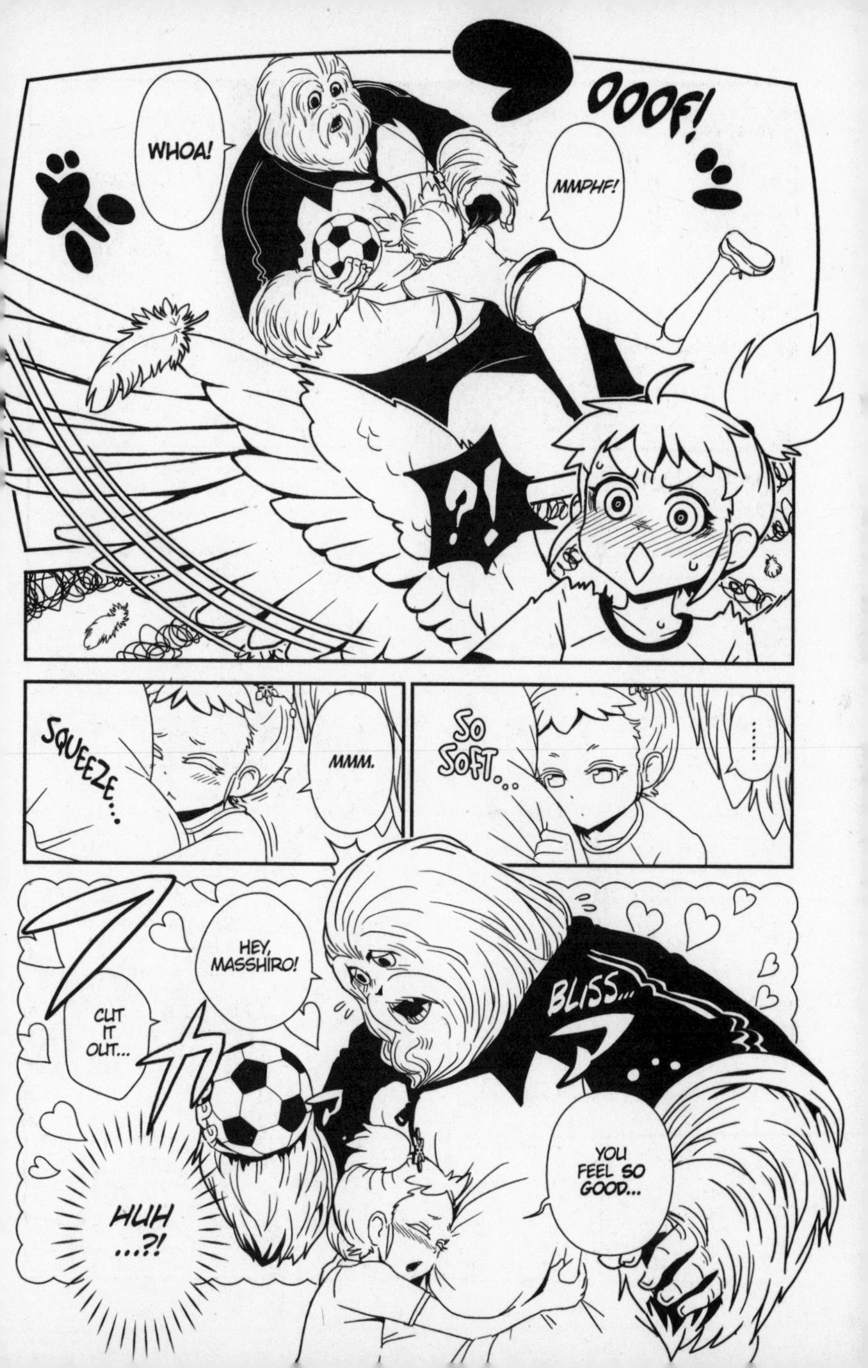
OOOF!
MMPHF!
WHOA!
?!
......
SO SOFT...
MMM.
SQUEEZE...
BLISS...
HEY, MASSHIRO!
CUT IT OUT...
YOU FEEL SO GOOD...
HUH ...?!

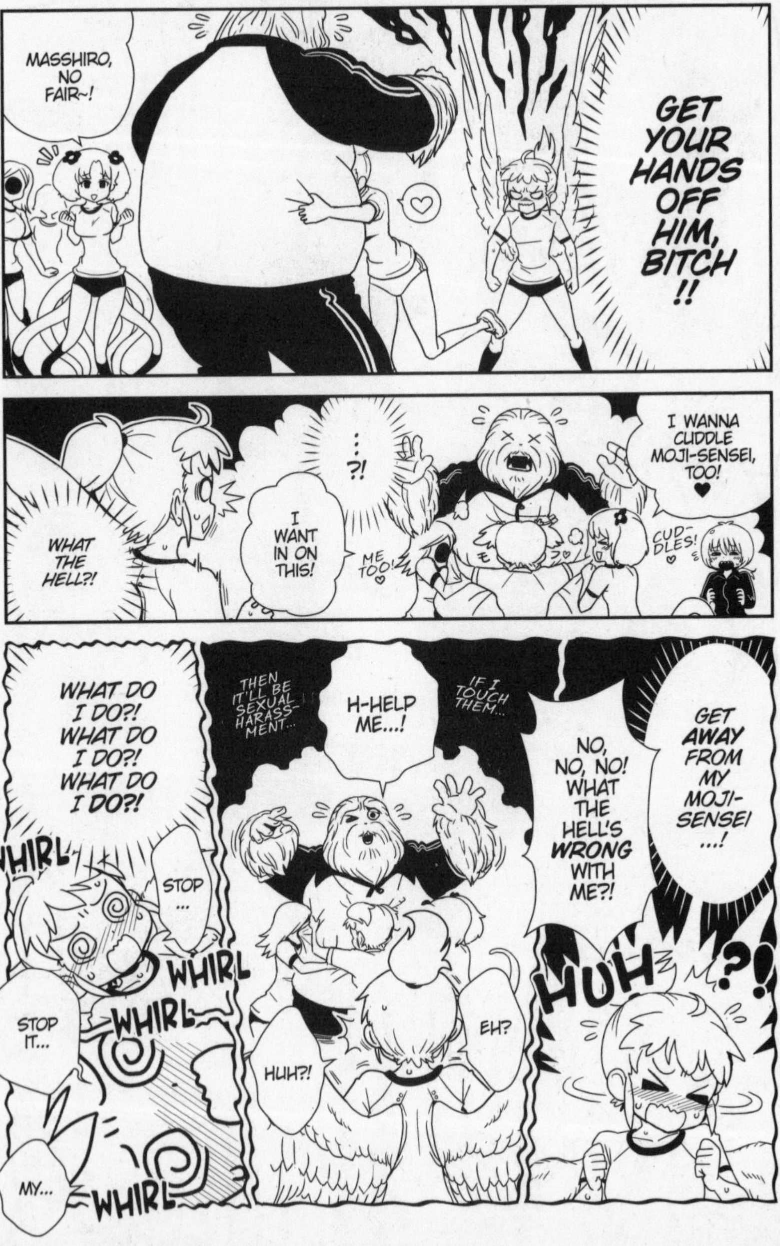
GET YOUR HANDS OFF HIM, BITCH!!
MASSHIRO, NO FAIR~!
I WANNA CUDDLE MOJI-SENSEI, TOO! ♥
CUDDLES! ♥
...?!
ME TOO! ♥
I WANT IN ON THIS!
WHAT THE HELL?!
GET AWAY FROM MY MOJI-SENSEI...!
NO, NO, NO! WHAT THE HELL'S WRONG WITH ME?!
HUH?!
IF I TOUCH THEM...
H-HELP ME...!
THEN IT'LL BE SEXUAL HARASSMENT...
EH?
HUH?!
WHAT DO I DO?! WHAT DO I DO?! WHAT DO I DO?!
WHIRL
STOP...
WHIRL
WHIRL
STOP IT...
MY...
WHIRL

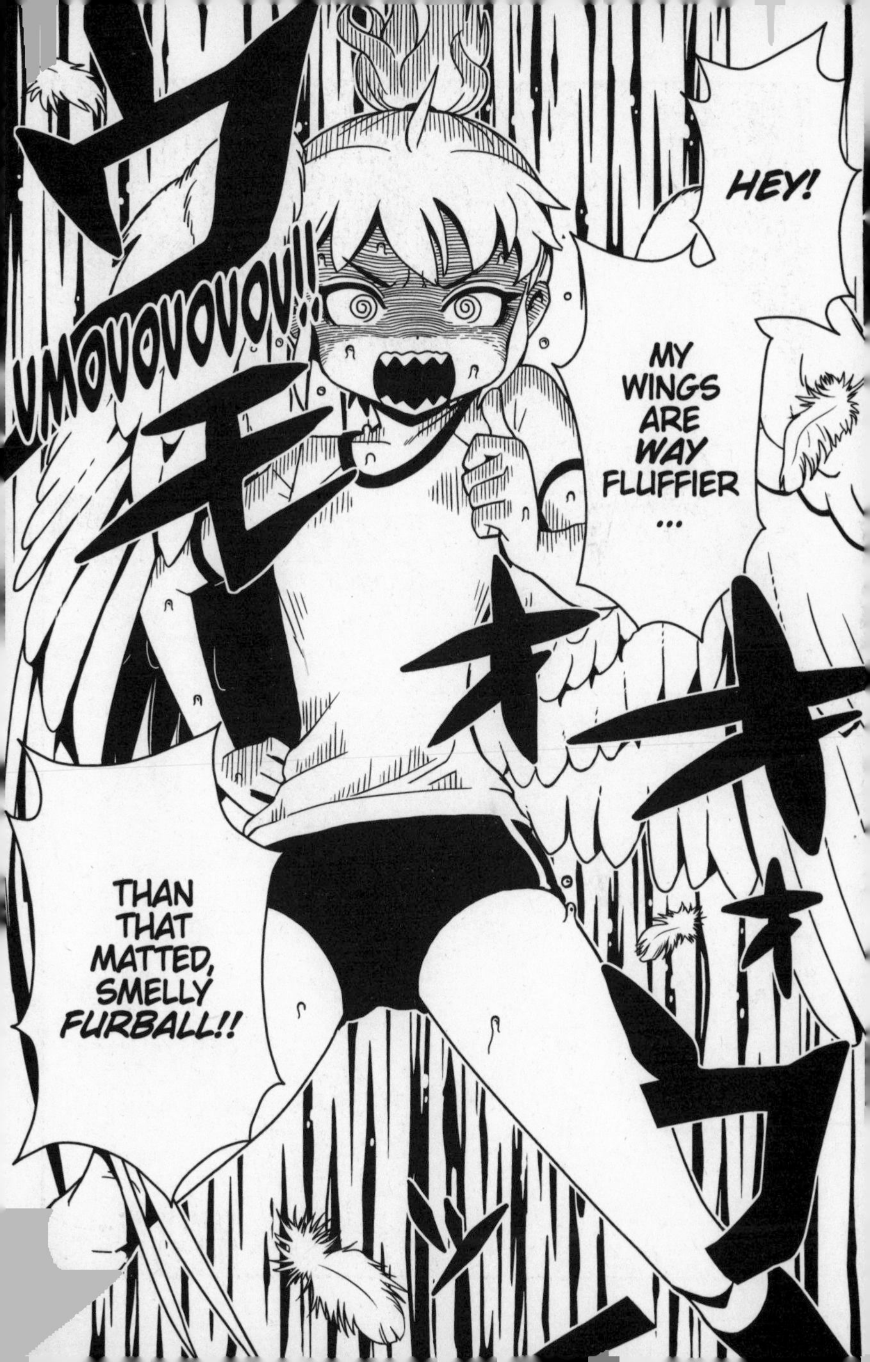
HEY!
MY WINGS ARE WAY FLUFFIER ...
UMOVOVOVOU!!
THAN THAT MATTED, SMELLY FURBALL!!

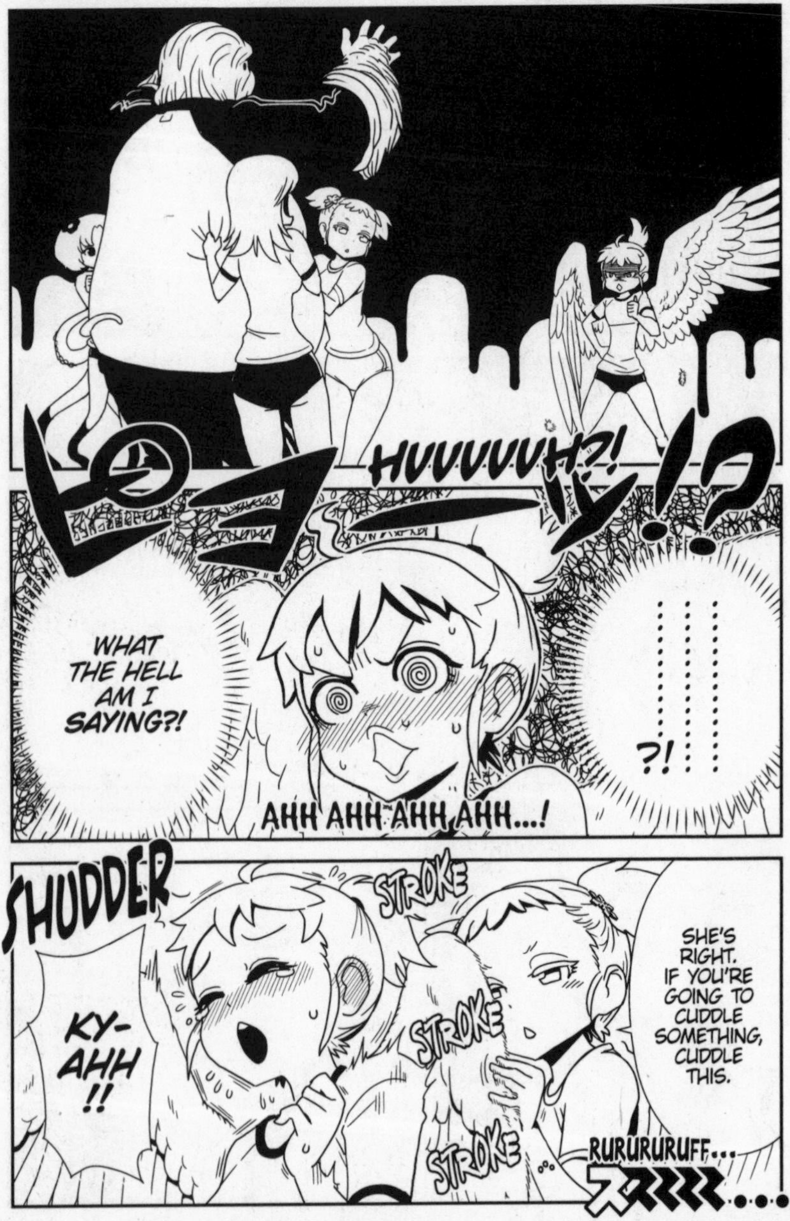
HUVVVVVH?!
WHAT THE HELL AM I SAYING?!
......
?!
AHH AHH AHH AHH...!
SHE'S RIGHT. IF YOU'RE GOING TO CUDDLE SOMETHING, CUDDLE THIS.
STROKE
STROKE
STROKE
RURURURUFF....
SHUDDER
KY-AHH!!

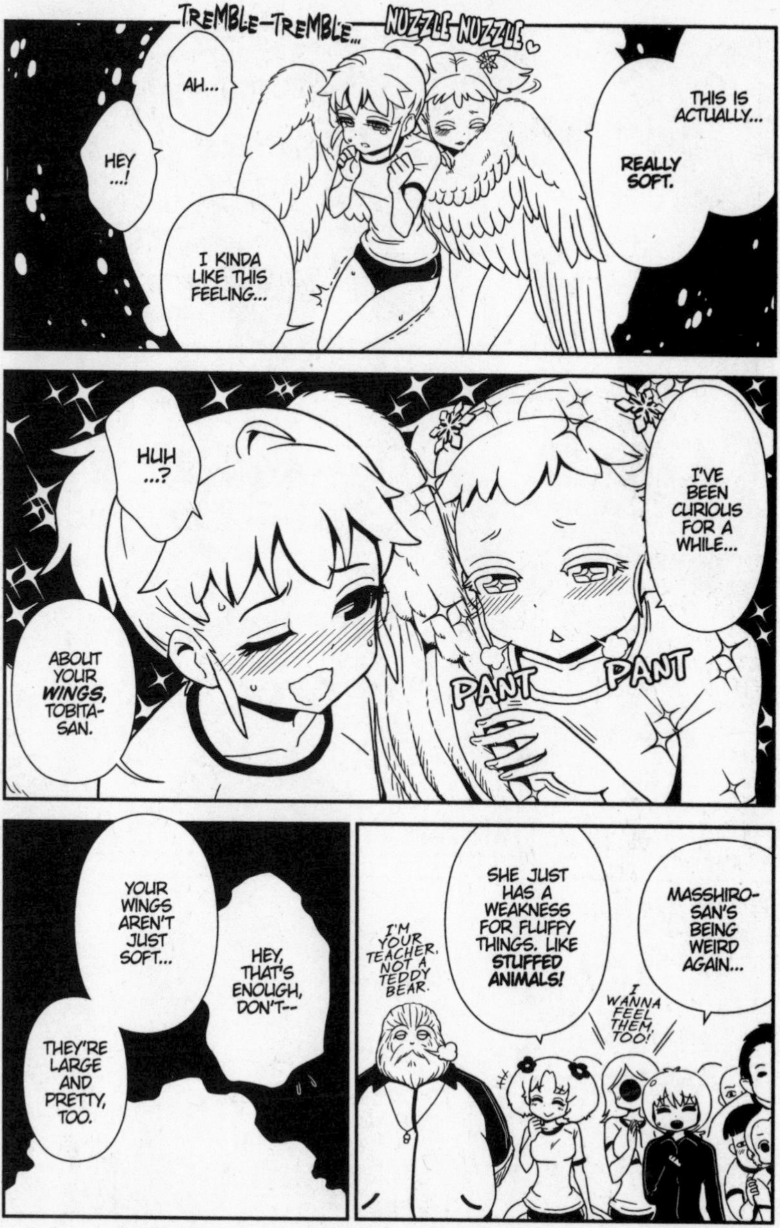
NUZZLE NUZZLE
THIS IS ACTUALLY...
REALLY SOFT.
TREMBLE-TREMBLE...
AH...
HEY ...!
I KINDA LIKE THIS FEELING...
I'VE BEEN CURIOUS FOR A WHILE...
PANT PANT
HUH ...?
ABOUT YOUR WINGS, TOBITA-SAN.
MASSHIRO-SAN'S BEING WEIRD AGAIN...
I WANNA FEEL THEM, TOO!
SHE JUST HAS A WEAKNESS FOR FLUFFY THINGS. LIKE STUFFED ANIMALS!
I'M YOUR TEACHER, NOT A TEDDY BEAR.
YOUR WINGS AREN'T JUST SOFT...
HEY, THAT'S ENOUGH, DON'T--
THEY'RE LARGE AND PRETTY, TOO.

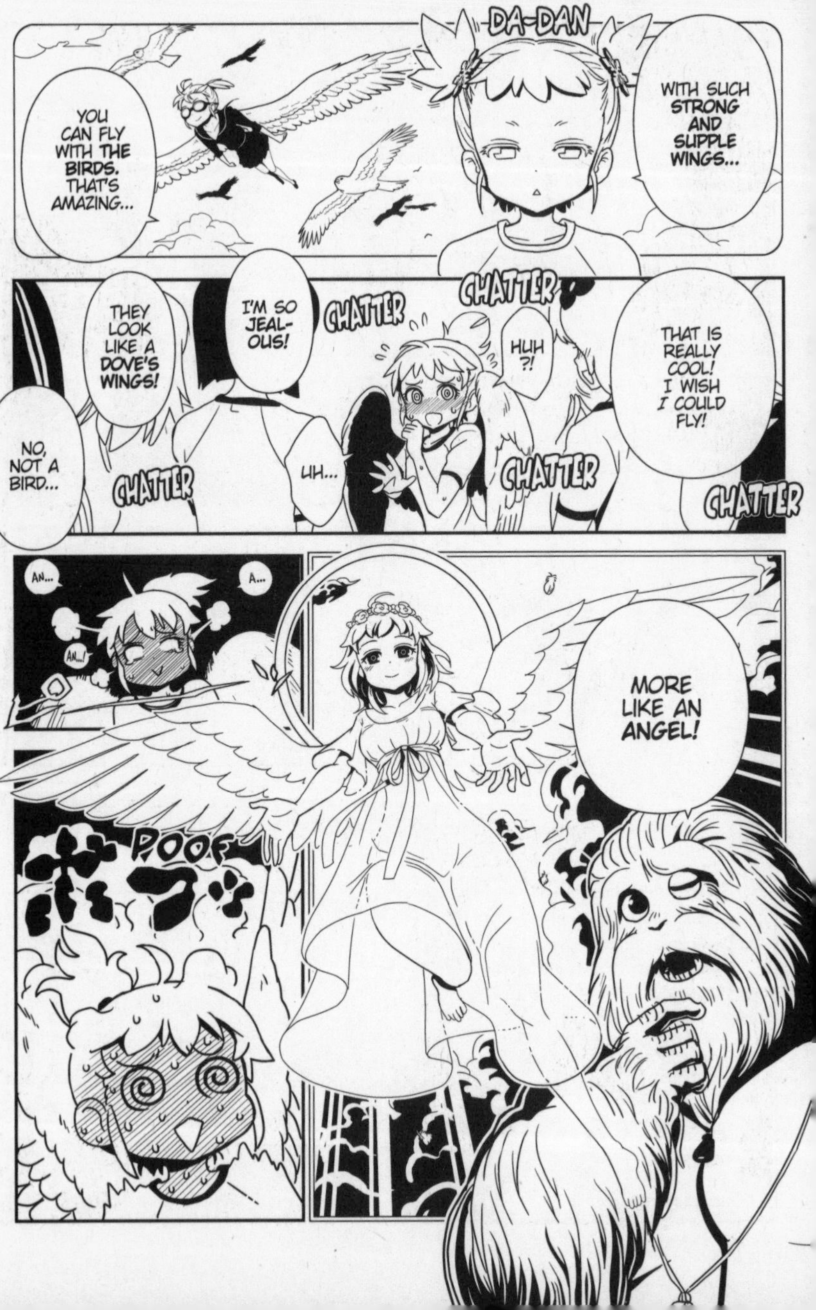
DA-DAN
WITH SUCH STRONG AND SUPPLE WINGS...
YOU CAN FLY WITH THE BIRDS. THAT'S AMAZING...
THAT IS REALLY COOL! I WISH I COULD FLY!
CHATTER
CHATTER
HUH ?!
I'M SO JEAL-OUS!
CHATTER
THEY LOOK LIKE A DOVE'S WINGS!
CHATTER
UH...
NO, NOT A BIRD...
CHATTER
MORE LIKE AN ANGEL!
A...
AN...
AN...!
POOF

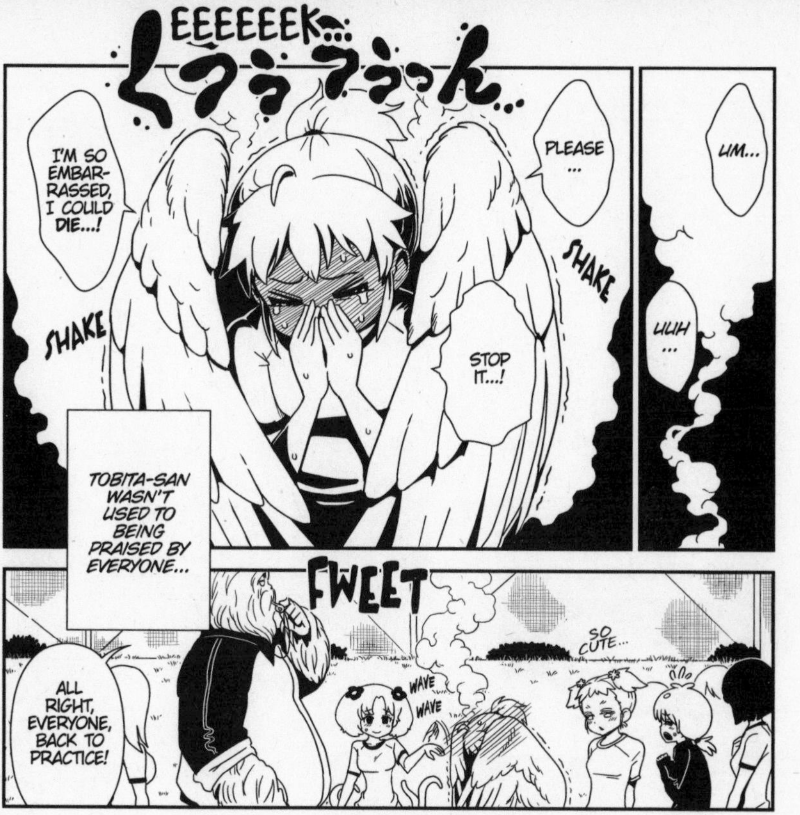
UM...
UUH ...
EEEEEEK...
PLEASE ...
SHAKE
I'M SO EMBARRASSED, I COULD DIE...!
STOP IT...!
SHAKE
TOBITA-SAN WASN'T USED TO BEING PRAISED BY EVERYONE...
FWEET
SO CUTE...
WAVE WAVE
ALL RIGHT, EVERYONE, BACK TO PRACTICE!

-THE NEXT DAY-

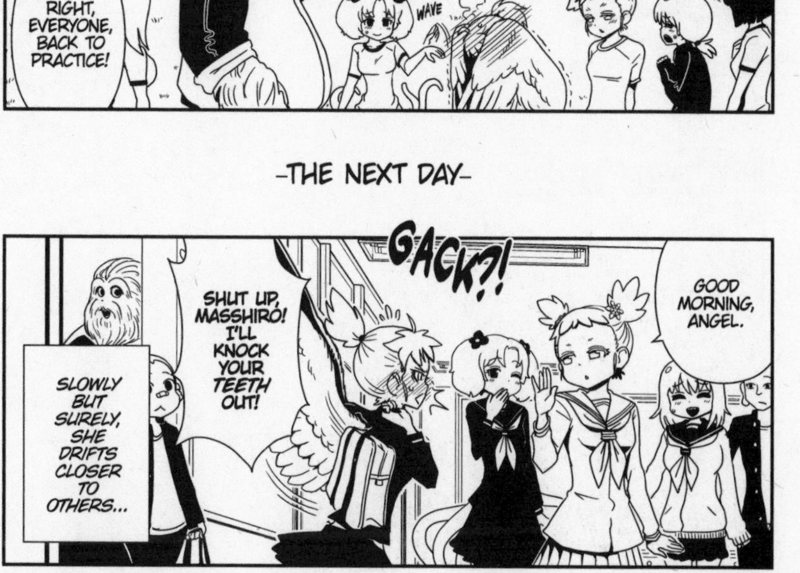
GOOD MORNING, ANGEL.
GACK?!
SHUT UP, MASSHIRO! I'LL KNOCK YOUR TEETH OUT!
SLOWLY BUT SURELY, SHE DRIFTS CLOSER TO OTHERS...

NURSE HITOMI'S Monster Infirmary

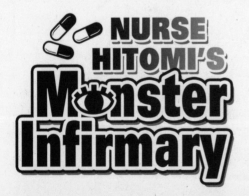

Student Health Record

May 201X

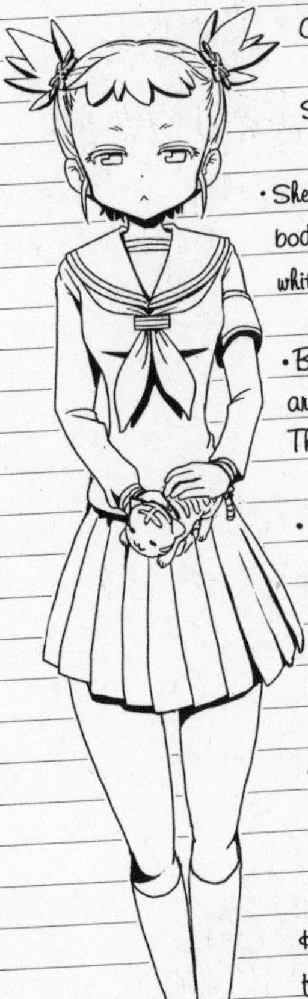

Class 2-B

Masshiro Nayuki

Snow White Girl

- She has a physical condition that makes her body white as snow. Anything she touches turns white as well.

- Because her body temperature and energy level are both low, she often seems aloof or indifferent. This is actually far from the case.

- She has a fondness for stuffed toys, children, animals, or anything soft or cute. When she sets her sights on something, she'll push herself in pursuit of it, no matter how tired she feels.

- She's the secretary of the student council executive committee. She writes all the reports.

Her recent favorite toy is Mii-chan.

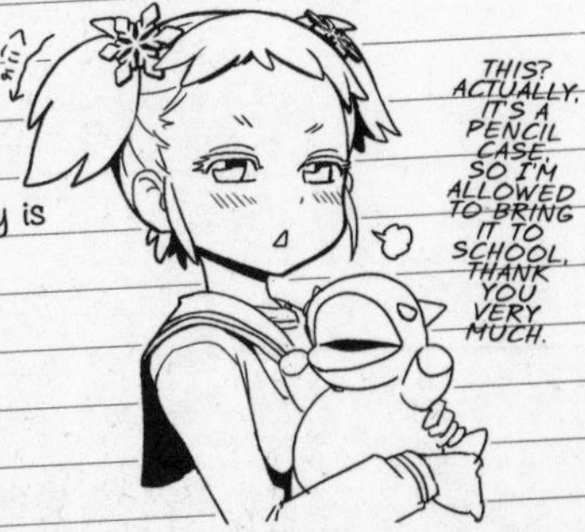
THIS? ACTUALLY, IT'S A PENCIL CASE, SO I'M ALLOWED TO BRING IT TO SCHOOL, THANK YOU VERY MUCH.

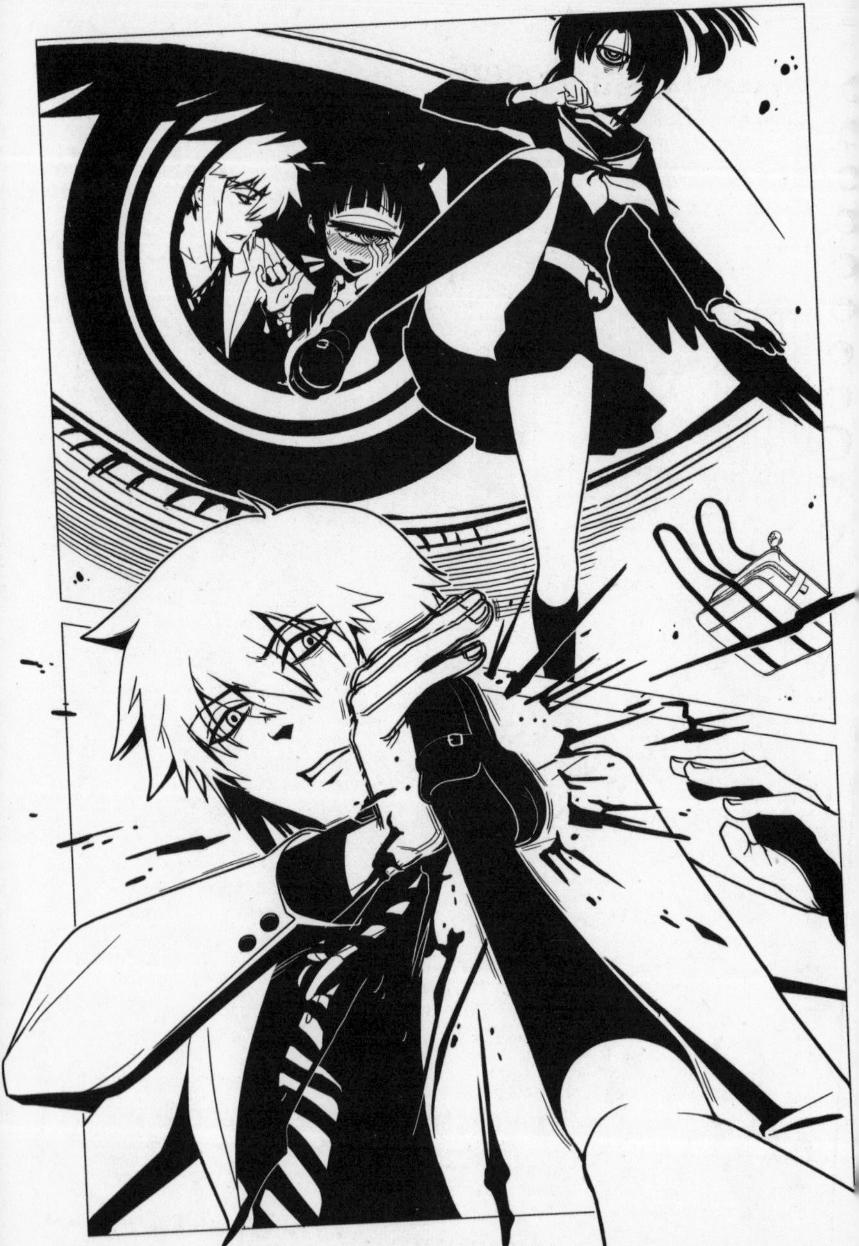

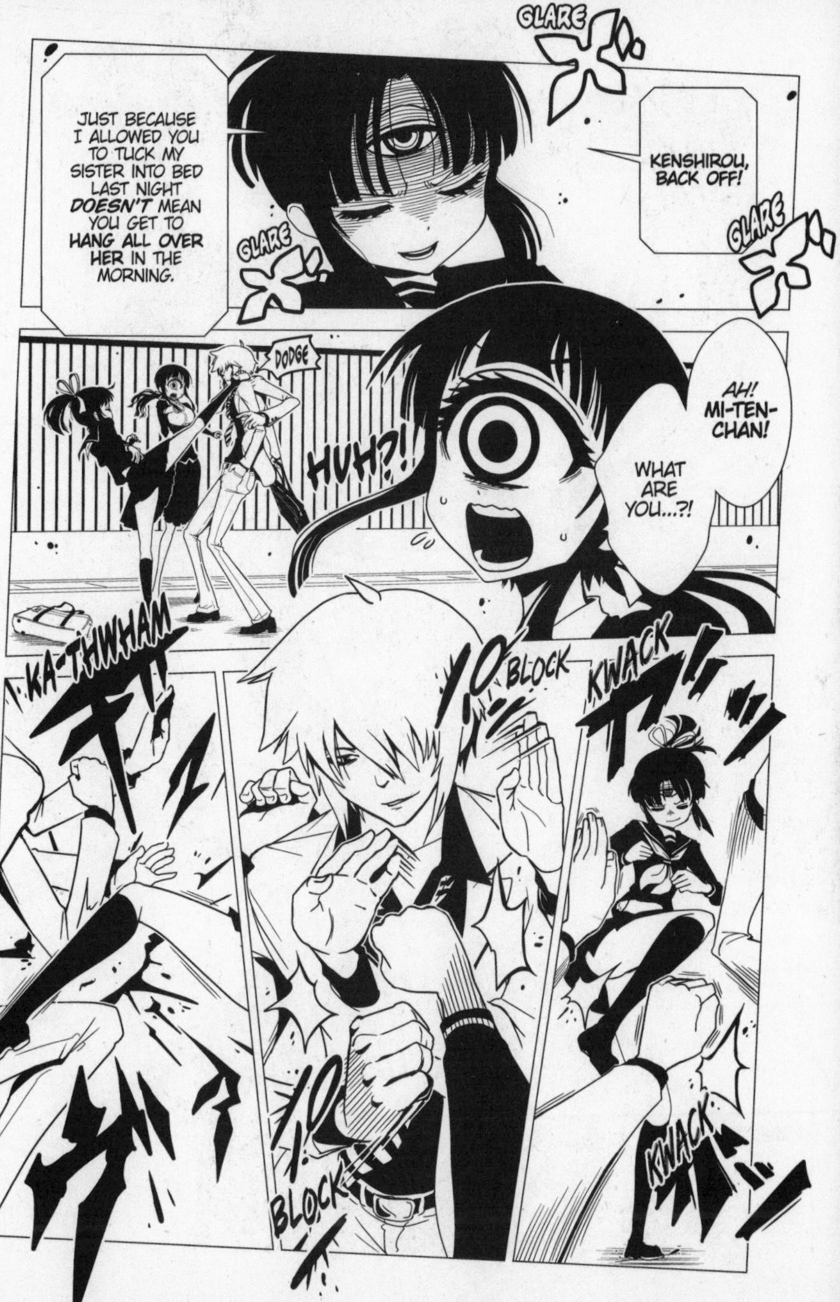
GLARE
KENSHIROU, BACK OFF!
GLARE
JUST BECAUSE I ALLOWED YOU TO TUCK MY SISTER INTO BED LAST NIGHT **DOESN'T** MEAN YOU GET TO **HANG ALL OVER** HER IN THE MORNING.
GLARE
AH! MI-TEN-CHAN!
WHAT ARE YOU...?!
HUH?!
DODGE
KWACK
KWACK
BLOCK
BLOCK
KA-THWHAM

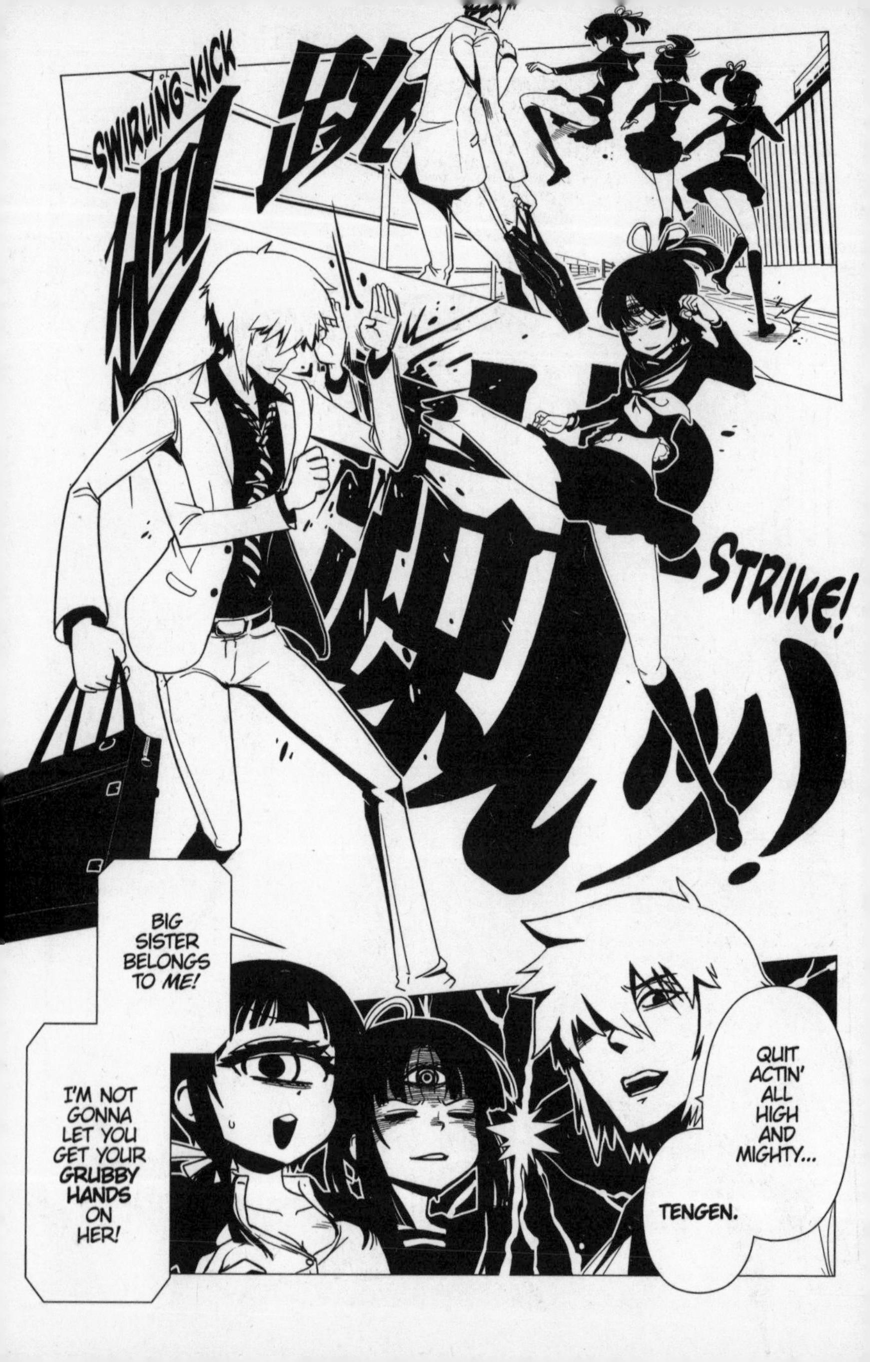
SWIRLING KICK
STRIKE!
QUIT ACTIN' ALL HIGH AND MIGHTY...
TENGEN.
BIG SISTER BELONGS TO ME!
I'M NOT GONNA LET YOU GET YOUR GRUBBY HANDS ON HER!

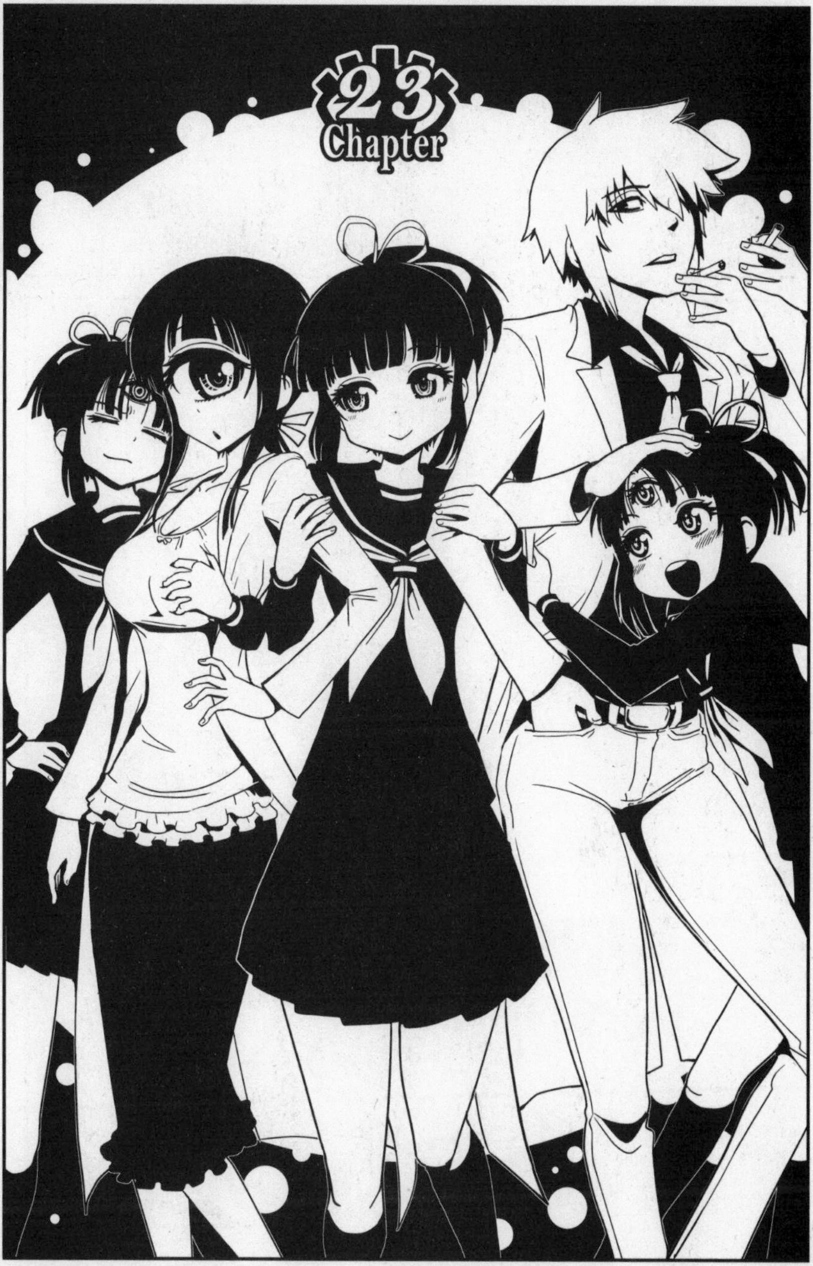
23
Chapter

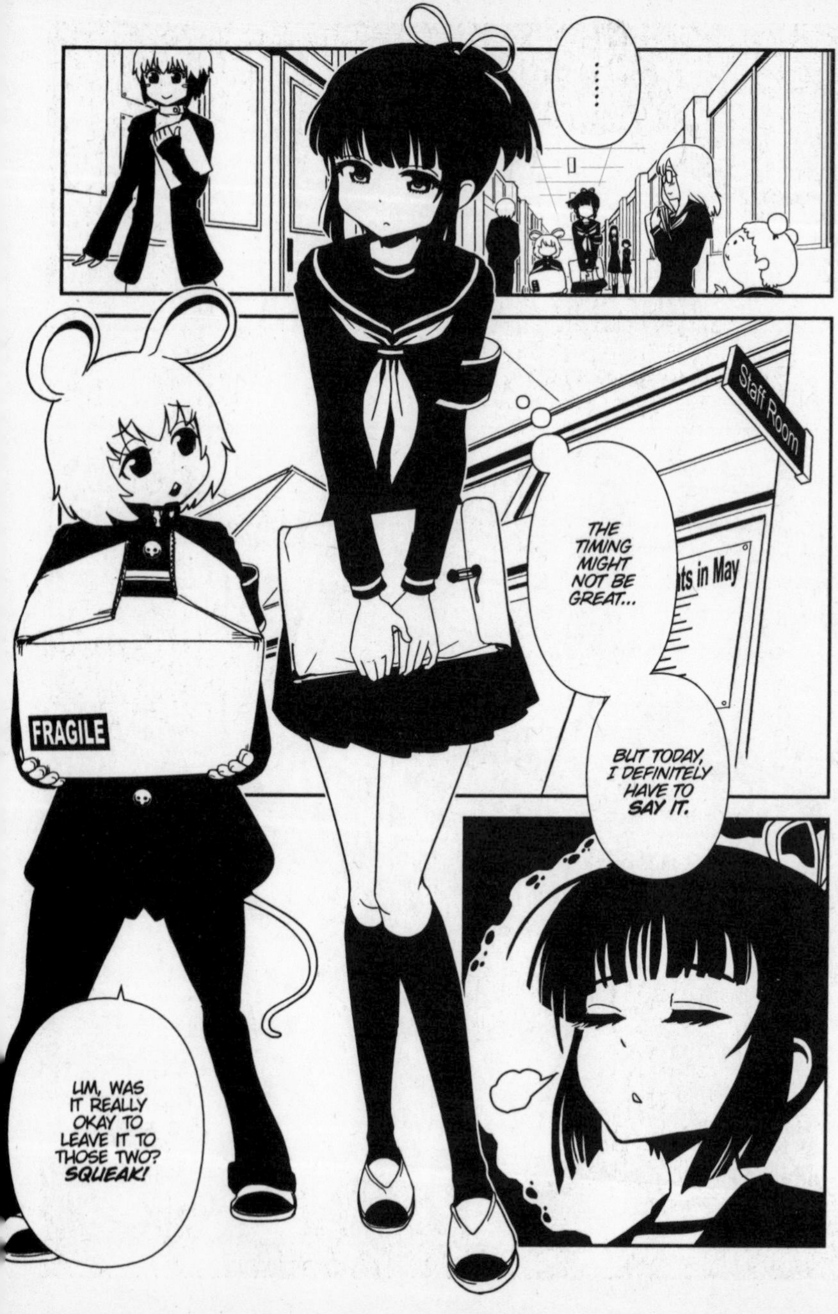
......
Staff Room
THE TIMING MIGHT NOT BE GREAT...
BUT TODAY, I DEFINITELY HAVE TO SAY IT.
FRAGILE
UM, WAS IT REALLY OKAY TO LEAVE IT TO THOSE TWO? SQUEAK!

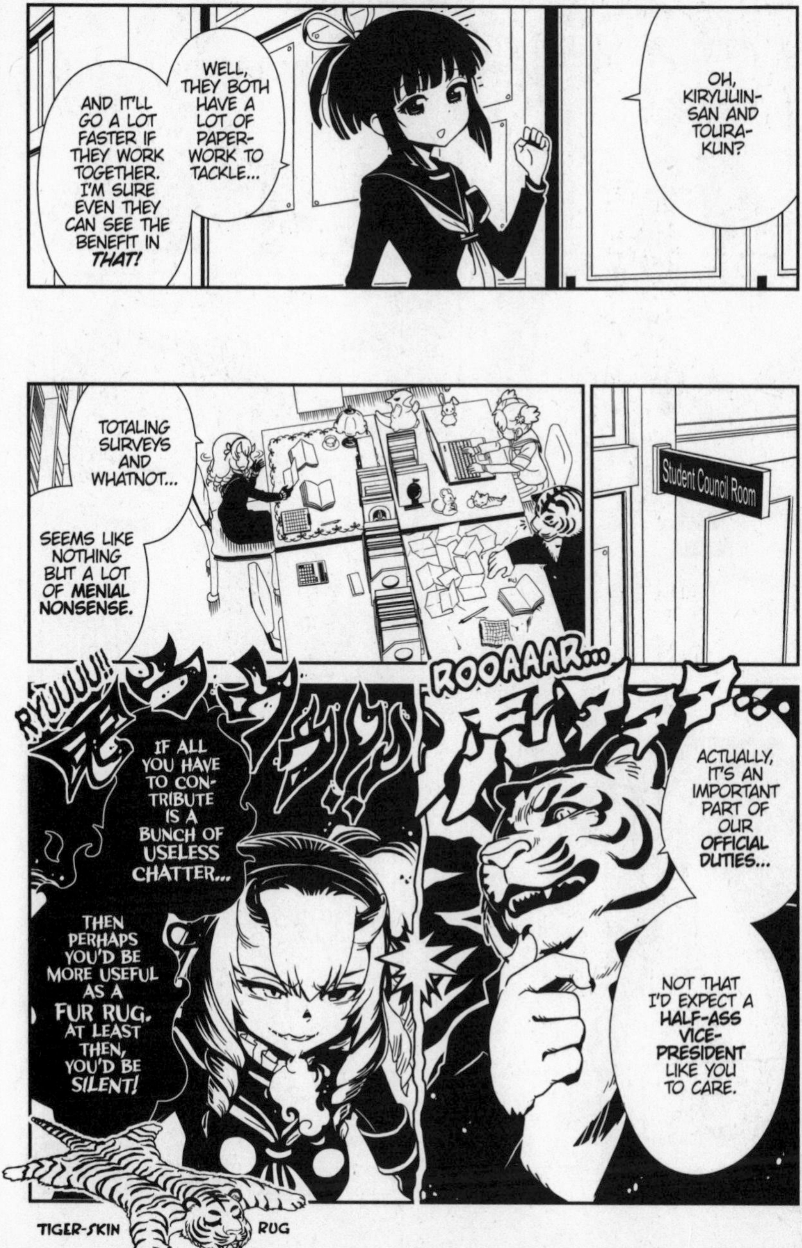
OH, KIRYUUIN-SAN AND TOURA-KUN?
WELL, THEY BOTH HAVE A LOT OF PAPER-WORK TO TACKLE...
AND IT'LL GO A LOT FASTER IF THEY WORK TOGETHER. I'M SURE EVEN THEY CAN SEE THE BENEFIT IN THAT!
Student Council Room
TOTALING SURVEYS AND WHATNOT...
SEEMS LIKE NOTHING BUT A LOT OF MENIAL NONSENSE.
ROOAAAR...
ACTUALLY, IT'S AN IMPORTANT PART OF OUR OFFICIAL DUTIES...
NOT THAT I'D EXPECT A HALF-ASS VICE-PRESIDENT LIKE YOU TO CARE.
RYUUUU!!
IF ALL YOU HAVE TO CON-TRIBUTE IS A BUNCH OF USELESS CHATTER...
THEN PERHAPS YOU'D BE MORE USEFUL AS A FUR RUG. AT LEAST THEN, YOU'D BE SILENT!
TIGER-SKIN RUG

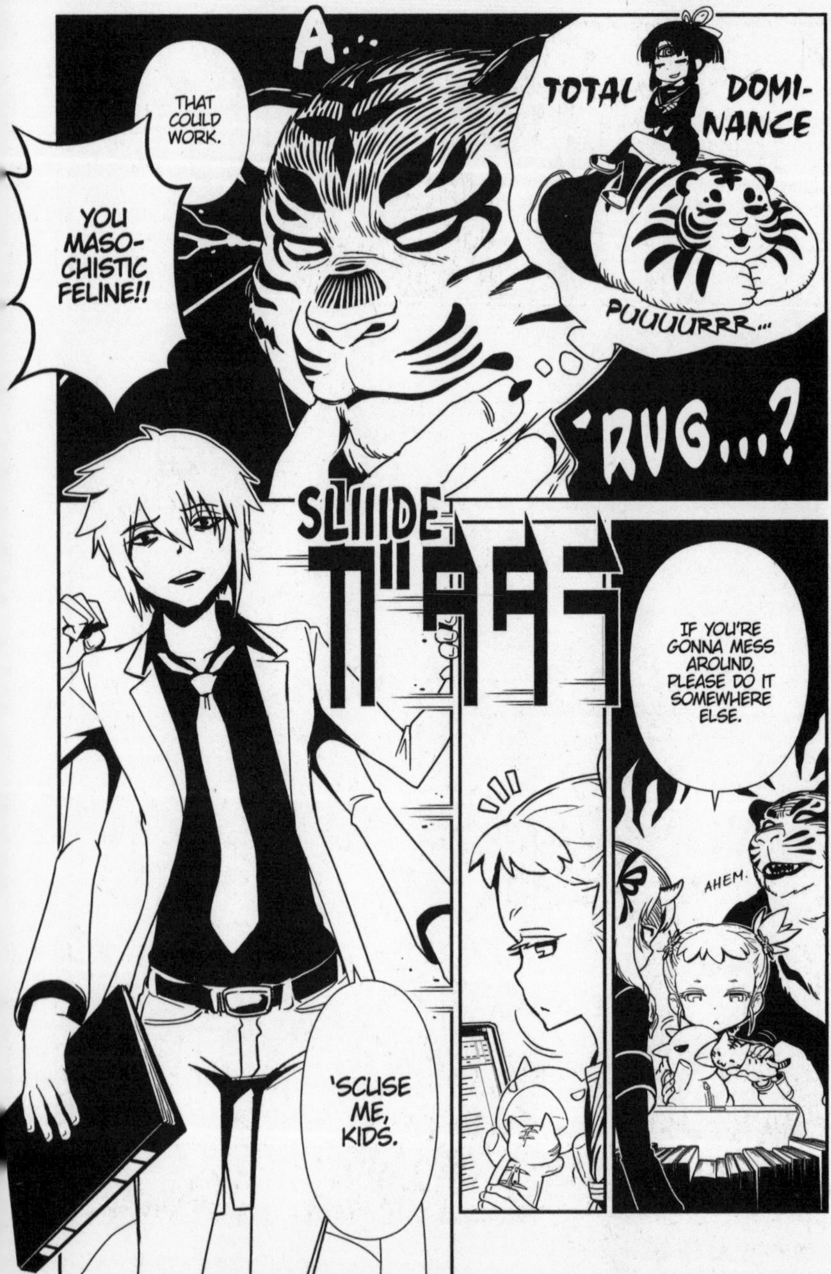
A...
TOTAL DOMINANCE
PUUUURRR...
'RUG...?
THAT COULD WORK.
YOU MASOCHISTIC FELINE!!
IF YOU'RE GONNA MESS AROUND, PLEASE DO IT SOMEWHERE ELSE.
AHEM.
SLIIDE
'SCUSE ME, KIDS.

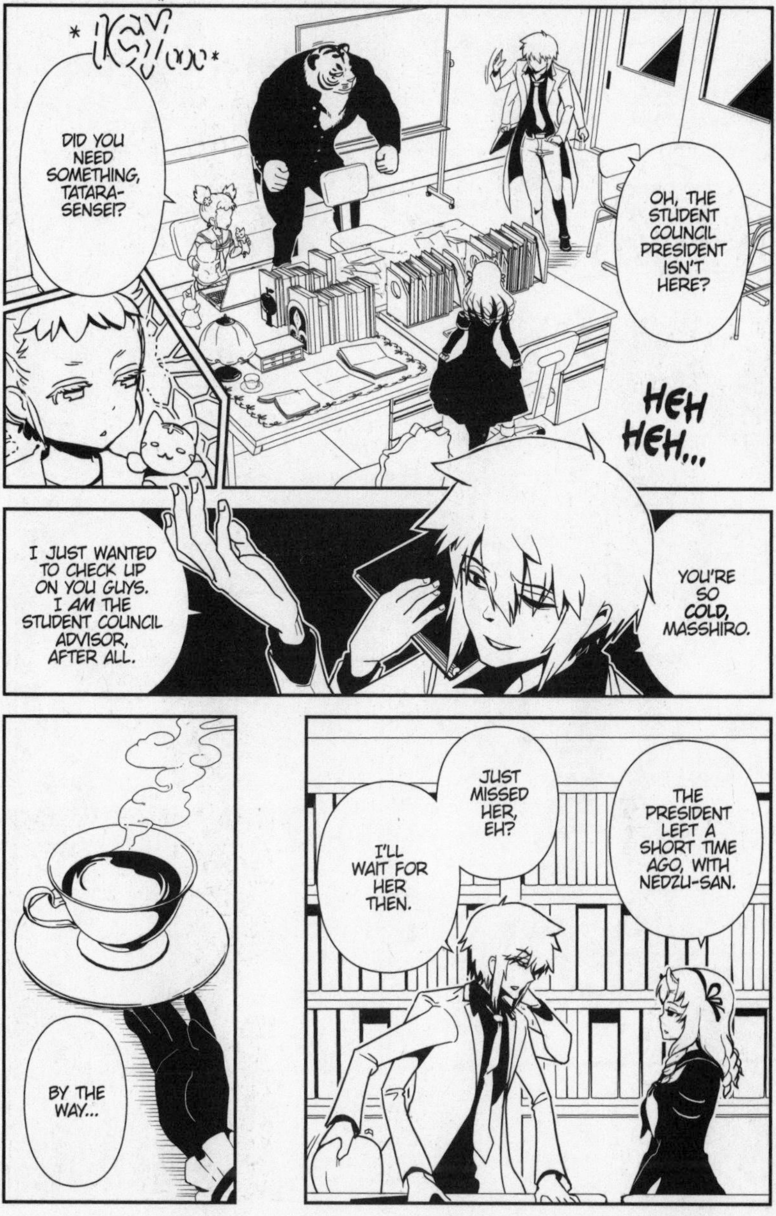
OH, THE STUDENT COUNCIL PRESIDENT ISN'T HERE?
DID YOU NEED SOMETHING, TATARA-SENSEI?
HEH HEH...
YOU'RE SO COLD, MASSHIRO.
I JUST WANTED TO CHECK UP ON YOU GUYS. I AM THE STUDENT COUNCIL ADVISOR, AFTER ALL.
THE PRESIDENT LEFT A SHORT TIME AGO, WITH NEDZU-SAN.
JUST MISSED HER, EH?
I'LL WAIT FOR HER THEN.
BY THE WAY...

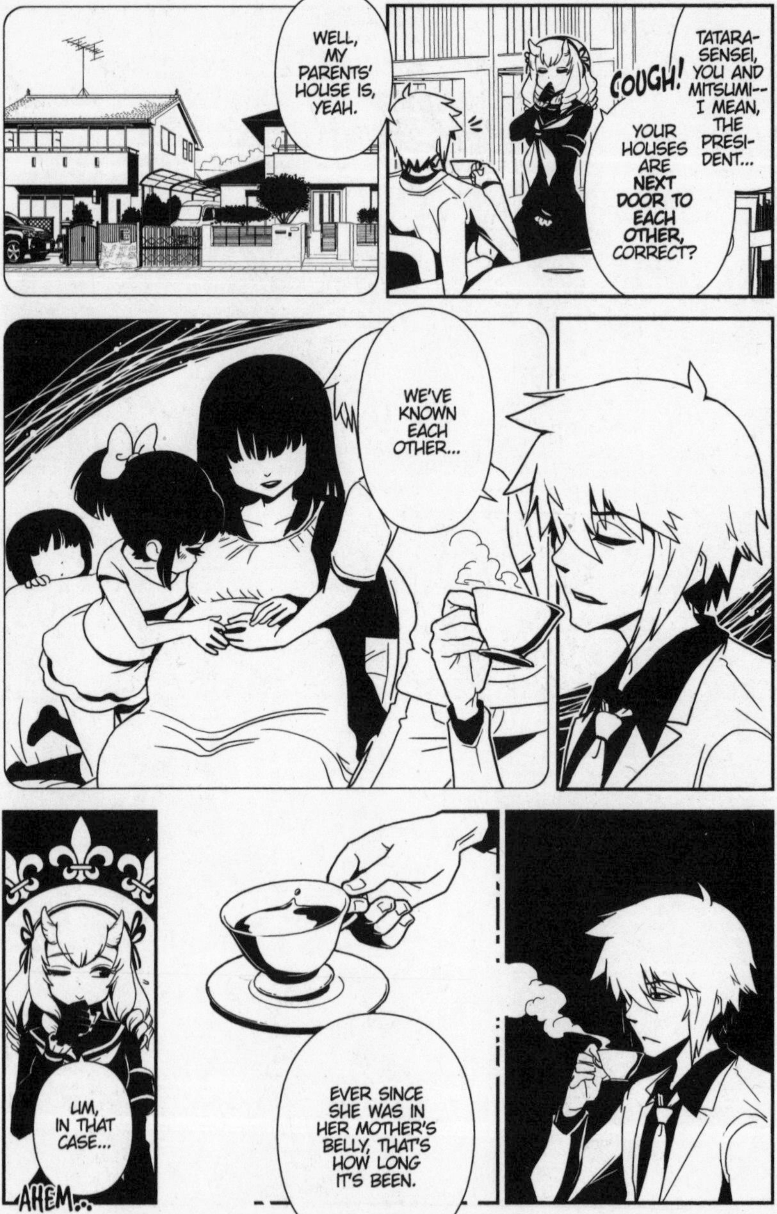
COUGH!
TATARA-SENSEI, YOU AND MITSUMI-- I MEAN, THE PRESIDENT...
YOUR HOUSES ARE NEXT DOOR TO EACH OTHER, CORRECT?
WELL, MY PARENTS' HOUSE IS, YEAH.
WE'VE KNOWN EACH OTHER...
EVER SINCE SHE WAS IN HER MOTHER'S BELLY, THAT'S HOW LONG IT'S BEEN.
UM, IN THAT CASE...
AHEM...

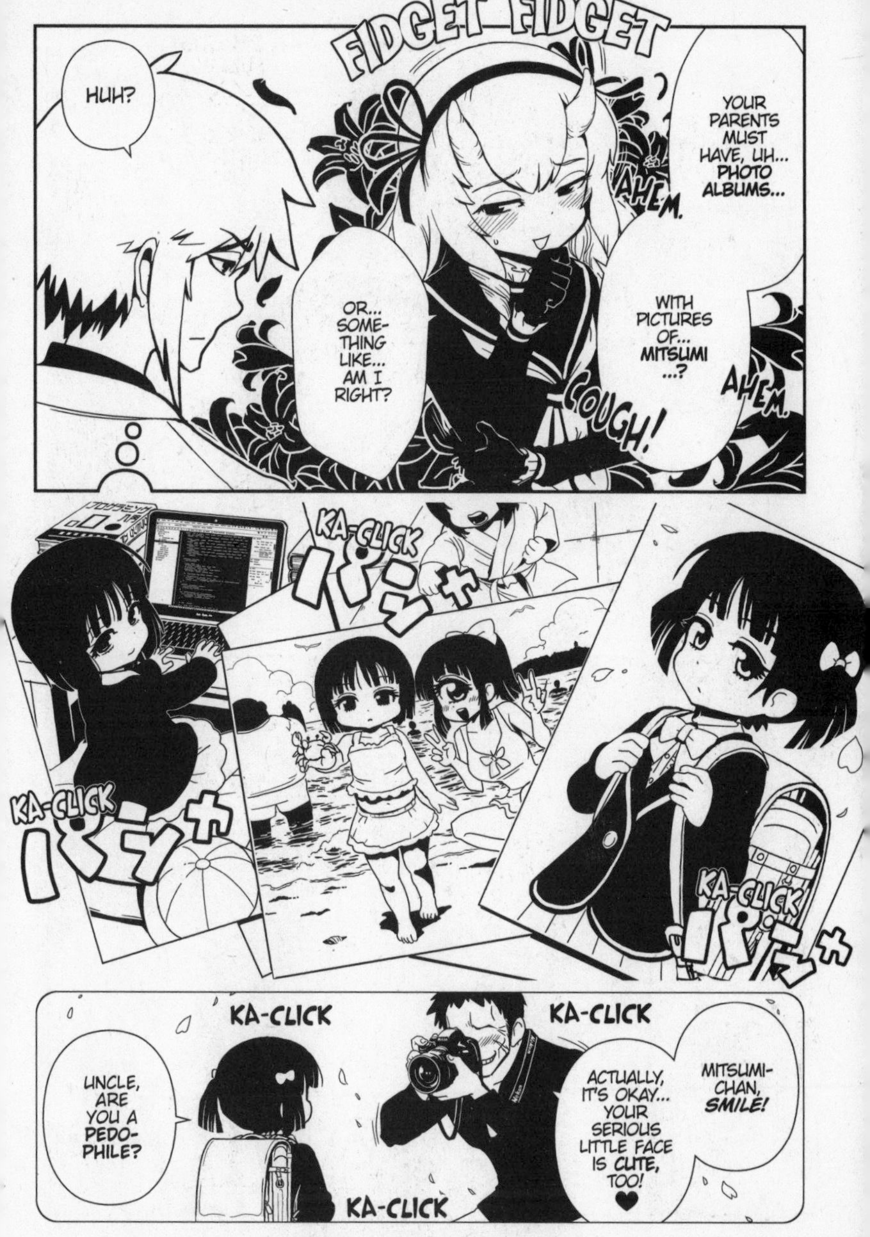
FIDGET FIDGET
YOUR PARENTS MUST HAVE, UH... PHOTO ALBUMS...
AHEM.
WITH PICTURES OF... MITSUMI ...?
AHEM.
COUGH!
OR... SOME-THING LIKE... AM I RIGHT?
HUH?
KA-CLICK
パシャ
KA-CLICK
パシャ
KA-CLICK
パシャ
MITSUMI-CHAN, SMILE!
ACTUALLY, IT'S OKAY... YOUR SERIOUS LITTLE FACE IS CUTE, TOO! ♥
KA-CLICK
KA-CLICK
KA-CLICK
UNCLE, ARE YOU A PEDO-PHILE?

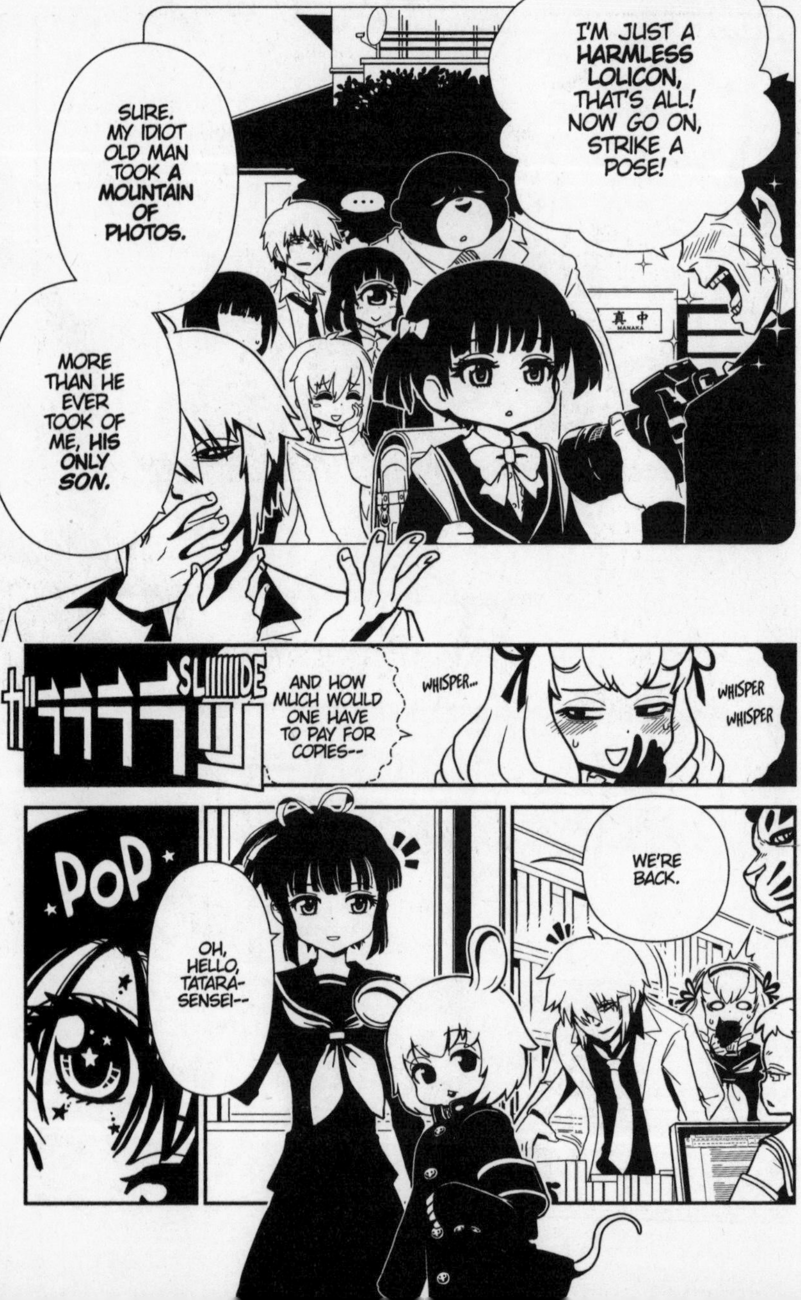
I'M JUST A HARMLESS LOLICON, THAT'S ALL! NOW GO ON, STRIKE A POSE!
真中
MANAKA
...
SURE. MY IDIOT OLD MAN TOOK A MOUNTAIN OF PHOTOS.
MORE THAN HE EVER TOOK OF ME, HIS ONLY SON.
WHISPER
WHISPER
WHISPER...
AND HOW MUCH WOULD ONE HAVE TO PAY FOR COPIES--
SLIIIIIDE
WE'RE BACK.
OH, HELLO, TATARA-SENSEI--
POP

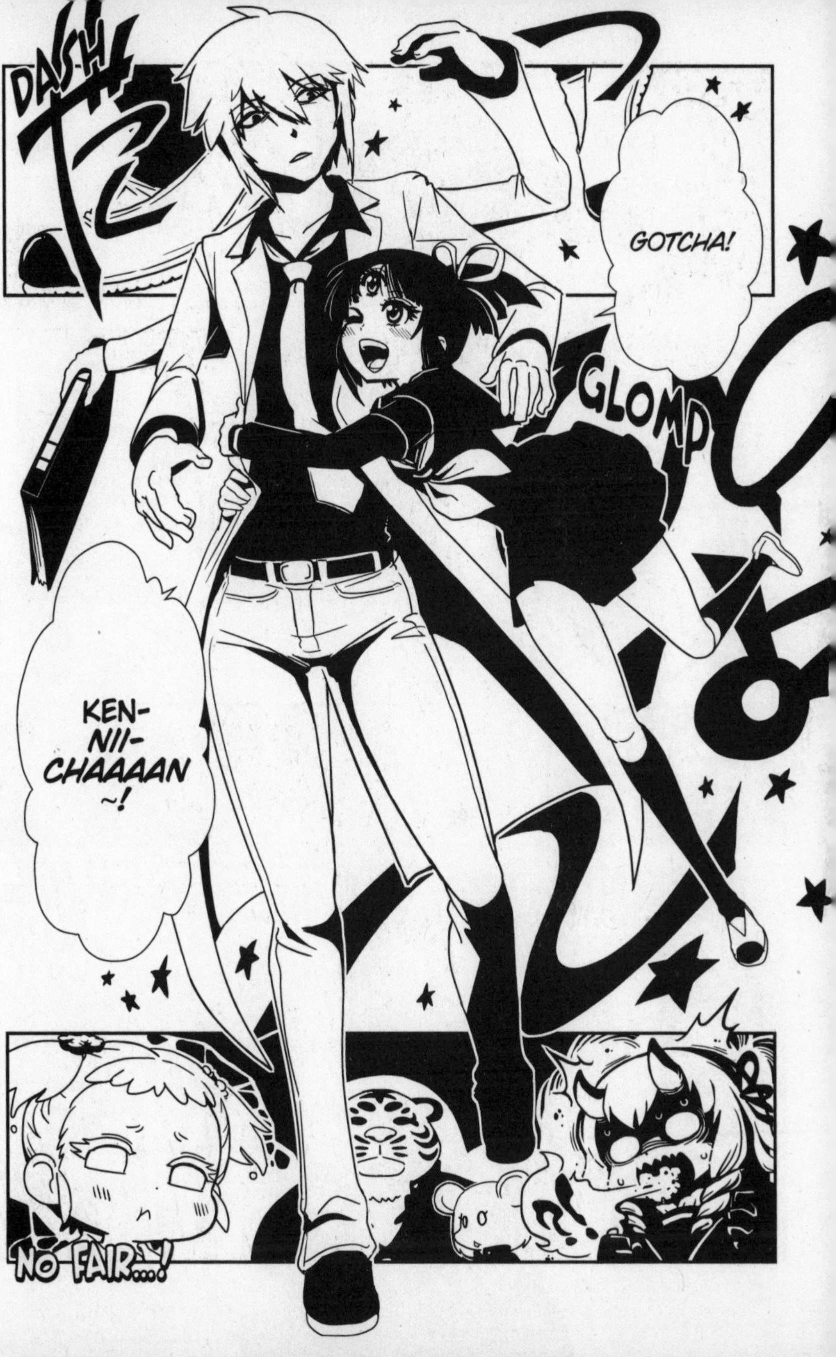
GOTCHA!
GLOMP
DASH
KEN-NII-CHAAAAN~!
?!
NO FAIR...!

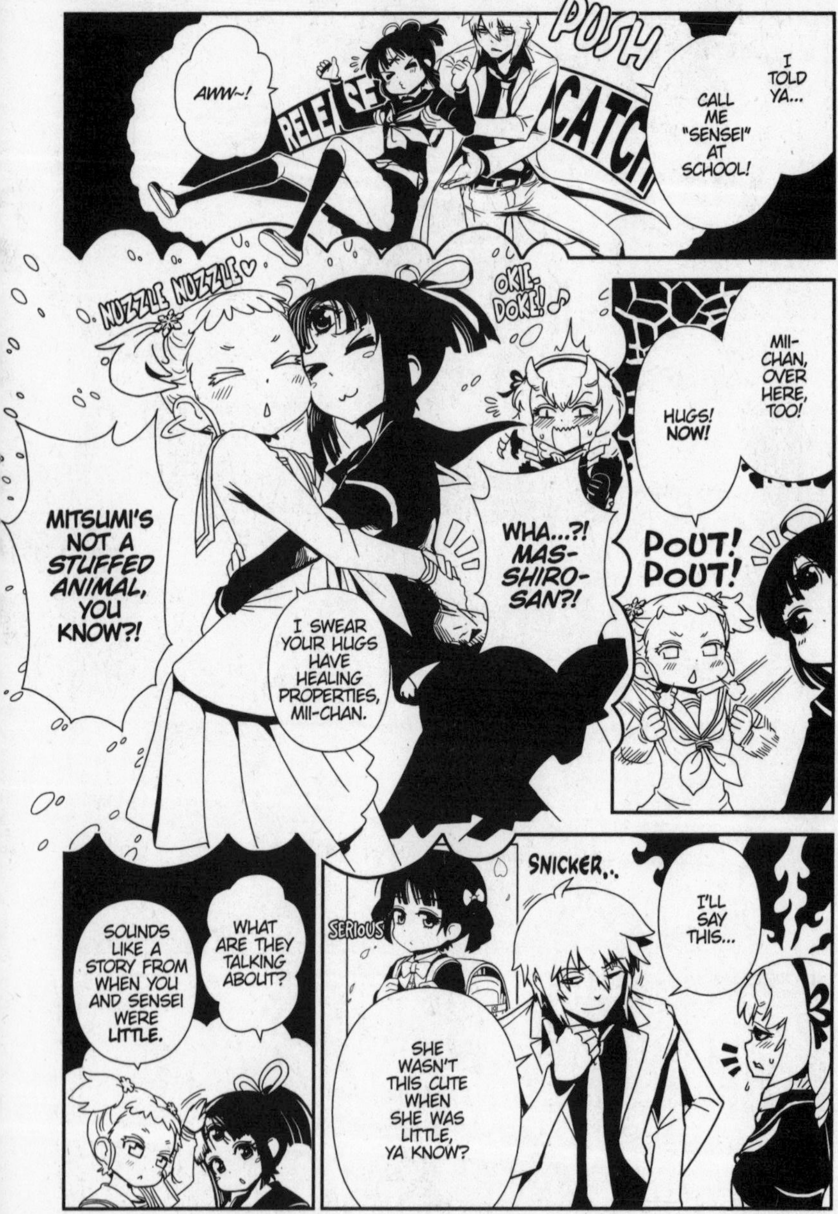
PUSH
I TOLD YA...
CALL ME "SENSEI" AT SCHOOL!
CATCH
RELE SE
AWW~!
MII-CHAN, OVER HERE, TOO!
HUGS! NOW!
POUT! POUT!
WHA...?! MAS-SHIRO-SAN?!
OKI-DOKI! ♪
NUZZLE NUZZLE ♥
I SWEAR YOUR HUGS HAVE HEALING PROPERTIES, MII-CHAN.
MITSUMI'S NOT A STUFFED ANIMAL, YOU KNOW?!
SNICKER...
I'LL SAY THIS...
SHE WASN'T THIS CUTE WHEN SHE WAS LITTLE, YA KNOW?
SERIOUS
WHAT ARE THEY TALKING ABOUT?
SOUNDS LIKE A STORY FROM WHEN YOU AND SENSEI WERE LITTLE.

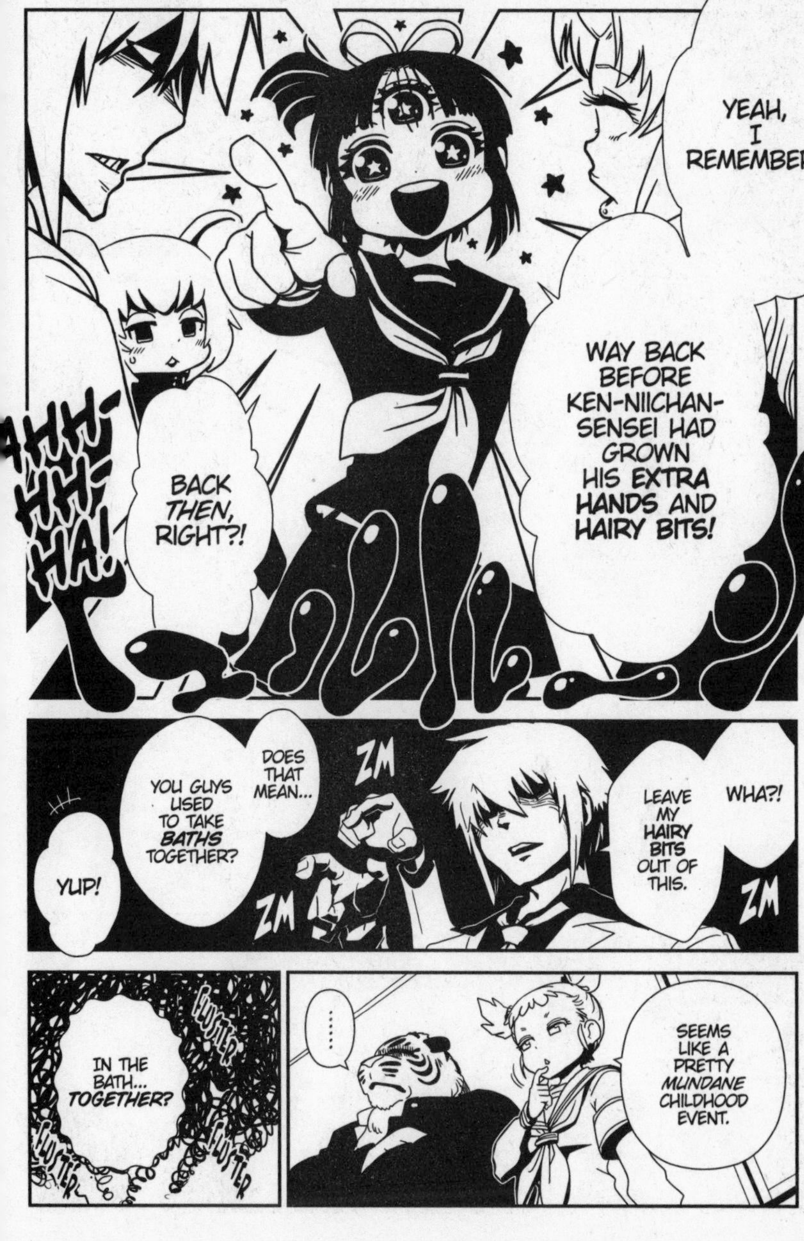
YEAH, I REMEMBER!
WAY BACK BEFORE KEN-NIICHAN-SENSEI HAD GROWN HIS EXTRA HANDS AND HAIRY BITS!
BACK THEN, RIGHT?!
HA!
WHA?!
LEAVE MY HAIRY BITS OUT OF THIS.
ZM
ZM
ZM
DOES THAT MEAN...
YOU GUYS USED TO TAKE BATHS TOGETHER?
YUP!
SEEMS LIKE A PRETTY MUNDANE CHILDHOOD EVENT.
......
IN THE BATH... TOGETHER?
FLUSTER
FLUSTER
FLUSTER
FLUSTER

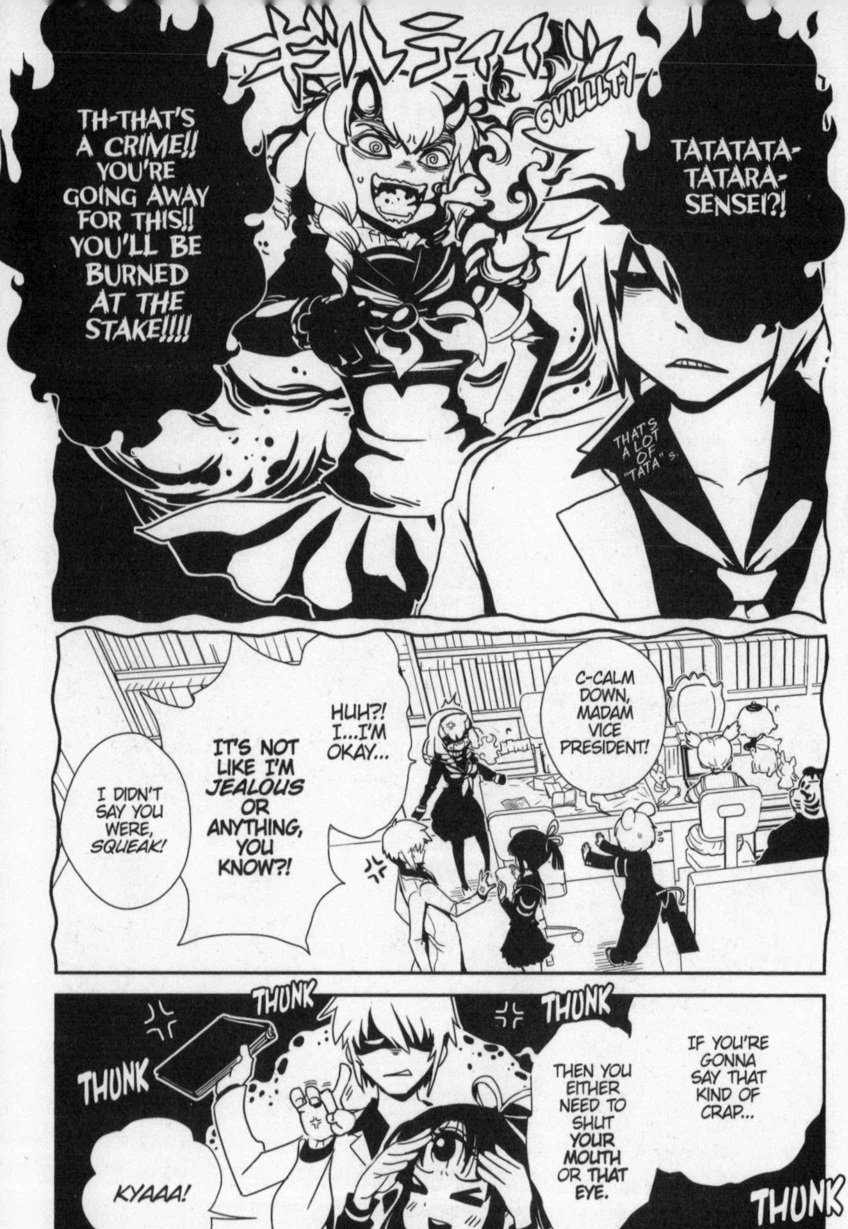
TATATATA-TATARA-SENSEI?!
GUILLLTY
TH-THAT'S A CRIME!! YOU'RE GOING AWAY FOR THIS!! YOU'LL BE BURNED AT THE STAKE!!!!
THAT'S A LOT OF "TATA"s.
C-CALM DOWN, MADAM VICE PRESIDENT!
HUH?! I...I'M OKAY...
IT'S NOT LIKE I'M JEALOUS OR ANYTHING, YOU KNOW?!
I DIDN'T SAY YOU WERE, SQUEAK!
THUNK
THUNK
IF YOU'RE GONNA SAY THAT KIND OF CRAP...
THEN YOU EITHER NEED TO SHUT YOUR MOUTH OR THAT EYE.
THUNK
KYAAA!
THUNK
THUNK
THUNK

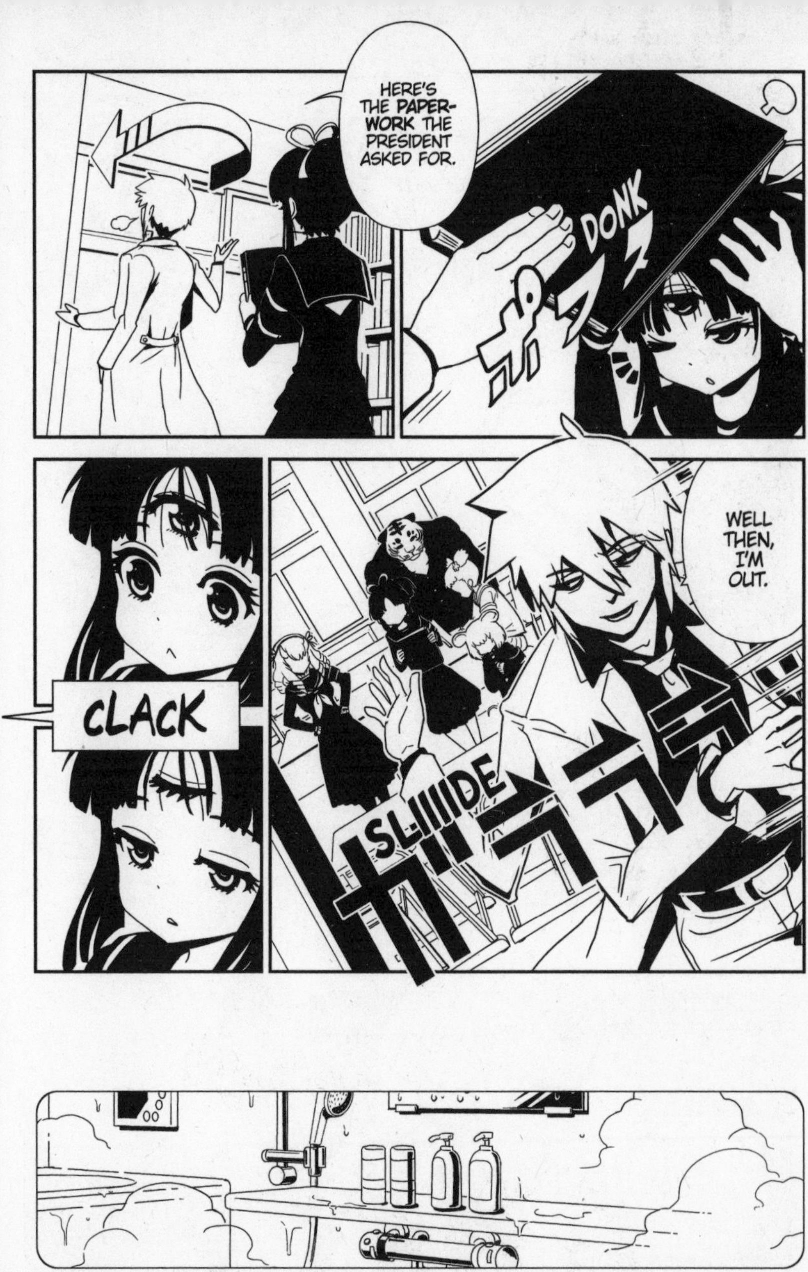
DONK
HERE'S THE PAPERWORK THE PRESIDENT ASKED FOR.
WELL THEN, I'M OUT.
SLIIIDE
CLACK

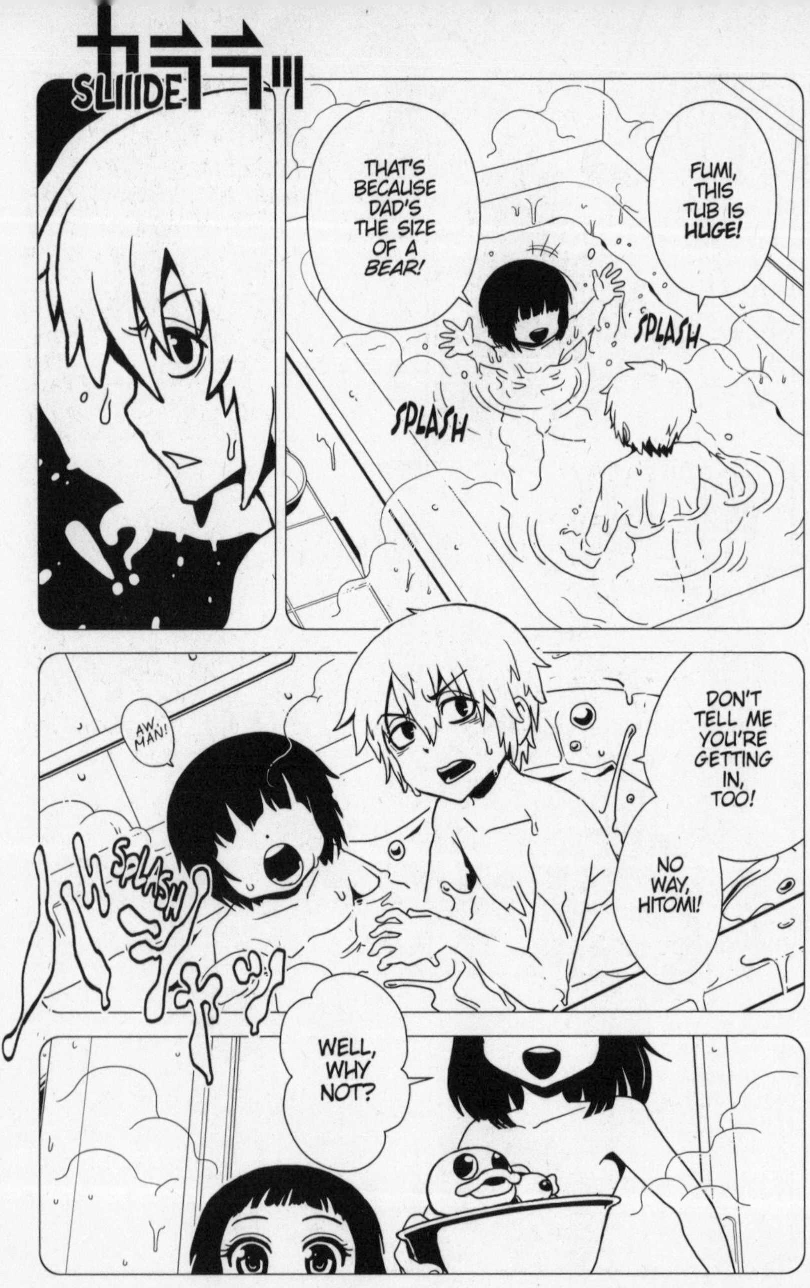
FUMI, THIS TUB IS HUGE!
THAT'S BECAUSE DAD'S THE SIZE OF A BEAR!
SPLASH
SPLASH
SLIIIDE
DON'T TELL ME YOU'RE GETTING IN, TOO!
NO WAY, HITOMI!
AW, MAN!
SPLASH
WELL, WHY NOT?

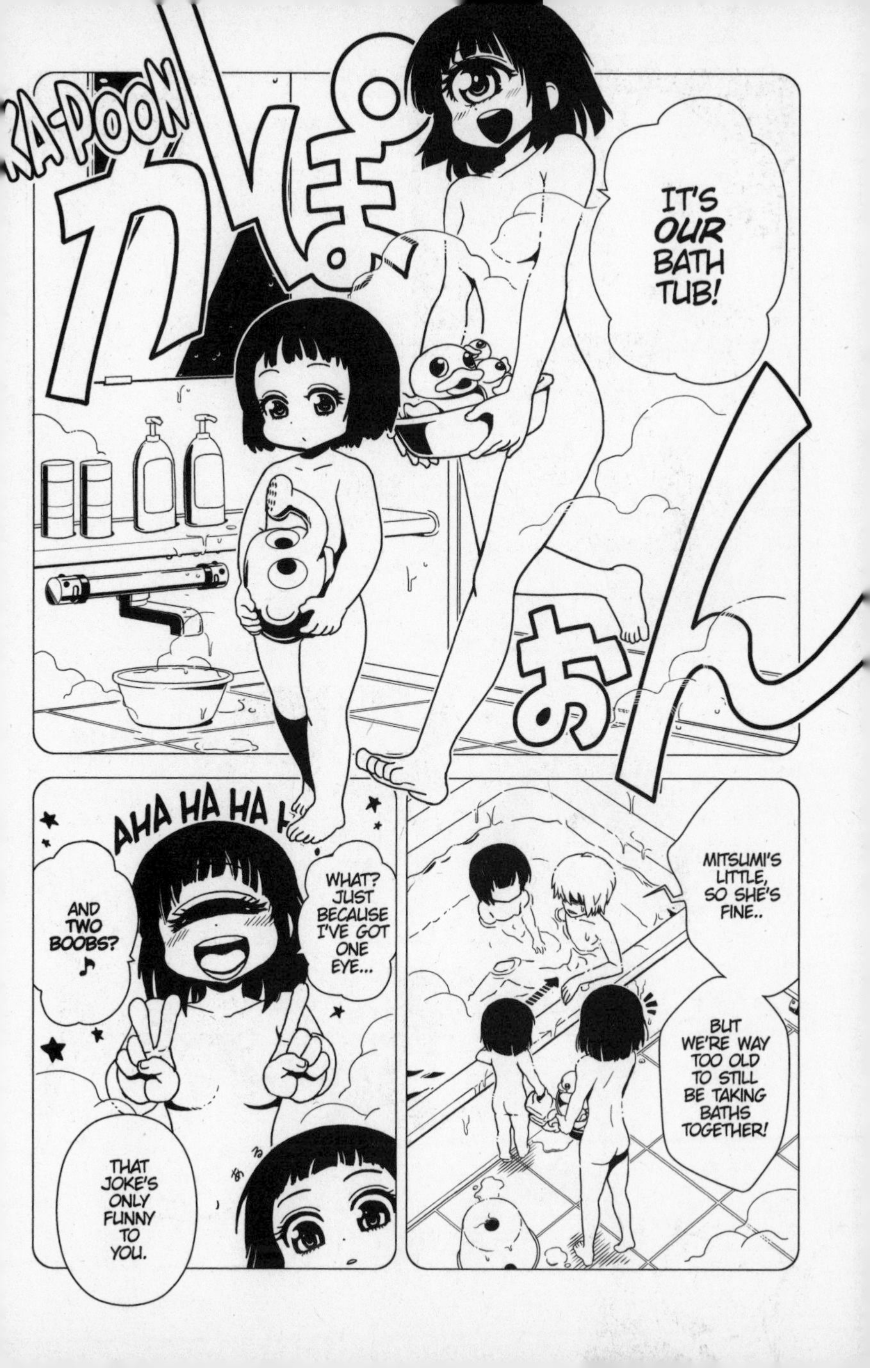
KA-POON
IT'S OUR BATH TUB!
MITSUMI'S LITTLE, SO SHE'S FINE..
BUT WE'RE WAY TOO OLD TO STILL BE TAKING BATHS TOGETHER!
AHA HA HA H
WHAT? JUST BECAUSE I'VE GOT ONE EYE...
AND TWO BOOBS? ♪
THAT JOKE'S ONLY FUNNY TO YOU.

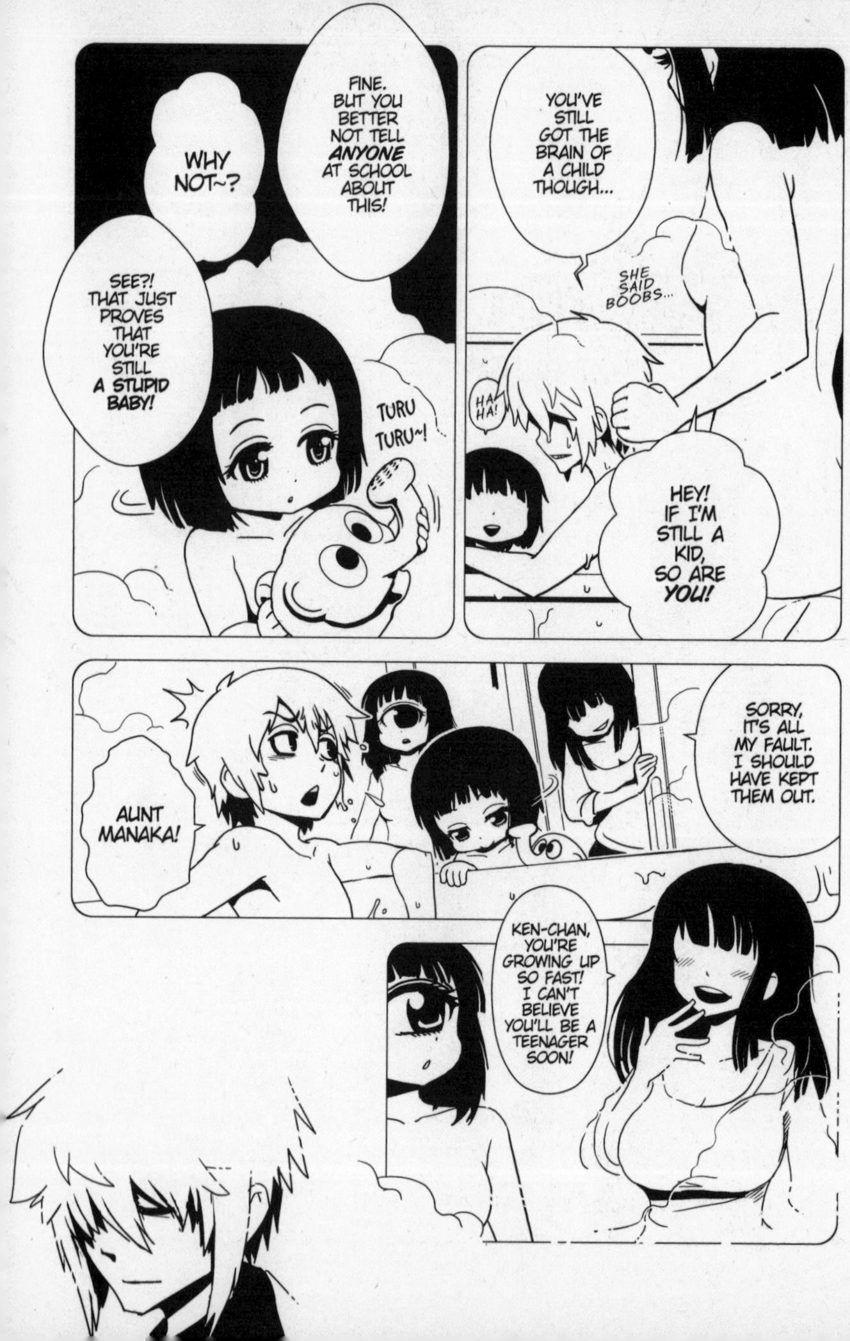
YOU'VE STILL GOT THE BRAIN OF A CHILD THOUGH...
SHE SAID BOOBS...
HA HA!
HEY! IF I'M STILL A KID, SO ARE YOU!
FINE. BUT YOU BETTER NOT TELL ANYONE AT SCHOOL ABOUT THIS!
WHY NOT~?
SEE?! THAT JUST PROVES THAT YOU'RE STILL A STUPID BABY!
TURU TURU~!
SORRY, IT'S ALL MY FAULT. I SHOULD HAVE KEPT THEM OUT.
AUNT MANAKA!
KEN-CHAN, YOU'RE GROWING UP SO FAST! I CAN'T BELIEVE YOU'LL BE A TEENAGER SOON!

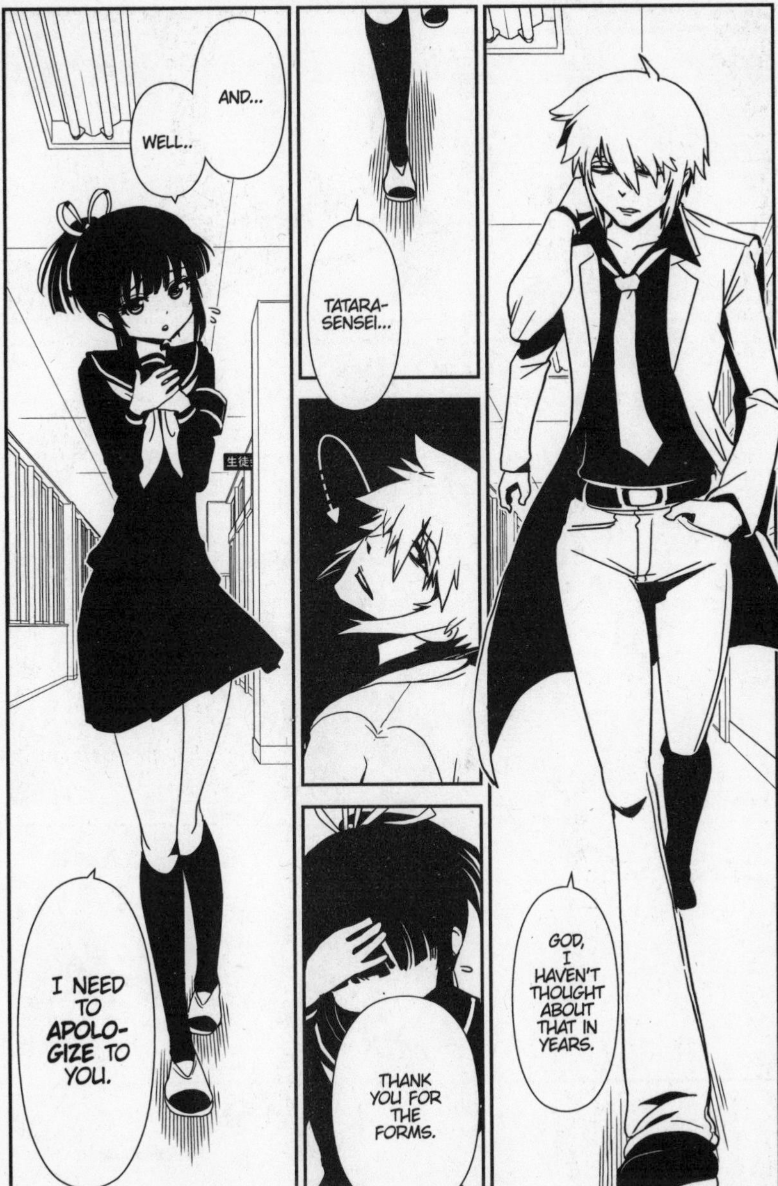
GOD, I HAVEN'T THOUGHT ABOUT THAT IN YEARS.
TATARA-SENSEI...
THANK YOU FOR THE FORMS.
AND...
WELL...
I NEED TO APOLOGIZE TO YOU.

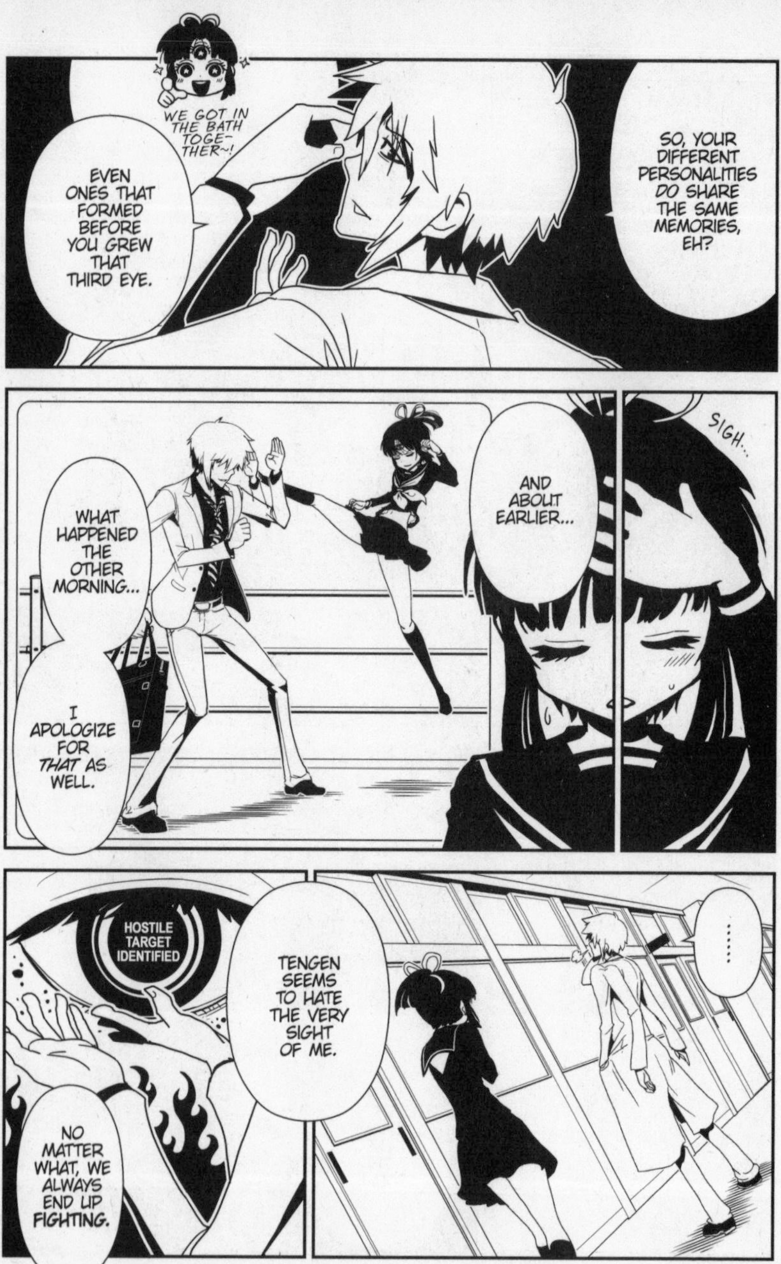
SO, YOUR DIFFERENT PERSONALITIES *DO* SHARE THE SAME MEMORIES, EH?
EVEN ONES THAT FORMED BEFORE YOU GREW THAT THIRD EYE.
WE GOT IN THE BATH TOGE-THER~!
SIGH...
AND ABOUT EARLIER...
WHAT HAPPENED THE OTHER MORNING...
I APOLOGIZE FOR *THAT* AS WELL.
......
TENGEN SEEMS TO HATE THE VERY SIGHT OF ME.
HOSTILE TARGET IDENTIFIED
NO MATTER WHAT, WE ALWAYS END UP FIGHTING.

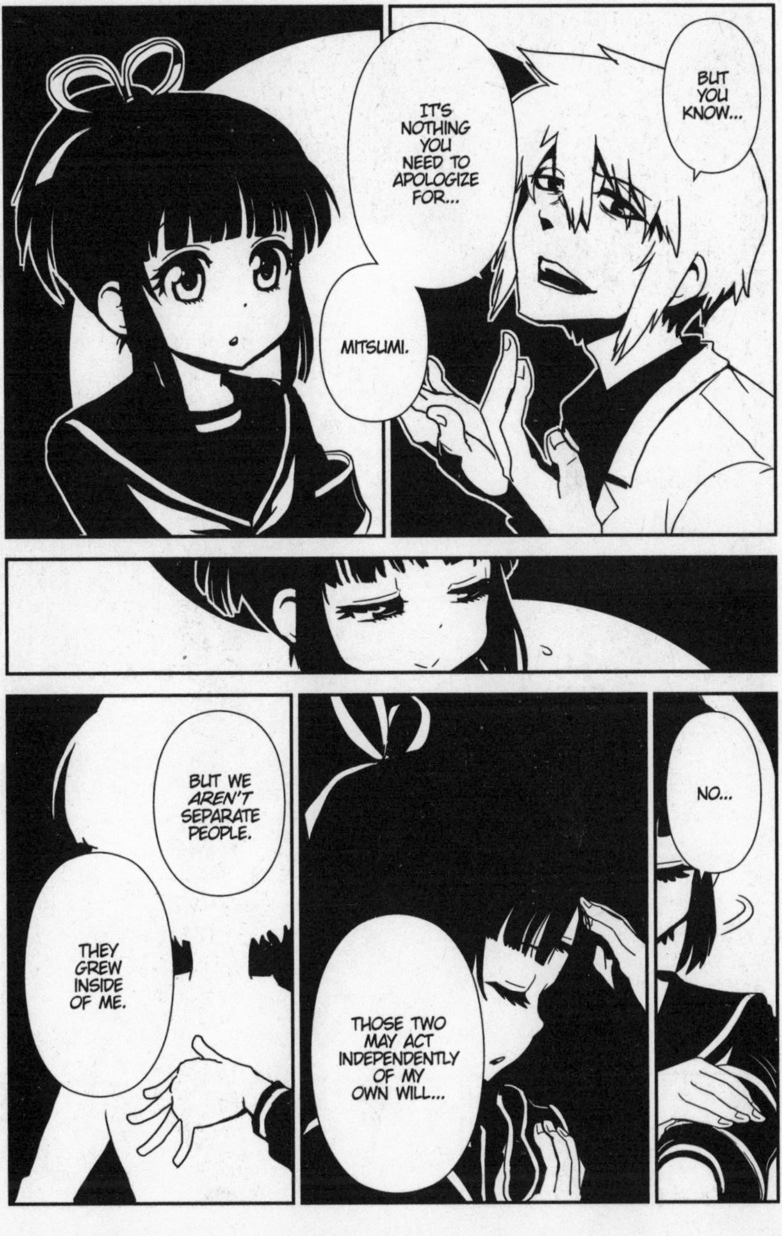
BUT YOU KNOW...
IT'S NOTHING YOU NEED TO APOLOGIZE FOR...
MITSUMI.
NO...
THOSE TWO MAY ACT INDEPENDENTLY OF MY OWN WILL...
BUT WE *AREN'T* SEPARATE PEOPLE.
THEY GREW INSIDE OF ME.

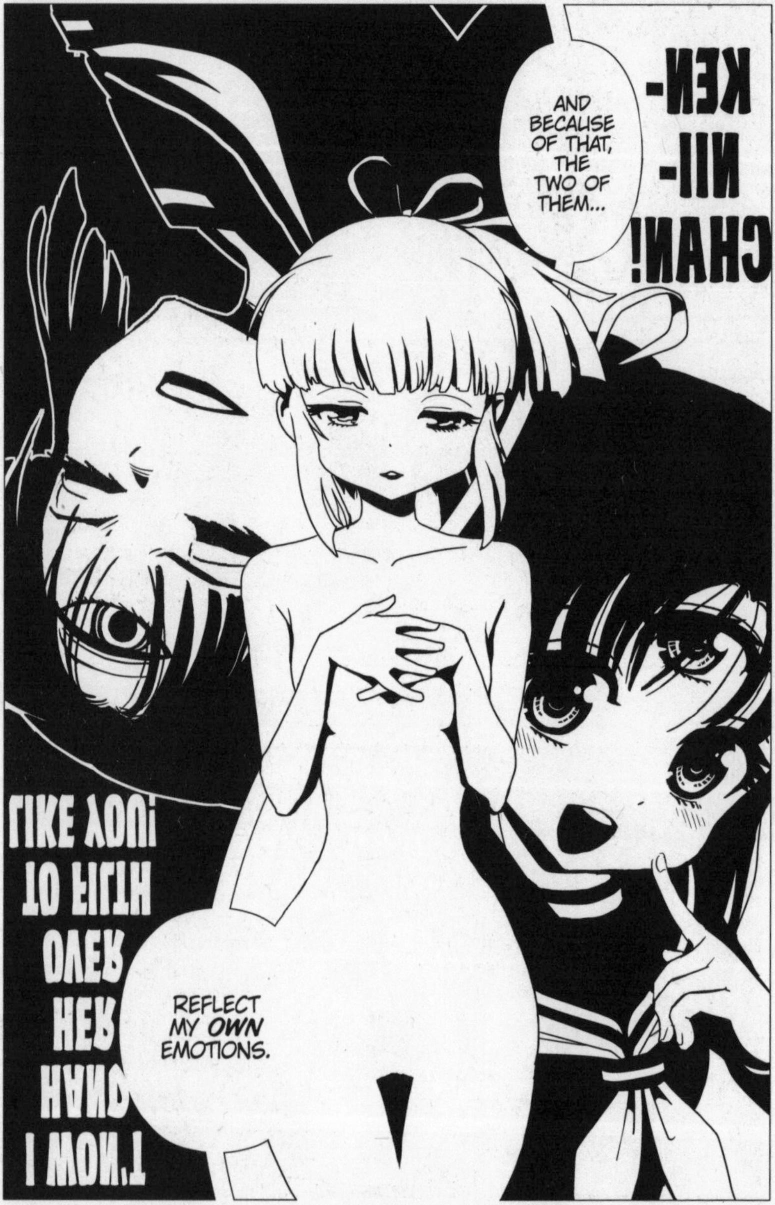
KEN-NII-CHAN!
AND BECAUSE OF THAT, THE TWO OF THEM...
REFLECT MY *OWN* EMOTIONS.
I WON'T HAND HER OVER TO FILTH LIKE YOU!

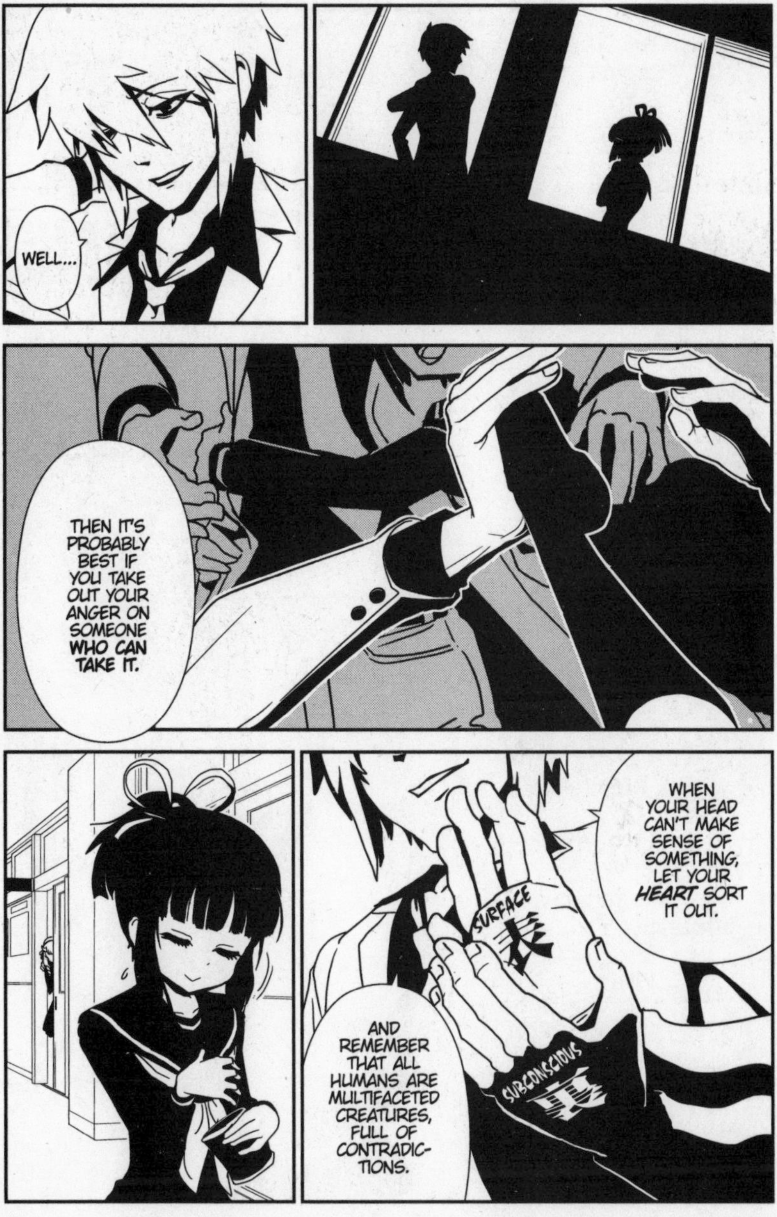
WELL...
THEN IT'S PROBABLY BEST IF YOU TAKE OUT YOUR ANGER ON SOMEONE WHO CAN TAKE IT.
WHEN YOUR HEAD CAN'T MAKE SENSE OF SOMETHING, LET YOUR *HEART* SORT IT OUT.
AND REMEMBER THAT ALL HUMANS ARE MULTIFACETED CREATURES, FULL OF CONTRADIC- TIONS.
SURFACE
SUBCONSCIOUS

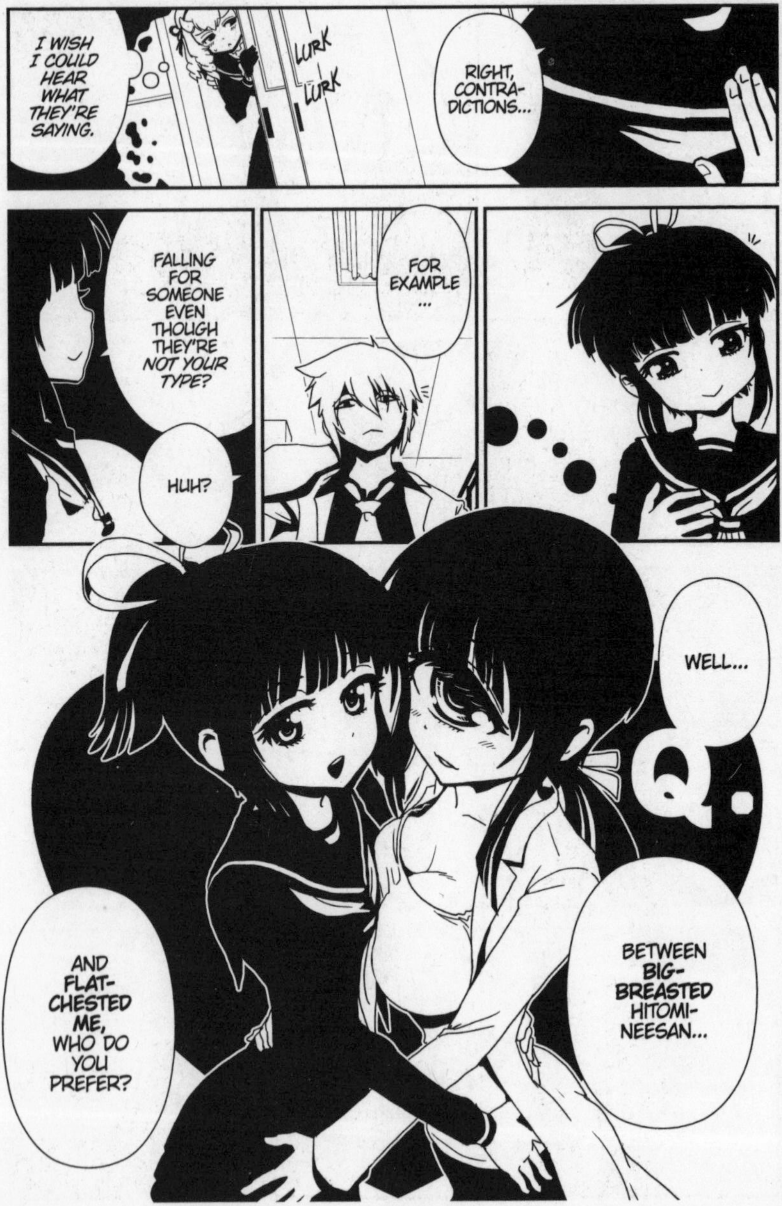
RIGHT, CONTRA-DICTIONS...
LURK LURK
I WISH I COULD HEAR WHAT THEY'RE SAYING.
FOR EXAMPLE ...
FALLING FOR SOMEONE EVEN THOUGH THEY'RE NOT YOUR TYPE?
HUH?
WELL...
Q.
BETWEEN BIG-BREASTED HITOMI-NEESAN...
AND FLAT-CHESTED ME, WHO DO YOU PREFER?

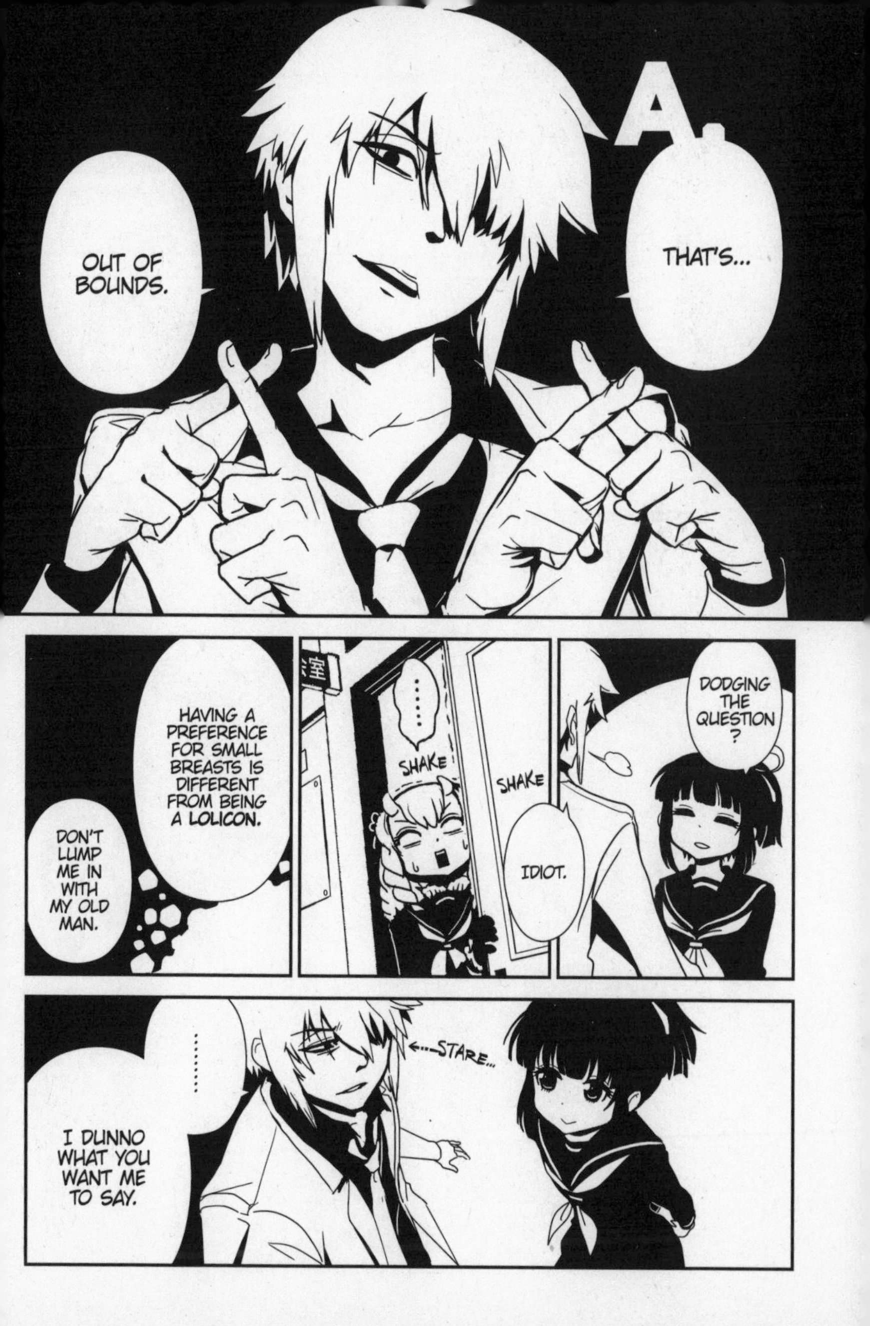
A.
THAT'S...
OUT OF BOUNDS.
DODGING THE QUESTION?
SHAKE
IDIOT.
......
SHAKE
HAVING A PREFERENCE FOR SMALL BREASTS IS DIFFERENT FROM BEING A LOLICON.
DON'T LUMP ME IN WITH MY OLD MAN.
←...STARE...
......
I DUNNO WHAT YOU WANT ME TO SAY.

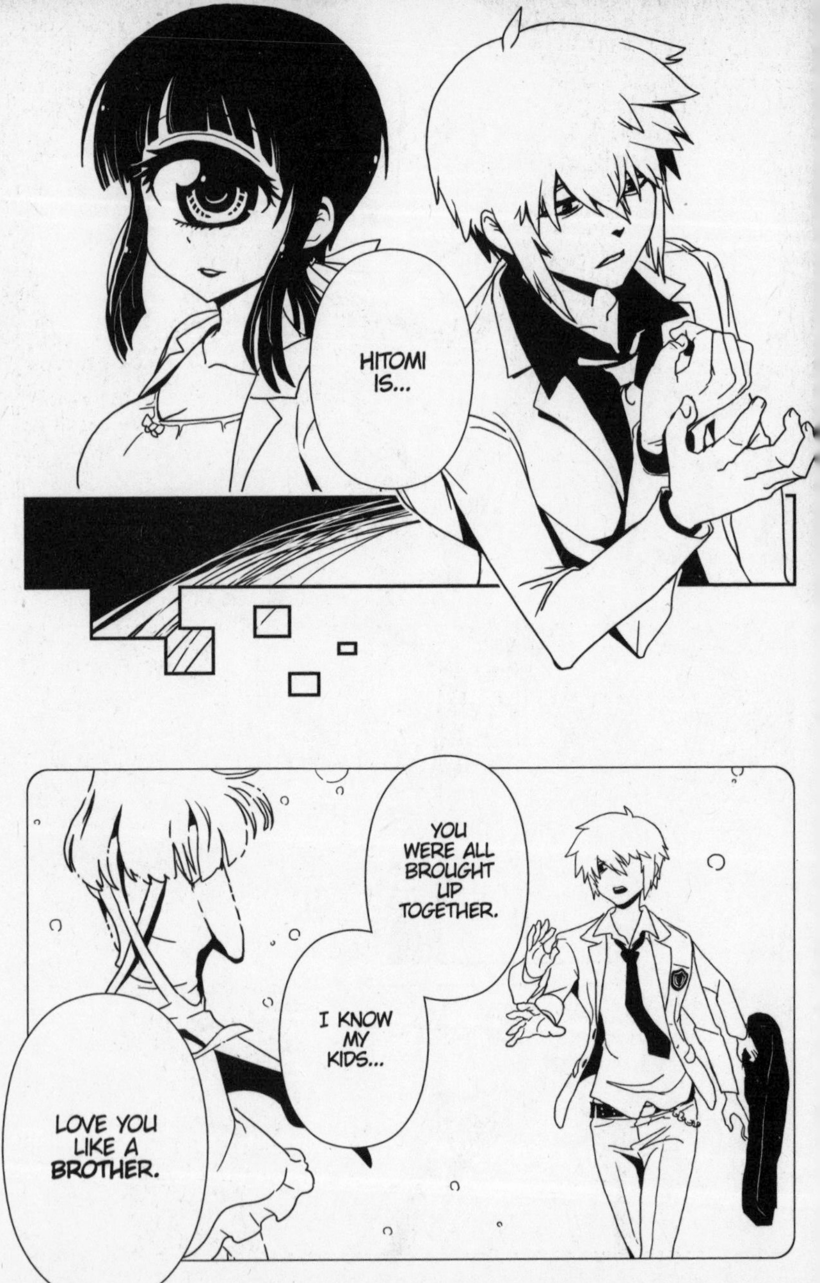
HITOMI IS...
YOU WERE ALL BROUGHT UP TOGETHER.
I KNOW MY KIDS...
LOVE YOU LIKE A BROTHER.

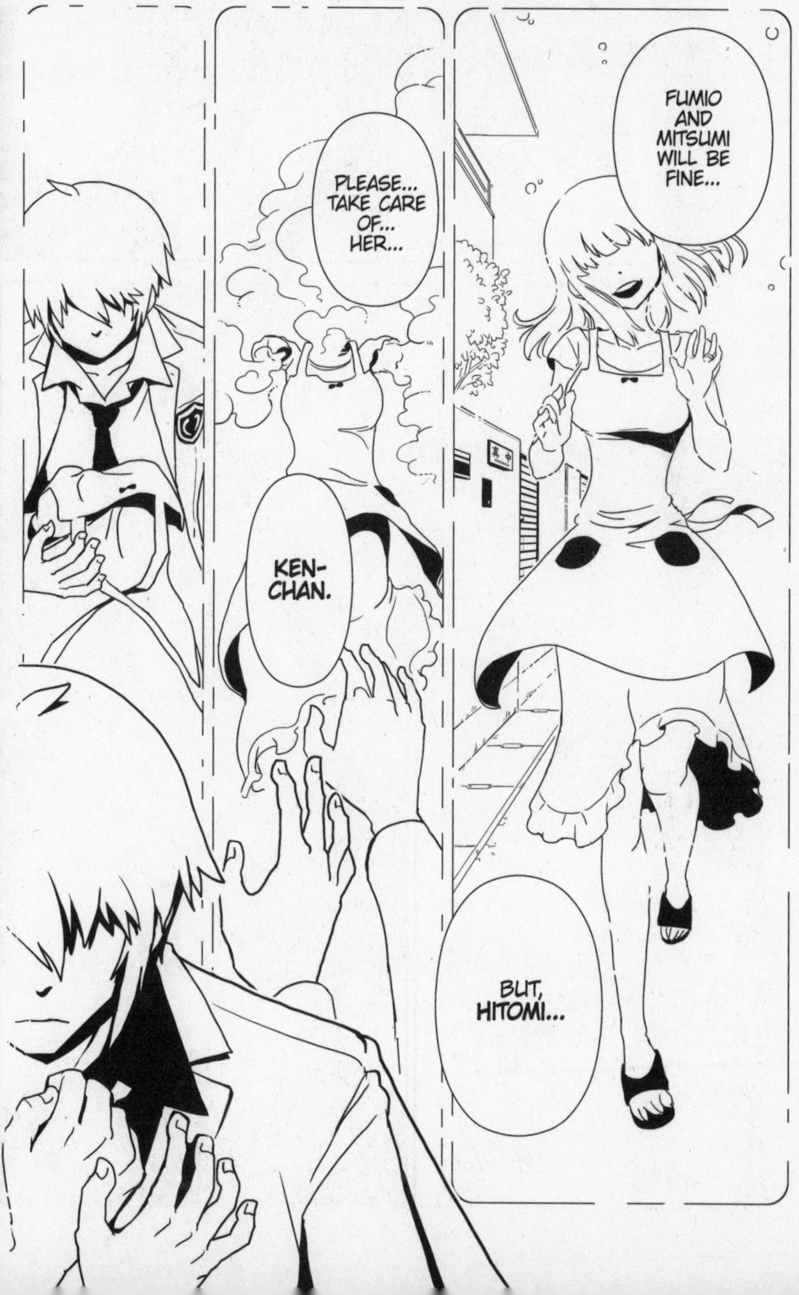
FUMIO AND MITSUMI WILL BE FINE...
BUT, HITOMI...
PLEASE... TAKE CARE OF... HER...
KEN-CHAN.

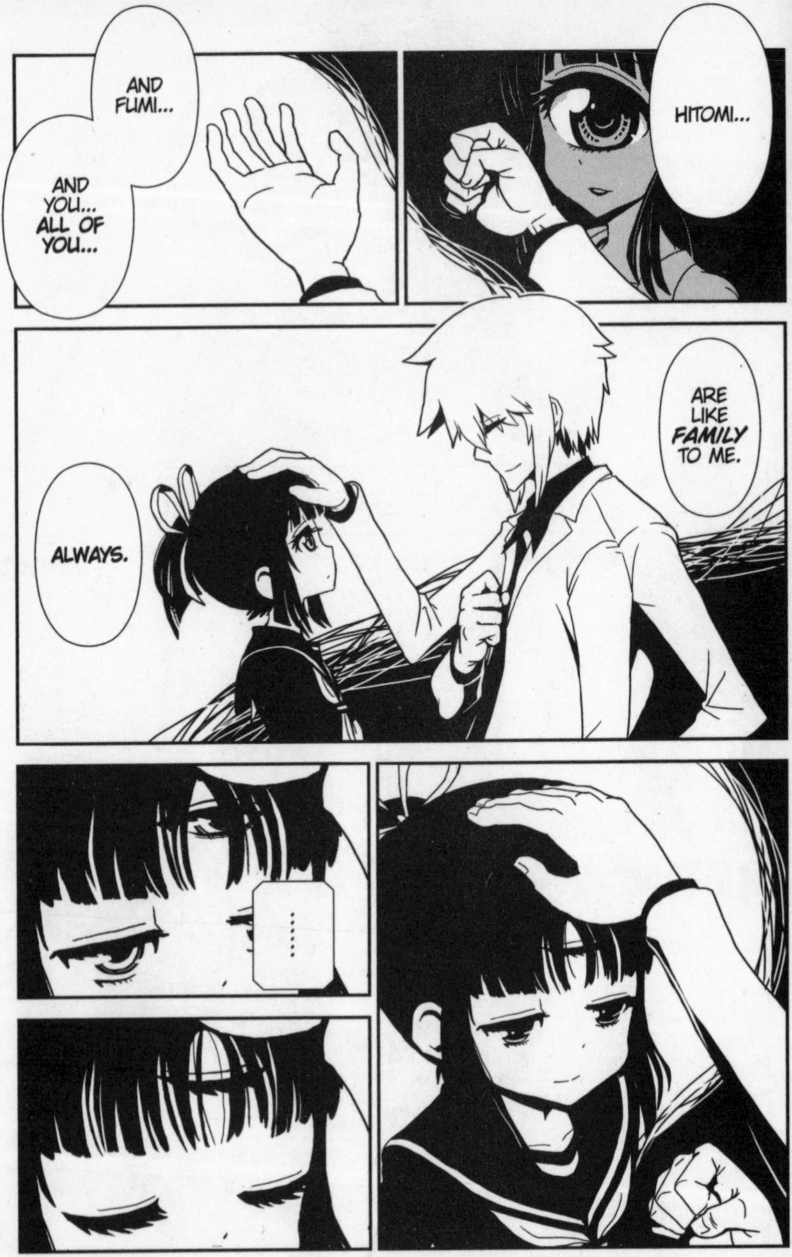
HITOMI...
AND FUMI...
AND YOU... ALL OF YOU...
ARE LIKE FAMILY TO ME.
ALWAYS.
......

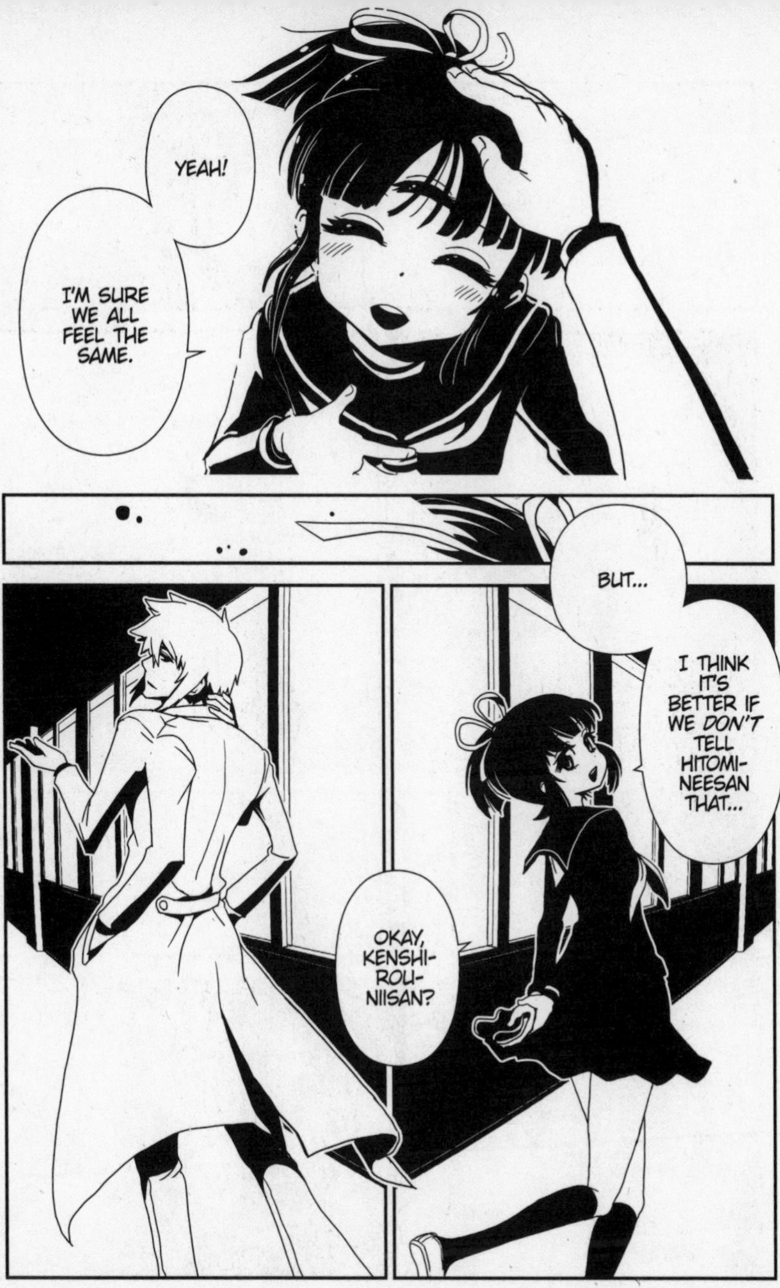
YEAH!
I'M SURE WE ALL FEEL THE SAME.
BUT...
I THINK IT'S BETTER IF WE *DON'T* TELL HITOMI-NEESAN THAT...
OKAY, KENSHI-ROU-NIISAN?

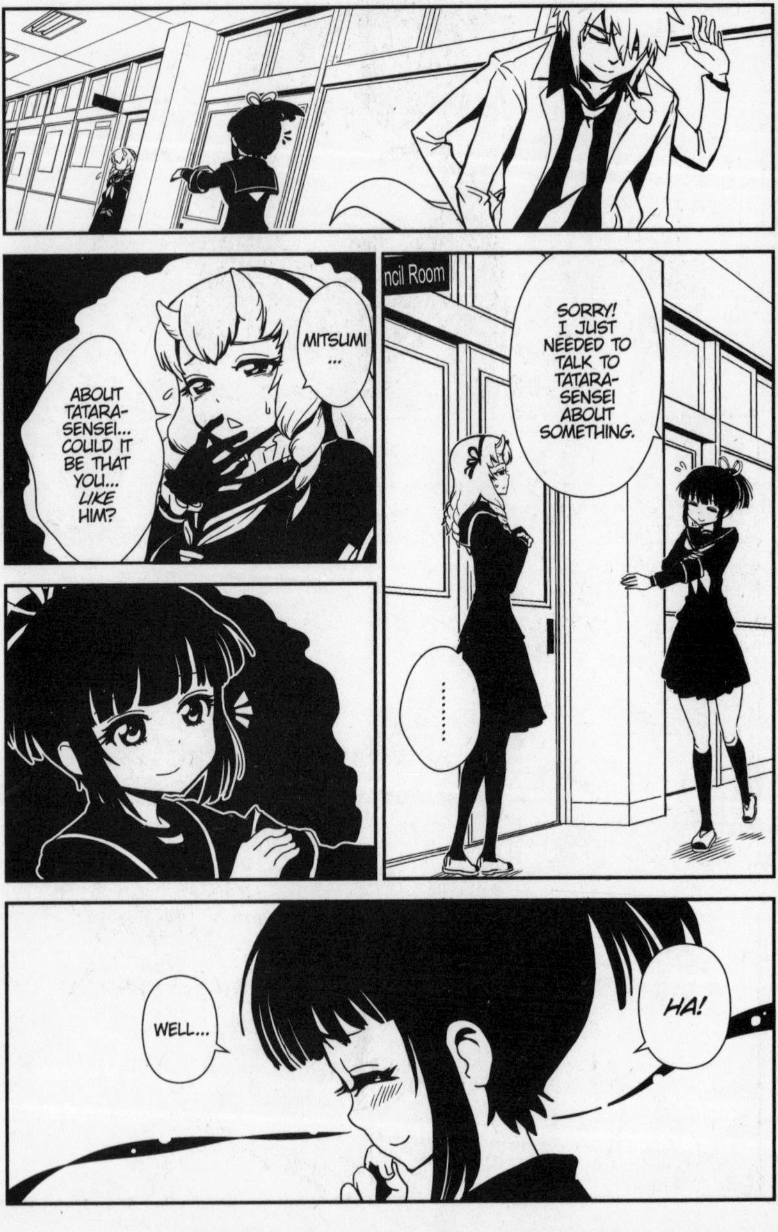
ncil Room
SORRY! I JUST NEEDED TO TALK TO TATARA-SENSEI ABOUT SOMETHING.
......
MITSUMI ...
ABOUT TATARA-SENSEI... COULD IT BE THAT YOU... *LIKE* HIM?
HA!
WELL...

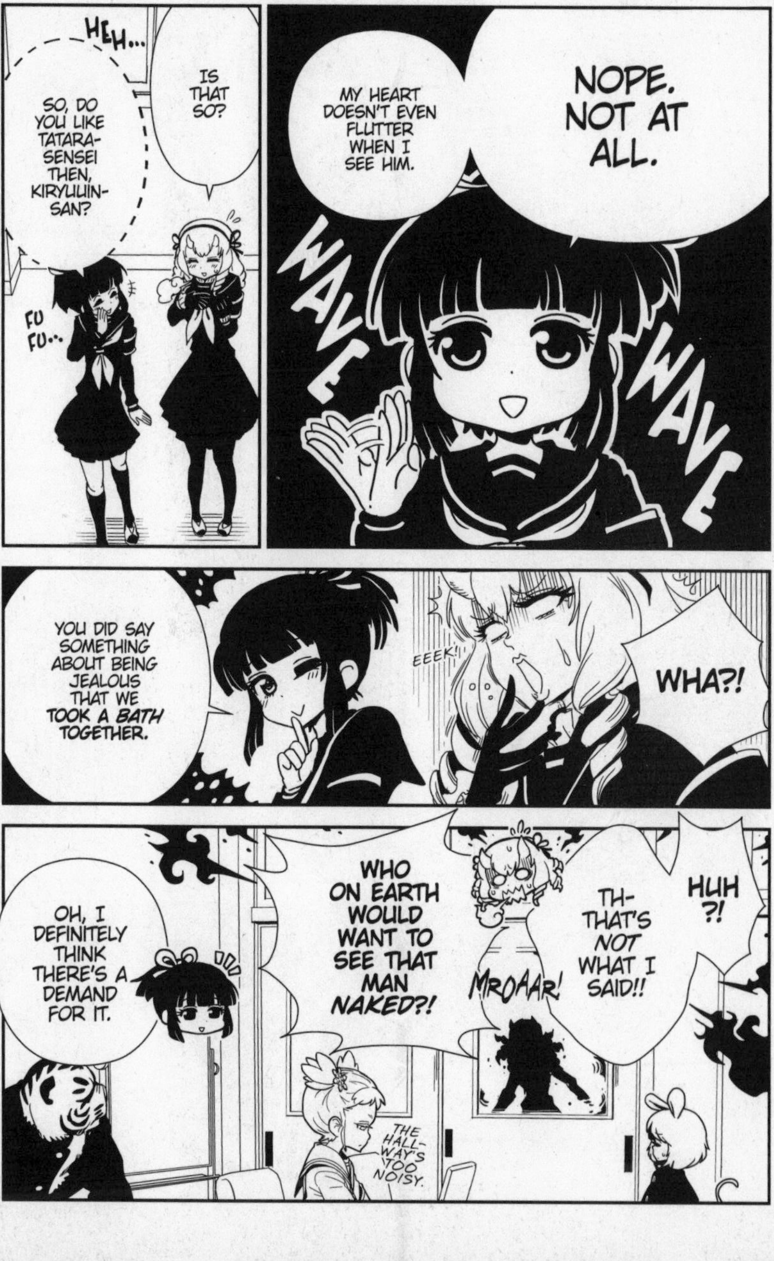
NOPE. NOT AT ALL.
MY HEART DOESN'T EVEN FLUTTER WHEN I SEE HIM.
WAVE
WAVE
IS THAT SO?
HEH...
SO, DO YOU LIKE TATARA-SENSEI THEN, KIRYUUIN-SAN?
FU FU...
WHA?!
EEEK!!
YOU DID SAY SOMETHING ABOUT BEING JEALOUS THAT WE TOOK A BATH TOGETHER.
HUH ?!
TH-THAT'S NOT WHAT I SAID!!
MROAAR!
WHO ON EARTH WOULD WANT TO SEE THAT MAN NAKED?!
OH, I DEFINITELY THINK THERE'S A DEMAND FOR IT.
THE HALLWAY'S TOO NOISY.

OMAKE

THIS IS A PICTURE I DREW FOR A SPECIAL EVENT.

INCIDENTALLY, WITHIN THE WORLD OF THIS SERIES THERE ARE LEGENDARY CREATURES SUCH AS ZOMBIES AND ANGELS AND CENTAURS.

THERE AREN'T *ACTUALLY* MONSTERS IN THE STORY, BUT THE ENGLISH TRANSLATED VERSION OF *HITOMI-SENSEI NO HOUKENSHITSU* DID COME OUT AS *NURSE HITOMI'S MONSTER INFIRMARY*.

GLOBAL!

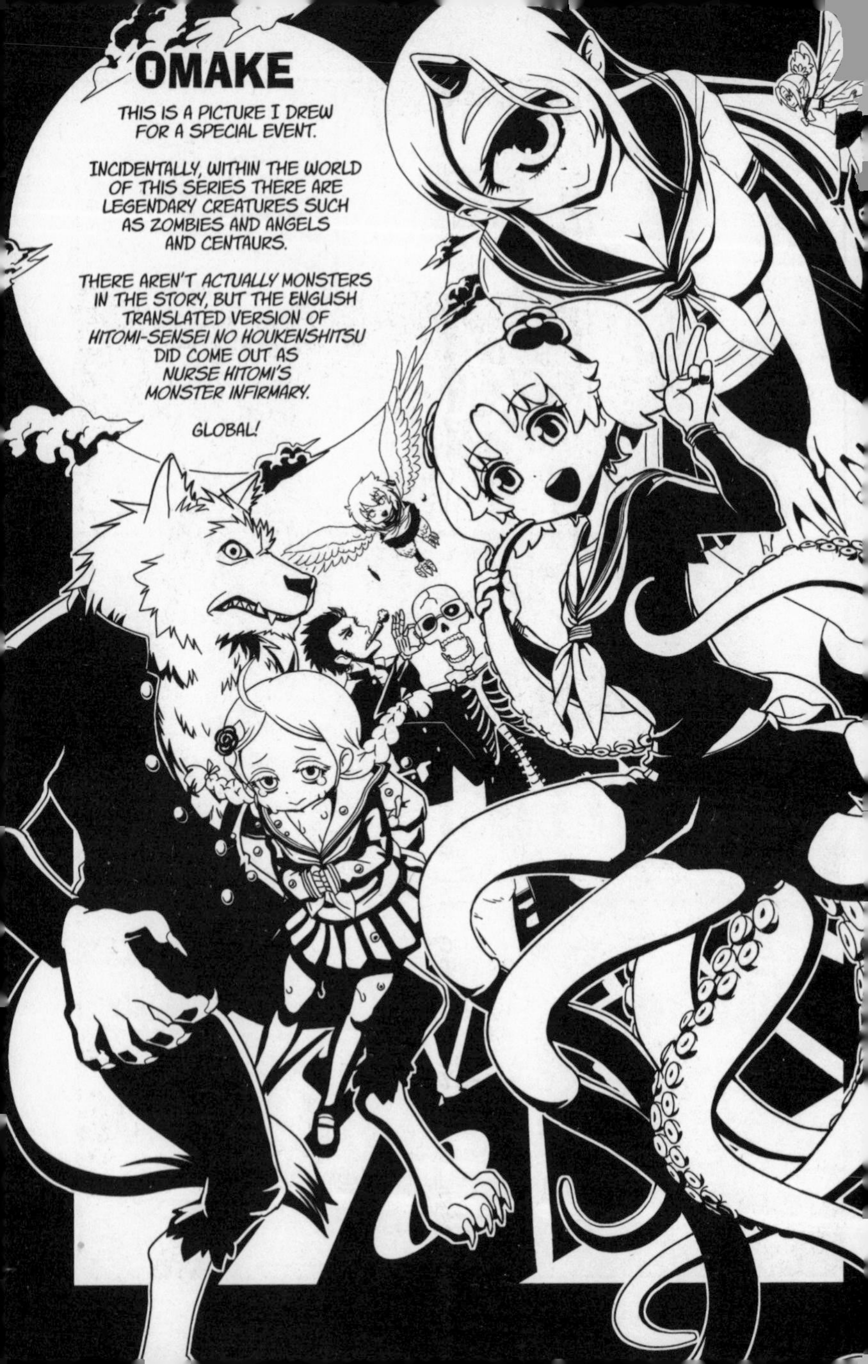

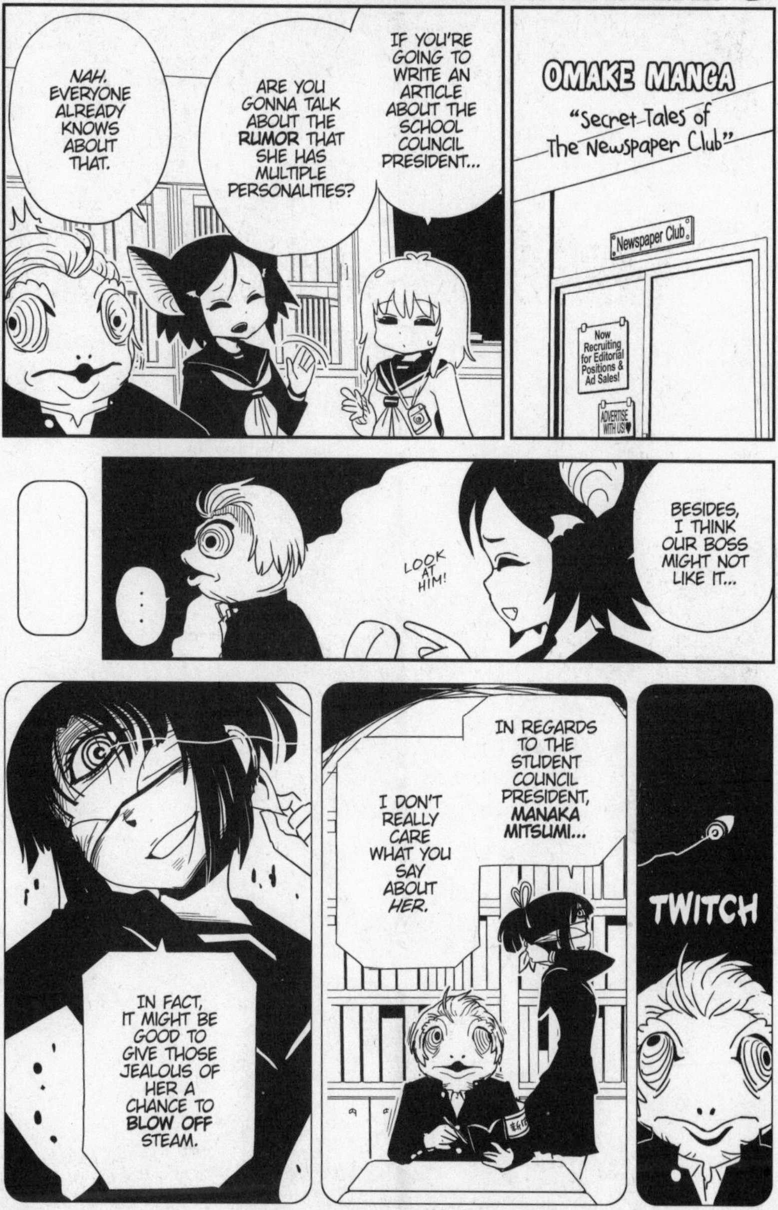
OMAKE MANGA
"Secret Tales of The Newspaper Club"
Newspaper Club
Now Recruiting for Editorial Positions & Ad Sales!
ADVERTISE WITH US!♥
IF YOU'RE GOING TO WRITE AN ARTICLE ABOUT THE SCHOOL COUNCIL PRESIDENT...
ARE YOU GONNA TALK ABOUT THE RUMOR THAT SHE HAS MULTIPLE PERSONALITIES?
NAH. EVERYONE ALREADY KNOWS ABOUT THAT.
BESIDES, I THINK OUR BOSS MIGHT NOT LIKE IT...
LOOK AT HIM!
...
TWITCH
IN REGARDS TO THE STUDENT COUNCIL PRESIDENT, MANAKA MITSUMI...
I DON'T REALLY CARE WHAT YOU SAY ABOUT HER.
IN FACT, IT MIGHT BE GOOD TO GIVE THOSE JEALOUS OF HER A CHANCE TO BLOW OFF STEAM.

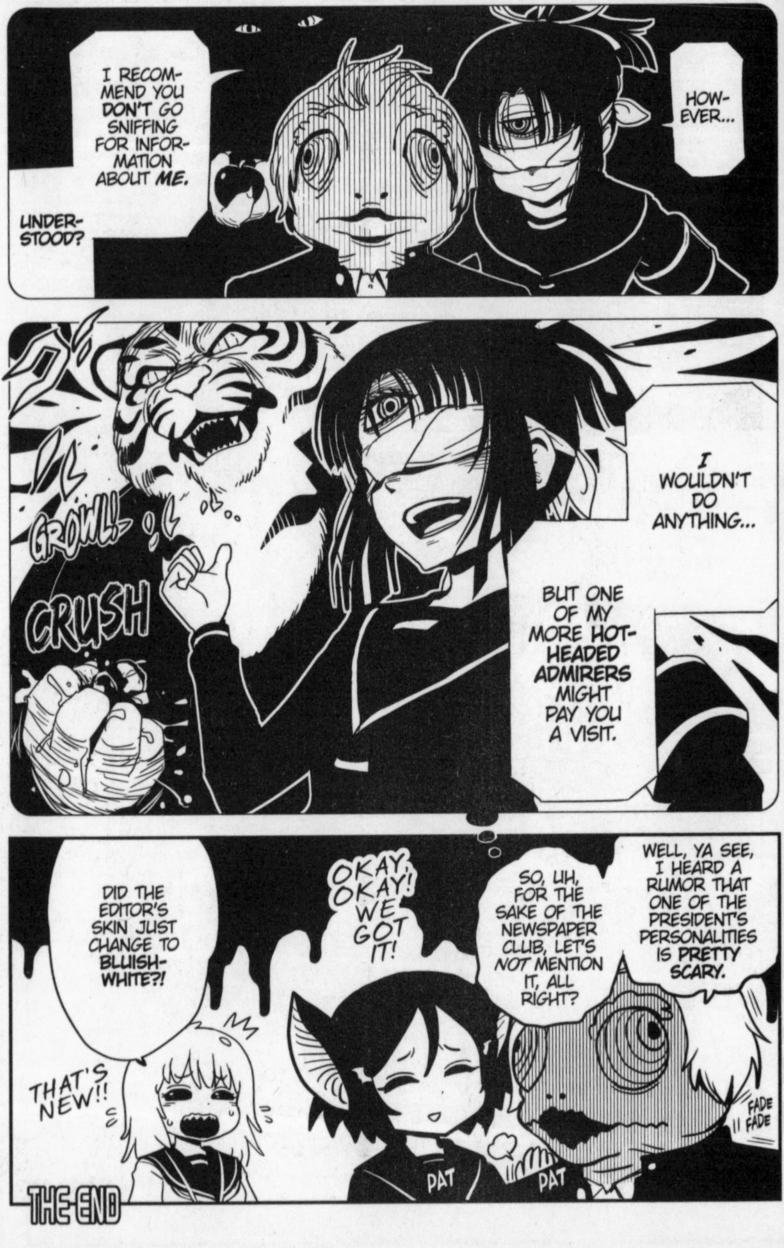
I RECOMMEND YOU DON'T GO SNIFFING FOR INFORMATION ABOUT ME.
UNDERSTOOD?
HOWEVER...
I WOULDN'T DO ANYTHING...
BUT ONE OF MY MORE HOT-HEADED ADMIRERS MIGHT PAY YOU A VISIT.
GROWL!
CRUSH
WELL, YA SEE, I HEARD A RUMOR THAT ONE OF THE PRESIDENT'S PERSONALITIES IS PRETTY SCARY.
SO, UH, FOR THE SAKE OF THE NEWSPAPER CLUB, LET'S NOT MENTION IT, ALL RIGHT?
FADE FADE
PAT PAT
OKAY, OKAY! WE GOT IT!
DID THE EDITOR'S SKIN JUST CHANGE TO BLUISH-WHITE?!
THAT'S NEW!!
THE END

SPECIAL ★ THANKS

- MY HEAD EDITOR, IKAI-SAMA
- FOR HANDLING PICTURES, JOU KURAYAMI-SAN, KYUU ARIHITO-SAN, TAMA MIZUKI-SAN, TARUHIRU-SAN, KOKONOTSU-SAN
- FOR 3-D IMAGES, USHI KANTO-SAN
- FOR BOOK DESIGN, AFTERGLOW-SAMA
- THE *COMIC RYUU* EDITING DEPARTMENT, MARKETING DEPARTMENT, AND ALL OF THE BOOKSELLERS.
- "HITO JA NAI (NOT HUMAN)" ♪
- EVERYONE SUPPORTING ME AND ALL OF THE READERS...!! I'M SO HAPPY FOR THOSE OF YOU RECOMMENDING THIS MANGA TO PEOPLE AROUND YOU!!

あとがき☆
AFTERWORD

GOOD EVENING. I AM SHAKE-O. THANK YOU VERY MUCH FOR READING VOLUME 4 OF *NURSE HITOMI'S MONSTER INFIRMARY!*

IN THIS VOLUME, THERE WERE MANY NEW AND RETURNING CHARACTERS. DID YOU ENJOY THEM ALL? BUT AS A TRADE-OFF, HITOMI-SENSEI DIDN'T PLAY A BIG ROLE THIS TIME AROUND. PLEASE CHECK OUT THE NEXT VOLUME, THOUGH!

IN THE MEANTIME, I BETTER START DRAWING IT...

2015. 9. 13 SHAKE-O

← AFTER THIS IS A FULL-COLOR SIDE-STORY ENTITLED "THE REVEALING WHITE LAB COAT"!!

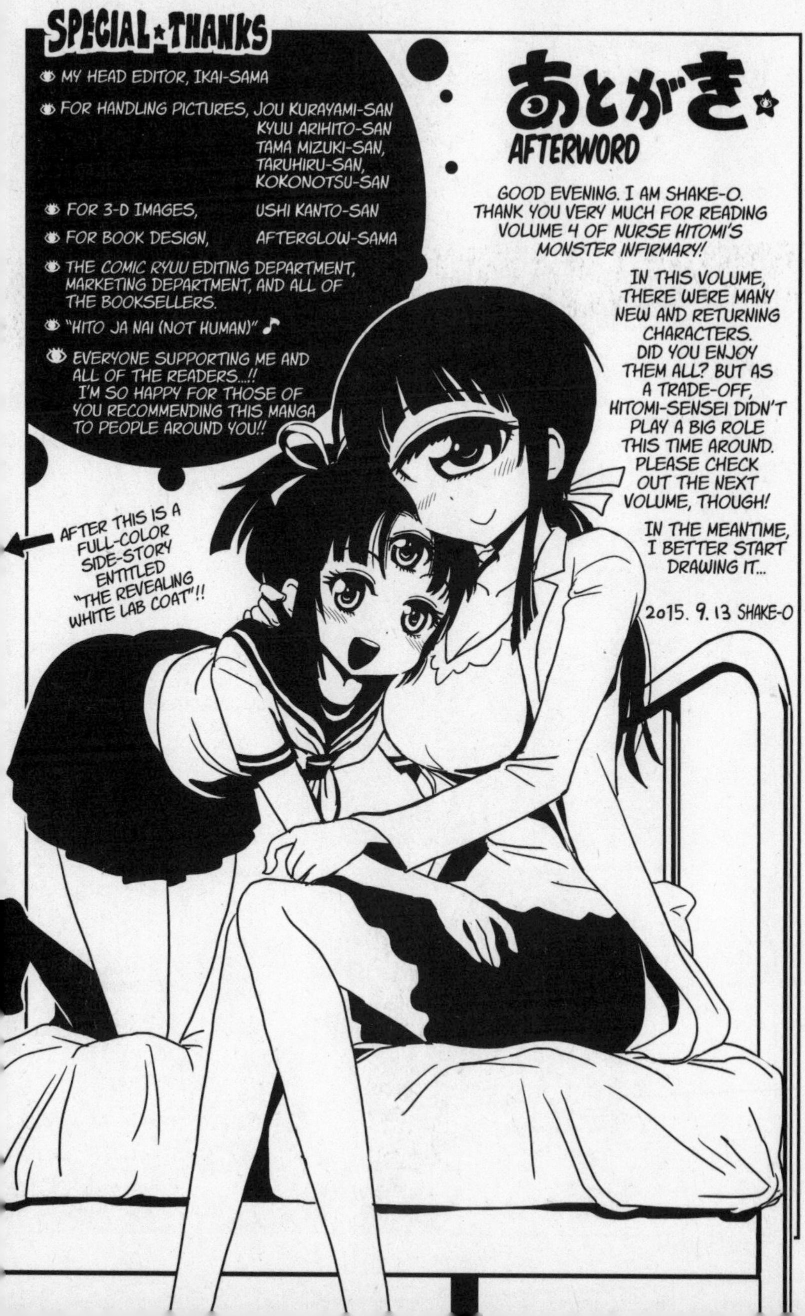

"The Revealing White Lab Coat"

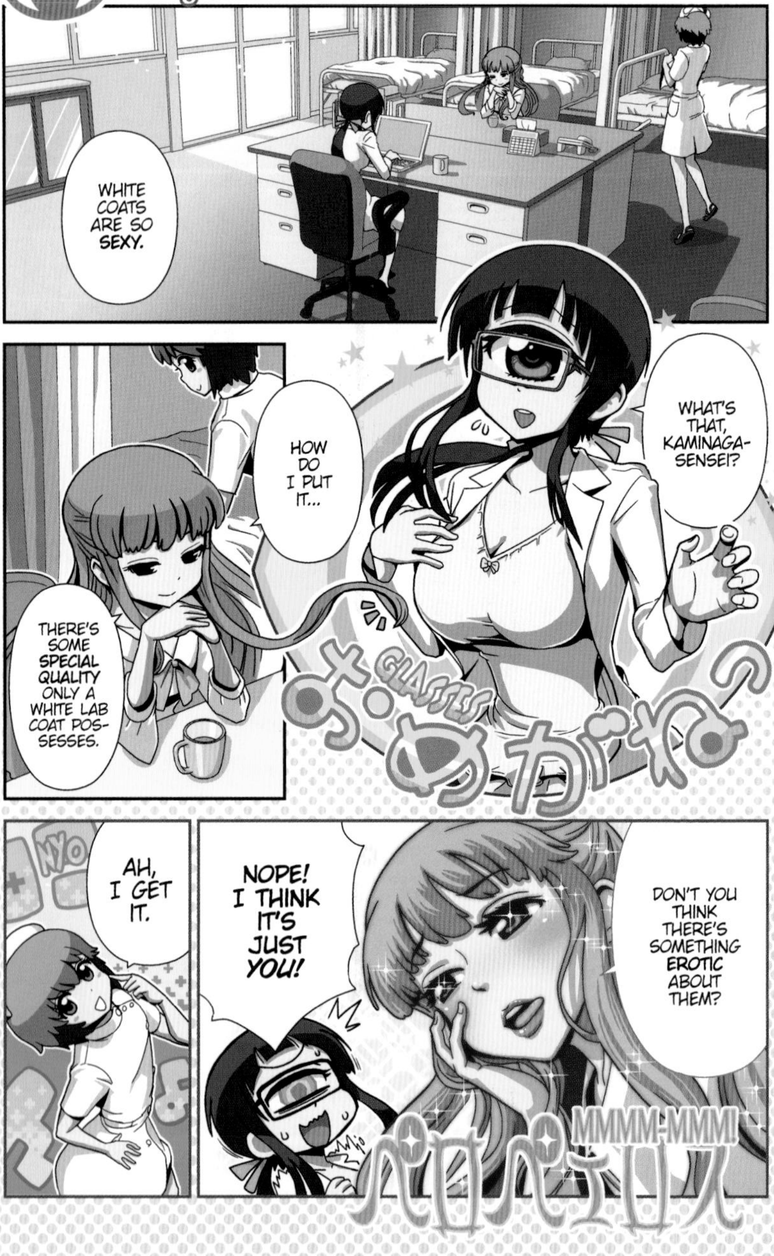
WHITE COATS ARE SO SEXY.
WHAT'S THAT, KAMINAGA-SENSEI?
GLASSES
HOW DO I PUT IT...
THERE'S SOME SPECIAL QUALITY ONLY A WHITE LAB COAT POS-SESSES.
DON'T YOU THINK THERE'S SOMETHING EROTIC ABOUT THEM?
NOPE! I THINK IT'S JUST YOU!
MMMM-MMM!
AH, I GET IT.

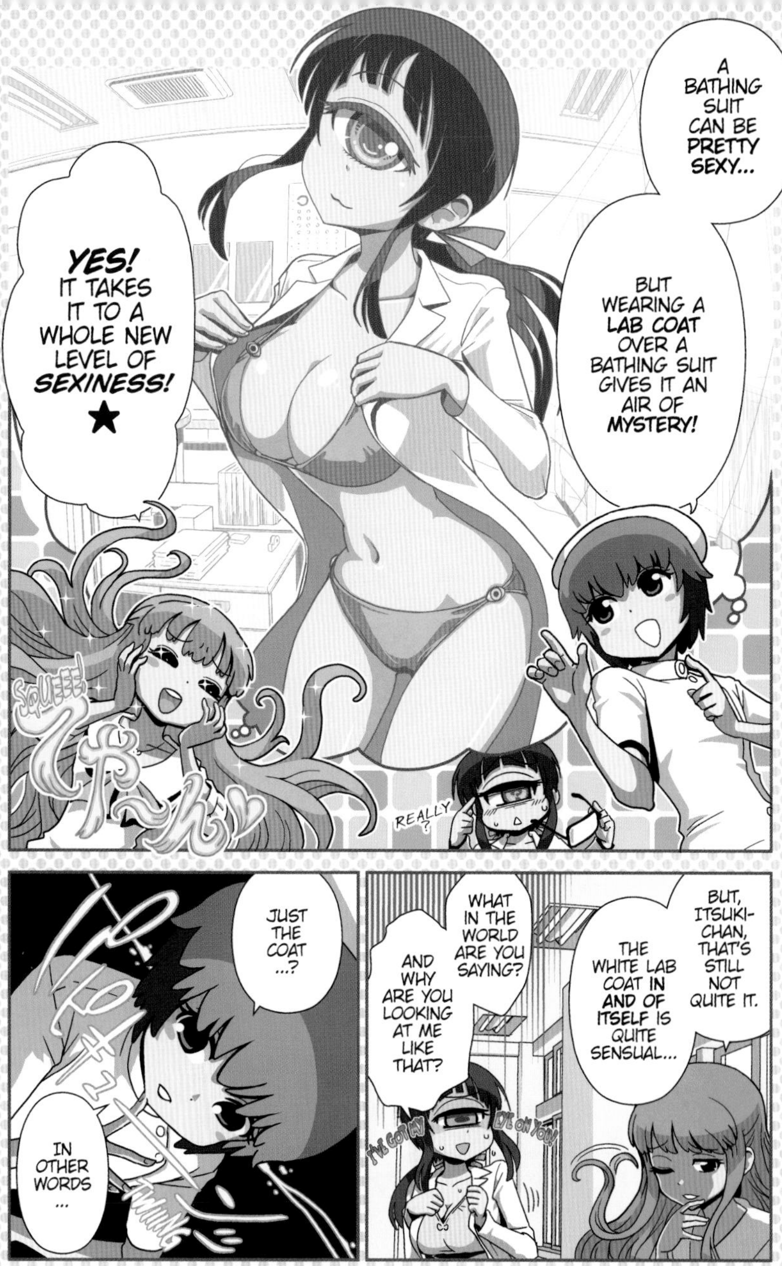
A BATHING SUIT CAN BE PRETTY SEXY...
BUT WEARING A LAB COAT OVER A BATHING SUIT GIVES IT AN AIR OF MYSTERY!
YES! IT TAKES IT TO A WHOLE NEW LEVEL OF SEXINESS! ★
SQUEEE!
REALLY?
BUT, ITSUKI-CHAN, THAT'S STILL NOT QUITE IT.
THE WHITE LAB COAT IN AND OF ITSELF IS QUITE SENSUAL...
WHAT IN THE WORLD ARE YOU SAYING?
AND WHY ARE YOU LOOKING AT ME LIKE THAT?
I'VE GOT MY EYE ON YOU!
JUST THE COAT ...?
IN OTHER WORDS ...
TWING

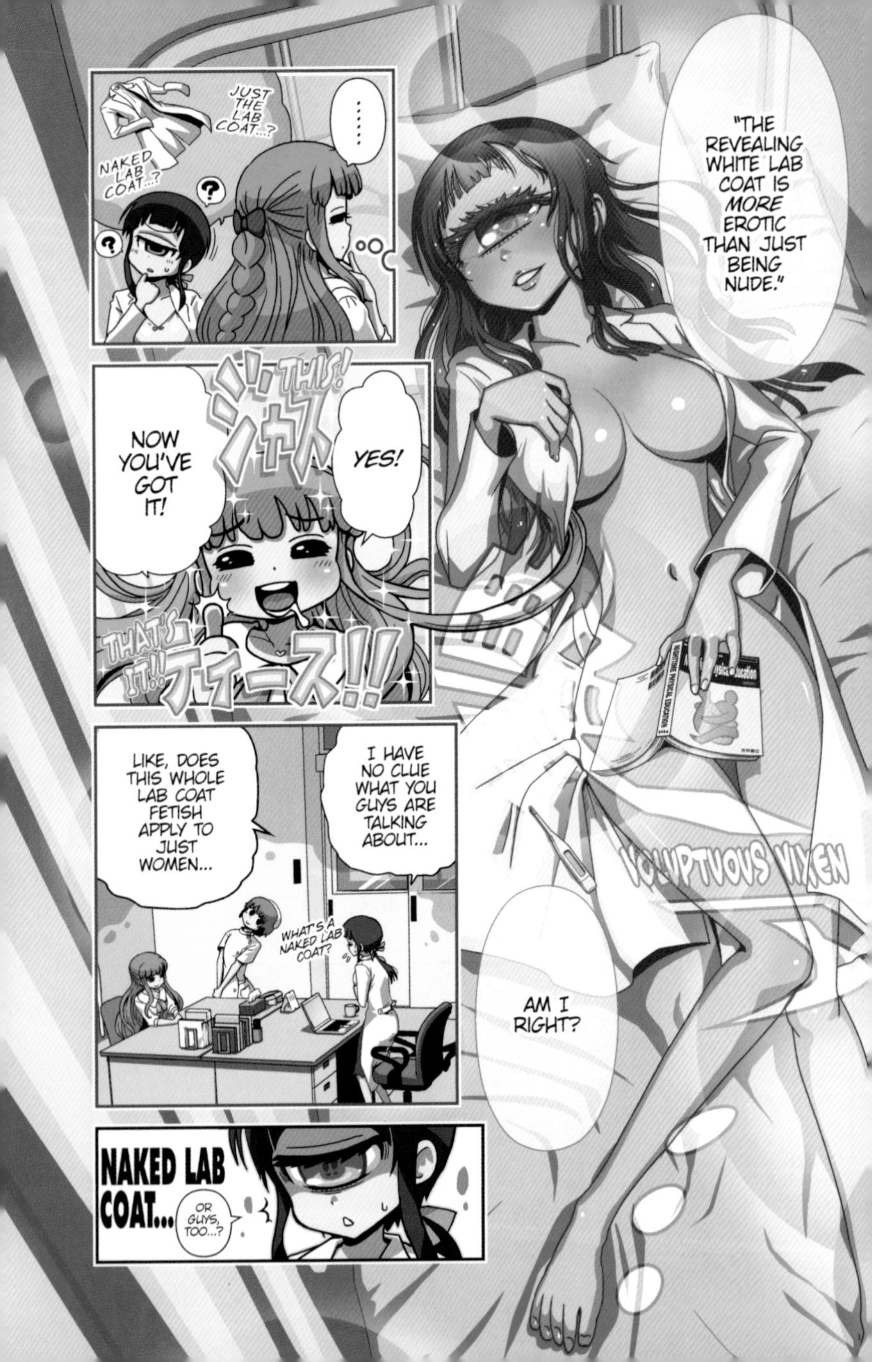
"THE REVEALING WHITE LAB COAT IS MORE EROTIC THAN JUST BEING NUDE."
NIGHTTIME PHYSICAL EDUCATION
VOLUPTUOUS VIXEN
AM I RIGHT?
......
JUST THE LAB COAT...?
NAKED LAB COAT...?
?
?
THIS!
YES!
NOW YOU'VE GOT IT!
THAT'S IT!!
I HAVE NO CLUE WHAT YOU GUYS ARE TALKING ABOUT...
LIKE, DOES THIS WHOLE LAB COAT FETISH APPLY TO JUST WOMEN...
WHAT'S A NAKED LAB COAT?
NAKED LAB COAT...
OR GUYS, TOO...?

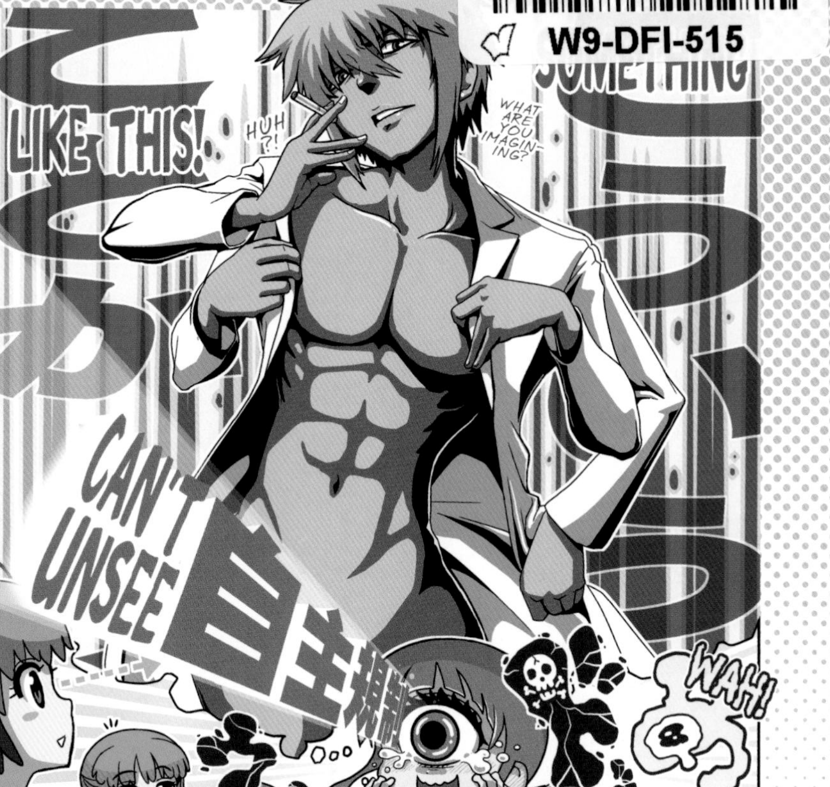
SOMETHING
WHAT ARE YOU IMAGINING?
LIKE THIS!
HUH?!
CAN'T UNSEE
自主規制
WAH!
BA-DUUUM

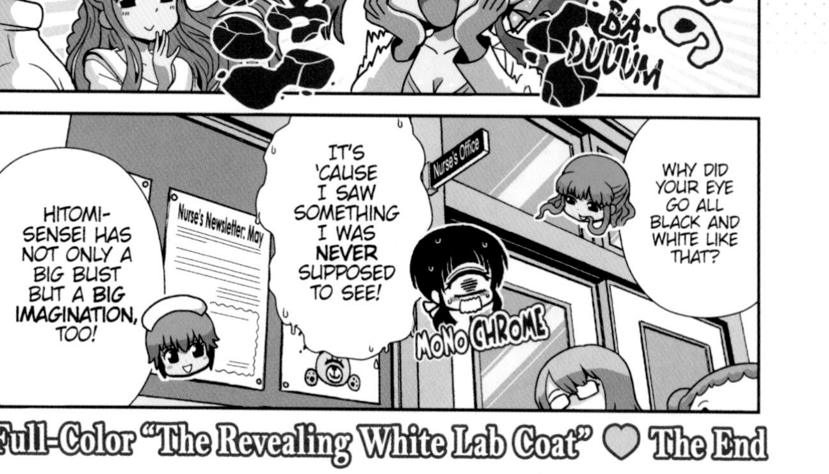
WHY DID YOUR EYE GO ALL BLACK AND WHITE LIKE THAT?
Nurse's Office
IT'S 'CAUSE I SAW SOMETHING I WAS **NEVER** SUPPOSED TO SEE!
MONO CHROME
Nurse's Newsletter: May
HITOMI-SENSEI HAS NOT ONLY A BIG BUST BUT A BIG **IMAGINATION**, TOO!

Full-Color "The Revealing White Lab Coat" ♥ The End